A SWEET TEMPTATION

For an infinite moment, the spell of silence wrapped around her. She became acutely aware of the young, vital man who held her, the kind of man whose embrace she secretly longed for in the night. She knew she'd overstepped the bounds of propriety by letting Wes touch her for so long, but try as she might, she couldn't relinquish the sweet, seldom-felt comfort.

For just one heartbeat longer, she told herself. For just one more fraction of her lonely, predictable life, she would allow this tantalizing breach of social conduct. Then she would summon a respectable show of outrage and storm inside to her empty bed.

But his hands shifted. She caught her breath as his fingers brushed her cheek, tucking a windblown strand of hair behind her ear. The feather-light gesture was so intimate in its innocence, that she stood frozen, uncertain whether to flee, to protest, or simply to glare. . . . Her feet stood rooted, though, as her limbs trembled like tempest-tossed leaves when his head lowered with mesmerizing slowness, and his lips parted to taste hers. . . .

Bantam Books By Adrienne deWolfe

TEXAS LOVER
TEXAS OUTLAW

Texas Lover

Adrienne deWolfe

BANTAM BOOKS
NEW YORK • TORONTO • LONDON • SYDNEY • AUCKLAND

TEXAS LOVER
A Bantam Fanfare Book / September 1996

FANFARE and the portrayal of a boxed "ff" are trademarks of Bantam Books,
a division of Bantam Doubleday Dell Publishing Group, Inc.

All rights reserved.
Copyright © 1996 by Adrienne M. Sobolak.
Cover art copyright © 1996 by Steve Assel.
No part of this book may be reproduced or transmitted in any
form or by any means, electronic or mechanical, including
photocopying, recording, or by any information storage and
retrieval system, without permission in writing from the publisher.
For information address: Bantam Books.

If you purchased this book without a cover you should be aware
that this book is stolen property. It was reported as "unsold and destroyed" to the publisher and neither the author nor the publisher
has received any payment for this "stripped book."

ISBN 0-553-57481-7

Published simultaneously in the United States and Canada

Bantam Books are published by Bantam Books, a division of Bantam
Doubleday Dell Publishing Group, Inc. Its trademark, consisting of the
words "Bantam Books" and the portrayal of a rooster, is Registered in
U.S. Patent and Trademark Office and in other countries. Marca Reg-
istrada. Bantam Books, 1540 Broadway, New York, New York 10036.

PRINTED IN THE UNITED STATES OF AMERICA

RAD   0 9 8 7 6 5 4 3 2 1

To my critique group and fellow authors, Pamela Ingrahm, Patricia Wynn, Cara West, and Janet Martin, without whom I'd still be peddling second-rate manuscripts.

Ladies, you're the best.

No book is written in a vacuum. This story, more than any other, required a special outpouring of love from my friends due to a physical setback I experienced. *Texas Lover* would not exist without the faith and encouragement of Paula Hudson; Aspen Bell; Donna Stephens; Frank Campbell; Pat Ricks; Diane Dwyer; Rachel and John Elam; Dr. Arthur Peterson; my typist, Laura "Kat" Fenton; and my parents, Edward and Diane Sobolak. These blessings whom I call friends rallied around me whether I laughed or cried, stumbled or soared.

My friends, I love you all.

LEGEND OF THE SWEETHEART TREE

If you would know your lady's heart,
The true depth of her caring,
Then take her to the woodland's midst,
The evergreen of sharing.

A tender kiss, a pledge of faith,
Then wait—that wise old tree,
Will crown its boughs with flow'rs of white,
If love is yours eternally.

—AMS

Texas
Lover

Chapter One

Bandera County, Texas
May 1883

*S*omething was wrong with this town.

Wescott Rawlins slung his saddle over his shoulder and dragged his weary, blistered feet out of the livery. His horse had gotten the fool notion to throw a shoe, and he'd walked the crockhead for ten miles to keep his appointment with the sheriff. Never in his twenty-four years had Wes been so happy to see a cluster of oakwood storefronts encroaching on the open range.

The town of Elodea, however, wasn't so happy to see him.

The blacksmith had been as friendly as a rained-on rooster when Wes asked for directions to Sheriff Boudreau's homestead. The liveryman had paled at the sight of Wes's matched pair of .45s and, claiming he had no horses for hire, had slammed the door in Wes's face.

Having his nose nearly smashed in by a tackroom door wasn't the worst part, though. The worst part was watching Elodea's womenfolk hurry past him as if he'd sprouted horns and a tail. True, he was caked with dust from his Stetson to his Justin boots, but he knew he held a certain appeal for the ladies. Years ago, as a gawky youth, he'd learned to compensate for his freckle-dusted nose and his auburn hair with flirtatious charm, but his most winning smiles were proving wastes of time on Elodea's fairest, and his friendliest "howdy's" were being answered by hunched shoulders and fleeing bonnets.

Yep. Something was *damned* wrong with this town.

"Mister! Hey mister, wait up. You dropped something," an eager young voice called, causing Wes to halt outside the doors of Sultan's Dance Hall.

A slender boy with possum-colored hair ran into the center of the road, where sunbeams glanced like shooting stars off a battered piece of tin. Swooping for the object, the boy gaped, his eyes growing round with excitement.

"It's a badge. A *Ranger*'s badge!"

Wes half smiled. Now here was the kind of welcome he'd grown used to during the past six years.

"Where'd ya get it, mister?"

Wes's vanity deflated a notch. "Austin, as I recollect," he said dryly.

"You mean you're a Ranger?" The boy caught his breath. "A *real* Ranger?"

"Reckon so."

Gray eyes doubtful, the boy watched Wes retrieve the badge and tuck it carefully into the inner pocket of his vest.

"Well, if you're a real Ranger," the boy said, "how come you're toting that old hunk of tin instead of a shiny new star?"

Shoving his hat back, Wes considered how to answer his young skeptic. Ten months earlier, his "hunk of tin" had deflected a bullet that should have been his ticket to the boneyard. Call him sentimental or just plain superstitious, but he didn't have the heart to trade in the scratches, dents, and faulty clasp for something showier. Of course, a young Ranger worshipper wasn't likely to understand how his hero could choose sentiment over glamour. Wes ought to know. He'd worshipped a Ranger himself in his youth.

"What's your name, son?" he asked solemnly.

"Danny Dukker."

"Well, Danny, a shiny new badge could reflect the

sun and warn off a road agent when I'm tracking him through the hills. Understand?"

Danny's brow furrowed, but he nodded. Wes sensed he'd just scored a point for the underdog, a sport that had always tickled him. Fishing in his pocket, he indulged Danny with a nickel.

"Much obliged for your help, Mr. Dukker."

The boy's eyes bugged out, but whether at the liberty head or the title of respect was hard to say.

Nodding good-bye, Wes pushed past the dance hall's swinging doors. To his surprise, Danny followed him inside, trotting at his heels like a faithful coonhound. Wes thought it strange that a boy who was maybe eight or nine years old could brazen his way up to the counter without the barkeep batting an eye. Why wasn't Danny at the local schoolhouse? Come to think of it, why weren't the half-dozen other boys he'd seen leapfrogging down Main Street poring over their readers?

Shrugging, Wes turned his attention to the corner of the mirror behind the bar. Monday's lunch menu, "ham an beenes," had been whitewashed on it in big, awkward letters. Apparently Danny wasn't the only one who needed schooling. Then Wes noticed how the barkeep was fidgeting and glancing at his Colts with their walnut-inlaid butts. Remembering that his badge was in his pocket, he sighed and tossed a quarter onto the bar.

"Bring me a plate of your special, will ya, barkeep? Oh, and shoot a cherry sarsaparilla down this way."

Danny, whose chin was just high enough to rest on the bar, wrinkled his nose in disgust. "Pete knows I don't drink that kiddy stuff. I'll have what you're having."

"You will, eh?" Wes caught the frothing mug before it could sail past him. "Looks like you'd best make that two sarsaparillas, Pete."

Danny's jaw dropped. So did the barkeep's.

Chuckling to himself, Wes shook the cherry foam from his hand and strolled to the traditional gunfighter's table: the one in the corner with a sweeping view of the door, street, and stairwell. In spite of his audience, he couldn't stifle another sigh as he eased the saddle from his chafing shoulder and parked his swollen feet. He couldn't remember the last time he'd had to walk a mile, much less ten. Hell, nobody walked in a place as big and hot as Texas.

Once that surly blacksmith got Two-Step reshod, Wes planned to pay a visit to Sheriff Boudreau's homestead. The sheriff had wired Ranger headquarters with the message, "Trouble's brewing. Send help." Nobody seemed to know what Boudreau was talking about, much less his reasons for being cryptic, so Wes had been ordered to investigate. The fact that he'd been happily stationed in Brownsville at the time, and about as far as he could get from his family's Bandera County cattle ranch, hadn't seemed to matter to his superior, Captain McQuade.

But then, McQuade was an old compadre of Cord's from the Civil War. And Cord had an irritating habit of meddling in his younger brothers' affairs. Suspecting Cord was behind the order to bring him home, Wes had taken his sweet time in leaving the Rio Grande Valley behind, and he planned to ride back just as fast as he was able. The last thing he needed—or wanted—was Cord showing up to show him up again.

Especially in front of Fancy.

"Ow!" Banging his knees as he usually did when he was distracted, Wes muttered a few choice oaths about tables. Chairs too. It seemed like furniture had started shrinking the day he turned thirteen.

Pushing back his chair, he let his boots stick out beneath the table and began to study his surroundings. The saloon was unremarkable, but he was determined to find something interesting. Something exciting.

Something to take his mind off his brother's wife.

Through the front window, he could see Milner's General Store across the street. A buckboard loaded with sacks of flour and bolts of fabric waited near the door. A young woman in a sunflower-print dress stood beside it. He couldn't make out her face beneath the brim of her straw hat, which she'd anchored to her head with a scarf, but she stood straighter than a rail, and was just about as slender. He noted the tiny cloud of dust that was rising around her square-toed shoe, as if she was tapping it, and the almost troubled way she turned her head, looking from one end of Main Street to the other. She seemed to be waiting for someone.

He watched her idly, sipping his soda and wondering which of the men he'd seen wandering about town might be her escort. That man would have to be comfortable looking up to a woman. She fairly towered over her wagon's bed, like a female Paul Bunyan, and yet she looked every inch a fine lady.

Just then, a handsome, long-limbed mulatto boy stepped out of Milner's store. Wes realized with a start that the youth was the first person of color—of *any* color—he had seen in Elodea. Carrying a hammer and a box of carpentry nails, the mulatto called out something to the woman and headed for the wagon.

The youth seemed to have attracted more than the woman's attention, though. A handful of young men emerged from an alley and strolled toward the buckboard, almost as if they'd been waiting for the mulatto to emerge from the store.

Danny chose that moment to reappear, planting himself like a wall in front of Wes.

"So tell me, Ranger," the boy challenged, biting off a mouthful of jerky, "how many men have you killed? And how many niggers and Injuns?"

Wes arched an eyebrow. Adventure-minded youths from El Paso to Galveston always asked the same question, but none had ever phrased it quite so crudely. For the first time, he noticed the uncommon crookedness of Danny's nose, as if a fist had once displaced the bone, and the fading bruises along the boy's jawline, where his stringy, collar-length hair half-hid them.

"I've always been of a mind," he answered carefully, "that what a man does with his gun is a private matter between him and his maker."

"Yeah?" Danny's face fell. His suspicious gaze raked over Wes's freckles and mustache, his two-week-old beard, and his guns. Finally it settled on the half-empty mug in Wes's fist, and Danny snorted.

"Well, it sounds to me like you ain't been a Ranger

real long. Either that, or them fancy guns of yours is just for show."

"You know a lot about guns, Danny?"

"Sure. My pa taught me. He killed his first nigger when he was fourteen. And Creed—that's my brother—he shot hisself a greaser about this time last year. Why, Pa and Creed just about run this town." Danny's chest puffed out. "And they sure don't drink no sarsaparilla."

Something cold settled in Wes's stomach. Setting his mug back down, he peered with new understanding over Danny's head. One of the young men held the wagon team's reins and the rest of the hecklers were circling its bed. The mulatto stood protectively in front of the woman, his jaw set and his fists clenched, while the leader of the gang, a stout, unattractive youth of about eighteen, sauntered forward.

"Look! There's Creed now," Danny said eagerly, pushing a chair out of the way and pressing his nose to the window. "And there's that uppity Shae. Thinks he's something special 'cause he's got some white-trash blood running through his veins. But Creed'll show him different. You jest wait and see."

The woman grabbed Shae's sleeve, but he shook her hand off. Creed laughed. So did his cronies. Spewing tobacco juice at Shae's boots, Creed made an obscene gesture that was clearly directed at the woman. Shae lunged.

The two youths collided, forming a windmill of limbs as they kicked and jabbed and grappled for advantage. Ducking, Shae broke free, and the two circled like baited hounds before the hooting spectators.

Wes started to rise, then hesitated, recalling a time when he was eighteen. Cord had exercised his guardianship over him by wading into a fistfight and dragging him off by his collar. Never in his life had he felt so humiliated. Fancy's honor had been at stake, but when Cord had demanded an explanation, Wes refused to provide one. He couldn't bear for Cord to know that some of the local boys had found out about his wife's former profession.

"C'mon, Creed! Give it to 'im!" Danny was shouting,

jumping up and down and swinging his fists like a prizefighter.

Torn, Wes gazed outside once more. As a lawman, he did have the pesky responsibility to keep the peace . . .

The combatants were on the street now, rolling in a cloud of dust. It looked like the two of them were determined to beat each other bloody, if not to mutilate and maim.

Damn.

Rising, Wes unhooked the trigger guards on his holsters and headed for the doors, but the woman had already taken matters into her own hands. She marched up to the flailing fighters and doused them with a bucket of water. The arena turned instantly to mud. Creed reared back, coughing and sputtering, and Shae heaved him into a puddle of ooze. The woman hurried between them, brandishing the hammer in warning.

Danny started cursing like a mule skinner. "Get up, Creed!" he shouted, pounding on the glass. "Get up and knock that Yankee on her bustle!"

Wes hesitated at the door as he noticed movement at the edge of the crowd. The spectators were falling back before a dark, squat, powerfully built man. A polished star glinted on his sweat-stained shirt, and a short-barreled Remington was strapped to his hip.

"Uh-oh," Danny muttered, becoming instantly subdued. "Pa looks mad."

Wes arched an eyebrow, his gaze darting back to the lawman. Dukker was the town marshal?

Snarling something at the woman, Dukker wrenched the hammer from her hands and threw it into the wagon bed. She straightened, seeming even taller as she towered over the marshal. Wes couldn't help but admire her as she inclined her head with a dignity reminiscent of Old World royalty. When she gestured to Shae, the young man stomped forward and handed her into the buckboard.

As the spectators hastily dispersed under the marshal's malevolent eye, Dukker was joined in the street by a rotund, laughing man who slapped him on the shoulder. They exchanged words for a moment before heading for the dance hall's front doors. Danny grew whiter than bleached bones.

"Uh-oh. Gotta go. See ya around, mister."

Wes frowned, watching the previously self-assured boy bolt like a jackrabbit for the alley.

Wes had reseated himself by the time Dukker and his companion entered the dance hall. The rotund man advanced toward Wes's table with a spritely step.

"Welcome to Elodea, stranger," he boomed. "Phineas Faraday is my name. I'm mayor of this fine town. And this here's Hannibal Dukker, our marshal."

Wes allowed the mayor to pump his hand, but he remained seated. He didn't much like politicians with wide, toothy smiles.

Apparently unconcerned by the slight, Faraday beamed at him as he adjusted his glasses. He had ink stains on his rolled-up sleeves and a smudge on his nose. It occurred to Wes that Faraday must be the owner of the local newspaper.

"Of course," Faraday went on, "you being a stranger, you probably aren't aware of our no-gun ordinance." His tone was amicable but the gaze he trained on Wes's Colts was wary. "If you don't mind my asking, what's your business here, mister?"

Wes delayed his answer as the bartender deposited a plate of greasy food before him. The man kept his eyes to the ground as he edged around Dukker and high-tailed it back to the safety of his bar.

"My name's Rawlins," Wes said finally. "I've got Ranger business with Sheriff Boudreau."

Faraday's eyebrows humped up like twin caterpillars. "Rawlins? Ranger *Cord* Rawlins?"

Wes tried not to grimace. Folks in Bandera County often confused him with his legendary, law-fighting brother. For the life of him, he couldn't understand why. Cord had left the force years ago. Besides, Cord was six inches shorter—not to mention fourteen years older—than he.

"Cord's a relation of mine," he answered coolly. "Anything else I can do for you, Mayor? I've got a meal waiting on me."

Dukker sneered, folding apelike arms across a barrel-sized chest. "Reckon you ain't heard then, eh, Rawlins?"

"Heard what?"

"You're late, that's what. Cousin Gator was expecting you two damned weeks ago. 'Course, he's dead now, so I reckon any business you got is with me."

Wes nearly choked on his mouthful of beans. "Boudreau's *dead*?"

"Yep." Dukker nodded ominously. "Shot and ambushed about twelve miles west of town. Hell, if you'd been doing your job, hunting down renegade niggers like you were supposed to, Cousin Gator would still be hunting and fishing with my boys."

Wes set down his fork. He didn't much like Dukker's accusation, mainly because there was a ring of truth in it. He could have ridden much harder, but he'd chosen to rest Two-Step during the hottest parts of the afternoon. He'd holed up for dust devils and lightning storms, and he'd even allowed a calico queen to lure him into an overnight stay. Could he have prevented the sheriff's ambush if he'd arrived sooner?

A pang of guilt stabbed through him.

"This is the first I've heard of Boudreau's death. Or of any renegades," he added cautiously. "Seems strange no one mentioned it to me while I was walking through town."

"Maybe no one mentioned it to you 'cause you ain't wearing a badge," Dukker retorted. "I reckon you Rangers get your jollies by strapping on big irons and scaring the living daylights out of unarmed folks."

Wes felt his neck heat. He knew he should allow for Dukker's grief at his cousin's death, but the man was making it hard.

"You've got a right to be angry. I apologize. Now you want to tell me why I had to bust my britches riding nearly two hundred miles?"

"I already told you it was renegades," Dukker snapped. "'Course, if those niggers had a lick of sense, they'd be halfway to New Mexico by now."

Faraday cleared his throat, his shrewd gaze darting to Wes. "You know we can't be entirely sure of that, Hannibal. And the county isn't within your jurisdiction—"

"A man's got a right to defend his property."

"Yes, but Mr. Rawlins has the *legal* authority to enforce the law until our new sheriff is elected. Perhaps before he rides off to track down Gator's killers, Mr. Rawlins can help you settle the trouble on your cousin's spread—you being so busy with the election campaign and all."

Dukker's face darkened. He seemed on the verge of a virulent protest until a cagey expression flickered in his eyes.

"Hell, you're right, Faraday. It's just that Gator was my boys' closest relation. Creed spent half the summer working those fields. Gator wanted his homestead to pass to my boy, and I'll be damned if I let some squatters lay a claim."

"Perfectly understandable, of course," Faraday said briskly. "No Texican is fond of squatters." He flashed Wes an apologetic smile, but his shoulders remained taut. "Perhaps now, Mr. Rawlins, you can see why Hannibal is so . . . er, quick on the draw. Since Gator's spread's only ten miles west of Elodea, none of us here wants trouble. What we do want is justice. And a Ranger can end this dispute. I can personally attest that Hannibal has been as patient as a man can be these last two weeks, but the Sinclairs—" Faraday sighed, shaking his head, "they're just—"

"A bunch of damned Yankees," Dukker interrupted, screwing up his face to spit.

Wes grimaced, pushing aside his plate. He didn't know which turned his stomach more: the greasy beans or Dukker. If Dukker's claim was legitimate—and the town mayor seemed to think it was—then Wes had a legal obligation to ride out to Boudreau's farm. He had a moral one, too, if the story of Boudreau's death was the gospel truth. But damn. Squatters. After riding two hundred miles, he deserved a more exciting mission than ending a property squabble.

"So what do you want me to do?" he asked, eyeing Dukker in disgust.

"Round 'em up," Dukker said. "Drive 'em out. Hell, shoot 'em if you have to. But don't hurt none of the live-stock," he added quickly, a covetous gleam lighting his wintry gaze. "I plan on selling it. Them goats and chickens ain't much, but they'll help pay for what needs mending. Ol' Gator wasn't good with roofs and windows and such, if you catch my meaning."

Wes's lip curled. He'd caught Dukker's meaning all right. "How 'bout if I just burn them out?"

Dukker bristled at Wes's sarcasm, but Faraday's quick laughter diffused the tension.

"That's a knee-slapper, Rawlins. Burn them out." He chuckled again, slapping Wes on the shoulder. "Tell you what. Instead of eating that day-old hash, why don't you come over to my house? My wife makes the best fried chicken in the county. And my Lorelei, why she's Bandera's prettiest belle."

Wes managed a thin smile. Any man who was a bachelor—and wanted to stay that way—didn't go sparking a virgin at her father's invitation. But the chicken sure was tempting. He'd gotten mighty tired of canned peaches and roasted rabbit on the trail.

"Much obliged, Mayor. I'd like to take you up on that." Wes stood and noticed with satisfaction that Dukker had to crane his neck back to look him in the eye. "But first I'd like to ride out to Boudreau's farm. Ask the Sinclairs what they know about his murder."

Dukker stiffened.

"Of course. Of course," Faraday said with brassy brightness. "Come on by the *Enquirer* when you're ready, and I'll escort you to the house."

Wes nodded.

Faraday turned to Dukker. "Buy you a drink, Hannibal?"

He gestured toward the bar with a wide smile, but the strain between the two men was hard to mistake. Considering that town marshals were typically hired by the mayor and his council, Wes found Faraday's kowtowing curious.

Keeping a wary eye on the two men, he stooped for his saddle. The sooner he rode to Boudreau's farm, the sooner he could get the coming unpleasantness over with. He planned to listen to the Sinclairs' story, of course, but he didn't have a lot of faith in the validity of their claim. If one could believe Faraday's testimonial, the law was on Dukker's side.

Heaving his saddle to his shoulder, he headed for the swinging doors. By sundown, hopefully, the squatter issue would be settled. He wanted to start tracking Boudreau's killer at dawn. With any luck, his manhunt would take him out of Bandera County before Cord and the rest of the family caught wind of his return.

Setting his hat on his head, he turned his thoughts to his meeting with Mr. Sinclair.

"Rider coming!"

The cry of alarm was the first thing Wes heard as Two-Step trotted up the drive of the Boudreau homestead. Somewhere a door slammed, then he saw a dozen or so boys and girls converge upon the yard, running from all directions, charging through squawking chickens and bleating goats. Every race and color seemed to be represented as the youngsters rushed by, clutching straw dolls and fishing poles, some clinging to another child's hand. Surprised, he reined in, throwing up an arm just in time to protect his hat from the frenzied flapping of a hen.

A squat black woman was gesturing frantically, shooing the children like chicks into the storm cellar by her feet. Every last one of the youngsters looked scared—if not of him, Wes noticed with growing concern, then of the yawning black pit below them. The woman was insistent, though, and she snatched up the smallest bawling child, kissing his hair as she hurried down the stairs after her wards. Two chubby brown arms reached past her, a pigtailed head bobbed, then the doors fell shut, sealing everyone in with a resounding bang.

Wes blinked.

Now if *that* wasn't the oddest damned thing he'd ever seen. . . .

"What's your business here, mister?"

His head snapped around at the sharp midwestern

accented voice. He'd been so bemused by the rush of little bodies that he hadn't noticed the statuesque woman beneath the magnolia tree by the front of the house. He recognized the sunflowers on her mud-spattered skirt, and for a moment, he allowed himself to admire what her straw hat had hidden from him earlier. A honey-brown sheaf of primly coiffed hair framed the classical features of her face, one that appeared to be a few years older than his own and striking in its maturity. Her high, thoughtful brow and elegantly chiseled cheekbones both bloomed pink at the moment, no doubt due to her agitation, and her firm, full lips were pressed together over a dimpled chin.

But the feature that struck him the most, the characteristic that downright stole his breath away, was her eyes: two fiery jewels of amber. And right now, those eyes were burning into him as if he were Satan's own messenger.

Which wasn't that far from the truth, he thought with a twinge of guilt.

Suddenly he remembered the badge in his pocket. A part of him cringed to think that in Mrs. Sinclair's eyes, his star would probably put him in a league with Hannibal Dukker. Still, he'd resigned himself early in his Ranger career to the fact that duty was rarely pleasant.

Thinking to save himself a lot of argument by proving his legal authority, he reached for his hidden star. The glint of steel froze him in midgesture. Warned of her .45 before Mrs. Sinclair drew it from her skirts, he spent the next heartbeat or so cursing himself for having fewer brains than a wooden Indian.

Then he smiled. He couldn't help himself.

He'd looked down many a gun barrel before, but never one held by a woman with the bearing of a queen and the courage of a mother cougar.

Chapter Two

"Keep your hands where I can see them, mister," Aurora Sinclair ordered. She locked her trembling knees and drew herself up to her full five-foot-ten, shooting the stranger her fiercest glare and praying to heaven that the children were all safely in the cellar.

For days she had drilled her charges in the emergency procedure, her distrust of Hannibal Dukker spurring her to take precautions. Although the marshal had yet to threaten her household, she feared his retaliation was only a matter of time. The night before, she had finally convinced him to take his courtship elsewhere; only that afternoon, Creed had given free rein to his envy of Shae.

Even if Rorie could have convinced herself Hannibal's courtship had been based on love—or his boys' desperate need of a mother—she would never have surrendered her orphans' guardianship simply to relieve her own loneliness. Even so, she had spent last night wondering if she had been prudent to reject Marshal Dukker. She would have had to suffer his suit for only another few weeks, until her more civilized beau returned from his cattle drive, or until Shae turned eighteen and could inherit the land she held in trust for him. If she had been wise enough to bide her time where Dukker was concerned, she might not be standing there now worrying that she had endangered the children.

Or that this dusty stranger, who had ridden out of town with twin revolvers on his hips, was part of Dukker's revenge.

Swallowing hard, she tightened her fists over the butt of the .45 and tried to hold it steady, as Shae had taught her. Her best gunfighter's stance only seemed to amuse the stranger, though. He was young, perhaps five or six years younger than she, but his accessories suggested he was an expert at destruction. In addition to his six-shooters, his cartridge belt, and the sheathed bowie knife that peeked from his boot, a Winchester rifle glinted against his saddle. No casual cowpoke carried so much firing power, even in Texas, the Braggadocio Capital of the South.

Cocking his head, the stranger grinned at her. "You planning on shooting me, ma'am?"

The very idea made her stomach roil. "If I must."

"You'll have to aim a bit higher then."

A slow heat crept up her neck. He was trying to intimidate her. She'd been practicing for two whole weeks, and she knew she could hit the side of a barrel—most of the time.

"You have yet to answer my question," she retorted in her sternest schoolmarm voice. "What is your business here?"

He doffed his hat. His hair was as thick as a lion's mane, and flared around his darkly tanned face with the red-gold glory of a sunset. For a moment, she simply could not tear her eyes away. She had stared down onto her former husband's shiny pate for so long, she had forgotten a man could be blessed with such magnificent hair.

"The name's Rawlins. Wes Rawlins," the stranger drawled in his rumbling baritone, one which might have been musical if not for its tiny twang of bluster. "I've come to see Mr. Sinclair."

"Then you have come to the wrong place."

"This is Gator Boudreau's homestead, isn't it?"

"Yes. Or rather, it was. But Sheriff Boudreau was—"

She bit her tongue. Prudence, she reminded herself. She had enough problems with Dukker; she would be inviting disaster if she accused him of complicity in Gator's murder without a single shred of evidence.

"Ma'am?"

Swallowing, Rorie forced herself to meet Rawlins's eyes. They were so startlingly green, they looked like polished emeralds set into the copper of his face.

"Did you know Sheriff Boudreau, Mr. Rawlins?"

"No, ma'am. I've heard talk of him, though."

"Gator was a good man. A decent, Christian man," she added firmly, knowing firsthand the damage gossip could do. "You would never have found him behaving like one of those rude, uncouth Rangers he often kept the company of."

A hint of amusement again crept across Rawlins's chiseled features. She noticed for the first time that he had a smattering of freckles on his nose. They blended almost to perfection with his tan.

"Do you know a lot of Rangers, ma'am?"

"I know a lot of lawmen, Mr. Rawlins. And I can't think of a single one—other than Gator—whom I'd consider trustworthy."

Rawlins frowned. His eyes bored into hers, and for a moment, she had the unsettling feeling that he knew more about her suspicions than she wanted to reveal.

Shae, for heaven's sake where are you? She wished the boy would come home. He'd been so furious with her for interfering in his fistfight that he had driven them back from town and unloaded the wagon without a single word to her. Then he had stalked off for a sulk. Of course, Shae or no Shae, Rorie would do what had to be done to protect the children. She certainly would feel better about martyrdom, though, knowing Shae's shotgun was guarding the cellar. Even Gator hadn't been able to beat Shae in an honest shooting match.

"I'm real sorry, ma'am," Rawlins said, "about the way Sheriff Boudreau passed on." He inclined his head. "You must have been right close to him, Mrs. . . . . er, Miss . . . ?"

"For the last time, Mr. Rawlins, what do you want?"

She had amused him again. There was a winsome charm in his smile, a youthful appeal that was more than a little disarming. She tried to steel herself against it. She recalled Gator's tales of Billy the Kid, a young man who had always smiled before he killed.

"Well, for starters," Rawlins said, "how 'bout putting down that equalizer before you shoot your foot off?"

"I assure you, Mr. Rawlins, I am not the one in danger. Now I suggest you ride on."

"You're not from around here, are you, ma'am?" Leaning forward, he winked in a conspiratorial manner. "I can always peg a Yankee lady by the way she doles out hospitality."

Rorie felt her face flame. *Well!*

" 'Course, I meant no offense," he continued, with that lilting vocal swagger of his. "And I sure don't want to put you out any. It's just that I've had a long ride and I'm real thirsty. Do you think we might call a truce so I can get a dipper of water? Shoot, I'll take my gun belt off, if that'd make you feel better."

Oh, he was a clever one, this Wes Rawlins. He'd gone straight to the heart of her female pride—her hospitality. How in good conscience could she refuse him water? By the looks of him, he *had* had a long ride. And the nearest body of water, Ramble Creek, was another mile to the west.

"All right," she said. "You may go to the well. But keep your hands away from your guns."

"Sure thing, ma'am. Whatever you say."

He was humoring her. She felt it as surely as she felt the growing fatigue in her arms. She worried she wouldn't be able to draw a straight bead on him much longer. She worried, too, about the heat and the darkness in that cellar. Poor Ginevee probably had her hands full, trying to ease the qualms of a dozen monster-fearing children.

"Please hurry, Mr. Rawlins, before my well and my patience dry up."

He swung a leg over his saddle, and her heart quickened as he unfolded. True to his word, he kept his hands high, but his cooperation wasn't what imprinted itself on her senses. She realized suddenly that he was taller than Shae—at least four inches taller, and Shae was six-foot! She couldn't remember the last time she'd had to tilt her head back to look a man in the eye.

Rawlins bent his head and grinned down into her flushed face. "You mind if I use my hands now? On the dipper, I mean."

Her insides fluttered at the provocative warmth in his voice. "Of course not."

"Much obliged . . . Mrs. Sinclair. It *is* Mrs. Sinclair, isn't it?"

"I am Aurora Sinclair," she admitted grudgingly, less annoyed by the reminder of her failed marriage than by the rush of her silly pulse.

Those green eyes laughed at her as he started to turn away. To her surprise, he limped. His easy masculine confidence couldn't conceal his grimace, and her annoyance ebbed slightly. He hadn't mentioned he was hurt. What had happened to him?

Chagrin trickled through her; she struggled against a swell of motherly instinct. Had she judged him too quickly? After all, he could have pleaded pain or injury and then, when her guard was down, he could have jumped her. If she were back in Cincinnati, where young men didn't wear revolvers during social calls, she would have known immediately where she stood with Wes Rawlins. But in Texas, a genteel, impeccably dressed gentleman might ride into town and dynamite the bank, while the grizzled, squinty-eyed type might turn out to be a traveling preacher. Rorie hated to pass judgment simply on appearances, but there was too much at stake in her cellar.

"So." He looked curiously around him, his gaze traveling from the chicken coop's half-hinged door to the cistern's rusting pump, and from the house's one boarded window to the fence's tumbled posts. "Are you running a school here, Mrs. Sinclair?"

"A school for some. A home for others."

He turned, dipper in hand, and rested his weight on the well. "A home? You mean you've made this old rat-trap into an orphanage?"

"The children have nowhere else to go, Mr. Rawlins, and our neighbors in Elodea are not inclined to charity."

"I see."

I doubt it, she thought, but she kept her peace. The Negro and Mexican farmers had always been kind to her, sparing what grains and livestock they could in exchange for their children's education. But the townsfolk of Elodea had yanked every one of their children from her tutelage. The parents had been aghast to learn that their precious Billy Bobs and Peggy Sues were sharing readers with her orphans. Preacher Jenkins and Mayor Faraday had tried repeatedly to replace her, but no teacher could satisfy the Elodean ideal.

"So how long have y'all been living here, if you don't mind my asking?"

"One year."

"That's all?"

She eyed him sharply. What kind of question was that?

"Well, if you must know, Mr. Rawlins, I was hired one year ago as Elodea's schoolmistress. But I was denied the house I was promised because certain elements in Elodea cannot suffer to live beside people of a different color. Fortunately Gator took the orphans in so we would all have a roof over our heads."

"And your husband?" Rawlins's face had darkened in a way that suggested anger. "Where was Mr. Sinclair when you were being booted out of town?"

In some whorehouse, no doubt. But she didn't need to tell Rawlins about Jarrod's peccadillos.

"My husband is none of your concern. And I will thank you now to leave our home."

Rawlins shook his head, and her heart leaped. Anxiously she watched him replace the dipper in the pail and let the pail sink into the well. The whizzing crank and groaning rope were the only sounds in the yard until several seconds later, when she heard a muffled splash.

"Begging your pardon, ma'am, but you seem eager to get rid of me. It kind of makes me wonder." Frank eyes searched her own. "Did I give you some reason to be scared? 'Cause even with this hair and all, I don't usually send children running and ladies reaching for their six-shooters. Not on purpose, anyway," he added with the tiniest, self-deprecating smile.

Rorie swallowed. For a moment, she spied concern, warm and genuine, in the jade recesses of his gaze. Guilt warred anew with her doubts. She started to wonder if, perhaps, she should try to explain. Or at least to apologize. She was on the verge of doing the latter when a sudden nerve-rattling howl made her jump.

"Flower bit me! *Flower bit me!*"

Rorie spun, her heart in her throat. She realized that the other children must have forgotten Po in their rush for the cellar. Sloughing off mud and petals, the two-year-old scrambled out of the rose bushes and rushed toward her with outstretched arms. After only three frantic steps, his shoes tangled in their unfastened straps, and he fell flat on his face with a thud. His howls crescendoed to an earsplitting pitch.

Rawlins chuckled, and his long legs outdistanced her as he hurried with her to the toddler's rescue.

"Here now, pardner," he said, undaunted by all the dirt, shrieks, and tears. "Let me see that flower bite."

"Hurt. *Hurt!*" Po wailed, his great, almond eyes gushing tears.

The gunslinger lifted the boy with the skill of a mammy, and Rorie halted, momentarily stunned. Discarding her .45, she planned to snatch Po away, but Rawlins had taken complete charge, turning over each muddy little hand for inspection.

"Aw, the tyke's just scared, ma'am. See? No scratches. No hurt," he told Po, who must have finally sensed he was being held by a stranger, not Shae. Whimpering, he reached for Rorie, and Rawlins obliged, lowering the child into her arms.

"What's his name?" he asked.

She cradled the boy, kissing his silky black hair. "Po. That's the name his mother gave him," she added defensively. "She was Cantonese."

She waited for Rawlins to back away as if Po had bubonic plague. To her surprise, he leaned closer instead, his smile turning wistful. Stretching out a freckled hand, he patted the boy's head.

"He's a cute little younker. Reminds me of my nephew Seth. Seth was always getting into trouble at that age, and Cord had to build a baby corral just so Fancy could—"

Damn. Wes bit his tongue, blushing furiously. He'd done it again. He'd sworn to himself he wouldn't reminisce about Fancy, but here he was, only a couple of hours later, mooning over her memory—and in front of another woman yet!

He glanced sheepishly at Aurora Sinclair, figuring he'd just made a first-class fool of himself. To his relief, he found a new acceptance warring with the suspicion on her face. She looked like she might even smile. Not that it mattered, but she would be pretty if she did. Downright beautiful, in fact. He didn't like grimness, especially in a woman, but he had to concede that Aurora Sinclair had better reasons than most. Her husband was missing; her protector—and lover?—had been gunned down; and the marshal of the local town was trying to ride her out on a rail.

What was Dukker's big hurry, anyway? Sure, the land might belong to him, but Aurora had orphans to rear. What difference did it make if she lived here a couple of weeks longer until she found them a new home?

He gazed once more into the big, watery eyes that peeked up at him from the hollow of Aurora's neck.

Something wasn't right here. Or, as Aunt Lally would say, "Son, there's a fox in the henhouse."

Thinking he might get some answers now, as long as he stayed circumspect, Wes prepared to ask about Boudreau's death. The scrabble of pebbles distracted him. A long, lean shadow poured across his boots, and he

tensed, reacting instinctively to being watched from behind. He had wondered what had happened to the
mulatto.

"You all right, Miss Aurora?" Shae asked. "I heard
Po crying."

"Yes. Yes, of course," she said a little breathlessly.
"I'm fine. And so is Po."

Wes didn't have to turn to understand the reason for
her agitation. A slender, polelike shadow had rippled outward from the youth's. He guessed it was a shotgun.

"You must be Shae," he said, turning as casually as
he was able. He saw instantly that he faced a marksman.
Despite the youth's swollen knuckles and blackened eye,
his grip was firm and his bead dead-on. Wes returned that
narrowed stare with a calm respect. The youth could have
blown him away if he'd wanted to, but Wes knew he
wouldn't. His gut told him so.

"That's right. I'm Shae. What's it to you, mister?"

"I saw you in town today. You put up some fight."

"Yeah?" Suspicion hardened the youth's jaw. "What
are you doing here?"

Wes glanced at Aurora. She had managed to hush
Po. Now she bit her lip as she gazed at the double-
barreled Whitney, trained with such precision on his
chest. Recalling the badge still in his pocket, Wes suffered
another pang of guilt. Unfortunately, this didn't seem like
the best of times to pull it out and pin it on.

"I'm here 'cause I heard there might be work for me
to do," he replied evenly.

"Where'd you hear that?"

"Oh, from someone who claimed Boudreau wasn't
much good at carpentry."

Shae's lips twisted, revealing startlingly white teeth.
"Carpentry, eh? Well, I don't know any carpenters who
wear double-holstered rigs, mister."

Wes hid a smile. Someone had taught the boy well.
"That may be, Shae. But a man can't be too careful these
days, what with renegades roaming the county, shooting
down the law. I figured it's the talk of all those renegades
that has Mrs. Sinclair so spooked. Am I right?"

Shae's gaze flickered to Aurora. She fidgeted.

"We don't need any hired hands," the youth said firmly.

Their evasiveness confirmed Wes's growing suspicions. There was more to their skittishness than a couple of Negro outlaws who, if they had ever even existed, were undoubtedly in the next county by now. And if there were no renegade Negroes, then another, more ominous question followed: Who had killed Sheriff Boudreau?

Feeling as responsible for the man's death as he did, Wes had more than an official duty to pursue that question. He suspected the answer could be found on Boudreau's spread. Or in Elodea. In either event, it didn't look like he would be leaving Bandera County quite as quickly as he'd hoped.

That realization helped him make a decision. He could put to good use the anonymity he had earned. If Aurora distrusted lawmen as much as she claimed, then she certainly wouldn't tell him anything if she learned he was a Ranger. He'd just keep his badge a secret from her and Shae for a while. In the meantime, he could try to settle this land issue in a peace-abiding way.

"I don't mean any offense, folks," he said, "but take a good look around you. You need a hand, all right. Luckily for you I've got two here, and they're just as good with hammers as with guns."

Po was yawning now around his thumb. Shifting him to her other hip, Aurora finally flashed the smile that Wes had been waiting for. It tugged at his heartstrings. Just as he'd imagined, it had the potential to be beautiful, but right now it looked weary. And strained.

"The truth is, Mr. Rawlins, we don't have the money to pay you."

He gazed into her eyes, those breathtaking, tawny eyes, and his heart twanged again. Only this time, the vibration moved through every nerve and fiber, going deeper than he had ever felt a feeling go before. The sensation was discomfiting. Hastily he donned his roguish grin, the one that never failed to fan pink fire beneath a woman's cheeks.

"Well, you can cook, can't you, ma'am? 'Cause all I need is a hot meal. And a place for me and Two-Step to bed down."

"For how long?" Shae demanded.

Wes forced his attention away from the pretty shade of rose that made Aurora look softer and younger, and a whole lot more appealing than her frowns did.

"That's hard to say. As long as it takes, I reckon. You wouldn't want any of those little ones falling through a rotted floorboard, would you? Or stepping on some rusty nail?"

Shae pressed his lips together. "Miss Aurora?"

Wes could see the uncertainty in her eyes. She looked down at Po, then up at Wes. He suspected he'd just about won her over—until she sighed.

"It's not my decision, Shae. The land is yours now."

Wes's brows shot up. *Shae's* land? Dukker hadn't mentioned anything about Shae contesting his title to the property.

"Excuse me, ma'am. Did I hear you right? I thought your husband was laying claim to this spread."

She tensed, and the look she shot him would have stiffened fresh cream. "As I told you earlier, Mr. Rawlins, my husband is none of your concern."

"You'd best keep your nose out of other people's business if you want to work for me," Shae said, the faintest of threats in his tone. "If a night of sleep doesn't change your mind, come back tomorrow morning around seven. I'll be starting the roof of my barn about then."

"Your barn?"

"That's right."

Now wouldn't Pa Dukker have a screaming fit to hear a mulatto talk that way? Wes mused. A tiny smile tugged up one corner of his mouth. He was beginning to like Shae better each minute.

"I've got to ask you, son," he said, " 'cause this is a fair piece of land in spite of all the wood rot. How'd you scrape up enough money to buy it?"

Wes waited expectantly. If the boy was squatting, or

if he was simply covering up for Mr. Sinclair's lies, Wes figured he would know by a shifty eye or a stammer.

Shae met his gaze head on, and his speech rang as clear as a church bell. "I didn't buy the land, Rawlins. It was willed to me by my father. Gator Boudreau."

Chapter Three

It was a good thing Wes had worn his high boots, because the manure was piling up pretty thick around Elodea.

After Shae claimed Gator Boudreau was his father, Wes's jaw had nearly hit the dirt. Not once, in the eight years since his family had moved their cattle outfit from Bosque County to Bandera, had Wes heard any rumor about Sheriff Boudreau fathering an illegitimate child, not with a white woman or a black one. The conviction in Shae's manner, though, had made him think twice about challenging the boy.

Back in Elodea, Wes made some discreet inquiries about Shae's background at Sultan's Dance Hall. He made a few more at the public bathhouse, while getting a haircut and shave for his dinner engagement at the Faradays. According to patrons of both establishments, Shae "sure as shootin'" must have been one of "them renegade niggers" who'd ambushed and murdered the "poor sumbitch" he'd had nerve enough to claim was his pa.

The townsfolks' opinions of Aurora Sinclair weren't much better. If one listened to Elodea's queen mud dauber, Mrs. Minerva Faraday, Aurora was the original serpent from Eden. Mrs. Faraday was only too happy to repeat the most sordid of the rumors while she piled Wes with chicken, fried okra, and cornbread. She staunchly defended public belief that Aurora had been sinning with Boudreau long before his wife passed away four short months ago. It was Aurora, Mrs. Faraday insisted, who had put Shae up to his outrageous lies. After all, Boudreau had never once mentioned he'd spawned a bastard boy. Hannibal and Creed Dukker could both vouch for that.

"Now don't go getting me wrong, Mr. Rawlins," Mrs. Faraday said in her honey-dripping voice. "As a Christian woman, I can certainly allow that Mrs. Sinclair must have her finer points too. It takes a special breed of woman to rear darkies who aren't even wanted by their own kind."

Mrs. Faraday plopped a slab of sweet-potato pie onto his plate and leaned closer. "But truly, sir, wouldn't you question the decency of a woman who buries her—" she paused delicately, "*friend* on a Sunday afternoon, and by Monday evening has entertained his cousin?"

"Mama, please." Lorelei Faraday's pretty young face screwed up in disgust. "Marshal Dukker is the one whose decency you should question. Shae said the man has been making a downright nuisance of himself ever since—"

"Lorelei." The reprimand came from her father, who dropped his bushy eyebrows so low they seemed to perch on the tops of his spectacles. "Did I not tell you, for safety's sake, to keep your distance from Shae McFadden?"

In surprise, Wes caught Lorelei's eye. A crimson blush spread across her porcelain face.

"I'm sorry, Papa." Ducking her head, she fiddled with her fork. "But I couldn't very well avoid him. He was coming out of church after the service for Sheriff Boudreau."

Mrs. Faraday puffed up like a bullfrog. "The *nerve* of that Shae McFadden. Showing up in God's house after his boldfaced lies. Claiming he was spawned by Gator was bad enough, I must say. But then that awful boy insisted that Gator named him his heir in some preposterous deathbed will! Why, poor Gator must be turning over in his grave. Everyone *knows* he intended for his farm to go to Creed Dukker."

"I don't know that, Mama."

"Lorelei!"

The girl's backbone stiffened. "It's Shae's word—and Mrs. Sinclair's too—against the word of Creed and Marshal Dukker."

Mrs. Faraday snorted. "As if there was ever a doubt. Lorelei, I'm appalled. Why are you listening to such rubbish? And Father, when are you going to put an end to Shae McFadden's lies? That boy is poisoning the mind of our daughter, and in our own church yet!"

"Now, Mother." Faraday looked mildly uncomfortable as he sliced a second helping of pie. "The boy has a right to religion. And the right to free speech, as I understand it, under the law."

"Well, I think Shae McFadden and his kind should take their blessed rights someplace else!"

Lorelei made an exasperated sound. Wes was hard-pressed not to do the same. The taste of sweet potatoes had turned bitter on his tongue, and he pushed back his plate.

"Oh, dear." For a moment, Mrs. Faraday looked positively stricken to see a large portion of his pie go uneaten. "Is there something wrong, Mr. Rawlins?"

Wes forced a smile. "Not at all, ma'am." In truth, he preferred his aunt Lally's pie recipe, not to mention her company. The Rawlins matriarch never judged a man by his skin color, and she'd taught Wes to do the same. "It's just that this belt of mine needs a little loosening." He winked, leaning back and patting his belly.

Mrs. Faraday tittered. Lorelei's face fell. Standing abruptly, she pressed her lips together and began to gather serving platters.

The mayor looked up, his brow wrinkling in concern. "Lorelei? Is something wrong, child?"

"Of course not, Papa. Don't mind me. I'm sure you and Mr. Rawlins have a great many things to discuss."

"Nonsense, Lorelei." Mrs. Faraday's smile was tight with annoyance. "Mr. Rawlins has called to talk with you. The dishes can wait."

Mrs. Faraday practically forced Lorelei and Wes to sit on the porch swing together, and the dark-eyed, dark-haired beauty perched nervously on its edge. As the silence grew more awkward, Wes wondered how to remove himself so he could wire headquarters.

Finally Lorelei stopped worrying her bottom lip long enough to speak.

"I . . . hope you won't judge Mrs. Sinclair too harshly, Mr. Rawlins," she said, tossing an irritated glance toward the parlor window, where they could see her mother's stout silhouette. "In spite of the things Mama says, I can't help but feel sorry for Mrs. Sinclair. At her age, and with those children, she'd be uncommonly fortunate to do better than a Dukker."

Lorelei's shudder was almost imperceptible. Wes was quick to notice it, though, and he couldn't stave off a protective instinct toward the seventeen-year-old girl. Lorelei was the first Elodean he had met who displayed genuine sympathy for Aurora Sinclair . . . and who talked openly of her distrust of the Dukkers.

"Am I to understand, Miss Faraday," he teased gently, "that you've had some experience entertaining gentlemen callers named Dukker?"

She drew in a quick breath, and her color rose rapidly. "You might as well know, Mr. Rawlins. Elodea is a very small town. There aren't that many young men who are eligible to come calling."

Wes bit his tongue on "That's a shame." He might feel empathy for Lorelei, but he didn't want to be shotgunned into marrying her. Or anyone else, for that matter.

Lorelei raised troubled, doelike eyes to his. "Papa says you won't be staying here for long. He says you're a Ranger and you've come to drive Shae off the land. Is that true?"

"Well . . ." Wes considered the silent plea in her gaze. He wondered if she was asking him to stay and court her, or if she was begging him to leave Shae in peace.

"I'll be here until I can figure out who's got the legal claim to Sheriff Boudreau's spread, if that's what you mean. 'Course, if there's a will like young Shae says, I won't need to hang my hat here for long."

Lorelei shook her head and sighed. "Honestly, Mr.

Rawlins, Shae isn't one to stir up trouble. I daresay he has more honor than the whole clan of Dukkers combined."

"Sounds like you know a lot about Shae."

He waited expectantly, noting the wistfulness that flickered across her features. She cast another wary glance at the window.

"We're . . . of a same age."

"I see."

She blushed once more. "You mustn't get the wrong idea," she said quickly. "It's just that . . . Well . . ." The pink ruffles on her bodice trembled in her agitation. "People in this town won't give Shae a chance and I don't think it's fair. Did you know he wants to go to that new Negro college when it opens in Prairie View next year? And someday read the law? Why, all that Creed Dukker wants to do is distill lightning whiskey!"

Wes found this piece of news interesting, to say the least. It occurred to him that Lorelei's uncommon friendship with Shae probably accounted for her parents' determination to pair her up with another male caller. Even a wild and woolly one like him.

But if Wes found the intrigue in Lorelei's young life interesting, he found the mystery in Aurora's more mature world fascinating. Had she really become Boudreau's mistress—and under the nose of his wife yet? Was there truth in the rumor that she'd conspired with Shae to keep Boudreau's homestead for herself?

Was she really as scarlet as the town wanted to paint her?

Bidding good night to Lorelei and her parents, Wes rode to the telegraph office and pounded on the door until the operator roused himself from the bedroom upstairs. The man was nervous and uncooperative, no doubt due to his interrupted sleep, so Wes paid him extra to send a wire to the county seat, asking for information about the sheriff's death and a verification of his will.

Next, Wes wired Ranger headquarters in Austin for news of any outlaw gangs that might be operating in and around Bandera County.

Then, his skin prickling with thoughts of Dukker, he decided against dropping his guard long enough to sleep in Elodea's hotel—or worse, at Sultan's Dance Hall. Riding several miles out of town, he pitched a camp beneath the pecan trees, chokecherries, and cedars, and tried to catch some sleep.

A gunshot exploded to the west.

Wes sat bolt upright, nearly blinded by the rising sun. The report had come from the direction of Boudreau's homestead. For a moment, his vision swam with the image of frightened little faces, of trembling bodies racing for the storm cellar.

The children.

He was on his feet, grabbing for his gun belt and his cartridge case even as the second report rolled down ominously from the hills. Grabbing the leads of Two-Step's halter, he vaulted onto the gelding's back and spurred him to a gallop. Wes left behind his saddle, bedroll, and even his hat. He would have time to retrieve them later. All he cared about now was the children.

And getting his sights on any bastard who might have ridden out to hurt them.

"Sons of thunder."

Rorie stomped her foot. She rarely resorted to such unladylike outbursts, but the strain of her predicament was beginning to wear. She had privately conceded she could not face Hannibal Dukker with the same laughable lack of shooting skill she had displayed before Wes Rawlins. So, swallowing her great distaste for guns, and the people who solved their problems with them, she had forced herself to ride out to the woods early, before the children arrived for their lessons, to practice her marksmanship yet again.

It was a good thing she had.

She had just fired her sixth round—her *sixth round*—and that abominable whiskey bottle still sat untouched on the top of her barrel. If she had been a fanciful woman—which she most assuredly was not—she might have imagined that impudent vessel was taking great pains to provoke her. Why, it hadn't rattled once when her bullets whizzed by. And the long rays of morning had fired it a bright and frolicsome green.

If there was one thing she couldn't abide, it was a frolicsome whiskey bottle.

She snapped open her cylinder and fished in the pocket of her pinafore for more bullets.

Thus occupied, Rorie didn't notice the tremor of the earth beneath her boots. She didn't ascribe anything unusual to her horse's snorting or the way the mare stomped and tossed her head. Daisy was chronically fractious.

Soon, though, Rorie detected the sounds of thrashing, as if a powerful animal were breaking through the brush toward the clearing. Her heart quickened, but she tried to remain calm. After all, bears were hardly as brutish as their hunters liked to tell. And any other wild animal with sense would turn tail and run once it got wind of her human scent, not to mention a whiff of her gunpowder.

Still, it might be wise to start reloading. . . .

A blood-curdling whoop shook her hands. She couldn't line up a single bullet with its chamber. She thought to run, but there was nowhere to hide, and Daisy was snapping too viciously to mount.

Suddenly the sun winked out of sight. A horse—a mammoth horse with fiery eyes and steaming nostrils—sailed toward her over the barrel. She tried to scream, but the sound lodged in her throat as an "eek." All she could do was stand there, jaw hanging, knees knocking, and remember the unfortunate schoolmaster Ichabod Crane.

Only her horseman had a head.

An auburn head, to be exact. And he carried it above his shoulders, rather than tucked in a macabre fashion under his arm.

"God A'mighty! Miss Aurora!"

The rider reined in so hard, his gelding reared, shrilling in indignation. Her revolver slid from her fingers to the ground. She saw a Peacemaker in the rider's fist, and she thought again about running.

"It's me, ma'am. Wes Rawlins," he called as his horse wheeled and pawed.

She blinked uncertainly, still poised to flee. He didn't

much look like the dusty long rider who'd drunk from her well the day before. His hair was sleek and short, and his clefted chin was bare of all but morning stubble. Although he did still wear the mustache, it was his gun belt that gave him away. She recognized the double holsters before she recognized his strong, sculpted features.

He managed to subdue his horse before it could bolt back through the trees. "Are you all right, ma'am?" He hastily dismounted, releasing the reins to ground-hitch the gelding. "Uh-oh." He peered anxiously into her face. "You aren't going to faint, are you?"

She snapped erect, mortified by the suggestion.

"Certainly not. I've never been sick a day in my life. And swooning is for invalids."

"Sissies too," he agreed solemnly.

He ran an appreciative gaze over her hastily piled hair and down her crisply pressed pinafore to her mud-spattered boots. She felt the blood surge to her cheeks. Masking her discomfort, she planted both fists on her hips.

"Mr. Rawlins, what on earth is the matter with you, tearing around the countryside like that? You frightened the devil out of my horse."

He had the decency to blush. "I'm real sorry, ma'am. I never meant to give your, er, *horse* such a fright. But you see, I heard gunshots. And since there's nothing out this way except the Boudreau homestead, I thought you might be having trouble."

"Trouble?" She felt her heart flutter. Had he heard something of Dukker's intentions?

"Well, sure," he said. "The way you had those children running for cover yesterday, I thought you might be expecting some." He folded his arms across his chest. "Are you?"

The directness of his question—and his gaze—was unsettling. He no longer reminded her of a lion. Today, he was a fox, slick and clever, with a dash of sly charm thrown in to confuse her. She hastily bolstered her defenses.

"Did it ever occur to you, Mr. Rawlins, that Shae might be out here shooting rabbits?"

"Nope. Never thought I'd find you here, either. Not

that I mind, ma'am. Not one bit. You see, I'm the type who likes surprises. Especially pleasant ones."

She felt her face grow warmer. She wasn't used to flattery. Jarrod had been too preoccupied with self-pity to spare many kind words in the last two years of their marriage. And Dukker . . . Well, the things that had come out of Dukker's mouth had always made her feel vaguely threatened, as if being a woman was somehow a crime.

"I never expected to see you out here either, Mr. Rawlins."

"Call me Wes."

She forced herself to ignore his winsome smile. "In truth, sir, I never thought to see you again at all."

"Why's that?"

"Let's be honest, Mr. Rawlins. You are no carpenter."

He chuckled. She found herself wondering which amused him more: her accusation or her refusal to use his Christian name.

"You have to give a fella a chance, Miss Aurora. You haven't even seen my handiwork yet."

"I take it you've worked on barns before?"

"Sure. Fences too. My older brothers have a ranch up near Bandera Pass. Zack raises cattle. Cord raises kids. I try to raise a little thunder now and then, but they won't let me." He winked. "That's why I had to ride south."

She felt the tug of a smile on her lips. She was inclined to believe a part of his story, the part about him rebelling against authority.

"I see," she said.

"You aren't going to make me bed down again in these woods, are you, ma'am? 'Cause Two-Step is awful fond of hay."

He managed to look woeful, in spite of the impish humor lighting his eyes. She realized then just how practiced his roguery was.

Wary once more, she searched his gaze, trying to find some hint of the truth. Why hadn't he stayed at the hotel? Or worse, at the dance hall? She felt better knowing he hadn't spent his free time exploiting an unfortunate young prostitute. Still, she worried that his reasons for sleeping alone had more to do with empty pockets than any nobility of character. What would Rawlins do if Dukker offered to hire his guns?

What would she do if Rawlins agreed?

Maybe feeding and housing Rawlins would be more prudent than driving him off. After all, boarding him could steer him away from Dukker's dangerous influence—at least until the day when Rawlins got restless enough to ride off in search of adventure.

Besides, Shae could genuinely use help on the barn. And there was always the possibility that Rawlins was more swagger than threat.

"Very well, Mr. Rawlins. I shall withhold judgment on your carpentry skills until you've had a chance to prove yourself."

"Why, that's right kind of you, ma'am."

She felt her cheeks grow warm again. His drawl had the all-too-disturbing tendency to make her feel uncertain and girlish.

"I suppose you'll want to ride to the house now," she went on. "It's a half-mile farther east. Shae is undoubtedly awake and can show you what to do." She inclined her head. "Good morning."

Except for a cannily raised eyebrow, he didn't budge.

Rorie fidgeted. She was unused to her dismissals going unheeded. She was especially unused to a young man regarding her as if she had just made the most delightful quip of the season.

Hoping he would go away if she ignored him, she stooped to retrieve her gun. He reached quickly to help. She was so stunned when he crouched before her, his corded thighs straining beneath the fabric of his blue jeans, that she leaped up, nearly butting her head against his. He chuckled.

"Do I make you nervous, ma'am?"

"Certainly not." She felt her ears burn at the lie. "Whatever makes you think that?"

"Well . . ." Still squatting, he scooped bullets out of the bluebonnets that rose like sapphire spears around the hem of her skirt. "I was worried you might be trying to get rid of me again."

"I—I only thought Shae was expecting you," she stammered, beating a hasty retreat. There was something disconcerting, not to mention titillating, about a man's bronzed fingers snaking through the grass and darting so near to the unmentionables one wore beneath one's skirt.

"Shae's not expecting me yet, ma'am. The sun's too low in the sky." Rawlins straightened leisurely. "I figure I've got a half hour, maybe more, before I report to the barn. Just think, Miss Aurora. That gives us plenty of time to get acquainted."

His grin was positively wicked. He stretched out his hand, offering her the bullets. She realized that if she wanted her bullets back, she would have to pluck every single one from his palm. And that meant touching him. She glared up into his laughing eyes. Fortunately, she was no longer a green girl, and she'd learned a good deal over the years about diverting young men from their less-than-wholesome urges.

"I don't have time to get acquainted," she said tartly, fishing for new bullets inside her apron pocket. "I must finish my practice before my students arrive."

"Let's see what you've got, then."

"I beg your pardon?"

"Show me what you can do."

He pocketed her cartridges, and she gaped at him.

"You can't mean to stay and watch!"

"Well, sure. Why not? I figure with all the gun-powder you've been burning, that's got to be—what?—the fifth bottle you're about to blow to kingdom come?" He smirked, rocking back on his heels and hooking his thumbs over his gun belt. "I reckon I might even learn something."

Oh, he really was a cutup.

"Watching me would not be a good idea. . . ."

"Why's that? You said I don't make you nervous."

Rorie bit her tongue. She'd never been good at the polite little falsehoods nice people told.

"The truth is, Mr. Rawlins, I'm not very accurate—"

"Oh, don't worry about me. I'll stay out of harm's way."

"—and Shae is the teacher I prefer," she finished defensively. She couldn't think of a single better excuse.

"Shae, huh?"

"Yes. He's a crack shot."

"Well, even I've been known to hit a bottle once or twice at fifty paces. Go ahead. Draw your bead."

Rorie scowled. She would have much rather called him a name and marched into the sunrise. However, she couldn't resign herself to the guilt she'd feel afterward. Her father, a German immigrant who'd divided his time equally between his bank and his political aspirations, had drilled her rigorously in the essentials of discipline. Her mother, a timid, sickly creature who had passed on after her third miscarriage, had taught Rorie about dignity in the face of long suffering.

Thus feeling outfoxed and outmaneuvered, she walked to her marker. Rawlins whistled for his horse. She had hoped to use the gelding as another excuse, but when it trotted obediently out of the line of fire, she could only bite her tongue on an uncharitable epithet and pump bullets into her revolver's cylinder. She took her time, checking and rechecking the chambers, adjusting and readjusting her stance.

If she had hoped her delay would irritate Rawlins enough to drive him away, she was disappointed. He folded his arms across his chest and observed her ritual without comment. She suspected he was highly entertained by the whole procedure—a fact that irritated her to no end.

Since divine intervention was not likely to rescue her, and since she'd exhausted every other plausible reason for delay, she resigned herself to the inevitable. Clamping her left fist over her right, she raised her gun and took aim. The .45 exploded; she jolted; and a ripping, cracking sound came from the canopy of leaves above the barrel.

Rawlins held his tongue. She admitted grudgingly that he was showing inordinate restraint.

She waited for the smoke to clear, then ground her teeth and tried again. This time, nothing ripped, nothing cracked, and the bottle stood as staunchly as a soldier. She longed to vent her frustration with an unladylike oath.

No doubt valuing his hide, Rawlins refrained from his usual smirk.

By the time she was drawing her fifth bead, her palms had grown sticky and her muscles were quivering so badly, she could scarcely hold her arms straight. Feeling somewhat vengeful, she tried locking her elbows.

"Er . . . Miss Aurora?"

She tossed him a withering look.

"Would you mind if I gave you a piece of advice?"

I most assuredly would! she longed to shout, but the side of her that esteemed self-control subdued her tongue.

"Very well. What do you suggest?"

"First of all, you have to loosen up."

She blew out her breath. Shae had told her the same thing, several times.

"And second?"

"Well . . ." Rubbing his chin, he seemed to consider. "I reckon you might try some dry firing next. You know, without any beans in your wheel. That way, you can get used to squeezing the trigger rather than jerking it."

"But how can I ever learn to aim straight if I don't fire bullets?"

The plaintive note in her voice made her wince. She wished she could contain her feelings as well as Papa had. Every morning since Gator's death, she had dragged herself out there for the dreaded practice. She felt obligated to put the children's safety before her own principles. The problem was, her aim wasn't improving.

Shae tried to help. He accompanied her every few days to give her suggestions, but his patience would inevitably wear thin, and she wound up feeling clumsy, foolish, and a trifle stung by his exasperation. As fond as she was of the boy, she had to concede Shae was no teacher.

Rawlins, on the other hand, was smiling at her. Smiling kindly, in fact. The expression was in such contrast to his recent roguery that she wondered what he could possibly be thinking. After all, she was a woman with a gun. In Cincinnati, females with firearms were considered no better than floozies.

"Aiming isn't so hard," he said affably. "It just takes practice. You don't want to rush a shot. That's the secret.

Right now, you're anticipating the recoil. And that makes you jolt before your bullet clears the muzzle."

She considered this analysis. It sounded reasonable.

"If what you say is true, then . . . how do I correct the problem?"

"Here. I'll show you."

Two strides brought him to her side. He seemed even taller standing scant inches from her shoulder. She felt her pulse leap, and it was all she could do not to flinch when he drew his gun and dumped out the bullets.

"See?" Turning, he extended his right arm on a line with her target. Now his broad chest faced her own. "Nice and relaxed, an easy pull." He demonstrated a few more times, clicking empty chambers.

It was amazing what one noticed when one was under duress, Rorie decided. She could scarcely keep her eyes on his trigger. Her gaze kept stealing toward the unfastened button at his neck, where red gold hairs peeked out. She noticed the way his shirt, a faded cornflower blue, hugged his ribs and accentuated the leanness of his waist. She indulged in a shy glance at his gun belt and the way it wrapped his hips like the arms of a lover.

The indecency of such a thought made her insides flame, so she hastily raised her eyes. His arm should have been safe to observe, except that all its rippling musculature bore testimony to a supple strength, one that no doubt stemmed from long hours of cattle roping and log splitting. Or whatever else young men did on ranches near Bandera Pass.

She found herself wondering more about him. Studying his profile, she decided he was handsome. Not in the classical, almost beautiful way Shae was, but in a rugged, robust manner. His attraction went far deeper than physical good looks. There was a magnetic energy about Wes Rawlins, something that emanated from the core of his being and twinkled like starshine in his eyes. That something reminded her of laughter. And youth.

And all the other things she secretly missed in her life.

". . . the slow and steady way. You try it this time, ma'am."

She started. He'd been speaking, and she hadn't

heard a word. Not a *word*! What was the matter with her, letting a young man disturb her concentration so?

"Go on," he said. "Give it a whirl."

His tone was encouraging, but his gaze was all business. The contrast between his manner and her thoughts made her feel ridiculous, and a bit deflated.

"Thank you," she said primly. *Rorie, for shame. You're acting like a randy old woman!*

Determined to nip her inappropriate behavior in the bud, she moved away and took her stance. Her arms were more rested now, and when she fired, she managed to strike the barrel. Splinters flew into the air. The bottle trembled.

"Better," he said. "But try not to grip the gun butt so tight."

She nodded. Shae had given her the same advice.

Focusing all her concentration, she fired her last shot. The bottle actually jumped. She had come no closer to shattering it, though.

"Foot." She grimaced and started to pull out more bullets.

"Never mind that. Come back over here."

She eyed him uncertainly, but he waved her forward, still clearly bent on his lesson.

"Are you locking your knees?" he asked. "I can't tell."

A new warmth crept up her neck. He'd been staring at her skirts! She hastily shook her head.

"Good girl. Now all we've got to do is get you to stand still. Let's try something. Hold out your arms, like you were taking aim."

She bit her lip and obeyed.

"Good." He stepped behind her. "Your bead's on target. Now go ahead and pull the trigger."

The barrel clicked.

"See how your muzzle's jumping up?"

No, she hadn't. She was too worried about what he was doing—or going to do—behind her.

"But the gun's lighter without the bullets," she protested weakly, glancing over her shoulder.

"Doesn't matter. You're still trying to compensate for the kick. Here. I'll show you."

Before she could stop him, before she could even think to protest, his arms circled her shoulders and his chest fused to her back. She was so stunned by this intimacy—this *audacity*, she corrected herself sternly— that she was rendered speechless when he clamped his hands over hers, holding them prisoner around the butt of her gun.

"See this?" He pushed her arms up, out of alignment with the bottle. "This is what you've been doing."

"*Mister* Rawlins—"

"Now this," he continued, fitting his finger over hers and squeezing the trigger, "is what you want to do. Feel the difference? See how your elbow takes the shock after you fire?"

Her heart, which had nearly catapulted out of her chest when he all but embraced her, was now slamming painfully against her ribcage. He held her so firmly, so steadily, she couldn't have broken free if she'd tried.

Her perverse side resurfaced then, noticing curious things. There was the warm, off-key rumble of his baritone voice in her ear, and the way his breaths teased an errant strand of hair, spreading shivers from her neck to her toes. She couldn't help but note how snugly his arms wrapped her shoulders, and the pleasant, if scandalous, heat that pooled between her buttocks and his thighs.

A woman with a less hardy constitution might have fainted dead away at such a trial, but Rorie had always disdained displays of weakness.

"I see precisely," she replied in her best no-nonsense voice. "You may release me now."

"Why don't you give it a try first?"

Was there a hint of amusement in his tone?

"Very well." Unable to see his face, she couldn't verify her suspicions.

Obeying his directions, she fired, reasoning that the sooner she could satisfy him, the sooner she could flee with her last shred of dignity intact.

A strange thing happened, though. With his arms as buffers, she realized he was right. Each time she pulled the trigger, her spine butted ever so slightly against his chest. Shae had never mentioned she'd developed this bad habit.

"I'm . . . not recoiling quite as much now, am I?"

"Nope. You're squeezing that trigger like a professional lead chucker now."

It was high praise indeed, she thought, judging by the burgundy warmth in his voice.

"Here." He pulled his left gun, the loaded one, from its holster. "Try it with bullets."

When he passed the weapon to her, their hands brushed. His touch was electric, shooting tiny sparks through her limbs. She felt her stomach flip, and told herself that his gun was to blame.

Tentatively, she wrapped her fingers around the cool walnut-inlay butt. The gun was a work of art, a custom-made piece. The butt itself had been designed for the hand that used it most.

Forcing such distractions from her mind, she aligned the gunsight with the bottle. His Colt was weighted differently. She didn't know much about six-shooters, but she suspected his Peacemaker was balanced better than her old Smith and Wesson.

She hesitated, uncertain once more.

"You can do it, Aurora," he said quietly. "Go on. Just like before."

He was still behind her, around her, his heat flowing through her. The sensation was unnerving—and strangely comforting. She realized then just how much she wanted to strike that bottle. She wanted to do well, really well, and not just for the sake of the children.

Releasing a ragged breath, she focused. She relaxed. She did everything he had instructed her to do.

And when at last she pulled the trigger, she forced herself to stand like stone.

The bottle exploded into a hundred pieces.

"I did it!" She laughed, spinning toward him, so excited that she nearly danced. "*I did it, Wes!*"

"You sure did."

He smiled, and she caught her breath. For a moment she stood spellbound, absolutely dazzled by the coppery shimmers that sparked like fire in his hair. In that instant, with the rays of morning ablaze around him, he looked like Apollo stepping out of the sun.

"Want to try again?"

His voice had turned husky. She felt rather than heard it, and a wave of tingles gusted over her skin.

"Uh ..." She realized, to her embarrassment, that she was staring. "I don't have another bottle."

"Too bad." He cocked his head, and his eyes, peridot green now with a trace of wistfulness, seemed to delve past all her pretenses. "Another time, then?"

She nodded, still too dazed to command herself.

He chuckled, retrieving his Colt. With a speed and a flare that appeared second nature, he spun the .45 over his forefinger and into its holster. She felt her heart trip, then it sank to her toes.

Clearly, she'd been nursing false hopes. Her Apollo was a gunfighter.

Chapter Four

After retrieving his gear and breaking camp, Wes set off a half hour later toward the Boudreau homestead.

Only he didn't do it at Aurora's breakneck pace.

The woman had gotten a burr under her saddle again, he mused. Over what, he wasn't certain, considering he'd been about as fine a gentleman as he knew how to be. After all, he'd taught her how to shoot straight, hadn't he? And he'd kept his peace while she tried to gun down half the county's chokecherry trees.

Wes shook his head. Maybe he was an idiot for teaching her how to defend her children with a Peacemaker. After all, town gossips would like him to believe she'd conspired in Boudreau's murder. But after seeing her ineptitude with a gun twice in two days, he doubted whether she herself could have shot down a renowned deadeye like the county sheriff.

There was the possibility, however, that she could have masterminded a conspiracy to kill Boudreau. Wes had no doubt she was clever enough for such a crime, even though she didn't lie particularly well. Her blush gave her away each time.

In fact, her blushes made her appear too damned vulnerable and appealing for his peace of mind.

The woman was an enigma, that was certain. Part

ferocious mother, part wide-eyed innocent—and part murdering Jezebel? The puzzle pieces just didn't fit. If she'd conspired to kill Boudreau, what had been her motivation? According to the less discreet people he'd talked to in Elodea, Aurora had flaunted herself as Gator's mistress, serving openly as lady of the house after Mrs. Boudreau's death. Had Aurora and Gator had a falling out? Had he threatened to throw her and her orphans into the wilds?

Wes had a hard time believing even a desperate Aurora would murder to keep a roof over her children's heads. Still, he'd heard of stranger things happening in the heat of passion. Maybe her priggish style of flirting was a clever ploy to throw him off her trail.

He almost laughed aloud. Surely she wasn't *that* accomplished at scheming.

Amused by the absurdity of his thought, he began to hum, and then to sing:

> *Come you midwestern girls, listen to me,*
> *Don't lose your fair heart to them Texan boys.*
> *When they go a'courtin', they make a great noise,*
> *Wear old leather coats, patched-up holes in their drawers.*
> *They ain't got much grace, and they sure got no poise,*
> *Those wild, unruly west Texas boys.*

As Two-Step trotted up the drive, Wes's rusty singing was accompanied by the sound of steel striking wood. He sang his last note with raunchy gusto, and Shae paused in his work to make a face.

"You're late, Rawlins."

"Reckon I am."

Shae climbed to his feet, balancing himself on the barn's sloping roof. He wore the look of a busy man who'd just decided his day was going downhill.

"You got some kind of explanation?"

"Oh, I always have an explanation."

Shae grimaced, and Wes had the sneaking suspicion that his young boss was more irritated at him for showing up than for being late.

"Would this explanation of yours have something to do with a whiskey bottle?"

"Well . . ." Wes dismounted and pushed back his hat with his thumb. He couldn't very well lie. " 'Fraid so," he said solemnly, trying not to smirk at the memory of Aurora, stomping her foot after every missed shot.

"Miss Aurora doesn't like drinking."

"Is that a fact?"

"A genuine fact, mister. So if you're thinking about cutting your wolf loose each night, you'd best turn around and head back where you came from."

Wes hiked a brow. Now that had to be the third attempt since sunrise to steer him clear of this spread. He supposed he could put Shae's mind to rest by confessing he hadn't touched a drop of whiskey for over eleven months. Bad things always seemed to happen when he got cork high and bottle deep. The first time, when he was sixteen, Zack and Aunt Lally had been kidnapped by outlaws and their Bosque County ranch had been burned to a cinder while he'd been staggering around the local saloon. That night had been the worst one of Wes's life. Of course, the evening a year ago when he got drunk enough to punch Cord's lights out certainly ran a close second. Tarantula juice had a nasty way of sneaking up on him. He'd made the decision to avoid it, but he doubted whether Shae would believe him.

"Much obliged for the warning, Shae. I'll keep my wolf leashed and muzzled for now.

"On second thought"—he anticipated his next clash of wits with relish—"I should probably go apologize to Miss Aurora before I muzzle anything."

He turned to lead Two-Step toward the corral.

"Rawlins!"

He glanced up. Sunlight glinted on metal, distracting him from the boy. Against the weather vane, within an arm's reach of Shae, leaned the double-barreled Whitney.

"I'll be watching you," Shae said grimly.

Wes steeled himself against his rising annoyance. Did the boy always pack a scattergun when he worked? Or was the weapon a precaution born of guilt . . . and fear of capture by lawmen?

"Fair enough, Shae." Wes matched the boy stare for

stare. "But just be sure, while you're watching, you don't let the real badmen sneak by."

Feeling somewhat vindicated, he unsaddled Two-Step and turned him loose inside the fenced-off pasture, where the Sinclairs' few barn animals had been temporarily relocated. True to his name, the gelding danced around Aurora's nag, two goats, and a disgruntled-looking heifer to claim the sweetest, most tender clover for himself. Wes watched the rascal fondly for a moment before it occurred to him that no children were in sight. He wondered with wry amusement if Aurora had whisked them into the storm cellar again. After all, he *was* prowling the grounds once more.

"There's an ax near the woodpile up by the porch," Shae called from his bird's-eye view. "You can start by breaking up some of these rotted timbers."

Wes nodded, hiding his smile as he slung his saddle over the corral's top rail. It looked as if he was going to get his opportunity to snoop sooner than he had expected.

Hooking his thumbs over his gun belt, he strolled up the drive, whistling as he went. Although his stride was long and leisurely, his gaze darted into every shadow, registering information about his new employers. He deduced from the struggling magnolia, with its freshly spread and watered fertilizer, that someone cared a great deal for the tree.

He noticed the clattering tin-can sentinels around the vegetable garden and the fresh nibble marks of the rabbits that had apparently overcome their fear of the noise. He suspected Aurora was waging a losing battle.

A busted chain hung from the porch roof, where the fallen swing must have swung. Wes wondered if the wood shavings that had been swept so neatly behind the cane seat had been hidden or simply forgotten by the small-footed person who had left a print there.

When the fluttering of clothes on a rope caught his eye, he noticed several junior-sized shirts and trousers, but nothing that suggested a man lived and worked there, except, perhaps, for the colorful quilt with its wedding-ring design. Boudreau's, he wondered, or Aurora's?

Once again Wes found his curiosity piqued by the anomaly that was Aurora. She had admitted to having a husband. So where was the man? Had he run off or passed on?

Forcing his thoughts to his work, he found the ax exactly as Shae had described it. However, Wes was far more interested in the aroma of something sweet wafting from somewhere inside the house. A sweetness like pecan pie, to be exact. Now when had Aurora had time to bake a pie?

An unbidden vision of Aurora, flushed and dusted with flour, appealed to him almost as much as the prospect of filling his belly with a hot, fresh slab of his favorite treat. He tossed a sideways glance at Shae. The boy was watching him like a hawk. Wes's contrary side surfaced, and he grinned, waving gaily. Turning the corner, he disappeared from Shae's sight.

With the instincts of a bloodhound, he sniffed out those pecans, tracking them to an open window with fluttery white muslin curtains. He wasn't disappointed. Four heavenly pies lay cooling on the sill. Only Aurora wasn't guarding them. Instead, a formidable-looking black woman stood by the window, a rolling pin held primed and ready in her fist. Wes recognized her as the woman who'd herded the children into the storm cellar the day before.

He edged another step closer and flashed his most engaging smile. " 'Morning, ma'am."

The woman looked him up and down. A bit on the short side for her ample girth, she was, nevertheless, a faded beauty with two keen brown eyes sharp enough to bore through a man. Wes thought she resembled Shae with her high cheekbones and long-fingered hands, but since she was at least thirty-five years the boy's senior, she was less likely to be Shae's mother than his grandmother.

"I take it you're Rawlins?" she said.

He tipped his hat. "Yes, ma'am. Pleased to meet you, ma'am."

"Humph. More likely you're pleased to meet my pie. Was that you I heard out there caterwauling about men's drawers?"

He chuckled. "Aw, I didn't sound as bad as all that, did I?"

"Like a burro with a head cold."

His grin turned lopsided. Aunt Lally had always told him the same thing. "Well, you know what they say, ma'am. Practice makes perfect. Want me to sing another verse to get it right?"

"You trying to scare me, son?"

"Naw. But I sure would be pleased to have you call me Wes, ma'am."

"Wes, huh?" Amusement began to twinkle in her cagey eyes. "And where did a villain like you learn good manners?"

"From my aunt Lally, I reckon. She always taught me to treat ladies real fine, 'cause she said each and every one was a heaven-sent angel."

"An angel, eh?"

"Yes, ma'am. Don't you agree?"

A smile tugged at the corners of her lips. "This aunt Lally of yours sounds like a wise woman."

"Oh yes, ma'am. One of the wisest." He felt his heart warm with fleeting memories. "I reckon you'd like her."

"I reckon I would." She locked her frank, discerning gaze with his once more, only this time, he saw the glimmer of acceptance there.

"So it's a piece of my pie you're wanting."

"Well, ma'am," he said, donning his best martyr's look, "I wouldn't want to impose or anything. But it sure would help to keep my mind off singing. . . ."

"Now that would be a blessing." A dimple flirted in her cheek. "I reckon I could cut you a slice to keep the peace around here."

"Much obliged, ma'am."

She chuckled, at last giving full rein to her amusement. "The name's Ginevee. I'm Shae's Maw-Maw."

A quarter of a pie, and a full conquest later, Wes was smacking his lips and heading back for the barn, when he nearly collided knee-first with a copper-skinned child of about seven years. The girl craned her head back, her Indian-style braids brushing her skirt, and regarded him with the biggest, most honest eyes he had ever seen in his life.

"You are very tall," she said, her hands clasped behind her back.

His mouth quirked. "I reckon I am."

"I am Merrilee," she said in that same grave, wiser-than-her-years voice.

He squatted down before her, but even then her gleaming black head only came up to his chin. "Pleased to meet you, Miss Merrilee. My name's Wes."

She nodded, then considered him for a moment. "Can you climb trees?"

He heard a titter. Seeking the sound, he spied three other children half-hidden behind the magnolia tree, all listening eagerly. There was a Mexican girl, also in pigtails, of about thirteen years, who tittered again and blushed profusely, dropping her eyes from his gaze. Her hand was gripping the collar of a muddy, shoeless, eager-to-run Po. Beside them, with his arms folded across his chest stood a tow-headed boy, maybe nine years old, whose jaw jutted in a manner reminiscent of Shae's.

"Well . . ." Wes gazed once more into Merrilee's enormous brown eyes—everything about the child was pint-sized except those eyes—and felt a tug on his heart-strings. "Sure, I can climb trees."

"Ask him, Merrilee!" the boy whispered loudly, pronouncing "ask" with a noticeable lisp. "Hurry up before Miss Aurora comes back."

"Miss Ror-wah! Miss Ror-wah!" Po shouted gaily, jumping up and down.

Wes nearly laughed at the toddler, but the nine-year-old's speech—and his freckles—sobered him. He hoped the boy would outgrow both afflictions soon.

"Is there something I can do for you, Miss Merrilee?" he asked the girl.

She nodded gravely, then produced what she'd been hiding behind her back, a cup-shaped nest of thorny twigs and dry leaves. Inside it were a few gray feathers, two speckled blue eggs, and the unfortunate remains of at least one more.

"The mama mockingbird lost her babies. And Topher can't climb the tree."

"I can too!" the boy called defensively. "Only Miss Aurora won't let me."

"She won't, eh?" Wes said. "Well . . ." He took the nest carefully and straightened, giving Topher a friendly smile as he approached the tree. "You can't go blaming Miss Aurora."

"I can't?"

"Naw. Seems to me there's a law about tree climbing somewhere."

"There is?" the Mexican girl asked, instantly turning crimson again when he glanced her way.

"Yep. You have to wait till you're as tall as me."

"Why's that?" Topher demanded suspiciously.

Wes thought fast, tickled by the challenge. "I guess it's 'cause trees consider us tall folks kind of like their next of kin."

Topher seemed to accept this explanation, albeit reluctantly.

Meanwhile, the irrepressible Po was beating on Wes's leg. "I wanna help!" he commanded in a voice at least three times his size. The boy's red-faced caretaker hastily dragged the child back, but not before, Wes noticed in amusement, baby handprints had decorated his thigh.

"Let's see," he said good-naturedly. "Do you think you could hold this for me?" He tugged off his neckerchief, surrendering it to Po's eager, grasping hands. Next, he slipped off his hat.

"And I'd be right honored if you'd hold this for me, miss," he told the Mexican girl. " 'Course, I'd be even more honored," he added, "if you'd tell me your name."

She giggled. Although she was plump in some places, Wes decided she would be a real beauty in a couple of years, when she finished sprouting into womanhood.

"Juanita," she answered shyly. "But everyone calls me Nita, mostly 'cause Po can't say the 'Juan' part."

"Nita, Nita, Nita!"

"Quiet, Po," Topher said in a low, cross voice. "Next thing you know, Miss Aurora will be over here asking why you're so dirty, and then I'm gonna be in for it, 'cause I went digging for worms instead of—" He broke off abruptly, seeming to recall that a member of the enemy camp—a grown-up—was listening. "Well?" His chin jutting out again, he eyed Wes in challenge. "Are you gonna climb that tree or aren't you?"

"I'll give it a try." Chuckling to himself, Wes hung his gun belt well out of the children's reach and swung up onto the lowest bough.

Back in the dining room, which served as her schoolroom, Rorie got her first hint that mischief was afoot when the mantel clock chimed a quarter past the hour, and her students had still not scrambled madly for their seats.

Her second clue came when she heard Ginevee call out the kitchen window, her tone unmistakable in its disbelief. "Land sakes! That boy's up in the tree!"

Rorie quailed. Visions of Topher, his head gashed and bloody, flashed before her eyes. She dropped her slate and rushed outside, praying that God would keep the boy surefooted until she could coax him back to earth—and give him a piece of her mind.

But as Rorie raced across the yard, scattering chickens with the flurry of her skirts, she saw Topher's sunbleached hair surrounded by a half-dozen gleaming black heads. Her four orphans and three of her students, all from neighboring farms, encircled the rain-thirsty magnolia tree. Giggling and pointing, they were shouting encouragements to the mischief-maker who was prowling the boughs. She couldn't see the rascal clearly through the canopy, and she worried that the older boys had dared chubby Bernardo Garcia to scale the tree. A nightmarish image of Nardo falling quickly blanked out her earlier vision of Topher. She began framing a frantic apology to Nardo's mother as she reached the children's circle. She arrived in time to see a lean, male torso swoop through the leaves.

"Mister Wes! Mister Wes!" Po shouted, jumping up and down.

Rorie scowled. She should have known.

He was suspended upside down from a limb, grinning while he reached playfully for Po's straining fingers.

For a heartbeat, she didn't know which was worse: that her children were watching her new handyman break her ironclad rule against tree climbing, or that she'd caught herself sneaking a peek beneath his gaping shirt, where his rock-ribbed planes melted into the valley of his waist.

"*Mister* Rawlins."

"Uh-oh," Topher whispered, nudging Merrilee.

The children hastily made way for her as she swept forward, endeavoring not to huff like a locomotive after her run.

Wes noticed her then. "Why . . . hello, ma'am," he drawled in that provocative baritone of his. "You sure got pretty hair."

Her hand flew to her to coiffure. When she found the tumbled ruins of her once neatly coiled braid, she blushed so hotly her face felt scalded. The children snickered, and Wes at last curled upward, displaying an abdominal strength that made such athletics look easy.

Rorie folded her arms. It would never do to let the children believe he could disturb her. For their sakes, she had worked hard to remain unruffled by Dukker's coercive courtship after Ethan Hawkins had ridden off on his cattle drive without making the marriage proposal she'd hoped for. She had also staunchly hidden her hurt when faced with the townsfolks' speculations about Ethan's intentions—or lack thereof. Having managed these feats of diplomacy, she felt certain she could handle with aplomb one redheaded rogue with trouble on his mind.

"Mr. Rawlins," she began crisply, "kindly explain what you're doing in that tree."

He reached above him, retrieving the gun belt, which, thankfully, he must have taken pains to keep from the children.

"Helping a lady in distress," he said.

Before she could fully comprehend his answer, she felt a tug on her skirt.

"You aren't mad, are you, ma'am?" Merrilee asked, her innocent brow furrowed with habitual, well-meaning concern. "The mama mockingbird lost her nest last night, and I asked Mr. Wes to—"

Topher nudged Merrilee again, and she reddened, her confession stuttering to a halt.

"I see," Rorie said more gently. Merrilee was always trying to rescue some wounded creature or another, and it drove Rorie to distraction worrying that the child might be bitten by some pain-crazed rabbit or squirrel. Nevertheless, she always found herself torn between lecturing and praising Merrilee. After all the unkindness the Indian girl had been shown, it was a miracle she possessed so much compassion.

Rorie decided to save her ire for Wes. Gazing once more into the tree, she leveled her best no-nonsense glare at him. "If you have accomplished your mission, Mr. Rawlins, then please remove yourself from our tree."

To her amazement, he obliged, and her heart leaped when he plummeted past her, landing catlike at her side. His all-too-masculine warmth was as tangible as the heat that flooded her neck. She stumbled backward, but the children crowded around him, their faces upturned and eager.

"Do you think the mama mockingbird will come back?" eleven-year-old Abraham asked doubtfully.

"What about the daddy?" asked his twin sister, Sarah.

Nardo, who must have joined the group during Wes's acrobatics, reached around the two black children and tugged on Rorie's skirt.

"Miss Aurora," he began in his froggy voice, "where do baby mockingbirds come from?"

Wes made a strangled noise that sounded suspiciously like laughter. She shot him a dark look.

"From eggs, children," she said briskly. "Nita, please take everyone inside and start the spelling lesson."

Topher looked mutinous. "We did spelling yesterday."

"Yes, well . . . Mr. Rawlins has work to do, Topher, and so do you."

"Grannies," he muttered under his breath.

Rorie arched an eyebrow. She'd learned to squelch the boy's oaths, even the most innocuous ones. Otherwise, she'd have to listen to Po gaily parrot them a hundred times a day. "I beg your pardon, young man?"

"I didn't say nothing. Ma'am," he added sullenly, snatching up his fishing pole. He hurried after Nardo and the twins.

Meanwhile, Nita was having a hard time getting Po to surrender Wes's neckerchief. By the time she had scooped the screaming toddler into her arms and started for the house, only Merrilee was left.

"You are very nice to help the mama mockingbird," she said solemnly. "Thank you, Mr. Wes."

"You are very welcome, Miss Merrilee."

Wes winked, and a shy smile curved Merrilee's lips. It lingered on her face when she turned and began her slow, painstaking limp after the others.

Rorie blew out her breath. At last they were alone, and she could tell Wes Rawlins exactly what she thought of him. She rounded on him, words like *scoundrel*, *reprobate*, and *ne'er-do-well* poised on her tongue.

When she thought to launch those invectives, though, the expression on his face made her stop. His teasing smile was gone, and he was frowning after Merrilee. The concern in his gaze was so intense that for a moment, Rorie imagined another Wes Rawlins had stepped from behind the tree.

"What happened to her?" he asked quietly.

Rorie hesitated. Merrilee's condition was none of his business, and yet, robbed of the momentum of her anger, she found herself moved, and not just a little surprised, by the empathy he seemed to feel for the child.

"Merrilee's parents were killed by white men when she was four," she said, struggling to keep her tone matter-of-fact. "She remembers little of the incident, other than that she was thrown against some rocks and left for dead."

Wes stiffened visibly. She could have sworn he grew taller by an inch.

"And her leg?"

Rorie glanced after Merrilee, her heart aching for the child. "It was injured in her fall. Fortunately, a traveling preacher and his wife happened across the campsite and found Merrilee before the coyotes did. They did what they could, but they were no doctors. By the time they brought her to Jarrod, the bone had set and there was little he could do."

"Jarrod?"

"Yes," she said coolly, her guard on the rise again. "My husband."

Those keen, searching eyes at last focused on her, and Rorie fidgeted, although she couldn't say why.

"So your husband was a doctor, eh?"

"He still is."

Surprise registered on his features. "Was Jarrod the same sawbones who treated Boudreau's gunshot wound?"

Rorie studied him narrowly, but she saw no reason not to answer. "No, Jarrod was long gone by then."

"I see."

She bristled at the speculation in his soft voice. "And now, Mr. Rawlins—"

"It's Wes, remember?" The mischievous light returned to his eyes. "At least, it was this morning."

An acute twinge of embarrassment pierced her chest. "Yes, well, I believe you have a barn roof to repair."

His grin was slow and lazy and filled with a heart-tripping warmth. "And a fence, and a swing, and maybe even a toy and a shoe."

She blinked, uncertain how to respond to his offer. She would have liked to say that Shae would fix the children's things, but ever since Gator's murder, Shae had been devoting his spare time to guns, which worried her immensely.

She needn't share with Wes her fear that Shae was obsessed with vengeance, she told herself. Nodding, she turned to hurry away.

"Miss Rorie?"

She hesitated, surprised to hear her childhood nickname. No one ever called her that anymore, although she remembered the last time clearly. It had been her fourteenth birthday, and her mother had whispered her name as she kissed her cheek. The next day, Mama had died, and Papa had relegated her to a nanny. Rorie had seen little of him after that, except, of course, when he needed an accomplished hostess for his political dinners.

Uncertainly, she glanced over her shoulder at Wes. "Yes?"

"He was loco, you know."

His voice was just gentle enough, just compassionate enough, to make her turn back around.

"Who?"

"This Jarrod feller. For letting you go, I mean."

Her throat tightened. For a moment, it was all she could do not to give in to tears. She knew Wes Rawlins had a gift for flattery, yet the sincerity in his manner was hard to discount. Maybe it was because she wanted so desperately to believe in that particular truth.

"Thank you. Wes."

He smiled again, looking pleased by her concession. Tipping his hat, he turned and strolled toward the barn.

It might have been the perfect reconciliation, except for one thing. He hooked his thumbs over his gun belt, and Rorie was reminded once again that her handyman was something more than he professed to be.

Chapter Five

Sometimes Wes amazed himself. The damnedest things could come out of his mouth.

Take, for instance, the wisecrack he'd made the day before when he said Jarrod Sinclair was loco. Wes didn't know where the hell *that* had come from, but after blurting it out to salve Rorie's feelings, he'd realized he meant it. Every word. Just like he'd meant his compliment, when he told her she had pretty hair.

Usually he flattered sweethearts, not murder suspects, and the lawman in him cautioned the flirt that he was taking too much pleasure out of this investigation. The last thing he needed, or wanted, was to feel sympathy for a woman he might have to arrest. Although the darker side of a female's nature had always appealed to Wes, he wasn't going to risk his badge or his personal freedom over a dalliance with Rorie—even if he did find evidence to clear her name.

Wes had always been careful to keep his sights off the marrying kind. A man could do a lot worse than a bawdily affectionate calico queen, and besides, Wes could always count on a whore not to complicate his life with expectations. Not that getting hitched was bad, he mused. He'd seen the good it had done Cord.

But Cord had married Fancy, and Fancy was one in a million. There wasn't a woman alive who could

compare with her, although there were times when he
rode up to a new cathouse filled with anticipation, hoping
that this was the place where he'd find her: that courageous, passionate, darkly sweet angel who'd steal his
heart from Fancy.

He smile mockingly at himself. Of course, that never
happened.

Maybe it was just as well. He didn't believe in
dumping a new bride on his doorstep so he could ride off
to collar renegades. When the time came for him to put
down roots—and that was still a long spell off—he would
be plenty sure he could give up outlaw busting without
regrets. No wife of his was going to walk the floor worrying he was dead. He'd learned the hard way how much
pain a man's absence could cause when he'd watched
Fancy stare after Cord's traildust.

The old anguish threatened, and Wes clenched his
teeth. Deliberately, and with a good deal of practice, he
shoved the feelings back down. He loved his brother. The
man could be overbearing and stubborn at times, but that
wasn't the problem. The real problem was that Wes had
let his feelings for Fancy get the better of him. And he'd
hurt Cord.

Never, ever could he go home and face his brother
again.

Wes drew a shuddering breath. It was better not to
think about home. It was better to get on with his
investigation.

Since Shae had dragged him off the previous evening
to fell an oak for lumber, Wes had missed the family dinner. With Ginevee scrubbing pans at one end of the
house, and Aurora tutoring Topher at the other, Wes had
also missed an opportunity to snoop through drawers and
cabinets.

But today was a new day. The sun, which had
climbed to its zenith, was hotter than the devil's branding
iron. Rorie had ended class early so the children could go
to the fishing hole at Ramble Creek. Only Merrilee remained behind, apparently content to pick wildflowers,
one of which she'd shyly presented to him.

Since Rorie and Ginevee were busy with laundry, and

Shae was fixing a dining room chair in the toolshed, Wes figured he'd have a good ten minutes to prowl the house undisturbed.

Whistling with practiced nonchalance as he climbed down from the barn roof, he strolled toward the privy, let the door bang loudly, then circled back through the trees to slink inside through the kitchen door. All this subterfuge was child's play to a man who delighted in tracking and stalking.

Since he'd come looking for clues, preferably written ones that might indicate discord between Gator, Shae, and Rorie, Wes stopped first in the stretch of floor space that served as sitting room, dining room, and schoolhouse. He could tell Rorie conducted her lessons there because of the slates stacked neatly on a pinewood sideboard.

A small desk stood wedged in one corner, and he started his search there, hoping to find a ledger that might indicate Gator's worth and thereby point toward a motivation for Shae and Rorie to kill him. Pulling open drawers, Wes rummaged among polished river stones, broken chess pieces, a bag of marbles, a limbless doll, and a variety of other junk that Rorie must have confiscated from inattentive students.

He couldn't help but be tickled when he found several marked playing cards and a piece of butcher paper on which Topher had scrawled, "cheating is wrong," about twenty times above his signature.

Opening the next drawer, Wes leafed through the paper cutouts, valentines, and dried flowers that had been carefully preserved between the tattered pages of an old reader. He suspected these items were Rorie's treasures, gifts that she had received from the children. It touched him in an unexpected way to see the value she placed on things of no monetary worth.

In the next instant, he was making a face at himself. Yep. His brain was most definitely turning to mush.

The remaining two drawers revealed little more than school supplies, so he turned his attention to the sideboard, with all its drawers and doors. He knew a grim sense of satisfaction when he found it was locked.

Apparently Rorie kept something in there that she valued even more than handmade gifts.

Removing his hat, he fished from the inner lining the widdy he had taken from a weasel-eyed stagecoach driver who tried to jimmy a passenger's trunk. Wes had a whole collection of ring shiners, knuckle dusters, shaved dice, counterfeit money, and other outlaw memorabilia back home in a box. He kept the widdy with him, though, because it was useful in detective work. He wasn't any Pinkerton, but he'd been known to turn up a fair share of verdict-clinching evidence with helpful gadgets like widdies.

Setting his hat back on his head, he went to work, jiggling the old, stubborn lock with his thief's pick. He'd no sooner swung open the door, when a bobbing, pigtailed shadow upon the sideboard caught his eye.

"Hello, Mr. Wes."

He didn't know what jumped harder, him or his heart. Turning, he found Merrilee standing in the open doorway holding a basket of flowers at least half her size.

"Hello, Merrilee."

He tried to smile, but it was hard to appear innocent when facing those big mahogany eyes.

"What are you doing in Miss Rorie's private cabinet?"

"Well, I . . ." He glanced down, straining to come up with a plausible lie, and noticed the wilted flower twined around his belt loop. Remembering the annoying honeybee he'd had to squash earlier, he looked back up at Merrilee. "I, er, was looking for medicine."

Merrilee's eyes grew even bigger, if that was possible. "Medicine? Are you sick?"

With a sleight of hand that a cardsharp would have envied, he slipped the widdy into his back pocket. "Not as sick as that honeybee is."

This humor was clearly lost on Merrilee. She frowned. "What's wrong with the honeybee?"

His smile was genuine this time as he struggled not to laugh. "That old bee had a run-in with my belly, and since I don't much like to be stung—"

Merrilee's gasp cut him off, and she dropped her basket, spilling flowers all over her moccasins. *"Bee sting?"*

She was backing for the door, and Wes saw instantly that he'd made a mistake.

"It wasn't a very big bee sting—"

"I'll get Miss Rorie."

"Merrilee, wait!"

But she was already hurrying down the hall, her pigtails bouncing behind her.

Wes muttered an oath. God love the child, she meant well, but he was going to have a helluva time explaining to Rorie how he'd opened her locked cabinet, not to mention why he was snooping in the first place. He didn't think she'd believe the medicine story, and that meant he would have to come up with some other whopper. Unless . . .

He smiled wickedly to himself.

Unless he found some way to distract her.

"Miss Rorie!"

Rorie started to hear Merrilee—shy, respectful Merrilee—call her by her childhood nickname. She supposed it was inevitable, though. The previous night during prayers, Topher had slyly tested the waters in front of the other children by asking God to bless "Miss Rorie."

That morning, she'd learned Topher's influence had spread to Po, when the toddler presented her with the biggest, ugliest toad she'd ever seen in her life and crowed, "Lookie, lookie! I named him Miss Wor-wee!"

Somehow, she'd managed to greet her new namesake with decorum.

In truth, Rorie didn't mind the orphans using her childhood name, since she'd often wished Jarrod would do the same as proof of his affection for her.

What Rorie did mind was the implication behind Wes's use of the name. She had no intention of encouraging a greater familiarity with her hired hand, nor did she want her children to. Unfortunately, the children had spent all of their play time the day before shadowing Wes. And Wes had spent his work time charming, entertaining, and *educating* them, God forbid.

She would have to speak to her hired hand about her children.

"Miss Rorie!" Merrilee called again, panting as she ran into the garden.

When Rorie saw the child's eyes, as big and dark as eclipsed suns, she knew immediately that disaster had struck. Jumping to her feet, she all but forgot Wes as Merrilee skidded to a halt before her.

"Bee sting!" the child cried.

"Where, Merrilee?" Rorie caught the girl's shoulders. "Where did the bee sting you?"

Shaking her head, Merrilee gulped down air. "Not me. Mr. Wes!"

Rorie frowned. "Mr. Wes?"

Merrilee nodded vigorously. "He was looking for medicine in your private cabinet."

Surprised by this information, Rorie decided she must have misunderstood. "You mean he's in the dining room?"

Merrilee looked close to tears. "Yes, ma'am. Hurry!" She tugged on Rorie's hand. "Mr. Wes could get very, very sick!"

Rorie obliged, letting the child pull her into the house. She knew Merrilee was remembering the previous summer, when Topher had been stung by a bee and had swelled up like a bull frog. The boy had been feverish for several days, and Merrilee had huddled by his bedside, afraid she would lose her playmate.

"It's all right, Merrilee," Rorie said soothingly. "I'm sure Mr. Wes will be just fine."

She'd no sooner said this, when a pitiful moan came from the dining room. Merrilee's uneven legs churned even faster as she pulled Rorie down the hall.

"Hurry, Miss Rorie. Hurry!"

Much to her secret amusement, Rorie spied Wes sitting on her desk, swinging a long, muscular leg and frowning perplexedly at the taffy box she'd filled with sewing notions.

"Damn," he muttered before realizing he'd acquired an audience.

"Does it hurt, Mr. Wes?" Merrilee asked, dragging Rorie all the way to his side.

He nodded woefully, but she saw the amusement dancing in his eyes. Rorie suspected then that there'd been no bee and no sting, and that he was the only pain.

Merrilee stepped up onto the stool by the desk and pressed a small palm to his sun-baked cheek. "He's real hot, Miss Rorie!" The child turned anxiously to her for guidance.

Wes had the audacity to smirk behind the child's back. "That's not the only place I'm hot, Miss Rorie."

She shot him a quelling glare. "Merrilee, sweetheart, why don't you gather up all your flowers and put them in a vase for Ginevee."

The child looked torn between her patient and her chore.

"Go ahead, Miss Merrilee," Wes said in a brave voice. "Miss Rorie will fix me."

I'll fix you, all right, she thought, helping the child fill her basket.

When the flowers were all gathered, Merrilee hesitated once more, glancing back at Wes. "Would it be all right if I draw your pony?"

"You mean Two-Step?" He chuckled. "Why, I think ol' fiddle foot would be right pleased to have his portrait made."

Merrilee turned eagerly to Rorie. "Can I, ma'am?"

Rorie nodded. What harm could come to the child as long as she stayed clear of the gelding's hooves? Besides, Rorie had been encouraging Merrilee's gift for drawing. It was the only way to get her to discuss the phantoms in her nightmares.

"You may take a slate to the corral," Rorie said, "but you must promise not to go inside."

"I promise." Merrilee eagerly retrieved a board and chalk from the table and slipped them into her basket. "Thank you, ma'am. 'Bye, Mr. Wes."

After Merrilee had left, Rorie planted her fists on her hips and glared at the scapegrace sitting on her desk.

"Ah, my angel of mercy."

"Mercy's the last thing you'll get from me, Wes Rawlins."

"You sure have a lot of flash in those eyes. Reminds me of a Winchester when its brass receiver catches the sun."

"Don't change the subject." She tugged the taffy box from his hands. "Don't you have any scruples?"

"Now don't go spitting smoke. I was only going to eat one tiny little piece . . ."

She glowered at him, but it was hard not to be distracted by his ruggedly sensual beauty.

"That is *not* what I meant and you know it well. Lying to the child that way—"

"What, you don't think I have a bee sting?"

She blinked, her reprimand faltering on her tongue. It had never occurred to her he really might.

"Do you?"

"Yes."

She wasn't sure she liked the silky tone of his voice. "Where?"

"On my belly."

For the first time since arriving in the room, she noticed the wilted Indian paintbrush tucked inside his belt loop. A bee sting in such a tender area probably throbbed worse than a sore tooth.

She sighed. Why hadn't he said he was hurting in the first place?

To her embarrassment, she realized he had.

"I see." She cleared her throat. "Very well. Unbutton your shirt while I get the salve."

She stepped to the cabinet, too flustered by her self-recriminations as she unlocked the doors to notice the upside-down book above the medicine shelf. He must think she was completely heartless, she berated herself. First his limp when she'd met him, now his bee sting, and she hadn't offered him care for either.

The idea that a gun-toting, wisecracking rogue like Wes Rawlins could be as vulnerable as Topher, or even Po, touched her in a way that did serious damage to the barrier of distrust she was trying to keep between them. It took all of her hard-won prudence, caution forged by her husband's betrayals and lies, to keep herself from begging Wes's forgiveness. After all, she didn't want any gunfighter getting too comfortable in her home and staying long enough to give Topher or Shae romantic ideas about shoot-outs.

All those thoughts flitted through her mind in the space of a few heartbeats. In fact, she couldn't have turned her back on him for more than half a minute while she'd unlocked the cabinet and retrieved salve from her collection of medicines. When she turned to face Wes again, though, he'd stripped off his vest and shirt.

Her jaw dropped.

The jar of salve nearly did too.

Perfectly at ease in all his bare-chested glory, he settled back on the desk, every sinew rippling in shameless display. She tried not to gawk, but it was almost impossible, given his striking virility. Apollo didn't do him justice today. He was more like the fabled Adonis, a Greek youth of such breathtaking beauty that Aphrodite herself had fallen in love with him.

Broad and brawny in the shoulders, lean and narrow in the hips, Wes had hidden a whole world of wonders beneath his faded cotton shirt: knotted biceps, corded forearms, and a rock-hard abdomen that would have taken a stinger of steel to scrape, much less pucker.

She swallowed, and he flashed a dazzling smile.

"You don't mind me unshucked, do you, ma'am? I figured with you being a doctor's wife and all, you'd grown kind of used to fixing up patients with their shirts off."

She clutched the jar like a lifeboat in a hurricane.

"Er . . . no." Her voice sounded too high, and she felt her face flood with color. "Of course not."

Think of him as Shae, she instructed herself sternly. *You've massaged salve into Shae's aching back a dozen times or more.*

She took a step closer, then forced herself to take another. He began swinging his leg again, an incongruous combination of youthful exuberance and manly sensuality. It drew her gaze to the thickened trunks of his thighs, which spread apart oh-so casually, on a level with her warming womanhood. The realization had a devastating effect on her pulse.

"Where, uh, were you stung?" she asked, relieved to hear her pitch had lowered, although it sounded a bit too husky to her ears.

"Here." He touched a reddened spot a hairbreadth higher than his buckle.

"Oh."

During times like this, she wished heartily that she'd learned how to curse. To treat his bee sting *there*—assuming it was a bee sting, of course—she'd have to walk right up to him and . . . and stand between his thighs!

She glanced uncertainly at his face, which he'd smoothed into stoic lines. She suspected his solemnity was a mask behind which he'd hidden a wealth of mirth, all at her expense.

She, however, wasn't about to let him see how much he could disturb her.

Besides, her virtuous side was protesting, a man didn't plan to get stung in such a delicate location. And, he would have asked for her help if he'd been plotting to torment her like this. Instead, he'd kept the injury to himself and had sought out medicine without bothering her.

Men. Why were they such exasperating creatures?

Drawing a steadying breath, she marched herself into the danger zone. She tried to keep her eyes focused on her hands, which, she realized to her mounting frustration, were not only sticky damp, they were fumbling.

"Need help?" he drawled.

She actually considered his suggestion until she pictured calling Ginevee and explaining why she was so flustered. "Er, no. Thank you."

After all, if she could endure Hannibal Dukker's less-than-appealing advances, she could certainly brave Wes Rawlins's.

Not that Wes *had* made any advances toward her. Not really.

That realization brought a rush of new frustrations. They were born as much from her traitorous disappointment as from her chiding to remember her station and her age.

She stole a glance upward—not at his eyes, for she wasn't quite nervy enough for that—but at his chest, the chiseled work of art that God himself had crafted. An auburn dusting of baby-fine hairs clung to the pale gold of his flesh. They curled enticingly over every ridge and plane of his chest. Never in her life had she seen anything so perfect—until her furtive gaze was arrested by the jagged, circular scar on his left shoulder. She caught her breath. Another scar, not far below it and ominously close to his heart, looked much fresher. She'd never seen a bullet hole before, but she knew with gut-wrenching certainty that these were gunshot wounds.

Her gaze flew to his. "Wes, you could have been killed."

He stared into her eyes for what seemed like forever. Only inches away, she could see all the shades of green in his eyes, from pine to jade, to emerald, bursting outward in concentric circles from their pitch-black center.

That dark core of his gaze mesmerized her. It was the doorway to his secret self, a portal where shadows flitted past like phantoms fleeing the light. She thought he might be hiding some secret he didn't want her to know. When his red-gold lashes fanned downward like a veil, intuition told her she'd touched on truth.

"Naw." His voice was husky, low. "No little bitty honeybee could send me to the boneyard."

He hadn't come close to fooling her. She knew that he knew it too.

"How did this happen?"

Of a will all their own, her fingers touched that second scar. She had never seen anything like it. Two odd triangular impressions, the lower one less distinct, angled outward from each other. They marred his perfect flesh like a cookie cutter might have marred soft dough. "This wound can't be more than a year old."

"Eleven months," he corrected her in a strangely hushed voice. "I remember, because . . ."

His voice trailed off.

"Does it hurt to talk about it?" she asked gently.

His heart jumped hard beneath her fingertips, its rhythm growing ragged. "A little," he admitted.

His gaze moved beyond her, growing dark with some haunting memory. "A man doesn't forget being bush-whacked and left for buzzard bait. Or lying helpless, unable to stop a blood feud from becoming a family massacre," he added with uncharacteristic grimness.

She swallowed, too shaken by his admission to press him further. She had expected the memory of his near death to be unpleasant, of course, but she hadn't expected it to make him look so hard . . . or so fierce.

Silence wrapped around them. He spared her the gruesome details of the nightmare he'd lived through, and yet his refusal to share his feelings and let her try to ease his hurt made her feel strangely shut out and alone.

"Wes, don't take such risks anymore." The words blazed a path from her heart to her tongue; she couldn't have stopped them if she'd tried. "You're too young—"

"I'm not that young."

She caught her breath. His voice held a razor-keen edge, a stab of warning so sharp, one might have thought she'd challenged him.

"I'm sorry. I meant no offense."

She retreated a step, retrieving her hand. She had meant what she said. Her worry for him had been genuine too, she realized in growing confusion. Wouldn't she be wiser to be wary of this dark and dangerous side she had glimpsed behind his glib charm?

Trying to stave off a fresh wave of chaotic thoughts and feelings, she focused once more on the jar. When she reached for the lid, though, he caught her fingers, and she met his gaze uncertainly. His haunted expression was receding, leaving in its place something just as discomfiting. Those forest-green depths gleamed now with a primal intensity, one that he couldn't entirely hide behind his fallen-angel's smile.

"I like when you touch me," he said, his voice deep and rumbly.

He raised her hand to his lips, and her pulse leaped. She was so disconcerted by the moist connection of his flesh tasting hers, that for a moment she couldn't breathe. She couldn't think. He raised her hand higher, pressing a damp kiss into her palm, and her knees went dangerously weak.

"Wes," she protested feebly.

He wouldn't release her hand, though, or free her from the smoky promise in his eyes. Turning her arm over, he applied gentle pressure to her palm with his thumb. The tip of his mustache, so provocatively soft, followed the sinfully wet brush of his tongue across her knuckles. She'd had no idea that goose bumps could make one feel so giddy.

"Wes, please," she whispered, "it's not proper."

He pressed her now moist and trembling hand against the hard, fierce beating of his heart. "You mean 'cause I'm so young?"

The earthy cadence of his murmur gusted fresh shivers down her spine. She was no blushing innocent, and yet this man—dare she say this young man?—had made her feel like a maid. She suspected he'd done so intentionally. She also suspected he'd gotten a ripsnorting thrill out of making a barren old spinster randy.

She flinched at the thought.

"Are you quite finished?" she demanded, snatching her hand away.

He arched his brows, looking for all the world as if her outrage surprised him. "Well, that depends. Are you going to touch me again?"

She nearly choked. She *had* started the whole thing, and there was no canyon on earth that was deep enough to hide her from the light of knowing in those foxy eyes.

"Do you, or do you not, want salve for that bee sting?"

"Hmm. As I recollect, my aunt Lally used to suck the stinger out when I was a boy. Me being so young and all, you might want to try that first."

"I think not!"

"Then I guess I'll settle for the salve."

He looked inordinately amused and much too smug for her peace of mind.

"Here." She shoved the jar into his hand. "You can salve the sting yourself."

"But from way up here, I can't tell if there's a stinger," he pointed out affably. "You aren't going to leave me with a stinger in my belly, are you?"

She ground her teeth. He did have a point. If he got some kind of infection, then she'd be nursing him back to health for days. Maybe even weeks. She didn't think she could bear his wickedness that long . . . much less resist it.

"Very well," she said. "I'll look for a stinger."

"You won't have to look far."

Heat coiled through her insides at his innuendo. "Kindly behave yourself."

"I'm trying, ma'am, but you make it so consarned hard for a man."

She folded her arms across her chest in silent warning.

"All right. You win. I'll behave—to the best of my ability."

She didn't find this concession reassuring, but the longer she stood between his legs, the longer she would have to endure his wayward sense of humor. That in itself was reason enough to expedite her task.

With a wariness she usually reserved for loaded six-guns, Rorie dragged her gaze to the flesh in question. Red and swollen, the bee sting lay well below her line of vision, and she realized, that glancing at him simply would not be enough. She would have to move closer, stoop, or worse, kneel between his thighs, to bring her eyes close enough for her inspection. There was no way on God's green earth that she could accomplish her task by keeping her face a respectable distance from his crotch.

She bit her lip to keep from groaning. Why did she have the sneaking suspicion that she was the only one having palpitations at the thought?

"Something wrong?" he asked.

She didn't have to see his face to know he was smirking.

"No." She silently vowed if she found more than one stinger thrusting out of his nether region, she'd make him wish that honeybee had sent him to the graveyard.

Knotting her hands in her skirt, she mustered her

courage and did the unthinkable: she lowered her head between his thighs. As hard as she tried, at such proximity, it was impossible to keep his fly out of her field of vision. An unsettling mixture of relief and disappointment washed over her when she spied no evidence of a straining, robust bulge.

"See anything?" he asked.

"Not yet," she replied, turning scarlet a heartbeat later when she realized where her eyes and thoughts had been trained. Hastily she focused on the bee sting.

"Maybe it would help if I loosen this—"

He was reaching for his buckle, and she grabbed his hand, straightening so fast, she nearly butted her head against his chest.

"Don't you dare!"

His deep, rich laughter was intoxicating. "Aw, Rorie, I don't bite."

She heated like a furnace, and not just at the use of her nickname. "You . . . take far too many liberties, sir."

"Me?" His voice lowered to an intimate murmur. "But you're the one touching me."

She glanced down and realized, to her utter mortification, that he was right. How or why her left hand had found a resting place on his thigh was a thorough mystery to her.

She jerked it away, then next tried removing her right hand from his neatly turned grasp, but he held on, making her feel like a mouse to his cat.

"You're enjoying this entirely too much," she accused him.

"Aren't you?"

"No, I most certainly am not!"

"Oh. My mistake."

His thumb was stroking her palm. It was the barest whisper of flesh against flesh, yet his touch shot confused signals through her body. Her insides shivered while her skin burned.

"You are no gentleman," she said hoarsely. "If you were, you wouldn't be touching me so."

"You mean a gentleman wouldn't hold a lady's

hand?" His eyelids drooped, hooding the stare that she felt like a hunger on her lips. "Or give it a little kiss?"

"Y-yes."

"Being a gentleman doesn't sound like very much fun."

She gulped a breath. He'd finally freed her—which was precisely what she'd wanted, she told herself.

Mustering her wits, she prepared to make a hasty but dignified retreat. Unfortunately, her feet had tangled in his discarded vest and shirt lying on the floor. When she tried to turn, she staggered instead of stepping.

It all happened so fast: one moment she was making a beeline for safety; the next, she was flailing, grasping at anything to keep her from falling. His neck proved the handiest anchor. Her breasts collided with his chest, and the air whooshed out of her at the stunning feel of hard, male musculature.

In that heartbeat, with her face so close to his, she could see surprise flare in his eyes. Then something very different, something primal and male, blazed to life in the depths of his gaze. She sank a fraction lower as his arms and legs cradled her, leaving little doubt in her mind that she'd had a stirring effect on him too. The gentle ridge of his manhood pressed against her woman's flesh, leaving her hot and shaken, scandalized and exhilarated.

His lashes swept down to hide the appetite lurking in his eyes. She had little time to form a coherent thought other than the nerve-jangling, pulse-firing realization that her lips were inches from his. . . .

"Oh, geez." The voice, which had come from the doorway, was filled with boyish disgust. "You two aren't going to smooch, are you?"

In that instant Rorie would have preferred facing a thousand raging honeybees than watching her four orphan children swarm into the room with their bright eyes wide and curious.

"Not now, I reckon," Wes said dryly.

She wrestled herself from his embrace, barely avoiding another tumble over his clothes, before she hurried to intercept the children.

"Is Mr. Wes's bee sting all better?" Merrilee asked, halting dutifully before her.

Topher, on the other hand, hardly glanced her way as he cut a swath around her, his fishing pole and catfish all dripping over his shoulder. "You got a bee sting, Mr. Wes? Where?"

"Topher, for heaven's sake." Rorie clasped her hands to keep from pressing them to her burning cheeks.

"Were you really kissing, Miss Rorie?" Nita asked, her avid gaze shifting from Rorie to Wes's torso.

"Of course not," she said sharply, wishing the earth would rise up to swallow her whole. "Topher," she added irritably, watching the boy bend over and peer at the welt above Wes's buckle, "what have I told you about bringing your fish in through the dining room?"

Topher didn't hear her. Either that, or he was ignoring her. He hooked his thumbs through his belt loops and rolled back on his heels—something she had never seen him do before.

"I did what you said, Mr. Wes. I spit on my bait, and I got four of the biggest catfish this county's ever seen."

Wes chuckled and dutifully inspected Topher's catch before shrugging into his shirt and vest. "Well, you see? I told you spitting on the line wasn't any old superstition."

"Topher!"

The boy cringed, glancing guiltily over his shoulder at Rorie. "Yes, ma'am," he said, then he turned his shining eyes back to Wes.

"Could you show me some more tricks, huh? Could you come fishing with me tomorrow, please?"

"Topher," Rorie said ominously, not sure what vexed her more: the boy's disobedience or his consultation with Wes over a matter she had absolutely no head for. "It is time to wash for dinner.

"All of you," she added sternly, glimpsing the not-so-childish admiration in Nita's eyes as she continued staring at Wes. "Nita, take Po to the washbasin."

But Po, Topher's constant shadow, abandoned the boy's side in favor of a taller champion.

"Me not want to go!" he said in his demanding, baby voice.

Caked with dirt from head to toe, he reached up a grubby hand and tugged on Wes's untucked shirt. "Pick me up!"

Rorie nearly died with embarrassment to see her child smear river mud all over Wes, but when she would have apologized, he surprised her yet again by lifting the filthy toddler into his arms.

"Is that better?"

"Yes!" Po shouted happily.

Rorie realized she was gaping and quickly hinged her jaw closed. Wes winked at her.

"Po and I will just mosey on down to the springhouse," he said, "and see what kind of mischief we can stir up in the shower bath. What do you say to that, pardner?"

"Yea!" Po said.

"I, er . . . Oh, very well," Rorie said. Getting that child washed without a fuss could well be an entry for the record books.

Nita looked disappointed—her new infatuation was leaving her behind. "You'll be back for dinner, won't you, Mr. Wes?"

He smiled at her as he walked past, then paused to pat Merrilee's head. The child blushed at this uncustomary male attention.

"Wild mustangs couldn't drive me away," he said.

Then his gaze slid to Rorie. She watched the light of a primitive hunger rekindle there.

"Especially from dessert."

Chapter Six

*D*inner didn't quite lend itself to the master sleuthing Wes had planned.

But then, all of his plans seemed to be going haywire that day. Merrilee had thwarted his search of the house; Rorie's shy, lingering touches had distracted him from the perfect opportunity to interrogate her; and the other children hadn't yielded a single useful piece of information during his various conversations with them.

The only thing worse than having his investigation drag on, going absolutely nowhere after two days, he decided, was saying grace as a fraud at a family dinner.

Shae had settled at the foot of the table, and Rorie began the prayers. Wes dutifully bowed his head, but he couldn't stop himself from peeking at the children's solemn faces as they recited the words. It had been a long time since he talked to God, and Wes wasn't sure he still knew how. And he wasn't so sure God would even listen to a Ranger who was lying about his badge, although he liked to think he had a damned good reason.

Other things he'd done weren't quite as easy to defend, though, like the way he'd been secretly lusting after his brother's wife for the last eight years. The devil had a mortgage on his soul, that was certain. He could pray until his tongue fell out, but what good would it do?

As the sweet reverence in Rorie's voice wrapped

around him, he fidgeted, growing more uncomfortable. He felt the sting of longing for the family he'd left behind. Although he tried to convince himself it was a momentary lapse, a passing weakness, a heaviness weighed his chest when he recalled what he missed: baiting catfish with his nephew Seth; giving shoulder rides to his niece Megan; spinning yarns for Cord's youngest boy, Bill. Wes had lost count of the days since he last helped Zack brand a steer or since he split a rail with Cord.

The realization that he would never again enjoy his brothers' camaraderie knifed through him. Until that moment, he had believed nothing could be more painful than denying himself the pleasure of seeing Fancy again.

"Mr. Wes?"

He was startled to hear Nita's hesitant voice at his left side.

"Don't you like fried okra?"

She was offering him a serving bowl. Judging by the other children's curious stares, he suspected she had been trying to attract his attention for several moments.

"Sure I do," he said, rallying his wits.

"So, how are you progressing on the barn?" Rorie asked, directing her question at Shae.

"There's a lot more wood rot than we expected," he said grimly. "Looks like we're going to have to tear up the loft and maybe even the north side of the barn."

Her face fell. "So much?"

Shae nodded, and she glanced uneasily at Wes.

"How long will that take?"

"A week," Shae said. "Maybe more."

Wes guessed she was really trying to gauge how much longer she would have to put up with him. The thought amused him. Although she could deny until she was blue in the face that she hadn't liked him kissing her hand, he'd felt the pulse leap in her wrist—and he'd seen the hunger in her love-starved eyes. A lady like her might not want to admit it, but he'd had a rousing effect on her. And damn if she hadn't had one on him too.

Nita passed him a tureen of gravy. "Maybe you could visit your folks before you leave, Mr. Wes."

Her comment caught him off guard. "My folks?"

"Uh-huh. Miss Rorie said they live near the county line."

Wes's humor abruptly ebbed. He avoided Nita's gaze and buttered a slice of bread. "I reckon I did tell her something like that."

Topher, who had scrambled to beat Po to the chair at Wes's other side, gulped down cider and wiped the back of his hand across his mouth. "How much folks've you got?"

Wes fidgeted. He could think of a dozen topics he'd rather discuss. "Two brothers. An aunt. A couple of nephews and a niece."

"What about your ma and pa?"

An unexpected sliver of hurt sliced through him. Childhood memories he preferred to forget resurfaced. Even though he'd been barely older than Po when his parents had died, certain images were emblazoned on his brain: Cord, at seventeen, looking pale beneath his tan; Uncle Seth, grim and rigid, with his arm around Aunt Lally's quaking shoulders; four-year-old Zack as confused and frightened as he'd been.

"Boys, we've had some news," Seth had said above Lally's sobs. "Seems like there were a couple of road agents hiding out near Houston. They came across the stage your ma and pa were on, and, well ... I'm sorry, boys. Your folks won't be coming home again."

"Mr. Wes?"

He shook himself, realizing that Topher, along with everyone else, was staring at him again.

"Didn't you hear me?"

"Yes, Topher. I heard. You see, my folks were mur—" He bit his tongue on the unpleasant, adult truth. "Er, they were killed when I was three."

Rorie's fork clattered against her plate. He glanced up in time to see the shocked look she exchanged with Ginevee.

"You mean you're an orphan? Like us?" Topher asked in awe.

"Reckon I am."

"Topher," Rorie interceded, feeling guilty for letting

the boy badger Wes into such a painful confession, "it isn't polite to pry into a person's private affairs."

Wes tossed her a grateful look, and she felt a good deal worse. When she decided to let the children's natural curiosity unearth the secrets she'd suspected him of keeping, she'd never dreamed his parents had been murdered, for clearly, that was what he'd intended to say. His haunted expression had confirmed it.

Meanwhile, Shae was studying Wes through narrowed eyes. "Seems like there's a cattle outfit up near the county line. I hear tell it's owned by a couple of Rawlins brothers. You wouldn't be one of those Rawlinses, would you?"

Wes jabbed a fork into his mashed potatoes. "I used to be," he mumbled, filling his mouth. He swallowed and flashed Ginevee a grin. "Mighty fine grub, ma'am. Ol' Two-Step's going to be jealous."

Rorie had seen Wes smile enough times in the last two days to realize his latest one was forced.

"You used to be?" Shae pressed his challenge. "What does that mean?"

Wes reached for his cider. Rorie suspected he was deliberately delaying his answer when he drained the mug dry. Finally, he faced the boy again, the warning in his eyes belying his mocking words.

"It means you make me feel so welcome, Shae, I don't ever plan on going back."

Nita looked delighted. Merrilee smiled, and Topher cheered. Po tried jumping in his seat, and Ginevee's lap was instantly doused with chicken broth.

"Messy!" Po said gaily.

The children all laughed at the comical look of despair on Ginevee's face, and Merrilee jumped up to fetch her a dish towel.

Everyone passed the rest of the meal in relative good humor, except perhaps for Shae. He didn't say another word all the way through dessert, and Rorie sensed he was brooding because Wes had put him in his place. She was grateful Shae had a cool enough head not to cause a scene and frighten the children, especially Merrilee, who was always so sensitive to the moods around her. But

Rorie worried Shae might try to provoke Wes later in private. The minute the meal was over, Shae retired to the front porch with a cleaning rag and his shotgun.

While Gator was alive, the men had traditionally sat outside on rockers while the women and children cleaned the kitchen. Given the tension between Shae and Wes, Rorie expected Wes to make his excuses and ride into town for a poker game or, at the very least, a shot of whiskey. To her surprise, he followed her into the kitchen instead, settling at the cluttered table and asking for a second cup of coffee.

Nita obliged him because Rorie had to collar Topher. As usual, the boy had been trying to avoid his chores, and she thrust a broom into his hand before he could sneak out after Shae.

"I reckon sweeping is better than reading some stupid history book," Topher grumbled.

Wes looked inordinately amused. "What's wrong with history?"

Topher gave him an exasperated look. "It's about old dead people."

Rorie hid her smile. "I'm sure Abraham is studying for the history test tomorrow. He told me he's going to be the one who wins that bottle of cherry sarsaparilla."

Topher scowled, giving a vicious sweep with his broom. "I hate history."

The back door banged, and Merrilee teetered inside, carefully carrying a brimming pail of water. Rorie watched the concern flicker across Wes's features. He started to rise, but Ginevee, who had been waiting for the child, hurried forward to help Merrilee with the pail.

"History's not so bad," Wes said to Topher. His thoughtful gaze followed Merrilee as she pulled her rag doll from her skirt pocket and limped to the corner to play. "After all, it's just a big, long string of yarns."

"Yeah?" Topher sounded doubtful.

"Sure. Take the story of Pocahontas and Captain John Smith."

"Who's Po-co-harness?"

"Pocahontas," Wes corrected him gently, "was a beautiful Indian princess."

"Oh."

Wes's answer may have disappointed Topher, but Merrilee raised her head, momentarily losing interest in her doll.

While Po scrambled up on Wes's knee, Nita edged closer, drying a plate with her towel. "Was Pocahontas a Comanche?"

Wes cast another sidelong glance at Merrilee. "I don't rightly know. She could have been, because she was strong and brave, and full of spirit like all Comanche squaws."

Merrilee smiled at his words, and Rorie felt her heart warm. She had opened her mouth to tell them that Pocahontas had been a Powhatan Indian, but thought better of it when she saw the pleasure Wes's words gave Merrilee.

Wes winked at her before smoothing his features into solemn lines. "Gather 'round your ol' Uncle Wes, children, and I'll tell you a little history."

"*Uncle* Wes?" Rorie paused in midreach for her sewing basket.

"Sure. Just like Uncle Remus."

Ginevee chuckled, and Rorie shook her head, settling at the table with yet another pair of Topher's ripped blue jeans. She suspected this would be one history lesson the children would never forget.

"A long time ago," Wes began, "in a land called Virginny, there was a beautiful Indian princess named Pocahontas. Her daddy was the mighty Indian chief, Powhatan, and her sweetheart was our hero, Captain John Smith."

"What did he look like?" Nita asked.

"Hmm." Wes cocked his head. "As I recall, Captain John was a tall, long-limbed man. He was strong, too, but gentle, and all the ladies liked him. They used to want to dance with him at the hoedowns and fandangos because they thought him such a handsome man. And . . ." Wes's eyes twinkled. "They'd never seen anyone with a finer head of red hair."

"*Red* hair?" Topher gaped in disbelief. "You mean like yours?"

Wes nodded, and Merrilee, who was kneeling at his feet with her doll, raised her hand. "Did he have freckles like yours, Uncle Wes?"

Wes made a great show of considering this question. "Yes, he did," he answered with an impossibly straight face. He raised his eyes to Rorie. "And that's why Pocahontas loved him so much."

Ginevee hooted, and Rorie blushed.

"Anyway"—Wes was smirking now—"that mean old Indian chief didn't like Captain John very much. Powhatan was jealous 'cause Captain John could outwrassle any puma, tiger, or bear in Virginny."

"What's a tiger?"

Wes turned his attention to Merrilee. "Why, that's a big striped cat with fangs out to here."

He made an exaggerated gesture down to his chest, and Topher folded his arms in a huff.

"There's no such thing."

A traitorous smile tugged at Rorie's lips. Shameless flirt, gunfighting rogue, and now Wes was proving himself a natural-born storyteller. Enthusiasm was etched into every line of his frame. His animation was magnetic, making the small room seem cozier. As she watched the show, she couldn't decide who was more entertaining: Wes, spinning his outlandish yarn, or the children, listening with such eagerness to his every glib word.

"What happened next?" Nita asked.

"Well, Captain John tried to be friends with the Indians, mostly 'cause he liked kissing Pocahontas, but Powhatan wouldn't hear of it. He sent his Indian braves out to capture poor John. When the braves brought John back, all trussed up like a turkey, Powhatan got a hankering for some of John's red hair, so he pulled out his scalping knife.

"But Pocahontas wouldn't let her father steal Captain John's hair. She threw her arms around John's neck and cried, 'Oh no, Daddy, you mustn't hurt my sweetheart!' "

Wes was speaking now in a high soprano voice. Nita and Merrilee both giggled. Topher rolled his eyes.

" 'I love him, and I want to marry him! We will hunt you many tigers and make you many grandbabies.'

"So Powhatan thought about that," Wes went on. "He thought about getting a striped tigerskin every month and bouncing a new freckled grandbaby on his knee every year. He decided that would be a pretty fair trade. So he let Captain John keep his hair, and he let Pocahontas marry John. And that's why, to this day, you can still find a freckled Indian or two living in Virginny."

He grinned at the end of his tale, and all the children clapped and cheered except for Topher.

"I liked it better when Captain John was wrassling tigers," the boy said.

"Me too," Po said, jumping up and down on Wes's knee. "More stories, Unca Wes."

Chuckling, Ginevee hung up her apron. "It's bedtime for you, young man."

She deftly scooped up the toddler in midbounce. Po's look of astonishment quickly vanished, and his wail drowned out Nita and Merrilee as they thanked Wes and said their good-nights.

"I'll tuck you all in after I help Topher study," Rorie said, not missing a single, sneaking footstep the boy was taking toward the back door.

He muttered an oath and stalked into the dining room.

Wes had been thoroughly enjoying himself, and he felt a pang of disappointment to see his audience go. He looked hopefully at Rorie, thinking she might linger over her half-finished coffee, but she was gathering up her sewing in preparation to leave the room. His earlier wistfulness struck him full force as he imagined returning to the solitude of that big lonely barn. Especially after Rorie's tender ministrations earlier that afternoon.

"So what did you think of my story?" he asked, trying to hold on to that sweet, homey feeling for just a few minutes longer.

She cast him a sideways glance, her lashes fanning down over the mirth in her eyes. "Well, it was certainly interesting. But that's not exactly the way the historians tell it."

"It's not?"

"No, it's not. Tigers in Virginia. Really. And Pocahontas was only twelve years old when she met John Smith. I assure you they never got married. It was a bunch of romantic nonsense, and I'll thank you not to fill the children's heads with it."

Wes chuckled. "So romance is nonsense, eh?" When she looked back down at her sewing, obviously discomfited by his teasing, he added, "You have to admit Captain John knew how to spin a yarn. Take that bit about Pocahontas throwing herself in front of the tomahawk that was meant for him. Chances are that Captain John Smith fella filled the history books with a whole lot more nonsense than that."

Rorie glanced up from her basket, one eyebrow raised in amused challenge. "Oh? Don't you think a woman is capable of saving a man's life?"

"Sure I do, on occasion. A woman saved my life once." His heart beat a little irregularly at the memory. "Never one to rest on her laurels, though, Fancy went on and saved Cord's and Zack's lives too. Thanking her didn't hardly seem like enough after that, not when a lady as smart and brave as Fancy was on the loose, so we decided one of us should marry her. We elected Cord."

Rorie's astute, curious eyes met his own. "So Fancy's your sister-in-law?"

"Yeah, that's right." In spite of his best efforts, his voice thickened with the old hurt. "Fancy's family now." He hastily donned a cocksure grin to throw Rorie off track. "I reckon you'd like Fancy. She's always been fond of drawing her gun on a man, same as you."

Rorie made a wry face. "I suppose you won't let me live that down any time soon."

She rose, and he rose with her, pleased to see she hadn't flown into one of her prim-and-proper snits at his jest. Now more than ever, he was reluctant to let her slip away when they finally seemed to be on civil terms. After all, he had a hundred questions that needed answers—and a loneliness that ached for relief.

Thinking fast, he lighted on a subject he hoped might woo her to stay. "You have a fine son in Topher, ma'am."

A strange sort of upset flickered across her features.

He sensed he'd just strayed into dangerous territory again.

"Thank you, but Topher isn't my son. He's an orphan, like the others."

Wes realized his blunder then. He'd assumed, because of the boy's fair hair and skin, that he was a relation of Rorie's.

"Well, he's still a fine boy," he said, uncertain why Rorie was splitting hairs. For all intents and purposes, Topher was her son now, so it seemed odd that she still referred to the boy—to all the children, in fact—as orphans. "I've never heard a name quite like Topher before. How did he get it?"

She toyed with the lid of her sewing basket for a moment, as if trying to decide whether to close it and the subject.

"Topher is the nickname I gave him," she said finally. "Two years ago, when Jarrod caught Topher stealing eggs from our henhouse, his speech was almost unintelligible. I thought it was cruel to call the boy Christopher, when he had such a difficult time pronouncing the name."

Wes was touched by Rorie's sensitivity. Although he had never lisped, he'd endured more than his fair share of heckling as a child, thanks to his freckles. To understand the shame and frustration Topher must feel because of his affliction didn't take much imagination.

"So Sinclair caught the little rascal stealing eggs, eh?"

Was it his imagination, or had the reminder of her husband made her even more uptight?

"Topher is no longer in the habit of stealing, I assure you." She closed the basket lid with a snap. "When I met Topher, he already had a long history of running away from the orphanage, but persuading Jarrod to let me teach the boy elocution was far easier than convincing him to let Topher live with us. Eventually, however, even Jarrod was forced to admit the boy might be shot by an angry farmer if he continued thieving to feed himself. So we adopted him."

Wes frowned. That was a hell of a cheap trick for Sinclair, taking on the responsibility of a child and then walking out the door. If Sinclair hadn't been ready for children, why had he filled his home with orphans? As far as Wes was concerned, if a man didn't want an obligation, he avoided entanglements. He himself had been careful to live by that creed, pledging himself to Two-Step and the state of Texas. That was it. That was all he wanted—except, perhaps, to get his hand on the louse who had abandoned Rorie to rear four children on her own.

"Sinclair hurt you pretty bad, didn't he?" he asked quietly.

She raised her chin, but her knuckles turned white as she gripped the handle of her basket. "The children and I have survived quite well without Jarrod since the divorce. So well, in fact, that we are beyond missing him.

"No," she continued with a brittle smile, "the damage Jarrod did by leaving must be weighed against the good he did by giving the children a home. I know Topher would never have been better off in the orphanage or with that swaggering, big-mouthed Ranger who sired him. From what I hear, Bill Malone left his mark in every town."

Wes winced. He knew of Malone and Malone's reputation. It seemed the man had trouble keeping his pecker in his pants—or rather, he'd had trouble. About six months earlier, Malone had gotten caught in the cross fire in a range war out in Tom Greene County.

Wes felt his face warm under Rorie's cool stare. As much as he would have liked to defend Rangers, he didn't dare. Not while he was keeping his own identity a secret.

"Topher is lucky to have you. All the children are," he added, feeling guilty for deceiving her. "If I'd been tossed in an orphanage, I would have run away too. A boy needs more than gruel and discipline to grow into a man. He needs a whole lot of love."

Seeing the ghost of pain on his face—a phantom not unlike the one she'd glimpsed when he told her of a massacred family he couldn't defend—Rorie felt her heart twist. She wondered what had driven this man who so clearly valued family away from the kinfolk he loved. "Wes, you were lucky, too, having an aunt and brothers to give you love."

He stiffened, and she knew she'd touched an un-healed wound.

He recovered almost instantly, though, flashing her a devilish grin and cloaking himself in the guise of a rogue. "I've always been lucky in love. Must be the star I . . . er, was born under."

His color heightened. She wasn't sure what had em-barrassed him, but she thought it must have something to do with his confession. She'd always heard hired gunmen were superstitious. Here was yet another proof of his profession.

She regarded him warily for a long moment before gathering the courage to demand the truth. "Wes, are you a gunfighter?"

He looked genuinely surprised by her question.

"If by that you mean do I sometimes fight with a gun," he said carefully, "then I reckon I am. But"—he held her gaze steadily—"if you're asking if I'm on the run from the law, no, I'm not. I'm not a road agent, Rorie. I'm not a gambler or a bootlegger or a confidence man, either. I wear these six-shooters to protect myself, and I wouldn't ever hesitate to use them to protect honest people who need me."

She bit her lip. She wanted to believe him. She told herself she shouldn't be so gullible, that she had nothing but his word. From long experience, she'd learned that a sweet talker's word was as changeable as the wind.

As she lost herself in the emerald fathoms of his gaze, though, a sweet comfort stole over her. She had prayed so long for a champion, one who would keep her and her children safe from the dragons, the Hannibal Dukkers of the world. Wes's armor might not be as shiny as some, but his gallantry certainly couldn't be denied. And by his own admission, as reluctant as it might have been, he held a deep and abiding respect for family.

Maybe she should give him the benefit of the doubt. Maybe she should learn how to trust again.

"I'm . . . glad to hear it, Wes. I was a little worried, you know. Losing Gator was a terrible blow to the chil-dren. They looked up to him, and they want to look up to you. So whether you like it or not, you're going to have an influence on them. That's why it's important for you to set a good example."

She waited, half-expecting him to bolt for the door. Instead, his expression turned wistful.

"No more tigers in Virginia, eh?"

She smiled, shaking her head. "No more tree climbing either, I'm afraid."

He chuckled, reaching for his hat. "Well, I reckon it could be worse. I reckon you could have told me no more bee-sting salve."

She felt her face warm.

He tipped his hat. "Good night, ma'am," he drawled, giving her a naughty wink. "Pleasant dreams."

Chapter Seven

*L*ater that Wednesday night, Wes could have kicked himself for nearly telling Rorie he wore a star. He'd gotten too damned close to her mesmerizing eyes and the private hurt she tried to hide to remember the questions he'd meant to ask about Gator.

But he had learned a bit more about the enigma she posed, and why Elodea's gossips stayed busy at her expense. She'd been divorced.

Piecing together what little information Shae had told him about the children over the last two days, Wes suspected Po and Nita, like Merrilee, had wound up on Rorie's doorstep because of Sinclair's medical practice. Yet, while Sinclair might have mended their broken bones and tended their fevers, Rorie clearly had been the one to open her heart to them.

Just like she'd opened her home to him.

Wes winced, needled by guilt. The more he learned about Aurora Sinclair, the more he wanted to close his investigation and clear her name. In truth, he had a hard time reconciling his suspicion of her as a murder conspirator with the reality of her as a protective, caring parent.

A woman who cared that much about homeless children—and scarred young gunslingers—couldn't possibly be cold-blooded enough to conspire against the man

who'd put a roof over her head. Hell, if she could have
killed anyone, it would have been her husband, yet
even he seemed to rate a redeeming quality or two in her
fair mind.

Only against the Ranger force did that mind of hers
show bias.

Wes frowned. He was bothered by Rorie's virulent
dislike of everything he stood for, just as he was bothered
by folks who claimed Rangers preferred keeping the peace
to enforcing justice. He was proud of his badge and the
men who had worn it—Samuel Walker, Big Foot Wallace,
Rip Ford, and, of course, his brother. Even Bill Malone
had been one hell of a lawman, in spite of his other
foibles.

All of those men had made names for themselves by
doing legendary deeds, and Wes wanted to follow in their
footsteps. He didn't want Rorie to despise the entire
Ranger force because of one man's indiscretions. In truth,
he felt honor-bound to prove to her Malone was the exception rather than the rule.

Wes figured he could accomplish this mission over
the next few days while he determined beyond a shadow
of a doubt whether Shae was a viable suspect. In the
meantime, he'd have to buy himself time if he didn't want
Dukker riding onto the property and demanding the
Sinclairs' eviction. Keeping Rorie and the children safe,
though, shouldn't be too hard if the wire from Bandera
Town proved the legitimacy of Shae's claim.

The trick would be getting to that wire without raising Rorie's alarm or Shae's suspicions. The two of them
had just been to Elodea on Monday for supplies, and Wes
needed a good reason to go back—preferably before Shae
sneaked off for a romantic rendezvous with Lorelei.

As he bedded down in the barn, he decided he'd
wake himself a couple of hours before dawn the next
morning, ride into town, and demand to know from that
surly telegraph operator whether he'd received his wire.
Unfortunately, he slept like a log that night, waking less
than an hour before dawn on Thursday with a stiff back
and his arms sore from two days of unaccustomed labor.

Since he couldn't possibly ride into town and back

again before Shae stirred, Wes decided his next best course would be to sneak inside the house and poke around again, looking for clues that might prove Shae capable of extreme violence. Gator's old law reports, letters, or even a journal would be ideal, assuming, of course, that Shae hadn't burned them.

He shrugged into his shirt, then spent a few minutes working the kinks out of his muscles. Outside, the early morning air was pleasantly cool, with one of those pristine, clear skies that rolled across the hills forever. The stars were still bright, without a single cloud to mar their winking, jewellike beauty. On a night like this, he mused, a man could find himself longing for a sweetheart.

The thought was a dangerous one, and he hastily girded his defenses against the vision that was sure to follow: his sister-in-law's blue-black hair and violet eyes. Instead, honey-brown hair and golden eyes shimmered into view. He blinked, shaking his head. God help him, now he knew his brain was going soft. He was fantasizing about a marriage-minded lady with four children!

A soft mewing interrupted his thoughts. The cry sounded like that of a kitten . . . or a small child. He frowned and glanced sharply around the yard, spying a huddled form in a white nightdress weeping against a post of the corral. Judging by the long black hair that tumbled to her waist, Wes thought the child was Merrilee. She looked so small and alone, even with Two-Step, kind-hearted brute that he was, standing watch over her.

"Merrilee, sweetheart, what's wrong?" Wes asked, hurrying to kneel by her side.

She seemed startled by his appearance and retreated from his arms. "I'm sorry I woke you, Uncle Wes."

He smiled to reassure her. "You didn't, honey."

She bowed her head, staring shamefully at the ground, and he touched her shoulder.

"Merrilee, why are you crying?"

"I had another nightmare," she said in a tiny voice.

"Do you want to talk about it?"

She sniffled, nodding. "It was about the bad men. The ones who came and burned our house."

Wes felt a sickness in his gut. It burned its way to his heart. "That sounds scary. What did the bad men do?"

She shuddered, at last shifting a few inches closer. "They hurt Mama. And Papa too."

She slipped her hand into his.

"Is that why you're afraid?"

She nodded again, at last meeting his eyes. "Miss Rorie said I would be safe here, that the bad men wouldn't come back. But Marshal Dukker comes here, and he's a bad man."

Wes frowned at this intelligence. He didn't like the idea of Dukker frightening Merrilee. "Why do you think he's a bad man?"

"Because Marshal Dukker came here when Shae was away. He asked Miss Rorie to marry him, and when she said no, he yelled at her and called her bad names. He pushed her and tried to kiss her, just like the bad men did to Mama. Only Mama fell down," she whispered anxiously, "and the bad men fell down with her. That's when Mama told me to run away."

Bile rose to Wes's throat. Pulling the child into his arms, he held her fiercely. "I won't let that happen to Miss Rorie, Merrilee. I promise."

She peeked up at him through tear-moistened lashes. "Even if the bad man comes back?"

"Especially if the bad man comes back."

A long moment passed before she sighed, snuggling closer and resting her head on his shoulder.

"I miss my mama. Do you miss yours?"

He stroked her hair. "Yeah. I reckon I miss all my folks."

Merrilee pulled back to look at him. "Miss Rorie said you don't have to miss your folks. She said when people die, they go to heaven and become angels. Angels watch over you. See those two big stars over there?" She pointed at the constellation of Orion. "Those are Mama's eyes. And Miss Rorie told me Papa's eyes are over there."

She pointed next at the Big Dipper, and Wes smiled, warmed by the proof of Rorie's creativity.

"Is that why you came out here? To see your mama and papa?"

She nodded vigorously. "I always talk to Mama outside so I won't wake up Nita or Ginevee."

Two-Step, who was apparently miffed at being ignored, leaned over the top rail just then and nuzzled Merrilee's head. She recoiled in surprise, and Wes pushed the gelding's nose away.

"Here now, you old whey-belly. Did Miss Merrilee say you could eat her hair?"

The child giggled.

"Looks like Two-Step likes you, Merrilee."

She shyly stretched a hand for the velvet snout. "You have a very nice pony."

Two-Step nudged her, revelling in the attention, and Wes shook his head. If he hadn't known better, he would have sworn Merrilee had an apple or a lump of sugar hidden up her sleeve. Two-Step wasn't inclined to be kind to somebody unless he figured there was something in it for him.

"I finished drawing Two-Step," she said suddenly. "Do you want to see? It's inside."

Wes had forgotten all about her request to sketch the gelding. "Sure."

She wrapped her arms around his neck, and he lifted her, hardly noticing the protest of his aching shoulders. He thought maybe he would whittle a wooden sole for her shoe to see if he couldn't ease her limp.

"It's inside," she whispered. "We have to be very quiet," she whispered, "so we don't wake anybody."

Tickled when she asked him to tiptoe, he let her ride high on his hip as he strode with her across the yard. Merrilee chattered happily in his ear, telling him about Fuzzy the burro and how Miss Rorie had had to sell him; and how Daisy, the nag, missed Fuzzy.

"Do you think Two-Step likes Daisy?" Merrilee whispered as he slipped inside the door, careful not to let it bang behind them.

"Don't know. Reckon I'll have to ask him."

Merrilee sighed, helping him light a lamp. "I hope they'll be good friends. Then they can get married."

Wes smiled at her innocence. Somehow, he didn't

think Daisy would be too happy having a gelding as a husband.

They reached the dining room, and Merrilee headed for Rorie's desk.

"I left my picture here to surprise Miss Rorie," she said.

Merrilee set down the lamp and reached for the stack of slates beside a vase of fresh wildflowers. "See?" she whispered.

Wes raised his brows as he looked at the drawing. He had been expecting a stick figure with a loop for a head and a broomstick for a tail, much as his niece always drew with her writing papers and fine pens. But Merrilee, in spite of the lump of chalk she'd had to use, had captured Two-Step in all his irascible glory. With his ears thrust forward, his head held erect, and his front hoof pawing the dirt, Two-Step was ready to charge off the slate. Wes whistled long and low. Merrilee had talent. More than that, she had a gift.

"This is very good, sweetheart. May I keep it?"

Her pleasure ebbed to regret. "Oh no, Uncle Wes. This is my school slate, and I must use it for my lessons."

Wes frowned. Didn't Rorie have any writing paper for the child to play with? He gazed at the slate once more and realized Merrilee had written something in the corner. "What does this say?"

She gazed at him curiously, then back at the slate. "It says, 'Two-Step the Pony is Mr. Wes's horse.' "

He couldn't help but chuckle. *Horse* was spelled *h-e-a-r-s-e*.

"Can't you read, Uncle Wes?"

He was about to tell her he could read just fine, when a leather-bound book caught his eye. It was peeking out of a partially open drawer in Rorie's desk. The spine had no writing on it, and, curious, he opened the volume to the light.

"That's Miss Rorie's journal," Merrilee whispered uneasily. "We're not allowed to play with it."

"Her journal, eh?" he said, and began flipping through the pages.

Rorie's writing was neat and precise, much as she

was. He found a three-year-old entry with tear stains on
it. Skimming it, he learned of one of Jarrod's apparently
many affairs. Wes's lip curled. The more he learned of
Jarrod Sinclair, the less he liked him.

Thinking Rorie might have noted some of her suspicions regarding Gator's murderer, Wes flipped quickly
toward the current month's entries.

Merrilee tugged on his jeans. "Uncle Wes, what are
you doing?"

"Looking for pictures," he answered absently.

His attention focused on an entry dated nearly three
weeks earlier.

> There's just no reasoning with Cousin Hannibal,
> Gator says. I know he feels badly. Hannibal's the
> only parent Creed and Danny have left. For their
> sakes, Gator has bent over backwards, giving
> Hannibal countless oportunities to mend his ways,
> but Hannibal always scoffs at Gator's threats.
>
> Gator has tried talking to Creed about the whis-
> key still, but Creed got so mad at him for "playing
> him against his pa," that he never made an appear-
> ance at the church barbecue, where Gator announced
> he would run again for sheriff. Not having Creed's
> support ate Gator up inside. But I think it hurt him
> worse when Hannibal stood up and proclaimed his
> own decision to run for sheriff. Now it looks like
> Gator will have to choose between his duty to the
> law, and his duty to his family—

"What do you think you're doing?" a female voice
snapped from the doorway.

Merrilee must have jumped five feet. Wes did too.
Turning, he found Rorie glaring at him from a pool of her
own lamp light. He had the fleeting impression of bare
feet, a softly clinging nightgown, cascading hair that fell
in a flattering way across one delightfully uncorsetted
breast, and two narrowed eyes hot enough to incinerate
him. He donned a sheepish grin.

"Er, looking for pictures?"

"Uncle Wes made my nightmares go away," Merrilee said, rising to his defense.

Rorie seemed to notice the child then. Setting her lamp on the dining table, she hurried forward, kneeling and placing her hands on Merrilee's shoulders.

"Sweetheart, you know you can come to me when you're scared. Why didn't you wake me?"

Merrilee hung her head. "I'm sorry."

"You don't have to be sorry." Rorie's voice was much gentler now. "It's just that I worry about you."

"I didn't want for you to worry," Merrilee said, "so I went and talked to Mama."

"I see."

Wes heard the disappointment in Rorie's voice, although she quickly masked it in her expression.

"Besides"—Merrilee put on a brave smile—"Uncle Wes helped me a lot."

Wes fidgeted as Rorie's eyes met his. He slipped the journal back into place in the drawer.

"We must thank your uncle Wes," she said dryly. She rose, taking Merrilee's hand in hers. "As for my journal, sir, I'd like to know—" She broke off abruptly as Merrilee tugged on her gown. "Yes, Merrilee. What is it?"

"Please don't be mad at Uncle Wes, ma'am. He can't read."

Wes felt his face heat. He didn't know what was worse, the fact that the child was lying, albeit unwittingly, to protect him, or that Rorie was gazing at him as if journal riffling was the most heinous of crimes.

"Is that true? Can you not read?"

Wes shuffled his feet. "Well, as a matter of fact—"

A creaking floorboard interrupted him. Topher, dressed in red longjohns, trundled into the room, knuckling the sleep from his eyes.

"Who can't read?" he asked around a yawn.

"Uncle Wes," Merrilee said promptly.

"Topher." Rorie looked at him with surprise and concern. "What's the matter? Why aren't you in bed?"

Topher shrugged. "I'm done sleeping. I'm hungry. What's for breakfast?"

Rorie sighed, obviously struggling to be patient. "Topher, it's too early for breakfast. Run along to bed."

Topher looked mutinous. "I can't sleep with all your noisy whispering. Besides, Merrilee's not in bed."

Suspecting Rorie was at the end of her rope, Wes stepped in.

"Topher does have a point, ma'am." Winking at Rorie over the boy's head, he draped his arm around Topher's shoulders. "If the boy can't sleep, there's no sense in sending him to bed. He can get a head start on his shower bath instead."

Topher stiffened, betraying the disgust any self-respecting boy his age should feel toward bathing. "The shower bath?"

"Sure. I'll even walk over there with you if you like."

"I went swimming yesterday. I don't need no shower bath."

"It's your choice, son," Wes said. "Either you can get up and take a shower bath, or you can go back to bed."

Appreciation flickered across Rorie's features, but Topher scowled. He tugged free of Wes's arm.

"I hate shower baths," he grumbled, stalking toward the hallway.

Merrilee, meanwhile, was tugging on Rorie's gown again. "Are you going to teach Uncle Wes how to read?"

Rorie arched her eyebrow, and Wes couldn't quite hide his grin. Bless Merrilee's little heart, he thought. She didn't realize it, but she had just provided him with the perfect opportunity to get to know Rorie better—all for the sake of his investigation, of course.

"I don't know if Miss Rorie's up to such a big challenge," he said to the girl.

Suspicion still glimmered in Rorie's eyes, but it was being rapidly replaced by compassion. The softness in her expression gave her a hint of vulnerability, a fragile elegance. He wondered why he hadn't noticed it before. Maybe it was the halo of lamplight that made the difference, or her loosened hair, framing her cheeks like a mass of honey-colored silk. Or maybe it was the utter simplicity of her gown, with its ribboned bodice and empress waistline.

"Reading is not difficult, Wes, I assure you, if you just give it the time and study it requires."

"Miss Rorie can teach anyone how to read," Merrilee said. "She even taught Abraham and he sees things backwards."

"Is that so? Reckon I've come to the right place then." Wes patted the child's head, unable to resist an admiring glance at the soft mounds and slender curves that receded shyly beneath Rorie's cotton muslin.

He felt his heart quicken as he dragged his gaze higher, past the ties that fluttered in rhythm to the rapid rise and fall of her breasts. He noticed the pulse in her throat was beating a little fast.

"When shall we start?" he asked, surprised by the huskiness in his voice.

"Well, I, er, was thinking we might begin after dinner," she said. Her own voice sounded breathless.

"Good idea. We can put the children to bed first, so we won't have any distractions."

She blushed prettily. "Ginevee and Shae will still be about."

He let his gaze steal down her length once more. "Oh, I'm not worried about them." He met her eyes deliberately. "Tell you what. Why don't I wait here while you put Merrilee back to bed, and then we can start our shooting lesson."

She started, the spell broken. "The shooting lesson! I'd forgotten we were going to have another one. I'll have to change my gown and—"

"Don't go to any trouble on my account."

She glared at him again. How he did love it when those tawny eyes of hers flashed.

"On second thought," she said crisply, "I promised Ginevee I would help her can preserves."

He donned his best hangdog expression. "Too bad."

"Come along, Merrilee. I'll tuck you in."

She urged the child toward the stairs, then hesitated on the first step. Turning suddenly, she walked back into the room and reached past him for the journal. He got a whiff of rose petals and lavender as her breast brushed his arm. His loins stirred, but she recoiled as if she'd been burned, clutching the book to her chest.

"You might consider the shower bath yourself, sir." She hiked her chin as if to hide the tremor in her voice. "I daresay it might help to cool you off."

He smiled, propping a shoulder against the wall, and indulged himself in watching the sway of Rorie's hips as she left. Apparently, he wasn't the only one who had gotten all fired up. He wondered idly if Rorie slept with any children in her bedroom. Then he began to wonder which window might be hers.

Topher reappeared, sticking his head around the corner.

"Pssst."

Wes raised his brows. "You talking to me?"

The boy nodded. "Is she gone?"

"I reckon so."

Topher blew out his breath. "Good." He pulled an oatmeal cookie from his pocket and began munching happily. "Did Merrilee have her nightmare again?"

Wes nodded, amused to see how rapidly the cookie was disappearing.

"That's what I figured. When I grow up, I'm going to be a lawman like Sheriff Gator and hang all those bad men who hurt Merrilee's family."

"You are, huh?" He wondered if Topher knew who his father had been.

"Sure. Then I'm going to marry Merrilee."

"Does Merrilee know about this?"

Topher shrugged. "I reckon," he said over a mouthful of cookie. "Don't get me wrong. I don't much like girls, but I figure I'm going to have to have one someday, and Merrilee ain't half-bad compared with most. She knows how to fish."

Topher pulled out two more cookies, hesitated, then reluctantly offered one to him. Wes chuckled.

"No, thanks, Topher. I've got a hankering for slabberdabs."

"Slabberdabs?" Topher frowned, and he actually stopped chewing for a moment. "What's that?"

"It's a secret," Wes whispered. "Want to find out?"

Topher nodded eagerly, and Wes took the boy's hand. As they headed for the kitchen, though, he couldn't resist one last glance toward the stairs—or a sigh.

Slabberdabs wouldn't be much consolation for a man with an appetite like his.

Rorie dressed mechanically. She hardly remembered rolling up her stockings or hooking her blouse. She was too busy thinking about Merrilee.

A part of her ached whenever the child gazed at her with those big earnest eyes and spoke about her mother. It wasn't that Rorie thought she could ever replace Merrilee's mother—far from it. It was just that Rorie felt the emptiness of her own womb so keenly that she longed for a deeper closeness with the child. Of the four children, Merrilee had had the most difficulty adjusting to her adopted home, no doubt because she was the only one who had known her parents, and she had witnessed the tragedy of their deaths.

For three years Rorie had tried to ease the girl's pain, but Merrilee always maintained a polite distance, wandering off for hours on end to talk to her dead mother. Rorie had also heard the child talking to the birds and the animals, the earth and the elements, in her native Comanche tongue. Unlike the fire-and-brimstone preacher who had found her, though, Rorie didn't frighten Merrilee with tales of hell to make her forsake her "savage ways." As far as Rorie was concerned, her first duty to the child was to help her heal her grief, not force her to accept a God who gave her little solace.

Rorie sighed, slipping on her apron and tying a large bow at her back. She supposed it was too late now to hope Merrilee might ever seek her out for comfort, as she would with a real mother. Jarrod, who'd never truly wanted to raise another man's child, had always insisted that the orphans call him "Mr. Jarrod," and her "Miss Aurora." For the sake of domestic peace, Rorie had resigned herself to the formal address. Now, hearing how readily the children were calling Wes "uncle," she wished she had put her foot down and had told the children they could call her Mama. Although, she thought sorrowfully, she knew she could never live up to such a lofty title. She loved the children, but she was well aware that her love was only a substitute for the love they should have known.

Turning toward the mirror, Rorie noticed the reflection of her journal, sitting behind her on the bedside table. The memory of Wes's snooping brought a rush of warmth to her cheeks. Maybe she'd been foolish the night before to forget her journal and leave it downstairs, but she'd never dreamed she might catch the scoundrel riffling its pages. Trust no longer came easily to her where men were concerned, and it stung to think she'd been humbugged by yet another male charmer. Why, only ten short hours ago, she'd convinced herself to believe in Wes!

Although Merrilee had defended him, claiming he couldn't read, Rorie wasn't so sure. Wes was too glib, too smooth, not to have some knowledge of letters. Of course, there was always the possibility he didn't read well. She hoped that was the case, since her insides turned queasy when she imagined him entertaining himself with her most recent entry.

> Wes—as he insists on being called—is an inveterate charmer who has the distressing ability to make me forget my God-given sense and agree to the most outrageous things, like hiring him in the first place. What is worse, my heart trips all over itself and my stomach performs the giddiest acrobatics whenever he smiles into my eyes. One would think, at the staid old age of 30, that I had at last become immune to sweet talk and swagger; yet though barely two days in our employ, Wes has made me recall again the secret kisses and stolen embraces I so enjoyed in my father's garden, when innocence was such a tedious burden and the nights were electric, not empty . . .

Rorie smiled ruefully. She was beginning to live up to her sordid reputation.

If the truth were known, she'd always enjoyed her marital relations—or rather, she had until Jarrod's frustration with her barrenness became so great, he stopped hiding his disgust for her big bones and angular frame. While he courted her, he had been quick to praise her height, calling her a goddess or an Amazon queen. It wasn't until much later that she learned the awful truth: her father, fearing she would never attract a husband, had offered to pay off all of Jarrod's university debts if he would consent to wed her.

Rorie swallowed the old bitterness with practiced efficiency.

Turning to her reflection, she straightened her pinafore and tucked a stray lock of hair into the knot at the nape of her neck. Neatness and poise, her father had always said, would stand a woman in good stead if her physical proportions weren't as pleasing as some men preferred.

She smiled mirthlessly. Her father had also stressed that she should cultivate a modest, unassuming attitude, and that she should refrain from voicing her opinions. Poor Papa would have rolled over in his grave if he knew she now carried a firearm and openly supported the women's suffrage and temperance movements. Was it any wonder, then, that her only suitors were bullies like Hannibal Dukker or men twenty years her senior, like Ethan Hawkins?

After a last resigned inspection of her patched-up calico skirt, Rorie blew out her lamp and headed down the stairs. She avoided the creaking floorboard in the dining room, more out of habit than necessity, and approached the kitchen door. She was intending to fetch the basket in which she always put her eggs, but the sound of voices stopped her.

"You got that batter stirred up, Topher?"

"Yeah, but . . ." Topher sounded mutinous. "I don't see why we got to do it. Men don't cook. That's women's work."

Wes's chuckle floated out to her. "And just who do you think cooks for the cattlemen, the Rangers, and the buffalo hunters when there aren't any womenfolk on the trail?"

Rorie felt a traitorous smile steal across her face.

She edged forward, her footsteps muffled by the rattle of pans, and furtively poked her head around the corner. What she saw nearly left her choking as she stifled her amusement.

The kitchen was in shambles. A bucket had been overturned beneath the sink, and one of the window curtains was twisted and wrinkled as if a small hand had grabbed it, probably to haul Topher up onto the sideboard to steal cookies. That hypothesis would explain why all the jars and bottles were in disarray on the top pantry shelf and why an empty cookie tin lay beneath a bench.

The picture grew more comical. On the table, nestled between little mountains of flour, were several discarded egg shells, each dripping the last of their remains into the powdery residue sprinkled across the floor. In fact, flour seemed to be everywhere. It decorated the milk pitcher in the imprint of a large masculine hand; it trailed footsteps to the butter churn and Ginevee's prized rack of spices; and it made Topher look like a ghost—or rather a raccoon, since his big blue eyes stared out from a pasty mask.

At the moment, Wes's back was turned to her. But after he slipped his head into the bib of Ginevee's apron, Rorie saw he had not been left untouched. The flour storm had blown into the crevices of his rolled-up sleeves and had rained down on his hair, giving him a sort of confectioner's halo. She had to clap a hand over her mouth to hold back a giggle when he brushed a rakish curl off his forehead, leaving a smear of white in its place. Then he grabbed a bowl and began filling it with the flour mountains inside, sweeping them off the table with his forearm and into the bowl.

Topher's brows furrowed, dribbling a few flakes of flour into the batter he was stirring. "Just what are slabberdabs, anyway?"

With a deft flick of his wrist, Wes broke an egg into his bowl. "Why, they're my pa's prized trail flapjacks. Pa passed the secret on to my brother, Cord, and Cord passed it on to Zack and me. Now I'm letting you in on the recipe. It's a time-honored tradition, son, and no women can ever know about it."

He fixed Topher with a stern stare. "You're going to have to take a pinky oath."

Topher's eyes nearly bugged out. "Gee, that's serious."

This time, Rorie clapped both hands to her mouth as Wes nodded gravely.

"Do you hereby swear to take to your grave the Rawlins brothers' secret slabberdab recipe?"

Topher linked his smallest finger with Wes's. "Ain't no woman going to pry it out of me until the worms eat out my eyeballs."

Rorie's mirth lodged in her throat when she heard a footstep behind her. She turned guiltily, blushing to think that Shae or Nita had caught her eavesdropping. Instead she recognized the squat, round form of Ginevee approaching through the lifting shadows of sunrise. Rorie hastily pressed a finger to her lips, grinning as she beckoned her friend closer.

Meanwhile, Topher was standing on a chair, straining to get a better view of Wes's bowl. "Whatcha got in there? Another secret recipe?"

"Naw. Just some biscuits. I could be making huckydummy, though, if I had raisins."

"We got raisins," Topher said brightly. Jumping back down to the floor, he blazed a trail through the flour drifts and stood on tiptoe to haul a tin container down from the shelves. "How many raisins you need?" he called as the metal lid clattered onto the floor.

"Well," Wes said thoughtfully, raising his spoon and watching the batter plop back into the bowl. "We got eight hungry people coming to breakfast, and I reckon they'll want at least two biscuits each. I figure we'll need about ten raisins per person; so how many does that make, Topher?"

The enthusiasm on Topher's face dwindled to confusion. "I don't know." He scowled. "Sixteen?"

Ginevee nudged Rorie as if to say, "That boy hasn't been doing his lessons," and Rorie shrugged helplessly. Topher had known the answer to eight times ten two weeks ago, when she tested the older children on their multiplication tables—or at least, he had seemed to. Had the boy been cheating again?

"No," Wes said gently. "Try again. Eight tens are how many?"

Topher's chin jutted. "I ain't any good at numbers."

"You want to know a secret?" Wes winked. "I'm not either."

The tenseness eased from Topher's shoulders. "You're not?"

"Nope. That's why I made up a song to help me. Want to hear it?"

Topher nodded eagerly. Grinning, Wes sang:

> Grisly's in the honeycomb,
> Queen bee, she's a bawlin',
> Hound dog treed a cougar cat,
> and kitty's up there squallin'.

In spite of Wes's total disregard for pitch, Rorie recognized the tune because it belonged to a childhood game she had played in Cincinnati. Wes had taken liberty with the lyrics, though. Either that or he was yodeling the Texas version, because she couldn't remember singing about grizzly bears or cougars in Ohio.

Perhaps it was just as well, she thought, delighted to watch the enthusiasm return to Topher's face. To hear the boy finally memorize his multiplication tables under Wes's tutelage, she had a hard time remembering how angry she'd been when she caught Wes with her journal. Her hired hand might be insubordinate, but he was gifted with children. What was more, Wes seemed to genuinely enjoy their company, unlike Jarrod, whose arm had to be twisted to pay them the slightest attention, or Gator, who had treated them with tolerant resignation.

Suddenly, painfully, Rorie realized Wes would make a wonderful father—the kind of father she would want for her own children, if she could have them.

Grinning from ear to ear, Topher threw back his head and joined Wes for the second refrain:

Ten times 5 is 50, ten times 6 is 60;
Ten times 7 is 70, ten times 8 is 80.

The combination of squeaky soprano and rusty baritone was so awful, so wonderfully blessed awful, Rorie
couldn't help herself. She snickered.

Ginevee, who was the county's uncontested fiddle-
playing champion, covered her ears and did the same.

The next thing Rorie knew, the two of them were
howling with laughter, clutching their sides, and staggering against the wall for support, tears of mirth streaking
their cheeks.

"Uh oh," Topher warned in a mortified whisper.
"Women!"

Wes broke off his singing as Topher leaped for the
empty cookie tin and kicked it behind the flour barrel.

"You can't come in here!" he called, racing to hide
his bowl behind his back. "No women allowed!"

Seeing the complete and utter panic on Topher's face,
Wes nearly laughed himself. After making the boy swear
a pinky oath, he supposed the least he could do was pretend there really was a Rawlins brothers' secret flapjack
recipe worth defending with his life. It was just so hard to
take slabberdabs seriously with Rorie all but oozing into
a puddle of merriment. The bright silvery peals of her
laughter sang through him, playing on his heartstrings
and flushing him with unexpected warmth. He realized
he'd never heard her laugh before.

"I do declare, Ginevee, isn't this a lovely surprise?"
Rorie called in a lilting voice. "These two fine gentlemen
are making us breakfast."

"It's a surprise all right," Ginevee quipped, casting a
meaningful glance at the chaos. "What do you suppose
the occasion is? I don't recall it being my birthday, and
I'm pretty sure it's not yours."

"Oh, dear. Then it must be just as I feared," Rorie
said, wringing her hands in mock consternation. "We've
met our competition for the Founder's Day baking
contest."

Ginevee hooted with laughter, and Topher sent them
a fierce look.

"Men can cook just as good as women," he said hotly. "Uncle Wes says so."

"Did he indeed?" Rorie turned to Wes. "I daresay he's right, as long as a secret family recipe's involved."

"She's been listening!" Topher hissed.

Wes folded his arms across his chest. "The young man is bringing mighty serious charges against you, Mrs. Sinclair," he said in his sternest voice. "What do you have to say for yourself?"

Her face was flushed with laughter, and her eyes shone as brightly as twin stars. It did strange things to his insides, seeing her happy that way.

"Am I on trial, sir?"

"With all due respect, ma'am, you've been caught smack dab in the middle of the act."

"Then I submit, sir, that there were extenuating circumstances, much like earlier this morning, when I caught you red-handed, reading my diary."

Wes has hard-pressed to keep his poker face in light of this reminder. It stirred in him the memory of lamplight shimmering on her amber brown hair, and shadows flirting with the modest nightgown that clung to her mile-long legs. She seemed to have forgiven him for snooping. He wasn't sure why, but he'd never been one to look a gift horse in the mouth.

He wagged a finger under her nose. "Don't go trying to cloud the issue with inadmissible evidence."

"Now you really *do* sound like a lawman."

He started, then mentally kicked himself. Lord, if someone were to put his brain in a grasshopper, it would jump backward.

He rallied with his wickedest grin and his smokiest drawl. "Do you like me better as a bad man?"

He heard the tiny catch in her breath, and the pulse at her throat quickened.

"I . . . think you deliberately distract us from the subject at hand," she stammered, "to avoid the comeuppance you and your partner in crime so richly deserve."

He arched his brows, enjoying the fresh spurt of color that rushed to her face. "And here I thought we'd been discussing how you and your lady friend listen at keyholes."

She laughed again, to his delight. Ginevee laughed, too, but Wes's eyes and ears were only for Rorie. He didn't think he'd ever heard a sweeter sound or watched a lovelier transformation. This playful, merry Rorie was aglow, a slice of heaven that twinkled within his reach. Here was the Rorie that Jarrod Sinclair must have known before all the burdens and woes, the heartaches and fears, had tamped down her spark of joy.

Her gaiety stirred something in him that went far beyond the civil bounds of admiration and respect.

He wanted her.

The realization hit him so forcefully, he heated from head to toe. Every nerve in his body tingled, and his private parts began to twitch. It was more than a little disconcerting to think he could get so randy over a woman's laugh, especially Rorie's laugh. The last thing she needed was some sagebrush Romeo to ride into her life and fill her belly with a bastard.

God knew, that was the last thing he needed too.

A loud thump jerked his thoughts and his eyes away from Rorie—and none to soon, he decided, furtively adjusting the skirt of his apron. Shae had pushed up the kitchen window from the outside and now leaned across the sill, irritation clearly etched on his face.

"Miss Aurora." He nodded at her and then at Topher, leaving Ginevee out of the greeting. Wes had a moment to wonder if the snub was deliberate before Shae's gaze raked him. "You planning on working today, Rawlins?"

Wes pursed his lips. Out of the corner of his eye, he had seen the hurt flicker across Ginevee's face. The boy had been noticeably cool to his kinswoman ever since Wes had ridden onto the property, and Wes didn't like it.

"Yeah. I'm working today, Shae."

"Glad to hear it."

The boy straightened and started to turn. Ginevee hurried forward, her hands clasped nervously before her.

"Shae."

He halted dutifully, but his features resembled carved stone. "Yes, ma'am?"

Ginevee fidgeted. "I'll have flapjacks ready in a jiffy if you—"

"I'm not hungry. Thanks," he said and continued on his way.

Wes frowned. He saw the compassion in Rorie's gaze and the discomfort in Topher's as Ginevee quickly turned to the stove and busied herself with the fire.

"Shae hardly ever eats with us nowadays," Topher complained, setting his bowl down at last. "Ever since he found out Sheriff Gator was his pa, it seems like he don't want to be part of our family no more."

Wes suspected Rorie's smile was forced as she knelt before the boy.

"Now, Topher. I'm sure that's not the case," she said, placing her hands on his shoulders. "Shae's just hurting that's all. He misses Sheriff Gator like the rest of us."

"And he plans on punishing me for it for the rest of his days," Ginevee muttered, shoving a frying pan across the stove.

Wes caught Rorie's eye. He saw the frustration and grief in her gaze, feelings she quickly repressed as she tried to comfort Topher and Ginevee. Seeing the three of them so worked up, when only moments ago they'd been happy, Wes wanted to wring Shae's neck.

He peeled off Ginevee's apron. "I'll talk to the boy, ma'am."

Rorie climbed quickly to her feet. "Wes, I'm not sure that's a good idea."

"Shae doesn't like anyone meddling in his business," Ginevee added with a mirthless laugh.

"That's never stopped me before." Wes winked, dusting off his hat and setting it on his head.

"Don't you worry, ladies. My knee's a lot taller than yours. It's just the right size for turning over a boy who's grown too big for his britches."

Chapter Eight

Wes caught up with Shae as he was dragging a ladder from the tool shed. Sleep apparently hadn't improved the boy's mood, for he looked as grim today as he had when he stalked from the dinner table the night before. In fact, Shae's features were screwed into a don't-mess-with-me look which Wes might have enjoyed ribbing him out of, if he hadn't been so riled up himself. The way he saw it, grief didn't give Shae the right to show his grandmother disrespect.

Halting beside the door, Wes curbed his immediate impulse to challenge the boy when he saw how Shae was struggling with the ladder.

"Need a hand with that?"

"Nope."

Wes suspected Shae was deliberately keeping his back turned as he heaved the heavy wooden planks to his shoulder. He hadn't balanced the weight, though, and he staggered. When Wes threw out a hand to help, Shae tossed him a dark look.

"I said I got it."

He turned toward the barn, and Wes ducked hastily to avoid being hit by the swinging ladder.

"Something eating you, son?" he asked, falling into step at Shae's side.

"Just busy, that's all."

"Too busy to be civil?"

The boy snorted. "Did I forget to wish you a good-morning, Rawlins?"

"I don't give a damn how you talk to me. Your grandmother has feelings, though."

"Sent you out here, did she?"

"I think you know better than that."

Shae averted his eyes. Busying himself with the ladder, he got it righted and propped against the barn wall. His movements were short and jerky, speaking volumes in his silence.

"You're mad at her." Wes made the words a statement, careful to keep the accusation from his voice.

"Wouldn't you be, if she'd lied to you all your life about your folks?"

"Maybe." He watched Shae intently. "Seems to me I could forgive her, though, if she loved me as much as she loves you."

Shae's jaw hardened. "What kind of love is that? All these years, she denied me the right to know who I am."

Wes heard more pain than anger in the boy's tone. Shae had been through a helluva lot, finding his father and losing him, as Wes understood it, all in the space of an hour. Still, Ginevee must have had her reasons for keeping such a weighty secret. Maybe Gator had forbidden her to tell Shae. Maybe she had thought she was protecting him.

"I can't pretend to know how deep your hurt is," he said quietly. "I've never been cheated quite that way before. Did you ever ask her why she did it?"

"Of course I did."

"And?"

Shae's spine went rigid. Turning abruptly, he pushed past Wes and walked inside the barn. "Leave it alone, Rawlins," he called over his shoulder. "It doesn't matter anymore."

"Yeah?" Wes followed at a more leisurely pace. "Then how come you're so spitting mad?"

"Because it isn't any of your business."

"Oh, I'll be the first to admit that," he said dryly.

"Then why can't you keep your nose out of it?"

Shae's voice broke, and Wes's heart went out to him. His original intention when he followed Shae out here had been to pump him for information. Now, Wes found his softer nature sneaking up on him again, making him more interested in helping Shae than condemning him.

"Because, son," he said in answer to Shae's question, "you're wound so tight, a tornado couldn't stick a straw in you. It might do you some good to talk about your father."

Shae's eyes narrowed to slits. "You want to know about my father? I'll tell you about him. He was good with his guns and good with his promises. That's how he got to be sheriff. Everyone said he was a fair man, and I reckon he was—with thieves, murderers, and such. But when it came to me, he never played square. He just couldn't bear for his childhood sweetheart to know he'd sired a black boy the spring before he married her."

Shae turned, reaching for the work gloves he'd left on the milking stool. "When mama died in childbed," he continued less harshly, "I guess some part of Gator couldn't make peace with the guilt. I remember how he used to come by the hotel where Maw-Maw cooked, bringing me candy, toys, and such. 'Course I never knew who he was then. Maw-Maw told me he was a peddler man who liked her rabbit stew.

"For thirteen years, Gator kept his dirty little secret—with Maw-Maw's help," Shae added acidly. "Then one day his wagon overturned, killing his real son and leaving Mrs. Boudreau an invalid. Gator couldn't nurse her on his own, so he wired Maw-Maw, asking for her help. She became his housekeeper, and I became his hired hand.

"That was five years ago." Shae's jaw twitched, and he turned away. "The bastard never did have the courage to admit who I was, until four months after his wife finally died. 'Course, that was the day he got shot, and he had to make peace with his maker."

Wes shifted uncomfortably. As much as he sympathized with the boy's grief, duty reminded him he still had an investigation to conduct.

"Well, Shae," he said with deliberate nonchalance, "at least you got Gator's land."

Shae made a guttural sound. Pulling on his gloves, he shouldered past Wes and headed for the door.

"I would rather have had my pa."

Wes watched thoughtfully as Shae clambered up the ladder. Reflecting on the hurt he'd heard in the boy's voice, he found it difficult to believe in his original suspicion, namely, that Shae had been one of the Negroes who'd killed Boudreau.

Besides, if given half a reason to believe in the boy's guilt, Dukker probably would have shot him. As for Shae's claim of kinship to Gator, well ... Dukker had every reason to discount it, skin color being only one of them.

Strolling outside, Wes picked up the box of nails Shae had left beside the ladder and climbed to the roof.

"I didn't realize you and Gator were so close." He watched the boy's shuttered features closely for some reaction. " 'Course, I never met the man myself, but it seems like him coming clean and naming you his heir was a good sign. He must have thought right highly of you. And Miss Rorie must, too, seeing as how she's stood by you all these weeks. Maybe it's time to put a cinch in all those wagging tongues and prove to Elodea you're who you say you are."

Shae said nothing.

"Gator did leave some kind of will, didn't he?"

Smiling mirthlessly, Shae pulled a hammer from his belt loop and began prying rotten pieces of wood from the weather vane's cupola.

"Yeah, he left a will."

"So where is it?"

"Well now, that's a funny thing." He gave a particularly vicious pull, and splinters of debris went flying. "Nobody seems to know."

"Then who witnessed the signing? I mean, if Gator named you his heir on his deathbed, then he had to scribble something down to make it valid. Who was there to watch him do it?"

"Hmm. Let's see," Shae said dryly. "There was me,

Miss Aurora, Hannibal Dukker—oh, yeah. And old Doc Warren."

"Doc Warren? Now he'd be an impartial witness. Where's he?"

Shae continued to smile, but the twitch in his jawline betrayed his anger. "Seems like nobody knows that, either."

Wes felt his skin prickle. "Do you think Dukker had something to do with Warren's disappearance?"

Shae's head shot up. Wes could almost see the boy's guard rise again.

"It doesn't matter what I think."

"It does to me."

Shae's eyes narrowed, and Wes had the fleeting notion words wouldn't go far in earning the boy's trust.

"What are you really after, Rawlins?"

"Just the facts."

"The facts aren't any of your business. My family isn't any of your business. Now, if you want my roof over your head tonight and my vittles in your belly, you'd best get yourself a hammer."

"Seems to me like you're pretty quick to take offense—"

"You don't listen so good, Rawlins. Get a hammer, or ride on."

Wes stiffened. He'd never much liked being told what to do. He liked lip from a boy even less. Part of him wanted to haul Shae down off the roof and teach him a lesson in manners he'd never forget. Another part couldn't help but admire the boy's grit. As abrasive as Shae's attitude was, Wes knew he had good reason to be wary. Shae had a household of women and children to protect, and not a single friend to stand by him—not that the boy made it easy to be his friend, Wes thought. If Shae didn't learn to muzzle that mouth of his, he was bound to get himself another black eye, if not worse.

"All right, son," he said, holding up his hands in a mock gesture of defeat. "Don't throw a duck fit."

"You've got a hell of a mouth, Rawlins."

He chuckled. "And here I was thinking the same about you." He swung a leg over the ladder, then glanced back at Shae, who was still glaring. "Don't get your hopes up, son. I'll be back."

Privately, however, Wes wondered it befriending Shae would be the most effective use of his time. Given the boy's level of distrust, he wasn't likely to reveal something useful about Dukker or the still for a good, long while. The children would be more open and honest, but they probably didn't know anything. As for Ginevee . . . If she could keep Gator's and Shae's kinship a secret all these years, he didn't have much hope of prying confidences out of her.

That left Rorie—and Rorie's journal.

His gaze trailed to the second story of the house, where three open windows welcomed the breeze into the family's sleeping quarters.

To think of climbing the trellis in the moonlight and prowling along the upper veranda while the others slept, did strange things to his insides. He suspected he would forget all about diaries, though, if he peeked in one of those windows and saw Rorie dreaming in her nightgown.

He quickly chided himself for such thoughts. Rorie was a lady, and as such, she was off limits. She would expect more from him than he was ready—or able—to give. The only thing he must seek from her was cooperation. Once she satisfied him she wasn't hiding anything to protect Shae, he could take his investigation elsewhere. He would hunt down the killer, win her appreciation, and ride off into the sunset, leaving behind a grateful Rorie and her four idolizing orphans.

At least, that's how the Rangers in the dime novels always did it.

Evening—and the inevitable reading lesson—approached much too quickly for Rorie's comfort. Torn between a giddy, girlish excitement and the pangs of spinsterly dread, she had tried to distract herself with the harried routine of an average Thursday.

Wes, however, managed to sneak into her thoughts no matter what she did. She couldn't conduct her history lesson without recalling his Pocahontas story and the

twinkle in his eyes. She couldn't peel potatoes without remembering his lopsided grin or the endearing smudge of
flour that had dusted his forehead. She couldn't water
Mrs. Boudreau's beloved magnolia tree without visions of
him swinging from its limbs, his firm abdomen and taut
thighs on shameless display.

What was worse, she lost all track of time as she
worked in the garden, sitting daydreaming rather than
weeding. Her gaze kept straying to Wes's powerful sun-
dappled frame, bending and stretching, reaching and flexing, above her on the barn. Even Po's indignant screeching
couldn't rouse her long from her mesmerized state, once she
learned Nita had merely taken his trowel away to keep him
from eating dirt.

As the day wore on, Rorie's heart tripped over the
silliest things—the sound of his voice, the passing of his
shadow. Her insides dissolved to a quivering jumble
whenever he climbed down the ladder to fetch water from
the well. He would stand behind her for endless pulse-
firing moments, his presence as tangible as the beads of
moisture on her palms.

She would feel his gaze upon her, but she didn't dare
look at him during those water breaks. It took every
ounce of will she possessed not to heed the silent calling
of his eyes. She never once flattered herself into thinking
his interest was serious. After all, a man with his good
looks, with his jovial nature and ready charm, had no
need of an over-the-hill castoff like herself.

Since scoldings and reprimands had done little to dis-
suade him, she told herself she needed a new defense
against his practiced roguery. She decided to laugh off his
flirtations and to treat them as he did: like amusing pastimes. The Lord knew, she could use a little amusement in
her life these days.

So when dinner came and his broad shoulders filled
the doorway, dwarfing every memory she'd ever had of
Jarrod, she carefully ignored the thumping of her pulse
and cast a welcoming smile his way.

When he gallantly held out her chair for her, she
made light of the way his hands brushed her shoulders.

When he smiled into her eyes, complimenting her

cobbler in a voice that fairly throbbed with another kind of hunger, she managed a gracious thank-you in spite of the sudden constriction in her throat.

At his every glance, his every contrived touch and compliment, she reminded herself Wes Rawlins was a natural-born roué who'd perfected the art of philandering. To make the mistake of taking his glances and innuendos seriously would only leave her looking like a fool.

As the clock ticked off the eighth hour of the evening, Wes's stories for the children finally drew to a close. Brer Rabbit saved the farmer from the monstrous chickie-lickie-chow-chow-chow, and the children, who'd huddled together in nervous apprehension throughout the tale, burst into claps and cheers.

Merrilee gave him a great hug and thanked him for the story; Topher made him promise to hunt worms with him on the morrow; and Nita said a bashful good-night as she caught hold of Po, who was running around in circles shouting, "Chow, chow, chow!" His cries could still be heard echoing from the stairwell as Ginevee led the children to their bedrooms.

Rorie had an attack of the jitters when she realized she and Wes were at long last alone. She hastily stacked her mending between them, then grabbed her sewing basket and busied her hands with the spools of thread inside.

"You've worked a long, hard day, Wes, so of course I would understand if you wanted to postpone the reading lesson."

"Shoot, no," he said with buoyant good spirits. "I've been looking forward to our reading lesson all day."

"Oh." She winced to hear how disappointed she sounded.

" 'Course, if you'd rather sit and talk—"

"No, that's quite all right," she said quickly. "A reading lesson would be just the thing." *To keep you out of mischief,* she added silently. "Let's go to the dining room." *Where there's a good deal more breathing room.* "Er, the books are in there."

She jumped up to fetch a peg lamp and was disconcerted when she returned to find he had swept all her mending into the basket and stood ready with the handle slung over his arm.

"Lead the way," he said.

She grudgingly obeyed. She didn't know which disturbed her more: the suspicion that he strolled behind her less for chivalry's sake than to watch the swaying of her hips, or the worry that she was in grave danger of losing control of this situation. Although she suspected they were evenly matched where innate cleverness was concerned, she liked to think she held the final advantage with her years of book learning. She just wished she could keep that book-learned brain of hers from conjuring up images of his naked chest.

"So what are we going to read?" he asked.

She crossed to her cabinet. Out of the corner of her eye, she glimpsed him swinging his leg over the back of a chair. His maneuver was so casual, so unconsciously youthful, it chose the book for her.

"I thought we'd start with one of Topher's favorites," she said, seating herself a judiciously safe three feet from his side. *"The Adventures of Tom Sawyer."*

Undaunted, he pushed her sewing basket out of the way and dragged his chair closer. "Tom Sawyer? Who's that?"

"He was, er . . ." Somehow, she resisted the urge to clutch the volume to her breast as his invasive warmth rolled over her. "He was a southern boy who got into a lot of mischief. I daresay he was a lot like you must have been at that age."

"So you reckon this story's about me?" Amusement colored his tone. He took the book and turned it over in his hands. "Is this the kind of stuff you like to read?"

"Oh, no." She laughed a little at the idea. "I keep *Tom Sawyer* and *Little Women* for the children. I prefer more serious fare, such as the essays by Susan B. Anthony, Elizabeth Cady Stanton, and Lucretia Mott."

Wes's brows knitted. "Aren't they lady suffragettes?"

She nodded, secretly impressed by his knowledge. "Mrs. Mott also wrote about women's rights in commerce. I was especially intrigued by her argument that male and female teachers should receive equal wages."

"Makes sense to me," he said. "I've had live dictionaries of both persuasions, and it would have been nigh on impossible to figure out who worked harder for an honest day's wage."

She was so surprised by his admission, all she could do was blink. She'd expected a heated debate on the subject.

"I also believe," she said deliberately, "that the so-called justice women receive from our courts is reprehensible. A man can be tried before a jury of his peers, yet a woman is denied the same basic human right."

"Oh, I'm all for women's basic human rights," he said wickedly.

She glared at him. "It's all very well for you to jest. You're protected by the law. Women, however, are still treated like chattel. Not long ago, I read an account of two offenders who were brought before a judge in this very county. One had stolen a pair of boots, the other had beaten his wife to the point of senselessness. The thief was sentenced to six months in prison while the brutalizer was released with a scolding from the judge."

She smiled mirthlessly. "Gator said the courts in this county rarely sink to such detestable lows. For the sake of us women who live here, I hope he's right. But as long as we are debased by unequal laws, we will continue to be degraded by our husbands, employers, and neighbors."

Wes frowned. "Rorie, I can assure you, if I'd been in town when that nonsense was going on, I would have hauled that judge back to Austin so fast—"

He broke off and fidgeted, as if thinking better of his words. "I mean, I would have made such a ruckus, they would have heard it all the way back at the Supreme Court building. A man like that has no business being a judge."

She leaned forward, excited by his words. "Then you agree a woman should be given the right to vote to protect herself from such outrages?"

Amusement tugged at the corners of his mouth. He leaned forward, too, so that their foreheads nearly touched.

"Considering how we've given the vote to immigrants—a lot of whom came from prisons and asylums," he added dryly, "I see no reason why we can't let our womenfolk jump on the voting bandwagon."

"Really?" She cleared her throat, embarrassed to hear how husky her voice had become. His potent maleness was demanding notice from her senses once more. "You're not just saying what you think I want to hear, are you?"

He chuckled and straightened, much to her relief.

"My aunt Lally has been a partner with my brothers in their cattle business for close to nine years now, and you can bet she gets a vote in everything they do. Sometimes two votes. And of course Fancy—"

He seemed to catch himself again.

"What about Fancy?"

He averted his eyes. The pain in his features was hard to mistake, even with the two bright spots of color staining his cheeks.

"Oh . . ." Waving in a dismissive gesture, he laughed, the sound sharp and forced. "Fancy never needed the law to tell her what her rights were."

Rorie watched him thoughtfully. This was the third time he had spoken of Fancy, only to become uncomfortable, even agitated, at her mention. What was it about his sister-in-law that upset him so?

"Are you and Fancy . . . close?" she ventured.

His head shot up, and his eyes narrowed. "I told you. She's family."

Rorie caught her breath, then furtively released it. Perhaps she was leaping to conclusions, but her female logic told her that Wes was in love with his sister-in-law.

"So tell me about this Dukker fellow," he said, abruptly changing the subject. "Is it true he asked you to marry him?"

Caught off guard, she blinked. How could he possibly have known . . . ? Oh, yes. He'd spent the morning with Topher and Merrilee.

"There's nothing to tell." She smiled ruefully. "Yes, he did, and I declined. Now why don't you turn to page—"

"How come?"

She arched her eyebrows. "Because you'll never learn to read anything unless you open that book."

"I was asking why you turned him down," he said with elaborate patience.

She suspected it would have been wiser to put him in his place the moment he broached the topic. Now she'd given credence to something she could have passed off as simply a young child's misunderstanding.

"As delightful as our conversation has been, Wes, we came here to read, remember?"

"Why don't you want to talk about Dukker?"

She squarely met the challenge in his gaze. "Why don't you want to talk about Fancy?"

For the tiniest fraction of time, his eyes widened.

"Hmmm," he murmured. "I reckon we might get started at that."

She smiled to herself. "Why don't you try reading a bit of the story to me?"

"You mean out loud?"

She nodded, hoping to soothe his fears. "I'm sure you'll do fine. But if you come across a word you don't know, I'll be here to help you."

"Well . . . all right."

Opening the book, he shook out the pages, then squinted hard at the type. Rorie reached over and turned the book right side up in his hand.

"Oh, er, thank you, ma'am."

Next he crunched down in his chair, his chin all but touching his chest as he stared at the page. Great furrows of concentration lined his brow. A full minute passed before he cleared his throat.

"What's this one?" He pointed to the first word on the page. Rorie leaned across his arm, trying not to let the elusive scents of sandalwood soap and leather distract her from her mission of enlightenment.

"*The*," she said helpfully.

"The," he repeated in a grave voice.

More squinting ensued. He cocked his head to the right, and then to the left. "Ah . . ." He pointed again to the page and looked at her piteously.

"Adventures," she said gently. "That's a rather

difficult word. When they're difficult, we try to break them into syllables." She taught him how to divide "adventures" into segments, then said, "Now let's turn to chapter one and try again."

"Chapter one?" he asked suspiciously. "What's that?"

She was beginning to suspect she had agreed to a Herculean task. "Chapter one is the beginning of the story. You've been reading the title page."

"Oh," he said in a mystified tone.

She glanced at him sharply. Was that the sparkle of merriment lurking in his eyes? Before she could decide, he'd averted his gaze and began thumbing through the volume.

"Let's see," he said in a voice that sounded a little too cheerful for her peace of mind. "Chapter one. I reckon that'd be about here." He grinned triumphantly.

He'd turned to chapter two.

She remembered her earlier thought, that he was too glib not to have had some exposure to education, and since he'd told her minutes earlier that he'd had both male and female teachers, she found it doubtful that a man who could multiply numbers and recount history didn't have a clue how to find the beginning of a book.

"Wes," she asked, "do you know your alphabet?"

"Sure I do." He nodded vigorously for emphasis.

Rising, she pulled a slate and piece of chalk from the shelf and handed them to him. "Why don't you show me?"

His face fell. "You mean now?"

The patience on which she had always prided herself began to wane. "Most certainly. Do you have a reason why you should wait?"

He fidgeted, reminding her of Topher when the boy had been caught in a lie. "Well, to tell the truth, ma'am, it would save us a heap of time if I just spelled out my name."

She arched a brow in question.

"It ain't quite as much trouble," he explained.

She cringed to hear his misuse of language, but she

didn't correct him. After all, reading, spelling, and grammar were a bit much to tackle in one lesson.

"Very well. Spell out your name."

Looking eager to please, he balanced the bottom of the slate on his abdomen and, hunching over the board, began sketching in large, bold strokes. He stopped once or twice in midgesture, rubbing out a mistake with his elbow, before continuing with his task. At last he finished his masterpiece, and beaming, turned the board around for her inspection.

A giant X filled the slate from top to bottom.

It was all she could do not to snatch the board from his hands. "That is *not* your name, Wes."

"It's not?"

He gazed at her in innocence, a state of being so completely unnatural to him, that she knew in an instant she'd been hoodwinked.

"Wesley Rawlins—"

"Wescott's my name."

She started. Momentarily robbed of her indignation, she blinked at him. "Wescott?"

He nodded, grimacing. "Mama was an angel, but she had the devil of a time naming boys. I got Wescott, Zack got Zachariah, and Cord . . ." He snickered, shaking his head. "Cord got Cordero. It means 'little lamb' in Spanish."

She didn't know whether to believe this absurd tale, but she was certain she could never stay mad at Wes for long. He was much too quick to deflect her ire with his charm.

"Very well, Wescott Rawlins," she said sternly. "Are you humbugging me?"

"Oh no, ma'am. That's Cord's real name. Honest."

She began tapping her toe. "That is not what I meant and you know it. Can you, or can you not, read?"

"Well . . ." He cast her a sidelong glance. "I reckon I can."

"I knew it!"

Undaunted, he sidled closer. "You know, ma'am, reading is powerful hard work." His gaze trailed provocatively from her eyes to her lips. "Why don't we rest for a spell?"

His lips strayed dangerously close—and kept coming. Gasping, she jumped to her feet. Her quick reflexes barely let her escape his kiss.

"It does seem to be getting rather warm in here," she said, tossing him a quelling look.

"Is that a fact?" He chuckled, leisurely unfolding his long frame. "Then maybe we should take a stroll outside."

"Very well." She raised her chin, determined this upstart of a hired hand wouldn't get the better of her. She would rather be tarred and feathered than let her silly biological processes make her capitulate to a randy young man.

Besides, he'd snooped, lied, and played her for a fool. She was not a wilting wallflower, and she would not suffer such roguish behavior without doling out the comeuppance he so richly deserved.

It was war now, her wits against his. Just as the dining room was bigger than the kitchen, the out-of-doors were infinitely larger than the dining room.

A general couldn't hope for a better field advantage.

Chapter Nine

*H*er head held at a regal angle, Rorie swept past Wes and out the door. He kept pace a few yards behind her, like a wolf trailing a nervous doe.

He wasn't exactly sure how she'd eluded his questions. Oh, she was quick enough on her feet, but he liked to think he wasn't any quarter-wit where interrogations were concerned. As best as he could figure, she must have used her perfume to unfair advantage, and he'd been just churn-headed enough to let its delicate floral scent tie his tongue in knots. Or maybe he'd been thrown off track by her defense of women's rights and the flash of righteousness in those tawny eyes. He'd so enjoyed crossing sabres with her that he never quite managed to work the conversation back to Dukker. God knew, his original strategy hadn't included trying to kiss her.

The more he thought about it, though, the more kissing her appealed to him. He figured after one cool peck on the lips from a prim-and-proper live dictionary like Rorie, she'd be out of his loins for good. Then he could finally concentrate on his mission.

His gaze strayed in reluctant fascination to the gentle rolling of her hips. For some reason, thoughts of his investigation kept slipping his mind.

Great gray clouds scudded across the moon as Rorie halted before the magnolia tree, her skirts flapping in the wind. Wes could taste the tang of rain in the air, and he muttered an oath. If the heavens unleashed themselves tonight, he'd have to wait for yet another opportunity to ride into town for his telegraph. He didn't like slogging through muddy downpours any more than Two-Step did, and that meant another wasted night.

"Is something wrong, ma'am?"

She'd been staring into the branches, her hand resting on the rough bark of the trunk. She started at his words, as if he'd pulled her from a deep well of thought.

"Er, no. Not really." She sighed, dropping her arm. "It's just that this poor old tree has lost so many leaves in the last few weeks. I worry about it with the coming storm."

Wes tipped his head back for a better view of the branches he'd romped through two days earlier. He'd been so busy showing off that he hadn't paid much attention to the telltale signs of brittle greenery or the occasional sparsely covered limb. Although this magnolia wasn't particularly grand compared to the ones that grew in humid east Texas, the tree had a certain feisty stubbornness that had allowed it to grow in a dry climate alien to its nature. Magnolias were evergreens, so it was unusual for the tree to be dropping its leaves—unless, of course, it was dying.

"What do you suppose is ailing it?" he asked, careful not to telegraph his private prognosis of doom.

"I don't know." She raised troubled eyes to his. "It was doing so beautifully up until Mrs. Boudreau passed on. Then it just seemed to fade away, as if it had lost its spirit."

Once more she turned to the tree, running a loving hand along its spine. Watching her caress the planes of that trunk, he felt a strange tingle in the pit of his belly. He wondered wistfully what her fingers would feel like some morning, stroking the stubble on his chin.

"She really loved this tree," Rorie said so quietly, he wasn't sure she'd meant for him to hear.

"You mean Mrs. Boudreau?"

She nodded. "She told me its story once, how she and Gator met as children when she went out to her father's yard to water the sapling he'd just planted there. She said there'd never been another man for her from that moment on. When she got old enough, Gator courted her formally and he asked her to marry him right under that tree. A few years later, he decided to try his hand at ranching in Texas. Mrs. Boudreau was so sad to leave her Louisiana home behind that Gator rode back to her papa's place and made arrangements for the tree to be shipped to his farm."

Rorie smiled at the thought. "I suppose he must have had the devil of a time hauling a twenty-foot tree all the way from New Orleans to Bandera County without the benefit of a train, but Mrs. Boudreau said Gator had a way with green things, even if he'd never had one with steers.

"I always thought that was such a beautiful story," she added, turning the warmth of her smile on Wes. "To meet Gator, you would never have thought the man had a romantic bone in his body. Yet he went to all that trouble to make his bayou bride feel at home in Texas."

Wes smiled too. He always liked a good story. "Well, that explains it. About the tree, I mean. It's doing poorly 'cause there aren't any sweethearts around."

She looked bemused. "I beg your pardon?"

"This here's a sweetheart tree." He could tell by her face, she didn't have the vaguest idea what he meant. "You mean you never heard the legend of the sweetheart tree?"

She shook her head. He did, too, in mock despair.

"Just what do you Yankee schoolmarms teach your young-uns up there?"

She opened her mouth as if to defend herself, but he held up both hands, staving off an earful.

"Never mind. That's what you book-learned folks like to call a rhetorical question."

Amusement flickered across her features.

"Now then, the sweetheart tree is a big ol' tree that's been around fifty or sixty years." Wes patted the trunk. "I'd say this one's just about old enough to be wise in the ways of folks like you and me."

Nodding gravely to emphasize his point, he took an oh-so casual step toward her.

"Being a sweetheart tree is a mighty big honor among the plant kingdom," he continued. "As I hear it told, those big fellas don't let just any old twig or bush sign up. You see, a sweetheart tree has got to know the difference between true love and . . . well, let's just call it unchaperoned sparking."

He watched her furtively for some sign of priggish outrage, and was encouraged by her peeking dimple. He took another step closer.

"Some folks will try to tell you that a sweetheart tree is a crabapple or a dogwood 'cause, come spring time, white flowers bust out all over them. But I beg to differ."

"You do, huh?"

"Uh-huh."

They were standing nearly toe to toe now, and he congratulated himself on his progress. "Oh, I'm sure that a crabapple or a dogwood could do in a pinch," he said with a lofty wave of his hand. "But a *magnolia* tree's got those Yankee pretenders beat hands down."

She crossed her arms, but her show of offense was belied by the glow in her eyes. "And why is that, pray tell?"

He gazed at her in mock surprise. " 'Cause magnolia trees have been around for ages and ages. Some book-learned fellas—you know, the kind that cut up fruits and stare at them through a magnifying glass—say magnolias are the granddaddies of all flowering plants."

He made one last strategic move, cutting her off from the most likely avenue of escape.

"Besides, magnolias are evergreens," he added. "They don't go to sleep all winter long, making sweethearts wait months on end to see if they've found their one and only love."

"Hmm." She sounded thoughtful. "And how does the magnolia achieve its grandiose mission in life?"

He decided to back her against the trunk. To his surprise, though, his graceful doe stood her ground. He almost frowned. It took all the fun out of being a predator if the prey didn't know she was being stalked.

Then again, maybe she did know, he thought in sudden wolfish triumph. Maybe all her ladylike airs were just a pretense, and deep down, she really wanted to be pursued.

"Well," he drawled in his best sparking voice, "the magnolia tree keeps a watch out for sweethearts. When a couple comes along, it takes stock of the way they hold hands, the way they look into each other's eyes . . ." He lowered his voice to a throbbing whisper. "The way they kiss."

He leaned closer, and still she didn't retreat. It was an exhilarating feeling, having her gaze up at him so sweetly. He couldn't remember her looking at him like that before, and he kind of liked it. But just as he drew close enough to kiss her, she threw a question between them like a gauntlet.

"So then what does the sweetheart tree do?"

His brows rose. So she'd played this game before, had she? The notion brought him a smug sense of satisfaction—until he realized she must have played it with Jarrod Sinclair.

"Let's see . . ." He could feel her skirt, whipped up by the wind, wrapping his calves like the long, silken limbs of a lover. The image brought a surge of heat to his groin, and he had to remind himself that he was kissing her for one reason and one reason only: To get her off his mind.

"The tree gives a sign, since it's so wise in the ways of true love. If a couple is meant to stay together for the rest of their lives, great white flowers start to bloom instantly, no matter what the time of year."

"How interesting," she said huskily.

She had leaned back ever so slightly from his advance. Now her eyelids drooped, as if she were staring at his mouth, and he imagined he could see the hunger behind her veil of lashes. A thrill of expectancy coursed through him, and he pressed forward once more, close enough for their thighs to brush. This time when he lowered his head, he reached for her waist too. That's when her tender smile stopped his heart.

"So what you're saying is, I should let Ethan kiss me under this tree."

If she had slapped his face, she couldn't have made him recoil faster.

"Ethan? Who's Ethan?"

She shot him a sly, coquettish look, one that he would have sworn her incapable of ten minutes ago.

"Why," she said in a honeyed voice, "Ethan Hawkins is one of my gentleman callers. He owns fifteen thousand acres and a modest herd of Hereford cattle on a range that starts about a dozen miles south of here."

Shock washed over Wes, then disbelief. Both were followed by a confused jumble of emotions that he couldn't entirely sort out, but which left him feeling as if he'd just been punched in the gut.

"Why would you want to kiss this Ethan Hawkins?" he asked, unaccountably irritated by the whole idea.

Rorie kept her eyes lowered. She used the ploy less to convey demureness than to stall for time to gather her wits. When she threw out Ethan's name, she'd been a four-star general playing a game of battlefield chess. Now she felt like a raw recruit who had just watched her bullet claim her first enemy casualty. She told herself remorse was ridiculous, not to mention lily-livered. After all, she'd been under attack all day long, and she had every right to strike a defense. The problem was, she hadn't expected Wes to look so . . . hurt.

"It's like you said," she answered lamely. "The sweetheart tree could tell me whether to let Ethan make his offer to me."

She dared to look at him then—which proved to be a mistake. His eyes were like shards of glass in the moonlight. She felt cut by their touch.

"Is that why you turned down Dukker? Because of Hawkins?"

She laughed weakly. More than twenty years her senior and hard of hearing, Ethan wasn't exactly her idea of a knight in shining armor. She had to admit, though, he'd never caused her to fear for the children's safety the way Hannibal Dukker had.

"Ethan is one of the reasons," she answered with well-rehearsed circumspection.

Wes frowned. "Do you love him?"

The conversation was taking a decided turn for the worse. By mentioning Ethan, she had hoped to put Wes in his place, to make him keep his distance out of respect for her serious beau. She hadn't intended to get into a discussion of her feelings for the man.

"Wes, really. That is hardly a matter for your concern." She started to turn away only to find her path blocked by a ramrod-straight arm that extended from his shoulder to the tree. She retreated—her next mistake. Her spine struck bark, and she became trapped between the magnolia's unyielding trunk and the imposing expanse of Wes's chest.

"What about the children? Is this Hawkins good to them?"

She caught her breath. She should have been outraged by his impertinence; instead, his show of concern brought a rush of warmth to her heart.

"Yes," she said quietly. "He's good to them."

He nodded, but he didn't look satisfied. There was an intensity about his hardened jaw and the taut line of his arm. If she didn't know better, she would have thought she'd made him jealous. But she was a realist, so she attributed his tenseness to youthful anger because she'd thwarted his kiss. Besides, she reminded herself, the man was pining away for his sister-in-law.

"I reckon there's only one other thing to ask then," he said less gruffly. "Is he good to you too?"

She swallowed. She hadn't expected this line of questioning. In truth, she hadn't expected him to care. As much as she would have liked to discount his concern, to attribute it to a wily philanderer's ace in the hole, she needed only to search his eyes to see that his regard for her and her family was not contrived. It was a painful revelation: this wild, young scoundrel, who'd known her less than four days, was showing more kindness toward her than her husband of seven years ever had.

Tearing her gaze away, she cast about frantically in her mind for some suitable answer. "He treats me well enough," she said, failing, in spite of her best efforts, to keep the defensiveness from her voice. "He's had a wife, and I've had a husband. Love only comes once in a lifetime, and we've already had our turns."

Wes looked incredulous. "So you're saying Jarrod Sinclair was the love of your life?" Snorting in derision, he shook his head. "Darlin', it sounds to me like you just haven't lived."

Her throat tightened. He'd come uncomfortably close to the truth, a truth that had smoldered in her soul ever since she realized she'd traded the oppression of her father's household for the degradation of her husband's.

Forcibly squaring her shoulders, she tried valiantly to disguise her hurt with anger. "You are in no position to judge me, or Jarrod, or . . ." Her vision blurred, and Wes swam out of focus. "Or anything that may have passed between us," she finished hoarsely.

"Rorie." His hands settled on her shoulders, warm and strong and gentle. "I didn't mean any offense. You have to know I'm on your side. It's just that . . . Well, shoot. Jarrod Sinclair should have the stuffing beat out of him for running out on you. I'd hate to see your feelings get all tangled over some other fella who might not treat you any better.

"You deserve a world of good things, Rorie," he said with surprising sincerity. "Don't marry some man who doesn't love you because you're afraid someone better won't come along."

She shook her head, trying to convey how wrong his insight was, but for all her hard-won stubbornness, she couldn't bring herself to meet his gaze. She wanted to believe his impudence was what made her so distraught, but the part of her that abhorred deceit refused to dole out blame. Wes had spoken to her secret fear.

Although a life with Ethan wasn't her fondest desire, she had witnessed his tolerance when he sat with his grandchildren at church. He might not be the kind of man she wanted holding her through the night, but at least she had no worries he might leave her and the children behind for some mythical greener pasture.

For an infinite moment, the spell of silence wrapped

around her. She became acutely aware of the young, vital man who held her, the kind of man whose embrace she secretly longed for in the night. She knew she'd overstepped the bounds of propriety by letting Wes touch her for so long, but try as she might, she couldn't relinquish that sweet, seldom-felt comfort.

For just one heartbeat longer, she told herself. For just one fraction more of her lonely, predictable life, she would allow this tantalizing breach of social conduct. Then she would summon a respectable show of outrage and storm inside to her empty bed.

Wes's hands shifted, though. She caught her breath as his fingers brushed her cheek, tucking a windblown strand of hair behind her ear. The featherlight gesture was so intimate in its innocence, that she stood frozen, uncertain whether to flee, to protest, or simply to frown. She could do nothing so decorous.

Instead, she found herself peeking up at him, past the shimmer of teardrops on her lashes, to gaze with girlish fascination at the dance of storm and shadow on his face. The sun god of two days earlier had been transformed by lancets of lightning. He'd become Thor, the fiery-haired king of the storm.

But Thor, she recalled, was half-brother to Loki, the master of mischief and mayhem. When Wes cupped her face in his hands and smiled, she knew she should run as fast as her feet could carry her. Her feet stood rooted, though, and her limbs trembled like tempest-tossed leaves when his head lowered with mesmerizing slowness, and his lips parted to taste hers.

His kiss was patient and kind, a sly, gentle plunder that left her dizzy with the rush of long-repressed desire. She swayed, her knees weakening faster than her resistance, and found herself clutching his shirt front. Just to brace her weight, she wanted to believe, until she realized that she, not he, was the one pulling closer, pushing her hips shamelessly into his.

Reason completely abandoned her then; good breeding left her in a cloud of dust. Never in her most sinful, decadent dreams had she imagined she might kiss a man the way she kissed Wes Rawlins. She twisted her fingers in his hair; she crushed her breasts against his chest. She demanded more of the mouth he slanted across hers and revelled in the thrust of his tongue. It gave her the most wanton, wicked pleasure to feel his solid length locked hard against hers. She'd never kissed a man who was taller than she was; she'd never felt her womanhood melt into the heat of brazen masculinity or thrill to the hardening of an unapologetic male. He was raw virility, ready for the taking; she was primal femininity unleashed.

She rubbed and arched, trying to appease her tender ache, and his restraint dissolved. With a feral growl, he flattened her shoulders against the tree, exposing her throat to his mouth and her breasts to his hand. She squirmed when his tongue's moist heat darted inside her ear, and she groaned to feel her nipple strain beneath his expert teasing.

His thigh was wedged thick and hard between her legs, and his fingers were making short work of the buttons on her blouse. In a matter of seconds, she would be bared to him, to the storm. The realization jolted through her like the electrical charges flashing around them.

Grasping wildly for the dignity she'd scattered to the wind, she raised a shaking hand and shoved against his chest.

"Wes, we have to stop," she said, gasping.

"The hell we do," came the rumble near her ear.

She nearly slid down the trunk when the top two stays of her corset burst free, and the leathery pads of his fingers closed over one very delighted breast. She grabbed his wrist, and it was all she could do to make herself deter his fondling.

"Wes, please," she whimpered, hating the sound and yet preferring it hands-down to the groan she'd made seconds earlier. "Stop."

His thumb challenged her resolve, nudging the swollen nub that jutted so eagerly into his palm. She came dangerously close to tearing open his buttons, then. In desperation, she threw her arms around his neck, dragging her body hard against his and pinning his fingers against the forbidden territory he sought to explore. She could feel his heart, as loud as the thunder, hammering against her own.

For several moments, his breath was hot and ragged in her ear. She sensed his inner struggle, the wanting that her response had roused in him, and she wished fervently that she'd had the good sense to act like the prude she'd always pretended to be outside her marriage bed. What was she to do with the man now? How was she to explain herself? For heaven's sake, he wasn't even her suitor!

"Lord have mercy on me." His raspy chuckle gusted goosebumps down her spine. "Where'd you learn to kiss like that?"

She squeezed her eyes closed, thankful he couldn't see her blush, and prayed he couldn't feel its heat when he rubbed his stubbled jaw against her cheek.

"I . . . had a husband, remember?"

"So that's what getting hitched does to a lady, eh?"

She wanted to die. She tried to wrench free, but he anchored her hips to his own with an arm as tractable as Bessemer steel.

"Steady, darlin'. I don't think you want to turn around just yet."

He reached for her buttons, presumably to fasten them. She was tempted to ask how he'd become so dexterous with ladies' clothing, but she decided she didn't want to know.

"I'll do that. Let me go."

"Shh," he murmured, his fingers working up her shirt more quickly.

She squirmed.

"Hold still," he whispered more urgently.

"Wes Rawlins, so help me God, if you don't let me g—"

His mouth swooped down to silence her. She reeled, too stunned to carry out her threat, which had something to do with a well-aimed knee. Then she heard the crunch of boots on the gravel behind her. Somebody coughed.

Rorie turned to stone. Wes fastened the button at her throat, and she prayed he hadn't missed one of the others.

"Sorry to barge in on you folks," the intruder said.

"Reckon you didn't hear me coming—er, 'cause of the thunder."

Shae! She groaned inwardly. Dear Lord, why couldn't it have been Ginevee?

Her eyes locked with Wes's. He gave her a lopsided grin, then casually stepped around her, blocking her dishevelled state from Shae's view. She silently cursed and thanked him at the same time when she saw her perfectly fastened bodice.

"Something I can do for you, Shae?" Wes drawled.

Rorie hastily patted her hair and smoothed down her blouse. Her skirts would have to pass muster the way they were now.

"As a matter of fact, I was looking for you," Shae said darkly.

Rorie glanced over her shoulder and saw he was balancing the shotgun butt-down on his boot. As harmless as his stance looked, the kick shot was a trick Gator had taught him, one that let him level the muzzle and fire lightning fast.

The realization suddenly made her clothing irrelevant.

"Shae, is something wrong?" Her voice quavered more from anxiety than embarrassment. She moved to shield Wes, and Shae's eyes narrowed.

"The fact is," he said, "I was going to ask you the same thing, ma'am."

Her laughter sounded ridiculously high and strained. "Don't be silly. Nothing's wrong."

He didn't look convinced. "You sure Rawlins isn't bothering you?"

"Oh, no. We were just . . . er . . ." She glimpsed Wes's hand sneaking playfully toward her waist, and she discreetly shoved it away. "We were just talking about ways to nurse the tree."

"Ways to *fertilize* the tree," Wes corrected her with his wayward sense of humor.

She gritted her teeth, wanting to slap him.

Thankfully, Shae was diplomatic enough to drop the subject. "There's a storm blowing in from the north. Looks like it might be a real duck drencher. I rounded up the animals and boarded the roof as best I could, but the barn isn't going to be too comfortable tonight. That's why I thought Rawlins might want to bunk with me and Topher."

"Why, that's right kind of you, Shae," Wes said.

The last thing Rorie wanted was Wes bedding down in the room next door, but what could she possibly say? "I don't care if it's raining bullfrogs and heifer calves, young man, you sleep outside so I'm not tempted to sin"?

"Yeah, well . . ." Shae glared at his hired hand as if to convey that his conscience was strictly a nuisance in this matter. "I reckon you can't get into too much trouble with me and Topher watching over you."

"I reckon," Wes agreed.

"But it's just for tonight, mind you."

"That suits me fine."

Rorie cleared her throat. "Wes will, of course, sleep in the barn again when the hay is dry enough. He'll want his privacy."

She wished she'd swallowed her tongue the instant she made the allusion.

"And lots of rolling-around room," Wes added drolly.

She choked. He smirked. Shae looked from her to Wes as if he'd just been swatted by a two-by-four. Finally, he shook his head.

"Whatever you say, ma'am. I'll be going to bed now, unless you think you need me . . . ?"

He tossed this last question to her like a lifeline, but Wes was quicker to jump on the bait.

"Oh, no. We're dandy here, Shae. Go on about your business. Just don't tucker yourself out by waiting up for me."

Now she wanted to throttle the scoundrel.

"Good night," Wes called jovially after the boy.

The front door banged, and she rounded on her tormentor.

"How dare you?" she exclaimed. "How dare you say such things and imply that we . . . that I . . . that tonight . . ." Her chest heaved. "Wescott Rawlins, you are a shameless rogue and a villain!"

"That's why you like me."

"*Oh!*" She stomped her foot. "You have no idea what I like!"

He leaned closer. "Oh, I think I do."

She jerked her head away, her lungs straining so hard beneath her corset that she could scarcely catch her breath. It took every ounce of self-control she possessed not to throw a temper tantrum like one of the outlandishly melodramatic females her father had taught her to disdain.

"Mr. Rawlins," she began again with considerably more aplomb, "you are mistaken if you believe you hold the key to my desires." She winced, wishing she hadn't put it quite that way. "What transpired tonight between you and me was, at best, a regrettable moment of folly."

"Folly, eh?"

"That's right."

"Not an invitation?"

She drew herself up to her most prim and proper pose. "Certainly *not* an invitation."

"So you mean to say you kiss Ethan Hawkins that way?"

"Good heavens, no!"

"I'm mighty glad to hear that."

She glared into his laughing eyes. This conversation was getting rapidly out of control again.

"I think the time has come for us to speak frankly, sir. I have a serious suitor in Mr. Hawkins, and I must insist that you lavish your spurious affections on someone else."

That sobered him a bit. He cocked his head and studied her. After a moment of silence, his appraisal made her blush.

"Do we understand each other?" She wasn't sure she liked the gleam that was kindling in his eyes. It smacked more of challenge than of understanding.

"What about the tree?" he asked, suspiciously nonchalant.

She frowned. "The tree?"

"Sure. If poor old Maggie's ever going to get well, she'll need a real couple of sweethearts."

She tried to look disdainful. "That's nothing but a Texas tall tale."

"Maybe." His eyelids lowered, and his hand raised to cup her chin. "But for Maggie's sake—for Merrilee, Topher, Po, and Nita—can you afford to take that chance?"

She swallowed. He'd struck at her weakness, the children, and she knew she should rally her wits to strike back. Instead, every nerve in her body tingled to feel that warm, callused palm connect with her flesh. She told herself he didn't really care what happened to her family, that he'd weave a dozen such quixotic tales if he thought they might win him a tumble in the barn. All he really wanted was a bit of sport, a bawdy release.

The thought made her feel like crying.

"Wes, don't." Drawing a ragged breath, she forced the lump from her throat. "Don't bait me with promises you don't intend to keep."

His lips paused in their descent, and contrition flitted across his features. She was surprised—and intrigued—when a tiny, pensive smile touched his mouth. He brushed his thumb across her cheek, then dropped his hand, finally stepping back.

"Fair enough," he said.

She should have been relieved. Instead, she felt a perplexing sense of loss.

"So . . . you and I understand each other at last?"

Rain drizzled from the clouds. The wind whipped droplets down her collar to slide along her breast, still tender and aching for his touch. She tried to ignore the sensation by pushing a strand of hair from her cheek, but the memory of his caress had left its imprint there too.

"In a manner of speaking," he answered, for once sounding grave.

She nodded. She didn't have the clear-cut victory she'd hoped for, but she told herself it would have to do. The rain began falling harder, more like pellets than drops, and lightning was rending great holes in the mist. She turned toward the house.

"Rorie, wait. There's something I have to tell—"

Thunder boomed. Above its echo, she heard a branch snap and fall from the magnolia.

"Hurry, Wes. It's not safe out here. Get your gear and come inside."

Wes didn't move. Instead, he watched her as she ran toward the porch. She looked back once in a blinding flash, but as the darkness returned, he heard the front door slam.

Inside the house a match flared. He saw her silhouette on the curtains in the sitting room. She peeked out the window, shaking her head as if she thought him as crazy as a sheepherder. Leaving a candle burning, she carried a lamp out of the room.

He waited a few minutes longer. The rain ran down his collar and soaked his jeans, but it didn't cool him off. He could see her silhouette again, framed by the glow of the oil lamp in a second-story window. Her arms rose, and her hair fell, a mass of sinuous shadow sliding down to her hips. When she reached for the buttons on her bodice, his mouth went dry, and he tore his gaze away.

God help him. What was he thinking? If kissing her had been a mistake, seducing her would be a downright sin. Rorie deserved a man who could give her more than a reputation. Even if he'd come clean before she ran into the house, telling her he was a Ranger, he couldn't in good conscience make a losing proposition seem attractive. This Ethan Hawkins had acreage and a couple hundred head of steers. All Wes had was . . . Two-Step. And a badge that made homesteading next to impossible.

He mentally kicked himself. He wasn't ready to hitch himself to one woman's bedpost. For Rorie's sake, he should be glad Ethan Hawkins was. He should be glad she had a serious suitor who was good to her orphans. Unfortunately, the idea of Rorie kissing some stranger kept sticking in his craw. Maybe it was because he didn't like to lose.

Turning, he winced at the chafing of his jeans and gingerly plucked the denim from his pecker. Come to think of it, he didn't like to start what he couldn't finish, either. The devil take the woman for kissing him like she had wildfire in her veins. Schoolmarms were supposed to be tame and demure, completely unworthy of a two-story climb.

But if he ever needed to make that climb, his wicked side reminded him, her bedroom was the first window on the right.

Somewhat cheered by the thought, he turned to wade through the puddles between the sweetheart tree and the barn.

Chapter Ten

*T*hat night was a restless one for Rorie. She spent half of it dreaming of flower-bedecked tropical islands where a red-haired pirate stole her kisses beneath lush green leaves.

The other half of the night, she strained her ears above the cracks of thunder, worrying she might not hear the stealthy sound of footsteps in the hall, wondering what she would do if she did. Every time a crossbeam groaned or a floorboard creaked, she shrank beneath her quilt and watched her door in a mixture of anticipation and dread. But the knob never turned; he never came; and she had to congratulate herself weakly that something she'd said must have stirred his conscience.

Either that, or he'd only been bluffing, and she'd never been in the least bit of danger of being debauched.

The thought was terribly deflating.

Wes didn't sleep much, either. The storm wasn't what bothered him—he thought it nice to have a roof over his head during one—and Shae's handily placed scattergun caused him amusement, not alarm.

He'd been kind of amused, too, when Topher, waiting impatiently for Shae to doze, had sneaked down from their bunks to crawl into his bedroll. The boy had demanded ghost stories, and Wes had obliged, whispering into his ear for a good hour or more before the little rascal tired enough to snuggle under his arm.

No, sleep evaded Wes mostly because his imagination broke loose, running wild with the taste and feel, the scent and touch, of Rorie. To his secret shame, visions of Fancy usually occupied his fantasies, so he wanted to believe his change of appetite was progressive. Instead, he had the nagging suspicion he'd traded one impossible craving for another.

He tried to tell himself Rorie's appeal came from being unattainable, but the words just wouldn't ring true. He was drawn to the fire that smoldered under all her refinement, and not just her sexual fire. Rorie had proven herself passionate about many things: politics, the rights of women, homeless children, oat-sowing Rangers . . .

He winced at that thought.

Maybe it was just as well the storm had kept him from unveiling his badge. Now more than ever he needed to prove the merits of Rangerhood so she would trust him and help him find Gator's killer. Unfortunately, he had a long way to go to show her he wasn't like Bill Malone.

Determined to be on his best behavior the next morning, Wes set out to win back the points he had lost. But Rorie, greeting him with cool serenity at breakfast, didn't look twice at him through the meal.

An hour or so later, she breezed past him at the well, nodding and smiling as if she were a queen on royal business and he was an infatuated nuisance standing in her way.

That put him in a sod-pawing mood.

By lunchtime, she had politely snubbed him two more times, and when he cornered her afterward for an explanation, she laughed off talk of their kiss, telling him not to trouble himself, since she'd "quite frankly forgotten all about it."

That put him damned near the end of his rope. He didn't kiss just any woman, by God, and when he did, he made sure she remembered it.

He was debating whether to give Madam Schoolmarm a biology lesson she'd never forget, when Nita burst through the kitchen door, wide-eyed and breathless.

"Miss Rorie, Topher's been in a fight!"

Rorie started, breaking free of Wes's wolfish glare. She frowned as she turned to the child. "A fight? But who—"

"Danny Dukker," Nita panted. "Down by the fishing hole. Topher took his puppy. You better come quick, 'cause Danny said he was sending Creed to lick Topher!"

Rorie's shoulders snapped back, and her eyes flashed like gunpowder.

"I assure you, Nita, Creed Dukker will not lay a hand on Topher. However," she added darkly, "I may."

Wes's wounded pride dissolved in a flood of concern for Topher, and he followed closely as Rorie headed for the yard. The first thing he noticed was that Abraham, Sarah, Merrilee, and Nardo had rallied around the boy like soldiers defending a flag. The next thing he noticed was Topher's split lip and the triumphant, albeit belligerent, gleam in his eye. He clutched a baby hound dog like a badge of honor to his chest, and only Merrilee was given permission to pet it.

"I didn't do nuthin' wrong," Topher said the minute Rorie halted before him.

"That's right, Miss Rorie," Sarah said fiercely. "Danny Dukker started it. He called me and Abraham woollyheads—"

"And me a smelly old bean eater," Nardo said.

"And Merrilee a feather duster," Sarah finished. "And then he kicked over our can of worms—"

"And broke Merrilee's fishing pole over his knee—" Nardo chimed in.

"And that's when Topher hit him," Abraham said in his older, wiser eleven-year-old's voice. "It was a fair brawl, if you ask me, seeing as how they're both the same age and size."

Rorie gazed down at them all in a mixture of exasperation and motherly concern. "And what did you do to provoke these attacks?"

"Nothing," they said in righteous unison.

Only Merrilee had remained silent throughout this elaborate defense. Rorie had apparently noticed it, because she fixed her judge's stare next on the Indian girl.

"Is this true, Merrilee?"

"Yes, ma'am, but ..." She raised troubled eyes to Rorie. "Danny was crying when we found him."

Everyone fidgeted, looking a trifle guilty, except for Topher.

"Why do you suppose Danny was crying?" Rorie asked more gently.

"Who cares?" Topher said. "Danny Dukker's a stinker."

"That will be quite enough of that, Topher," Rorie chided.

Wes hid his smile.

Standing in a neutral position between the children's and the grown ups' camps, Nita asked, "Can Topher keep the puppy?"

"Yeah, can I?"

"Well, I don't think—"

"I won him fair and square." Topher's chin jutted out, and he looked to a higher authority for support. "You'd let me keep it, wouldn't you, Uncle Wes?"

"Well ..." He glanced at Rorie, who was glaring a warning at him. He repressed the urge to chuckle and, squatting down before Topher, reached to pet the puppy. "Sometimes a man has to fight for the honor of his woman," he said. "And sometimes he has to fight to protect his home and family. But I don't know of any time when it's right for a man to hit another man to take something that doesn't belong to him, like a fishing pole ... or a puppy."

Topher pouted. "I did it for Merrilee."

"I'm sure you did, son." He gave the boy's shoulder a squeeze. "But keeping that puppy would be kind of like stealing. And you don't want to be any low-down, lizard-tailed thief, do you?"

"No," Topher said sullenly.

"Good man." He released the boy's shoulder and rose.

Shae chose that moment to join the group. "I hear there's been some trouble."

"Nothing Topher couldn't handle," Wes said, tousling the boy's hair.

Topher started to grin, and Rorie shook her head.

"That's just going to be the beginning if Creed rides out here," she said.

"Don't you worry any about Creed," Wes told her. "I'll take care of him."

Shae's expression was darkly forbidding. "This isn't your fight, Rawlins."

"Who said anything about a fight?" He lifted the dog from Topher's arms. "I'm just taking this puppy back to town."

Rorie bit her lip, and trepidation replaced the anger in her gaze. "Wes, you don't know how Creed can be. Or his father."

"That's right, Rawlins," Shae said. "They're my kin. You don't have any quarrel with them."

"And that's exactly how it's going to stay," he said firmly. "The Dukkers have no reason to lock horns with me, but things could get mighty contentious if you ride up to their back gate. Besides, there're some personal items I'd like to purchase at the general store. Since we're running low on nails, I'll pick up a box of them too."

Shae didn't look convinced, but Wes was determined to take advantage of this opportunity to ride into town. Fortunately, Rorie took his side in the argument.

"Wes is right, Shae," she said. "After the fistfight you and Creed had on Monday, I really think it would be best if you let Wes handle this matter. There's no reason why it can't be resolved peacefully."

"Except that Cousin Hannibal doesn't wear his gun belt for ballast," Shae muttered.

In the end, Wes had his way. The children gathered around him and Two-Step to say good-bye to the yawning puppy, which he'd snuggled under his vest. Shae surrendered a gold piece for the nails, which Wes interpreted as a sign of the boy's growing trust in him. Then Rorie edged closer, touching his sleeve.

"Be careful, Wes," she said, her big eyes glimmering with concern.

In that moment, Wes felt absurdly boyish. The wound to his pride was repaired, and his flagging spirits soared. There wasn't a man on God's earth who could have pulled him back down—or so he thought, until he made his long overdue return to Elodea.

Hannibal Dukker's likeness stared out at him from windows in every business on Main Street. The poster pictured him smiling like a snake oil salesman above the slogan "Clear the Coloreds From the County—Elect Dukker Sheriff." Wes got a blood rush at the very idea. What the county really needed, he thought angrily, was someone to clear out folks like Dukker. Thank God C. J. Jackson, a cattleman up near Bandera Town, had thrown his hat into the election ring.

Reining in before the telegraph office, Wes dismounted and reached inside his pocket for his badge. A sick feeling settled in the pit of his stomach when he found it missing. Juggling the puppy to his other arm, he slipped his fingers inside his vest once more and searched the lining for his star. No badge. Nothing.

"Confound it." He glared down at the hound, which gazed up at him with its big puppy eyes and wagged its tail in innocent response. The little mongrel had started fussing on the trail, and Wes had needed to stop more than once to let it do its business. Now he wondered if the dog might have knocked his badge out of his pocket. He didn't much like the thought of his good-luck tin star lying in the middle of the prairie for a buzzard or ground squirrel to snatch up.

Then another, more sobering thought hit him square between the eyes. He hadn't seen his badge since that morning, when Topher, whooping like an Indian, had pounced on him to wrestle. He groaned inwardly. What if his badge was lying in Shae's bedroom somewhere?

"Ranger Rawlins, how good to see you again," a sweet voice called behind him.

Starting guiltily, he turned to find Miss Lorelei Faraday strolling toward him from the general store next door. She broke into a surprised and delighted smile when she spied the dog in his arms.

"Why that's the Jenkins' puppy! Little Harold has been going from door to door, asking about it for the last three days." She reached a hand toward the furry head and was rewarded with a friendly lick. "Wherever did you find it?"

"Oh . . ." He refrained from making any dog-napping charges against Danny Dukker, even though he suspected that a barely weaned puppy wouldn't wander out to the children's fishing hole by itself. "The Sinclair boy found it down by Ramble Creek."

"So far?" Her finely brushed eyebrows drew together in a frown, then she shrugged. "Harold will be so happy that you brought it back."

"Just doing my job, ma'am," he said lightly. "Do you know where to find this Harold Jenkins?"

"Oh, of course. He lives in the rectory with his parents. I'm meeting Mama there to have tea with Preacher Jenkins and his wife. I'd be happy to take the puppy there for you."

"Much obliged, ma'am."

She laid the puppy against her shoulder and patted its back, much as she might have patted a human baby she had just finished nursing. Her pose was so tenderly maternal, it made Wes think of Rorie with Po. He fidgeted a little at this newest proof of his ill-advised and poorly timed calico fever.

Lorelei, meanwhile, was gazing up at him with shy, ocean-sized eyes that held just a hint of worry in them.

"How . . . are the Sinclairs?" she asked hesitantly. "Marshal Dukker has been saying such awful things in his campaign speeches"—she glanced toward a nearby poster, and a shudder rocked her petite frame—" and no one dares to cross him. It makes me worry for Shae McFadden. And Mrs. Sinclair too," she added hastily.

Well, that was one thing in his favor, Wes thought. Apparently Shae had been too busy watching him to sneak off for a rendezvous with Lorelei. He pasted on a reassuring smile. "Shae's just fine, Miss Faraday, and the Sinclairs are too."

"You mean you haven't forced them off the land?"

"No, ma'am. I'm still conducting my investigation."

She looked relieved. "I'm so glad to hear that, Mr. Rawlins." Her voice was warm and eager. "Papa printed a whole special edition just to let folks know Marshal

Dukker had sent you out to drive the squatters from the Boudreau farm. I was so upset with him for printing all the unkind things Marshal Dukker said about Shae, but Papa said news is news, and Rangers don't ride into Elodea every day."

Wes steeled himself against another groan. He had always fancied himself in the headlines one day for some courageous act of daring-do, not for driving orphans from their home. Now he was doubly glad he had convinced Shae to stay behind. If the boy had ridden into town and read the newspaper, Wes was certain he would have spent the afternoon picking buckshot out of his behind.

"I didn't realize I'd become so notorious," he said dryly. "I reckon I should stop by the *Enquirer* and see just what kind of stories your pa's been printing about me. Besides, there's a couple of things I would like to ask the mayor about. . . ."

Lorelei had stiffened visibly, and Wes, realizing she no longer was listening to him, turned his head in the direction of her gaze. Approaching them from the livery stable across the street was an unarmed Creed Dukker, his stride eager and his expression hopeful as he made a beeline toward the town's belle.

She glanced despairingly at Wes. "I knew my luck couldn't hold out for long. It seems every time I turn around, one of those Dukkers is following me—"

"Hullo, Miss Lorelei," Creed said bashfully, his ruddy features taking on a pink glow. "Gosh you sure are ragged out with all them purty she-stuffs you're wearing."

She inclined her head at this awkward compliment. "Thank you," she said coolly, and turned a shoulder on him. "Mr. Rawlins, it was nice to see you again, but the Jenkins are waiting and I really must go. I hope to see you again soon."

Wes tipped his hat as she started to walk away, but Creed stepped quickly into her path.

"Uh, Miss Lorelei," he stammered, "since I ain't got nothing better to do, I'd be right, uh, pleased to walk with you a spell."

Her distaste was thinly veiled. "Thank you, Creed, but I'm sure that won't be necessary."

Turning on her heel, she hiked her chin and swept away just as fast as her dainty boots could carry her.

Creed's hound-dog face fell noticeably, making him even less attractive than before. Wes shook his head. The boy had cupid's cramp, all right. He'd recognize that look anywhere, seeing as how he'd spent the last eight years staring at Fancy that way. He wondered if he'd begun to look at Rorie like that too.

"So you're Rawlins, eh?"

Wes gazed into two deep-set belligerent eyes as gray as a North Texas winter. The only difference between Creed's stare and his daddy's was the glimmer of sentiment that struggled for life in Creed's. Wes guessed the boy still had a thimbleful of conscience inside him somewhere.

"That's right," he answered.

Creed sneered. "I heard all about you, Ranger. So did you run off them coyotes like Pa told you?"

Wes's lips tightened. *Squatter* had always been an insult in Texas; *coyote* was a downright profanity.

"Well, now," he said. "That's a matter for me and your pa to discuss, son." He watched Creed's hackles rise. "Say, you wouldn't know where I could find Doc Warren, would you?"

"Doc Warren?" The boy's hostility changed instantly to wariness. "How should I know where that old still chaser is?"

Wes watched the boy's reactions keenly. "Well, you living in town and he being a resident of Elodea, I just naturally thought you'd know where to find him."

"You thought wrong."

"Is that so?" Wes rubbed his chin. "Maybe it's just this toothache that's got my thinking all muddled. I hear tell that old pill wrangler could crack jaws with the best of them. Sew up a man too like some kind of tailor. But then, you'd know all about that, wouldn't you, seeing as how you were there when Doc Warren tried to patch up Sheriff Boudreau."

Creed said nothing, but he grew stiffer than a new rawhide rope.

"I hear tell too," Wes said casually, "that you were the one who found your cousin facedown on the road leading back from Bandera Town. That's some kind of terrible thing, finding your kin shot from behind. Did you see the bastards who did it?"

Creed's gaze flickered away. "Nope."

"Hmm. So why don't you tell me just exactly what happened after you found Gator?"

"I slung him over my horse and I rode back to the farmhouse. Then I went and fetched a doctor. Pa too," he added tersely.

Wes frowned. "Knowing Gator was alive when you found him, did you ever ask him for a description of his killer?"

"He didn't come to."

"Now that's interesting, 'cause the Sinclairs said—"

"He didn't ever come to, I tell you. And he sure as hell didn't name some persimmon skin as his heir."

"How could you know that, son, since you were gone for an hour or so, hunting down Doc Warren?"

Creed's jaw tightened mutinously. "I just do, that's all."

"Then it would stand to reason Gator never told your pa who shot him either. And yet your pa says Gator was shot by a gang of renegade Negroes." Wes folded his arms across his chest and locked stares with the boy. "How do you suppose he figured that, seeing as how you didn't find any trace of the killers, and you're the closest thing to a witness I've got?"

Panic crossed Creed's face. "There were tracks."

"Tracks, huh?"

"That's right."

Wes shook his head. "I have to tell you, son, I've been tracking men for years, and I haven't learned yet how to tell the color of a renegade's skin by the hoof prints his pony leaves behind. You don't suppose your pa leaped to conclusions in this matter, do you?"

"My pa can track a man as good as you can, Ranger. By the sound of it, he can probably do it better."

Wes didn't bother to rise to this bait. Either Creed was as dim-witted as a possum, or he was lying about those tracks. The question was why?

"You know, Creed, it strikes me kind of funny that those renegades never tried to steal anything from your cousin. I mean, they left him with his saddle, boots, and badge. Why, as I hear it told, they even left him with his cartridge belt and gun. Why do you suppose they did that?"

Creed's lip curled. "They were jiggaboos, weren't they? We're not talking about the smartest of men here, Rawlins."

"So you figure these Negroes were bent on murder, not theft, eh?"

"Sure. Everyone knows those black bastards have murder on their minds from the day they're born."

Wes smiled ruefully. Pa Dukker had obviously been feeding heifer dust to his boy for a long time. The sad thing was, Creed seemed to believe it. "Well, I'm glad that's settled. Now tell me about this still of yours."

Creed's head shot up faster than a bull whip. "Gator shut it down."

Wes didn't need his sixth sense to know the boy was lying again. "I reckon that must have caused some trouble between you and your cousin."

Creed looked away. "We got past it."

"So you and your cousin were close, then?" he asked more gently.

"What's it to you, Ranger?"

The boy's hostility was back, and Wes realized he'd touched a nerve. Creed had a hair-trigger temper all right. No wonder he and Shae fought like wildcats.

"Oh, I don't know. Sometimes I just get to wondering about things. Take your brother Danny, for instance. An hour or so back, I was wondering why he was crying."

Something genuine, like concern, vied with the angry bravado on Creed's face. "What do you mean, crying? Where?"

"Down by the fishing hole. Seems like he was down there trying to hide the preacher boy's stolen puppy."

Creed started in surprise. "The hell he was. You've got no proof of that, Rawlins."

Wes didn't bother to point out the obvious. It wasn't Danny he wanted in wrist irons. Unfortunately, the boy was headed that way unless somebody tried to turn him around.

"You know, Creed, Danny's a fine boy, and he looks up to you. Seems like you could talk to him, maybe give him some counsel. Otherwise, he's just going to lie and steal and hate his way into a jail cell . . . maybe worse."

Wes suspected his six-shooters were the only things keeping Creed's fists out of his face.

"My brother ain't any kind of rounder," he said hotly. "You'd best keep your wisecracks to yourself, if you know what's good for you. Now move aside. I got business in Milner's."

With a smile that bordered on mocking, Wes refrained from further debate and sidestepped out of the boy's way. Arguing with Creed about Danny would clearly be a waste of time, and he had an investigation to conduct.

Creed's answers—or rather, his lies—had given Wes a couple of ideas, not the least of which was Gator had been murdered by somebody he knew. No self-respecting road agent would go through the trouble of an ambush and then leave the body for somebody else to loot. And since the bushwhacking happened so close to Gator's farm, the killer must have been worried about being recognized. Otherwise, he would have ridden right up to Gator's body to make sure he'd finished the job.

Thus, Wes felt safe in assuming Gator had been slain by somebody who lived in or around Elodea. Just to be safe, though, he decided to see if headquarters had sent any telegrams about hill-country outlaws.

Pushing open the door to the telegraph office, he nodded to the slender, spaniel-eyed operator with a drooping mustache. "Howdy."

The man took one look at Wes's guns and practically fell out of his chair in his haste to pull his boots off the counter and jump to his feet.

"You're, er, that Ranger, aren't you?" he asked in a

mousy voice, just one whisker shy of panic-stricken. "I remember you."

Wes frowned. One might have thought he'd held his equalizer to the man's head Monday night, rather than paying him double what his services were worth. "That's right, Mister . . . er—" he glanced at the copper name placard beside the door, "Bartlesby. I've come to see about the answers to my wires."

Bartlesby's Adam's apple bobbed above his starched winged collar. "Your wires, sir?"

Wes gazed narrowly at the man. Bartlesby might be a sight more civil by day, but he wasn't proving any less troublesome.

"That's right. One to Ranger headquarters in Austin and one to the clerk in County Records up in Bandera Town."

"Oh, er, yes. Let me look." Bartlesby hurried to a row of boxes against the rear wall, but he was already shaking his head and mumbling, "No, I don't see any," before he had lifted a single sheaf of paper from the box.

Wes watched these theatrics with rising annoyance. "I should have received answers two days ago."

"Yes, well, sometimes these things take longer—"

"Never mind." Wes cut him off with a wave of his hand. "I want to send another wire to a lawyer friend of mine, Mr. Jonathan Harrell, in Bandera Town."

Bartlesby glanced uneasily out the window. "A lawyer, Mr. Rawlins? Oh, but we've got a fine lawyer here in Elo—"

"I need someone who's friendly with the county judge, not to mention someone I can trust," Wes added under his breath. "Now, why don't you pull up your chair, and I'll spell out the message for you."

Just then, a cowbell clanged and the door swung open. Hannibal Dukker stood on the threshold, his left cheek swelled out with a wad of tobacco. He spat on the floor.

"So there you are, Rawlins, and minus your badge again too. Hell, you know better than to ride into Elodea without your star. Next time, I'm going to have to take away that fancy rig of yours or throw you in the calaboose."

Wes's eyes narrowed. There was nothing even remotely amusing about the lawman's threat, and he suspected that was how Dukker had wanted it to be.

"Mr. Rawlins wants to wire an attorney in Bandera," Bartlesby said anxiously. "One who knows the county judge."

Dukker arched an eyebrow. "Is that a fact? Well, you told him about the lines being down, didn't you, Simon?"

"Oh . . ." Bartlesby's gaze flitted between the two lawmen. "That's right. The lines are down." He nodded vigorously.

Dukker shot him a withering glare. "Simon, isn't that your wife I hear calling you?"

If Bartlesby had been a real spaniel, he would have tucked his tail between his legs. "Why, er, yes, Marshal. I do believe it is. Excuse me, gentlemen."

Wes watched as Bartlesby slinked for the back door and the stairwell that led to his living quarters. Apparently Danny had been right: Hannibal Dukker did own this town, or at least, he owned most of the men who lived in it.

"It's a good thing I ran into you here, Rawlins," Dukker said with a faint sneer. "I was starting to wonder about you. I thought maybe that white nigger boy out at Gator's had put a bullet through your head. If I hadn't been so busy with this damned county sheriff's campaign, I would have rounded up a posse and come out there looking for you."

"Much obliged for your concern, Marshal," Wes said dryly.

Dukker nodded. "So is that farm ready for me and my boys to move in?"

"Not exactly." Wes kept his hands loose at his sides and ready to draw. "As a matter of fact, I was just going to wire the county judge and ask for a court order to keep you off the property."

"You don't say?" Dukker spat another stream of tobacco juice, this time at Wes's boots. It missed only by a hairsbreadth. "Why would you want to do that?"

Wes felt his neck heat with his mounting outrage, but he steeled himself against a show of anger. "There seems to be some controversy over the legitimacy of your claim."

Dukker snorted. "Don't tell me you've been listening to that nigger's nonsense. Hell, what kind of lawman are you? If it ain't a crime for that boy to be strutting around the county, claiming he's Gator's next of kin, then I don't know what is. I don't care if Lorelei Faraday did swear on a Bible, I got my doubts Shae McFadden was out fixing the axle on her daddy's wagon about the same time Gator got shot. That girl has an unnatural attraction for that piece of trash, and I told Mayor Faraday he'd best lock her in her bedroom if he didn't want some jiggaboo baby toddling around calling him Granddaddy."

Wes felt his jaw begin to twitch. He was less concerned about Dukker's slurs against him than about the man's obvious hostility toward Shae and Lorelei. "Speaking of the afternoon Gator was shot," he said with passable nonchalance, "where were you?"

Dukker's eyes narrowed to reptilian slits. "What kind of question is that, boy?"

"An official one. You got some reason for not answering it?"

The two men squared off.

"You think you're so high and mighty, don't you?" Dukker said. "You think you got a license to come in here with your Ranger airs and put yourself above the local law. Well, I ain't going to stand for it."

Wes kept his eyes hooded, affecting a lazy expression, but his muscles tensed in grim anticipation. "You planning on giving me an answer sometime soon?"

Dukker's face darkened with menace. "Poker," he spat. "I was playing poker in the back room at Sultan's. Pete will vouch for me. Simon, lawyer Callahan, and blacksmith Kleber will too—not that I need some kind of alibi," he added, his lip curling. "I'm the law in this town."

"No, Dukker," Wes said quietly, "you just wear the badge."

"Why you smart-mouthed, rooster-headed prick—"

He reached, but Wes was faster, his Colt cocked and leveled before Dukker had even cleared leather. He had the satisfaction of watching the marshal's eyes grow as round as a terrapin's shell. Then Dukker barked with laughter, the sound dark and dripping with venom. "Well, now. I got to hand it to you, boy. You're fast. But can you aim?"

He strutted closer.

"Tell you what. I'll make it easier for you. Go ahead and shoot." He halted, his barrellike chest just inches from Wes's muzzle. "Don't let my badge stop you. After all, you won the draw fair and square." He slipped the buckle on his holster and tossed the Remington aside. "You can call it self-defense. Tell folks around town that's how you Rangers investigate murders, by gunning down the victim's next of kin. Or what's the matter, Rawlins?" he taunted, his voice like nitroglycerin. "Have you been spending so much time inside that icehouse Aurora Sinclair calls a twat that you've forgotten how to be a red-blooded man?"

Dukker had already established he wouldn't shoot an unarmed man, Wes thought. Now the bastard was testing him, trying to determine whether he was hotheaded and what his weakness was. Even knowing that, Wes couldn't let the slur against Rorie go undefended.

With careful deliberation he eased his gun hammer back into place, slipped his Colt inside its holster, then hauled off and hit the sonuvabitch, burying his fist in the soft paunch of Dukker's gut. The lawman wheezed, doubling over, only to rear up an instant later with a Bowie knife in his hand. Wes dodged, and the blade slashed harmlessly through his sleeve.

Grabbing Dukker's wrist, Wes slammed the marshal back against the counter, beating his arm on the wood until the knife slipped through Dukker's fingers.

"Now you listen to me, *old man*," he growled, grabbing Dukker's collar and effectively cutting off a tide of spittle-flecked vulgarities. "I don't care if you own every lawyer and telegraph operator in this county. I'm going to get that court order to keep you off Boudreau's farm. There's going to be a hearing before a judge, and Shae McFadden's claim is going to be given due consideration."

Dukker made a gurgling sound, and Wes contemptuously let him slide to the floor.

"You're just one man, Rawlins," Dukker panted, rubbing his neck and flexing his gun hand into a white-knuckled fist. "Just one man, and this here's my town."

"Well, now you've gone and made it personal, Hannibal." Wes met his lethal stare evenly. "Any time you want a face-to-face showdown, you just let me know. In the meantime, remember one thing: Aurora Sinclair, Shae McFadden, and the children living on that farm are under Ranger protection now. If someone so much as looks slantways at them, you can bet I'll be exacting a price from your hide. So you'd better hope everyone in your town treats them with tender-loving care."

He picked up Dukker's knife and kicked the holster out of the way. Swinging the door open, he paused on the threshold and gave the marshal a harrowing stare.

"Oh, and by the way, Hannibal," he drawled, the threat in his voice thinly veiled, "I don't believe there ever were any renegade Negroes committing murder in this county. And I'm going to prove it."

Chapter Eleven

*E*very light in the sitting room was burning when Wes rode into the yard. He cursed under his breath to see Shae and Rorie perched side by side on the porch steps as if they'd been anxiously waiting for his return.

He'd spent a damned sight longer than he intended in town, mainly because he had to track down the four men who Dukker had claimed were playing poker with him the day Gator was shot. They'd all supported Dukker's alibi, nodding vigorously and lying through their teeth. Short of breaking arms or bashing heads, Wes didn't see how he could get them to change their stories. Dukker clearly owned them.

Phineas Faraday, however, had given Wes hope that one Elodean, at least, showed promise as a man. When Wes found the mayor in his newspaper office, Faraday had greeted him with his usual booming joviality—until Wes challenged the inaccuracies Faraday had printed about him in the *Enquirer*.

"You forget," Faraday said, his tension not entirely disguised by his well-schooled diplomacy, "I was there when you agreed to help Hannibal get his land back."

"I agreed to ride to the farm and investigate," Wes said through clenched teeth. "I never said I was going to shoot any orphans."

"That's right. And if you'll read that article carefully, you'll see the shooting quote is attributed to Hannibal."

Wes scowled. "I want to rebut his lies."

"Sure thing. I have another issue coming out next week." Faraday's newspaperman's smile wasn't entirely benign. "Should I quote you directly in saying Hannibal's a liar?"

"I want you to print the truth," Wes growled back, "and see that justice is served."

"That's what I'm here for."

"Yeah?" He planted his hands on Faraday's desk and glared down into the mayor's bespectacled eyes. "So why did you pin a badge on a murdering sonuvabitch like Hannibal Dukker?"

Faraday's color rose. Looking away from Wes, he became extremely interest in the type he'd been setting—particularly the letter *b*, which he took extraordinary pains to adjust in the word *bullet*.

"Town council," he said at last, "felt it would be in the best interests of Elodea to hire a gunfighter as marshal, much like Abilene, Kansas, did when it hired Wild Bill Hickok to clean up its streets. Having a wife and children at the time, Hannibal Dukker seemed more settled and, er, tame than most."

Wes gazed at the man in exasperation. "Gunfighters live by the gun, not the law, Faraday, and it's nigh on impossible to teach an old dog new tricks. As you'll recall, Hickok was drummed out of Abilene a year later for shooting his deputy."

Faraday cleared his throat. "Yes, well, I understand that unfortunate incident was an accident."

"They're all accidents, Faraday, or they're always someone else's fault. Kind of like Gator's murder. Or Doc Warren's," he bluffed, hoping finally to get some confirmation.

Faraday's pudgy hand shook a bit as he reached for the letter *d*. "I can't imagine where you heard such a rumor. Since Doc tended to medicate his rheumatism with whiskey, Hannibal speculates Doc got a couple of swigs of oh-be-joyful in him, lost his way back from Gator's farm, and fell off the cliff at Ramble Creek."

"After Warren witnessed Gator's will? That would be just a tad bit convenient, don't you think?"

Faraday shrugged, but Wes could hear the nervous shuffling of the man's feet beneath his desk.

"Unless you find Doc's body or some other evidence, I'm afraid we Elodeans have no choice but to accept the findings of Hannibal's investigation."

Reflecting back on that conversation, Wes suspected Faraday knew something more than he was telling. The mayor struck him as being evasive rather than cowardly, so he guessed Dukker knew something incriminating about Faraday, and that was why the mayor was keeping quiet. If a well-respected, influential man like Faraday was scared to talk, Rorie must be terrified, Wes reasoned grimly.

The time was coming when he would have to broaden his investigation. That meant leaving Rorie and the children unprotected, which worried the devil out of him. He just prayed he'd put enough fear in Dukker to turn that bastard's attention away from them and onto him.

Wes realized he'd have to come clean about the lies he'd told Rorie, but he wanted to do it in the gentlest way possible, which meant calming down for a spell. As reluctant as he was to admit it, he cared what Rorie thought about him. He didn't want her to fear him the way she feared the town marshal . . . or hate him the way she hated Rangers.

Thus, his guilt, heaped on top of his sense of duty, had made him ride hell-for-leather for two hours to the nearest stagecoach station. He'd found there an honest telegraph operator to wire an attorney and get him to draw up the court order he hoped would pacify and protect Rorie and Shae. What Wes hadn't found, unfortunately, was a sign of his badge when he retraced his tracks from Elodea to the farm.

By the time he finally rode up the drive, daylight had all but slipped away. He hoped it was dark enough so Rorie wouldn't notice his ripped shirt. He didn't want her to think he couldn't handle himself in a fight—or worse, that he was a troublemaker, like Bill Malone and the other "rude, uncouth" Rangers she'd met through Gator.

After nodding his greeting, he hurried Two-Step into the barn, thinking to delay Shae's and Rorie's questions just long enough for him to strip off his shirt. Unfortunately, he hadn't quite slipped his last button, when a lantern flared behind him, and he heard the shuffle of feet through the door.

"Wes! Good heavens! What happened to you?" Rorie sounded more anxious than angry. "When you didn't come home in time for dinner we didn't know what to think ..."

For a fleeting moment Wes felt a warm confusion at her use of the word "home." Sentimentality quickly gave way to annoyance, however. He couldn't very well ignore her, and yet, to turn around would clearly reveal the slash in his sleeve. His only remaining option would be to strip to his waist and throw the shirt into a corner. He rather fancied that option, since his perverse side hadn't yet gotten over the idea that they had been as intimate as they were ever going to be.

"And then, trying to explain to the children that—"

Her breath caught when he shrugged from his shirt. As he turned to face her, he had the satisfaction of watching her blush. He could almost feel her gaze slide down every rib as he searched his torso for ... what? Old times's sake? He couldn't help but feel vindicated, knowing she wasn't as immune to him as she pretended to be.

"Did you see Dukker?"

He started, swinging around at the sound of Shae's voice, and found the boy standing with his hand on Two-Step's sweaty neck. Wes stifled another oath. Shae was standing at an angle that must have afforded him a clear view of the rended sleeve before he'd gotten the shirt off.

"Yeah. I saw him."

Shae was looking him up and down. "Any trouble?"

"Nope."

"You sure?"

He met Shae's gaze evenly. "Do I look like a man who's unsure?"

From the corner of his eye, Wes saw Rorie fidget.

"Then what took you so long, Wes?" she asked.

It was her turn to receive a bold, searching appraisal. "Well now, ma'am," he drawled in a tone designed to trigger another blush and send her huffing in moral outrage to the safety of the house, "a man like me isn't accustomed to going hungry for long. But I reckon you don't want to hear all about that kind of meal."

That shut her up. She actually pressed her lips together. But she didn't run away.

"You ate in town, eh?" Shae asked.

"That's right."

"You don't smell like smoke or rotgut. In fact you look damned sober. You want to tell me why your horse is so lathered?"

Caught in his lies, Wes could only heap on more. "Me and the boys had a little bet. Ran a race down the center of town. 'Course, wind is Two-Step's middle name, so he left that old bay grazing on his dust. You need to see the purse I won to prove it?"

Shae glared at him. "No."

"Good. Then hand me those saddlebags and I'll give you your nails."

Shae obliged, and Wes, grateful for an end to the questions, slung the bags over the nearest stall door and rummaged inside. When his fingers closed over a length of satin, he remembered with a twinge of embarrassment the other items he hadn't been able to resist buying at the general store.

"Oh, and here," he said gruffly, thrusting a bag and a tightly folded wad of paper at Rorie. "I got some candy for the boys, and some hair ribbons for the girls, and Mayor Faraday sent along some newsprint so Merrilee could practice drawing Two-Step."

Taken aback by the gifts Wes had shoved into her hands, Rorie gazed in amazement at the colorful array of peppermints and satins inside the bag. A warm, sweet jumble of emotion washed over her, leaving her disarmed and chagrined and completely bereft of the sensible use of her tongue. She stammered a thank-you as he shrugged and backed away.

"The children will be delighted, Wes, but you shouldn't have spent—"

"I told you I won a chunk of change betting on Two-Step," he said in a rough voice. "So in a way, I didn't spend anything."

She swallowed, glancing at Shae. He just shook his head. She could see he didn't believe Wes's tale about the expense any more than she had believed the farce about the horse race. Wes was too tense, too wary and defensive, for a man who had supposedly gambled his wages and won.

No, something had happened in town, something disturbing or unpleasant, judging by his rigid shoulders and squared jaw. She suspected Dukker was behind Wes's upset, and while it touched her deeply to know he was trying to protect her and Shae from the problem, the truth was, she felt responsible. She never should have allowed Wes to face Dukker alone over a matter that concerned one of her children. She was certain Dukker had been spoiling for revenge ever since she rejected his suit, and she'd had no right to send Wes into the proverbial lion's den, armed with only a few circumspect warnings. Dukker might very well be a murderer, and she should have prepared Wes for the worst before involving him in her and Shae's business.

"Er, Shae, would you mind taking these gifts inside to the children?" she asked, striving for discretion.

He seemed to understand her need to talk to Wes alone, and nodded. "Not at all, ma'am."

Hesitating as he turned to go, Shae cocked his head at Wes. "I could rub down your horse for you, if you like."

His offer was the next-best thing to an olive branch, and the tension in Wes's shoulders eased a notch.

"That would be right kind of you, Shae."

She waited for Shae to lead the gelding outside into the moonlight, all the while wondering how to approach a particularly touchy subject. When the door banged closed behind Shae, however, she was completely unprepared for the thick, weighty silence that fell around her and Wes.

He folded his arms across his chest. The gesture, she

was sure, was meant to convey impatience, yet the rippling contraction of all those manly muscles had to be the most unconsciously sensual display she'd ever seen.

She cleared her throat. His eyebrows rose in question. Her mouth went dry all over again. There was something in his eyes, something dark and primal—even dangerous—that she'd never seen before. Whatever quality or essence that had always made him seem so boyishly charming was gone. Before her stood a man of shadowy motives and unforeseeable intent, a man whose very presence made her pulse fire and her skin heat, melting away the iron core of her resolve not to touch him.

Or want him.

"Not that I'm complaining or anything," he said, his voice deep, "but if you keep staring at me like that, I'm going to get ideas in my head just like the ones I got last night."

She tore her gaze free. "That, of course, would be a mistake."

"How can you be sure? There you go again, not giving a fella a chance."

It was the old banter with a new edge. Swallowing, she moistened her lips. "Wes"—she was mortified to hear how husky her own voice had become—"please. I know you're upset about what happened in town."

"I'm not upset."

She caught her breath, then slowly released it to the count of ten. The tactic still left her feeling shaky inside, as if every fiber of her being were resisting some magnetic pull. She kept her eyes trained on his ear, knowing that to brave his stare again would dissolve the last of her defenses.

"I know something's bothering you," she tried again, "and I want to be able to help you, if I can."

"Now that's music to my ears."

Her cheeks burned at his provocative tone.

"You deliberately misunderstand me." She glanced uncertainly at his face. "I was talking about Dukker."

"Ah . . ."

Her palms grew moist beneath the tangible intensity

of his stare. "He's, er . . ." She shifted uncomfortably. "He's not someone you should provoke."

"Oh? And why's that?"

She forced herself to meet his gaze. "Because the law is just a convenience to him, and his badge is a means to an end. Gator was the only man in this county who wasn't afraid of him, and now he's dead."

Wes head tilted slightly as he continued to regard her. "Are you saying Dukker had something to do with Gator's murder?"

"I . . ." Her eyelids began to sting, and she blinked back tears. "I don't know. There's no proof, no evidence. It's just this feeling I have, and . . ." She swallowed again, fighting to control the quaver in her voice. "And Gator swore before he died that the man who gunned him down was white. I don't want to see you get shot in the back, Wes. Or anywhere else," she whispered tremulously.

One corner of his mouth quirked up at that. "Come here," he said quietly.

She bit her lip, unable to move.

"Come here."

His tone was gentler this time, yet there was an enticing enigma about its quality, one that lured her feet closer in spite of her better sense. He cupped her chin in one rough hand, and a gust of tingles breezed down her spine.

"I'm not one of your cubs, darlin'. I'm all grown up. And I've got some experience in these matters, probably even more than Gator had. So don't you worry yourself silly over me."

"I don't want you to get hurt," she murmured, her knees quivering shamefully.

"You know what I want?" His eyelids drooped, and he released her chin only to stroll a predatory step closer. "I want to know what you find so consarned interesting about this Ethan fellow."

She stumbled backward, and her spine struck the stall door. He reached a hand above her, bracing his weight on the wooden support beam, and leaned tantalizingly closer. Every muscle, every sinew was etched in ruddy lamplight, like a smoldering ember ready to burst into flame. Her heart hammered so loudly, she felt certain he must hear it, yet she couldn't make the rush of blood give life to her leaden feet.

"E-Ethan?"

"That's right. Ethan."

He was so close, so exhilaratingly, dangerously close, that she could touch him. She could map every plane and valley of his rock-ribbed frame, glide her fingertips along the satiny skin of his chest, or trail them through the red-gold hair that blazed a forbidden trail toward his jeans. The temptation was too much to bear. She knew she should run, but her feet remained as rooted as before. All she could do was sink helplessly against the door and ball her itching fingers into fists.

"Well? Don't tell me that fine mind of yours can't think of a single thing."

"Ethan's a good man," she said desperately.

"Yeah? And just what is he good at?"

He hadn't touched her yet. No part of their bodies was connected, yet she'd never felt so intimately bound to a man in her life. She breathed in rhythm to the mesmerizing rise and fall of his chest; her heart tripped in time to the pulsing cadence of the vein in his throat. Even that elusive quality, that energy she called her own, seemed to have merged with his, so that her skin was as sensitized to his flesh as if she had melded every pore into his own. She wondered if their connection was more than physical, if he could read her thoughts, if he knew how much she longed to touch him. Then she wondered how many other weak-willed spinsters he had seduced.

"You have a disturbing habit of—of twisting my words out of context." She forced the words past her trembling lips. "I came here to express my concern for you, not to—to repeat last night. I have tried my very best to be honest with you about that, Wes."

"Maybe." He bent his elbow, leaning infinitesimally closer, the warmth of his breath caressing her lips. "But if you're so all-fired fond of Ethan's courtship, then how come you chased away your chaperone? How come you're standing around in this barn with your half-naked hired hand?"

Her cheeks felt scalded at the truth of his words. She choked down a sob as he swam before her, and tears threatened to steal the last shreds of her composure. How could she answer without compromising herself further? How could she admit she felt lonely, that his laughter had reminded her of everything she'd ever wanted and his kisses had fanned the embers of her need? "I don't want to live my life alone," she wanted to shout. "I want a man to hold me and love me and fill my emptiness with joy. Is that such a crime?"

She shoved her way past him, stumbling for the door, and he threw out a hand to stop her.

"Rorie, wait."

She tugged her sleeve free, hurrying onward, and she heard his muffled oath. A steely forearm wrapped her waist, dragging her back against the granite hardness of his chest. She was so stunned by their contact that for a moment, all she could do was sag against him.

"Rorie, I'm sorry," he murmured against her hair. "Don't run away mad. I didn't mean to sound like such a cur dog. It's just that I wanted—"

He gave a short, bitter laugh, and she could feel his heart hammering against her back.

"Never mind. It doesn't matter what I wanted."

He released her, turning her to face him. Maybe it was just her tears, or the shock of being cradled for one heartbreakingly brief moment in his arms, but when she gazed up into his eyes, she could have sworn she saw a glimmer of melancholy much like her own in those misty-green depths.

"Thank you for worrying about me," he said with a faint smile. He gave her shoulders a gentle squeeze before releasing her. "It's nice to have somebody care about me again. It makes me feel kind of like I'm back home."

His confession touched a deep, hidden part of Rorie, the part that knew what it was like to be unwanted and alone. She searched for something to say, something to take away the pain that he clearly associated with his family, but he tore his gaze free and turned away.

"I reckon you'll be wanting to go in now," he said.

"I think I'll mosey on down to the springhouse and take a shower bath to wash off some of this trail dust."

She hesitated, and he glanced her way. For a moment, one endless, breathless moment, she could see the hope and longing in his eyes. They called to every female fiber of her being, and she was torn between what was right and what was proper, and what she wished she had more than anything else in the world. She asked herself what harm there could be in crossing over to him, in letting him know she'd accepted his apology, but he grinned. It was a purely wicked flash of white teeth and dimples.

"'Course, if you'd care to join me . . ."

She knew he was deliberately trying to provoke her again, and yet, even as her cheeks warmed, temptation flurried through her belly.

Not trusting her voice, she shook her head.

"Too bad." He winked with a hint of his old roguery. "I guess I'll see you in the morning then. Good night, ma'am."

She released a ragged breath and smiled, her reluctant feet dragging her away.

"Good night, Wes."

Wes had returned from town Friday night a changed man. Rorie couldn't put her finger on the difference, although there seemed to be a subtle wariness about him— that edge she'd noticed earlier—and he couldn't quite disguise it behind his easygoing charm. Even Shae remarked on the difference, confiding that Wes was a lot less talkative while he worked, and that he often turned his gaze to the road as if he were watching for someone or waiting for something to happen.

Even so, Shae seemed to make peace with this new Wes. After tucking the children in that night, Rorie spied the two of them together, chatting on the porch and engaging in the manly ritual of gun cleaning. She wondered uneasily if she should regard this traditional pastime as the foreshadowing of some ominous event to come, but on Saturday, Wes's behavior was nearly back to normal. When he wasn't scaling the roof or painting the barn's newly raised wall, he was riding a delighted Po on his shoulders, teaching an eager Topher how to whittle, or advising a downhearted Nita how to get boys to notice her after Shae, her primary infatuation, proved too busy to compliment her on the ribbons in her hair.

Rorie overheard Nita's conversation with Wes as she approached the front door to ring the angle iron for dinner. Although she hadn't meant to eavesdrop, Nita's dejected tone arrested her on the threshold. She quickly found herself too touched—and too confused—to make her presence known while Wes counseled the child.

"All fellas are different, Nita, so I reckon I can't speak for Shae," he said. "Now as for me, I like a woman who can talk to a man about more than she-stuff, a woman with spunk and some class—but one who isn't shy about laughing or smiling. My woman's going to have a Texas-sized heart, too, and she'll love a lot of children. 'Cause I'm going to have a lot of children someday," he added drolly, "and they're all going to have red hair."

"I like children," Nita said coyly. "And red hair too."

"You do, huh?" Pausing in his work, he measured the wooden sole he'd been whittling to help correct Merrilee's limp. Then he cast a sidelong glance at the thirteen-year-old sitting beside him. "Do you think Miss Rorie likes red hair?"

Nita gave his question grave consideration. "I guess so," she answered after a moment. "I've never heard her say anything against it."

Rorie bit her lip. She didn't know whether to laugh or cry. For Wes to ask such a question, he must have been thinking about her at least half as much as she'd been thinking about him. Why, after their encounter in the barn, she'd been so hot and restless in her bed, she'd skimmed guilty hands over her belly, touching her tangle of womanly hair, clutching her pillow between her thighs. A hundred times or more the previous night, she had imagined him: his warm leathery palms, his hot hungry lips, the velvet granite of his naked flesh.

She knew it was wrong to fantasize about one man when she was encouraging the suit of another, but she seemed especially drawn to Wes's new, enigmatic darkness—that primal shadow that lurked beneath his lighthearted facade. She didn't understand how she could long for a scoundrel when she could have the security and predictability of Ethan. A hard-working, honest rancher rooted in his land, Ethan was exactly what she needed for herself and the children.

But Ethan had never made her heart trip with his smile or her knees weaken with his glance. In fact, nothing about Ethan's mannerisms made her giddy, perhaps because he always conducted himself like a gentleman in her presence, rather than some shameless, cocksure flirt.

Maybe with the right kind of encouragement, she thought, Ethan could curl her toes. Wes was always telling her to give a fellow a chance. Maybe if she let Ethan kiss her, she would feel the same spark of passion for him that she felt for Wes.

One could always hope so, she mused ruefully.

That night, after dinner, Shae had to take Nardo home. The child had dutifully arrived after lunch with a basket of his mother's tamales as weekly payment for his lessons, and Topher had persuaded him to play chase—until Nardo twisted his ankle and abruptly ended the game.

As Shae hitched Daisy to the wagon, Wes showed the first sign that his easygoing manner still hid a lingering wariness.

"How long do you think you'll be away?" he demanded, casting a glance at the setting sun.

Shae's color deepened as he glanced at Rorie, standing near the wagon bed and holding Nardo's hand. She guessed Shae had hoped to use Nardo's ankle as an excuse to disappear for a while, doing whatever young men did on a Saturday night. She suspected Lorelei Faraday was the object of Shae's affection, but other than a cautionary word about "innocent young women" and "gentlemanly honor," she'd always been careful not to pry into his private affairs. Shae was a sensitive and intelligent young man, and she trusted him not to sire bastards all over the county.

"I don't know how long I'll be," Shae answered,

drawing himself up a little taller and meeting Wes's stare with a narrowed gaze of his own. "Why?"

Topher snickered, nudging Nardo in the ribs. "Shae's still sweet on your sister Rosa."

The boys tittered, and the tension seemed to ease somewhat from Wes's shoulders. He shrugged, pasting on a smile. "No reason. Just . . . keep your eyes peeled."

Shae nodded. He shoved his shotgun under the driver's seat only to have Wes hand him one of his Peacemaker's—much to Rorie's uneasiness.

"I expect you won't be needing it, son, since you're only driving out to the Garcias'," Wes said pointedly. His smile turned wry. "If I thought you did need it, you couldn't keep me from riding along."

Their eyes locked again, and some manly understanding seemed to pass between them.

"I trust you can keep an eye on things while I'm gone?" Shae said.

"Oh yeah." Hooking his thumbs over his gun belt, Wes tossed Rorie a mouthwatering grin. "I'll watch things real good."

So Shae and Nardo rode off into the sunset, leaving Rorie to fend for herself—against Wes. Fortunately, she had Ginevee and four more children to distract him from mischief. They all crowded around as he put the finishing touches on Merrilee's new, elevated shoe. Topher wanted to wear the shoe first, ostensibly to help Merrilee break it in. Seeing how self-conscious the girl had become, Ginevee chased Topher and the others from the sitting room.

Even so, Merrilee looked as if she'd prefer to run and hide. Wes must have murmured every tender encouragement he knew to get her to take her first hesitant step with him. His patience was truly extraordinary. Standing at the opposite end of the room, Rorie watched his ministrations with a mixture of misty-eyed gratitude and maternal distrust. Every time Merrilee teetered or stumbled, Rorie was tempted to run to the child, but Wes was always at her side, stopping her fall.

He must have worked for a full half hour, buoying Merrilee's confidence, before she finally set his hand free and paced the room's perimeter without his help. The look of joyous wonder on her face made tears stream down Rorie's own.

And when Merrilee completed her solo trip, throwing her arms around Wes's waist in an exuberant show of gratitude, Rorie was hard-pressed not to do the same.

A chorus of cheers and applause erupted from outside. Startled, Rorie turned to find Topher and Nita, Po and Ginevee, all peeking through the open window.

"That was ripsnortin', Merrilee!" Topher crowed.

"Bully for you," Nita chimed in.

"Bull-wee shortin'! Bang, bang, bang!" Po shouted, bouncing up and down in Ginevee's arms and brandishing the wooden gun Wes had whittled for him.

Everyone laughed, and Ginevee wiped a tear from her eye.

"I reckon this calls for a celebration," she said, her voice thick with emotion.

"Hoo-boy! Cookies!"

"Topher," Nita chided, "you just had dessert."

"So?"

Ginevee chuckled, waving the children inside. "I was thinking more along the lines of pie. Pecan pie."

"That's even better," Wes quipped, winking down at Merrilee. "But don't you eat too much, you hear? This being your fandango and all, I'm going to want the first dance."

"Wes, really." Rorie laughed, blinking away the last of her tears. She couldn't remember the last time a man had brought such happiness into her home. "I don't think Merrilee's up to dancing just yet."

"Sure she is." He kissed the back of the beaming child's hand. "Merrilee can do anything. It's Ginevee I'm worried about," he teased as the woman reappeared, herding the other children through the front door. "You think you can pluck out a boot-scootin' tune on that old fiddle of yours?"

Her eyes twinkling, Ginevee tossed her head. "Just try and keep up with me, clodhopper."

The children dashed from the kitchen back to the sitting room each holding a plate with a generous slice of pie on it. Wes joked that he didn't need sawdust on the floor since he had Topher's pie crumbs for traction. As he pushed the furniture against the wall, Ginevee rosined up her bow. There was a general hush of excitement as everyone waited for her to play. Even Topher stopped smacking his lips long enough to hear the first lively strains of melody—"Turkey in the Straw."

Wes threw back his head and laughed. "C'mon, Merrilee. We'll show Ginevee we're no lead-footed bumpkins."

Doubling over, he swung the child into his arms and spun her around the room. Laughter bubbled up in Rorie's throat as she watched his stomping and swaying. The man had rhythm, that was certain, and a carefree energy that stole her breath away. Just watching his whirlwind turns made her heart pound, and when he bowed next to Nita, she felt a trickle of jealousy that made her feel guilty and foolish.

Trying to ignore her muddled emotions, she bounced Po on her knee, clapping the toddler's hands in time to Ginevee's spirited bowing. The sun had set, and the lamplight sent Wes's shadow leaping and dancing across the walls. Her foot began tapping to the sound of his boots. She'd always loved waltzes and reels, but Jarrod had discouraged her enthusiasm after they were wed, saying it was scandalous for a married woman to "carry on so." As self-conscious as Jarrod was about her height, she'd often suspected he denied her the pleasure of dancing simply because he felt awkward leading a woman whose shoulder obscured his view. In any event, she could count on one hand the number of times she had danced in the past eight years.

"Not bad for a hayseed," Ginevee called to Wes. "You warmed up enough for some real foot stompin'?"

He grinned at her, releasing Nita's hand. "And here I'd thought you'd fallen asleep with that bow. Give me the best you've got, fiddler."

He was standing before Rorie now, offering her his hand, and her pulse took off like a runaway train. Thanks to Jarrod, she had never had a chance to learn the two-step that Texicans favored—and that Wes had been dancing with carefree enthusiasm. She clutched Po a little tighter.

"Thank you, Wes. But after all that pie—"

He snatched Po out of her arms and passed him to Nita.

"You'll work off that pie in a dance or two. On your feet, Mrs. Sinclair. Or can't a Yankee lady keep up with a Texican cyclone like me?"

She blushed at his challenge. "Well, to tell you the truth, we don't practice your particular, er, style in Cincinnati."

"Shoot. I'll teach you." He was dragging her out of her chair. "After you taught me how to read, that seems only fair."

She laughed at his jest. She couldn't help herself. Nothing she had ever learned in finishing school had prepared her for Wes. He was a homespun gallant, impossible to resist. And when his arm wrapped around her waist, pulling her breathlessly close to his chest, she forgot her reasons for trying.

"This isn't some fuddy-duddy waltz now," he teased in her ear. "You just might have to kick up your heels."

His heat spiraled through her as he turned her around the room. She quickly realized that two-stepping had all the vigor of a polka, minus one of the steps. Quick to learn, she had little trouble adjusting her feet to the pattern. But that freed up her attention, leaving her endless moments to concentrate on forbidden things, like him.

She knew it was wrong to enjoy the half circle of his arm, so audaciously possessive and yet strangely comforting as he anchored her waist to his; or the devilishly casual way his thighs brushed hers, making her pulse skitter each time he pressed her back in a straight line. She couldn't remember the last time she'd danced and looked up into an attentive, laughing face—rather than down into a glazed and distant stare.

A delicious shiver tiptoed down her spine. The glow in his gaze was intoxicating; she imagined she was valued and admired, even pretty, in his eyes. His smile dazzled her enough to believe it. She hadn't felt so exhilarated, so lighthearted or joyful in years.

She knew she was dangerously close to surrender, that all her high ideals and righteous principles couldn't save her from this man. As much as she tried to convince herself that latent desire was to blame, deep down she knew her loneliness had little to do with her attraction to Wes. Clever and winsome, sensitive and sensual, he'd razed the final barrier to her heart when he combined compassion and ingenuity for Merrilee's sake. Rorie tried to tell herself it was too soon to have such feelings, that she'd known him for only six short days, and yet, the same giddy question kept racing through her brain: Could she be falling in love with him?

It was her last thought before a shot rang out, smashing the window and showering glass all around her.

Chapter Twelve

"*E*verybody down!" Wes shouted.

Rorie barely had time to react before his hard body toppled hers, shielding her from the spray of glass. She dimly heard the whoops of mounted gunmen and the frightened cries of the children, and she fought the rush of her own panic as Wes scrambled to his feet. He drew his .45 and doused the lamps.

"Miss Rorie?" Merrilee's shaky whisper followed fast on the heels of a sob. As her eyes adjusted to the moonlight, Rorie spied the child huddled with her doll under the table. Crawling hastily to her side, she pulled Merrilee into her arms. Topher, his face ashen, scampered into her lap.

"McFadden!" It was Creed's voice, slurred from drink. "We got a score to settle, you nigger bastard. Come on out! I know you're hiding in there behind all those skirts!"

Amidst the cacophony of laughter, jeers, and revolver reports, she heard flames whoosh to life outside. In the light of the blaze, she glimpsed Ginevee clutching Po and Nita to her breasts.

Suddenly Wes's shadow leaped across the wall. Protective, fearless, and larger than life, it loomed over them all, much as Wes loomed in the window. His face was a mask of stark, raw fury. When he raised his Peacemaker, she held her breath.

Once, twice, three times, the muzzle spat fire. Each shot was followed by a howl, a yelp, or a curse.

"My leg!"

"My arm!"

"You didn't tell us the nigger could shoot. Let's get the hell out of here!"

A trio of centaur shadows rolled across the wall. Just as quickly as it had begun, the shooting was over. Creed and his band of bullies rode off to lick their wounds, and Rorie was left with a roomful of cowering, whimpering children. Her own limbs were shaking so badly, she wasn't sure she could stand.

"Wes!" Her voice cracked, and he hesitated in his rush for the door. "The children," she said hoarsely, too stunned and too awed by his ferocious skill to utter a single word more.

She watched his jaw twitch. His gaze flitted to the straw effigy, most likely Gator's scarecrow, burning in the dirt drive outside. Then his eyes met hers, and his features softened.

"Is anyone hurt?" He scanned the children's trembling bodies and tearstained faces in the effigy's eerie light.

Four little heads shook, but no one spoke. No one hardly dared to breathe, in fact, as everyone looked up at Wes, so authoritative and commanding, and so startlingly different from the flirt who'd danced with them only minutes before.

"It's over now." His voice was gruff, allowing no room for argument. "They're gone now, and they won't be coming back."

Rorie bit her tongue on her doubts, but Merrilee shifted under her arm, peeking up at Wes through her fingers.

"Was it the bad men?" she whispered tremulously.

Outrage vied with the tender concern spreading across Wes's face. "No, sweetheart." Holstering his gun, he squatted down before the child. "It was Creed

Dukker and some of his friends. They were out for a little sport, that's all. They weren't firing at anybody on purpose."

Rorie wasn't entirely convinced. Creed had come to make trouble with Shae. No doubt he'd intended to finish the fistfight over Lorelei Faraday that Rorie had interrupted on Monday.

Nita must have suspected the same thing, for she glanced anxiously up at Ginevee before turning her troubled gaze to Wes.

"But what about Shae?" she asked. "I mean, ever since that Miss Lorelei Faraday made it clear she'd rather court anyone—even a colored boy—over the likes of Creed Dukker, the whole town has been mean to Shae. It isn't even Shae that's causing the trouble!"

Rorie knew Nita's version of the truth was based on her jealousy. In reality, Shae had always been ambitious, which some Elodeans liked to term uppity. He hadn't discouraged Lorelei's calf-eyed glances, particularly after the Dukkers accused him of trying to rise above his so-called station.

Rorie knew Lorelei's attention flattered Shae, but she also knew the boy had no real interest in courtship and marriage at this time. College was his heart's desire at the moment.

"You needn't worry about Shae, Nita," Rorie said as firmly as her constricted throat would allow. "He's safe at the Garcias'. Besides, he's got one of Wes's revolvers and Gator's shotgun to protect him."

"Yeah, but Shae can't shoot like Uncle Wes can," Topher said, scrambling to his feet as Wes reached to help Merrilee. "Even Sheriff Gator never shot as good as you," Topher added, this time to Wes. Admiration replaced the dread on his still-pale face. "Three shots and three hits all on moving targets. And in the dark too! Can you teach me to shoot like that, Uncle Wes? Can you?"

The eagerness in Topher's voice made Rorie's gut knot. She met Wes's eyes uneasily.

"A man doesn't fire on another man unless he's ready to take a bullet himself," he answered firmly, offering Rorie his hand. "If I had my druthers, I wouldn't have hit anyone at all. Creed Dukker had to be taught he can't go around shooting up houses full of women and children. That was a low-down, cowardly stunt he pulled, son, and damned irresponsible too."

Rorie silently blessed him. Then his warm, strong fingers closed around hers, and she came dangerously close to tears. What if he hadn't been here when Creed came? What if he had ridden into town for Saturday-night recreation like any other red-blooded, unmarried man? What would she and Ginevee have done then?

"Are you hurt?" he murmured, his gaze anxious and questioning as he helped her rise.

Shaking her head, she stumbled on the glass. His arm wrapped her waist, pulling her against him. She squeezed her eyes closed, hating the moisture that lurked there. She wished she dared let him hold her to his heart forever, so she could absorb his comforting warmth and fill herself with his strength, but she had the children to think about. She couldn't let them see her grow weepy.

"It's going to be all right," he said huskily in her ear. "I won't let anyone hurt you or the children."

She nodded, pasting on a brave smile as she dragged herself from his embrace. "Of course not. You ... are very kind. And we owe you a great debt, Wes. One, I'm afraid, which we can't fully repay."

His brows knitted. "Rorie—"

She looked away. She couldn't bear for him to gaze at her with such tender concern. Not now, when she was struggling not to fling herself back into his arms.

"Ginevee, please help me put the children to bed."

"Rorie." He was more insistent this time, his hand closing over her sleeve. "I need to talk with you—"

"Not now, Wes, please." She glanced meaningfully at the children. "I need for you to put out that fire before the wind spreads it to the house."

His jaw grew harder at her rebuff. "All right."

She released a shuddering breath, relieved, yet disappointed as well, when he dropped his hand. Drawing herself up taller, she took refuge from the

umult in her breast by turning to the only haven she'd
ver had.

"Come along, children. I'll read you a bedtime story
before we douse the lights. Something with a happy end-
ng. Would you like that?"

Wes paced the porch like a caged puma. He kept one
eye on the door, hoping Rorie would come outside so
he could finally confess he was a Ranger. He kept his
other eye on the drive, wondering where the hell Shae
was and if the boy might not be in trouble after all.

Riding after Creed and beating the stuffing out of
him would have gone a long way to restoring Wes's hu-
nor. He didn't dare leave Rorie alone to fend for herself,
hough. When the window had shattered around her, he'd
eared she'd be pierced by the shards of glass or the bullet
hat had launched them, and terror had ripped through
his soul. In that frozen moment in time, when he was
helpless to do anything more than wrap himself around
her, a mindless rage had seized him. He would have
walked into a hail of gunfire naked and unarmed, just to
ear Creed Dukker limb from limb. That sonuvabitch had
been lucky. If four impressionable children hadn't been
watching, Wes might not have been so careful to inflict
mere flesh wounds on Creed's gang.

He scowled first at the sitting-room window, which
he'd had to board, and then at the charred remains of Gator's scarecrow. He'd seen similar debris a hundred or
more times after some drunken cowboys hurrahed a
town, but after seeing Rorie so pale and shaking, he
would never be able to forgive Creed's mischief. Rorie's
expression had nearly done him in. With her eyes so
misty pleading, he'd been certain she'd wanted him—
needed him—to console her. The minute he tried to comfort her, though, she'd turned coltish on him again. The
woman ran so hot and cold, it made his head spin. If
she were a born coquette or an accomplished schemer, he
might have thought she was indulging in some elaborate
tease. Instead, she'd taken great pains to be honest with
him about her intentions and Ethan. At least, that's what
she'd claimed two nights ago.

He scowled at the memory.

Maybe she didn't know her own mind. Or maybe she did, but what she secretly wanted, a man like him, frightened the living daylights out of her. Maybe that was why she kept trying to convince him her wanting didn't exist.

She wasn't fooling him, though. Not after their kiss. A river of passion ran through Aurora Sinclair, and the harder she tried to dam it, the more he wanted her. God help him. He wanted a proper lady with four children, more principled notions than he could count, and a hurting streak so wide, it made the Rio Grande look like a crack full of water. Had he lost his ever-loving mind?

The sound of a galloping horse pricked his ears and jerked his attention back to his surroundings. Grabbing his Winchester, he dropped behind the corner of the house where the shadows were dark and concealing. He didn't have to wait long for the rider to come into view. Recognizing Daisy's pale flanks and flattened ears, he marveled that Shae had left the wagon behind to spur the nag out of her habitually lazy gait.

The boy reined in hard when he saw the ashes and the window. Drawing Wes's .45, he jumped to the ground. He knelt for a moment, rubbing his fingers over dark splotches on the drive. Wes stepped forward in time to see the boy sniff what he'd found. Shae stiffened.

They regarded each other with long measured stares for what seemed like an uncommonly long time. Finally, reluctantly, Shae turned the borrowed revolver butt-forward and handed it back to Wes.

"So it's you," he said flatly.

"Heard the gunshots?"

Shae's smile was grim and wary. "Half the county heard. There's blood here. Whose is it?"

"Creed's . . . and some other fellas who came looking for you."

Shae started, his gaze rising to the lighted second-story of the house.

"The children are scared, but they're not hurt," Wes

said, answering the boy's unspoken question. "Do you want to tell me what the hell I've been protecting them from?"

Shae stiffened, but his chagrin gave way to ire. "You've got some explaining to do first, Rawlins."

He pulled a folded wad of newspaper from the bib of his overalls and tossed it at Wes's feet.

" 'Ranger Rawlins Ousts The Sinclair Squatters.' " Shae's voice was dry as he read the headline aloud. "Imagine my surprise."

It was Wes's turn to fidget. "You got this from Lorelei?"

"Does it matter? I knew you weren't any damned carpenter. Your name always did sound familiar, although it took me a week to remember why. There's a retired U.S. marshal named Rawlins who settled north of here awhile back. They say he has two brothers. One's a rancher, the other's a Ranger. I reckon the Ranger must be you."

Wes released the breath he'd been holding. He didn't know whether to be relieved or annoyed that the truth was finally out.

"Yeah, that's right. I'm the Ranger. And it's a damned good thing, too, since the law around here isn't worth a plug nickel."

"My pa was."

"Your pa isn't who I'm talking about."

Shae regarded him in a mixture of suspicion and shattered trust. Shoving the paper closer with his toe, he finally blurted out, "It says you're in cahoots with Marshal Dukker. That it was Dukker who sent you here with orders to shoot us so he could lay claim to Pa's spread."

"I don't take orders from Hannibal Dukker."

"Yeah? Then why the big secret? Why didn't you tell us straight out who you are?"

"You want the truth?"

"I figure you owe it to me."

"All right." Wes met his glare evenly. "Because I was told some renegade Negroes shot Gator. I thought you might have been one of them, to claim his land. You have to admit, it's pretty damned suspicious, you not having a shred of evidence to back up your kinship claim. And some mighty incriminating things are being said about you and Rorie back in Elodea."

Shae folded his arms across his chest. "So you rode out here to see what we're like, is that it?"

"Something like that."

"And your opinion?"

"I think you're one helluva fine man," Wes said more quietly. "And I think Rorie is the victim of some extremely malicious lies."

"Good answer."

Wes bit back an oath, steeling himself against his rising irritation. "Look, Shae. If I was going to run you off your land, don't you think I would have done it the first day I got here?"

"Maybe." Shae's tone was as sharp as his gaze. "Or maybe you thought you'd bide your time, catch a little amusement first on the side."

"What the hell is that supposed to mean?"

"I think you know damned well." Looking Wes square in the eye, Shae didn't mince words. "What are your intentions toward Miss Aurora?"

Wes felt his face heat.

"I've seen how you look at her," Shae went on grimly.

"Yeah? Well, she's an attractive woman."

"And vulnerable to the likes of you."

"You paint me as some kind of sagebrush Romeo."

"Are you?"

"No."

Shae cocked his head, as if he wasn't sure what to believe. "She's a lady, Rawlins."

"I know that."

"And she's a good woman."

"I know that too," he said less defensively.

"She doesn't take kindly to lies. She got a bellyful from her husband. From the little Maw-Maw told me, I gather Sinclair spent most of his Saturday nights drinking and whoring." Shae shook his head."You're going to have a helluva time convincing her to trust you after all the whoppers you've told."

"I had no choice," Wes said, averting his eyes. "My investigation came first."

"Well, for your sake, I hope she sees things the same way."

Wes frowned. Shae obviously thought the chances of that were slim to none.

"So when are you going to tell her who you are?"

"I've tried telling her three times already."

"No offense, but I suggest you try a little harder, Rawlins. Tomorrow being Sunday and all, she's bound to hear about you in church."

Wes groaned inwardly. Of course she'd hear about him in church! How could he not have considered that? Rorie would bundle every last one of the children off to the house of the Lord, even if the whole town disapproved of her so-called squatting. She was too strong a woman to let prejudice and spite stand in the way of her orphans' little souls.

"You're not going to spill the beans before that?" he asked sheepishly.

"Nope." Shae's tone, if not his manner, had softened. "I figure she has the right to hear it from you."

Wes swallowed, his smile weak. "Thanks."

An awkward silence lengthened between them.

"If it makes you feel any better, I think she's fond of you," Shae said grudgingly. "At least, she started smiling again after you rode in. That's got to mean something."

Wes was relieved by the boy's admission. He didn't know why, but it bothered him to think Rorie might never forgive him for his lies. Perhaps it was because he'd worked so damned hard to earn her trust. He'd seemed to be making real progress, too, since she actually loosened up enough to dance and flirt with him. Of course, Creed's poor timing had put an end to whatever Wes might have reaped from that flirtation. Was it any wonder he wanted to flatten the boy?

Shae was watching him with disconcertingly keen eyes. "You care about her, don't you."

The words were a bald, blunt assessment, not an indulgence in curiosity. Wes flinched, unable to deny to himself any longer what he feared was true.

"A man would have to have a heart of stone not to," he hedged.

Amusement lifted the corners of Shae's mouth, but just as quickly, his lips flattened into a solemn line. "Then you and I have something in common—besides a healthy distrust of Dukkers, I mean. Tell her who you are and get it over with, Rawlins. She'll be hurt, and she'll be bothered, but she's about the fairest person I know. She'll come around."

Wes felt an uneasy anticipation as he glanced at Rorie's window. When he realized the house was dark, disappointment vied with a guilty sense of relief.

Shae's gaze followed his to the blackened panes.

"Well, looks like you missed your opportunity," he said dryly. "But you can put the night to good use, studying that slander everyone will be talking about in church. Maybe then you can prepare her for the worst of what she'll hear."

Wes would have preferred to tear the paper to shreds, just as he had the first time he read it in town. But Shae did have a point, so he snatched up the rag and tucked it under his arm. "Damn Faraday."

Shae's mirth was fleeting. "He's no Mark Twain, that's true, but he's not entirely in Dukker's back pocket either. We have Miss Lorelei to thank for that. She's shared Miss Aurora's opinion of Dukker ever since last Christmas, when he came sniffing around as her caller."

Wes started, wondering if he'd misunderstood, but the hardened planes of Shae's face told him differently.

"Well, I reckon the wagon can keep till tomorrow. It's too rickety to be worth stealing." Nodding, Shae stifled a yawn as he stepped past Wes to take Daisy's reins. "Good night, Rawlins."

Wes watched thoughtfully as the boy led the mare to the corral. So Pa Dukker had courted Lorelei? Just what did Creed think about that? Wes remembered the stricken, puppy look the boy had worn when Lorelei hurried away from him in town. Maybe Creed and his pa weren't that close after all.

And maybe that could work to his advantage.

Chapter Thirteen

Sitting in the dark, Rorie waited impatiently for the creaking of Shae's mattress and the long stretch of silence that would indicate he slept. She'd been waiting for what seemed like hours for him to return, not daring to telegraph her private worries to Ginevee or the children. But the murmur of male voices below had reassured her Shae was safe and that she could retire in peace to her own sleep.

Unfortunately, she'd been afraid to close her eyes. The violent proof of Creed's jealousy toward Shae had shaken her far more than she dared admit to four frightened children and Shae's anxious grandmother. In her heart, Rorie knew she must convince Shae to give up the land—his land—the only thing he had left of his father. The realization caused her as much rage as it did grief. It wasn't fair Shae had enemies simply because his keen intelligence, good looks, and lofty ambitions threatened Hannibal Dukker's peace of mind. Even so, if Shae continued to live near Elodea, he wouldn't be safe. Rorie had experienced enough of life to know that people often feared what they didn't understand. And what they feared, they destroyed.

Swallowing hard, she peeked once more past her curtain toward the light radiating from the half-open barn door. She liked to tell herself that that burning lamp drew her only because of her urgent concern for Shae. Since Wes had earned the boy's respect, he might be able to help her make Shae see sense. That was why she must speak with Wes now.

But that was only part of the reason.

The shameful reality was, she was too frightened, too worried, too *lonely* to spend a single moment longer by herself.

And she couldn't think of anyone else she'd rather spend a lonely night with than Wes.

Gathering what was left of her courage, she tossed a modest shawl over her shoulders and hurried on shaking legs to the barn. As quiet as she tried to be, Wes must have heard her approach. Before she'd drawn enough breath to announce herself, his head snapped up, and he reached for his Colt. She nearly lost her nerve completely then, and it didn't help to see his surprise dissolve to embarrassment when he hastily shoved something into the straw behind his saddlebag.

It occurred to her that he was probably in the midst of his nighttime toilette, since he sat without boots. His feet with their dusting of freckles were almost as provocative in their innocence as the gaping of his untucked, unbuttoned shirt. Beneath the faded blue folds, golden light and auburn shadow cavorted in a tantalizing game of hide and seek. Her heart quickened to a dizzying rate, and she dragged her gaze to his face. All the implications, all the possibilities, of her visit to his resting place were enough to make her knees wobble.

"Rorie?" Concern crinkled the corners of his eyes, darkening them to a smoky shade of pine. "I thought you were asleep. Is everything all right?"

She nodded feebly, her tongue too swollen to answer. Although common sense told her she should be babbling apologies and backing out the door just as fast as her rubbery legs could carry her, she couldn't flee.

He rose and walked toward her with a lithe grace that was more like a ripple than a stride. She remembered how he'd stalked her beneath the magnolia tree, and how he'd cornered her inside the stall. A tremor of longing rocked her, and she wondered what it would be like— what it would *really* be like—to let him feed the sweet, hot hunger that his touch had ignited inside her.

"I'm glad you're here," he said, his voice a husky murmur. "I was hoping you'd come."

He was?

A tiny thrill danced down her spine. "I . . . need to talk with you."

He nodded, his gaze pouring into hers, filling her with warmth. "Me too."

He reached past her, pulling the door shut. For a breathless moment, the world fell away. There were no broken promises, shattered dreams, or scarred memories of days past. There were only starlight and silence, spilling in through the naked rafters, and the heady glow of something ancient and alluring in the unjaded eyes that held her own.

"Come sit awhile."

He took her hand, which pleased her far more than she had any right to let it. Leading her to the milking stool, he settled her there with all the consideration of a serious beau. His care made her heart ache for something more, something her mind didn't dare focus on for long. Otherwise, she might weep, recalling the lonely hurting that was such an inescapable part of her nights.

Dropping her eyes from the questions in his gaze, she clasped her hands in her lap and struggled for the composure to begin. "I'm so worried about Shae," she whispered, forcing the words past the lump in her throat. "If he had been at the window tonight instead of you, he . . . might be dead now."

Wes knelt in front of her, rocking back on his heels. He steeled himself against the pressing urge to comfort her with touches, as he had earlier, after the shooting. Her face still looked pale against the honeyed length of her waist-long braid, and the hollows beneath her eyes were shadowed by unshed tears.

For her to come alone to him in the middle of the night, she must have been badly shaken by the shootout.

The way she'd shooed him off with her usual stiff-backed practicality, he figured she'd gotten over the ordeal within a minute or two of the smoke's clearing. At the time, he'd marveled that she could be so nonchalant, but then he'd hoped it was a good sign, indicating she might just as quickly get over his confession.

"You're not alone anymore, Rorie," he said gently, "and neither is Shae. I told you my guns are for your protection. I told Hannibal Dukker, too, but I reckon Creed just had to find out the hard way."

She grew even paler. "Wes, you shouldn't have. You don't know what Hannibal's capable of, and with his badge to protect him—"

"He won't be wearing that badge for long. Not if I have my way."

Panic stole across her features. "What do you mean? You're not going to—to—"

"Shoot him like the cur dog he is?" He indulged in a wan smile. "I can't say the thought hasn't crossed my mind a time or two. But no, I don't put myself above the law. I told you I'm square, Rorie. And well . . ." He sighed, trying to keep the disappointment from his voice. "I was kind of hoping you believed me."

"I do," she said quickly, a spot of color returning to her cheeks. "It's just that I don't want . . . I mean, you could be . . ."

Her swallow was audible. For a moment, her eyes became so bright and luminous, he wondered how she managed to stave off the fresh onslaught of tears.

"Wes, please promise me you won't cross him. You could wind up dead, and I couldn't bear that . . . knowing it was because of me," she added tremulously.

His heart turned over, filling him with a giddy, tingly elation. Her plea was the sweetest thing he'd ever heard. An angel's song couldn't have lifted his spirits half as high.

"Now Rorie, don't you go worrying about me," he said, his voice gruff with pleasure. "I'm more than a match for that two-legged cockroach."

"No!"

She grabbed his shoulders. The strength in her hands surprised him, but what stunned him even more was the stark, wild terror he saw in her eyes.

"Don't talk crazy! Don't go gunning for him! He'll shoot you in the back a surely as night turns to day. Leave him to someone who knows about killing and bushwhacking. Leave him to one of his own kind—one of those awful, hateful Rangers."

Wes sucked in his breath. If she'd hit his head with a hammer, she couldn't have laid him so low.

"Rorie . . ." Easing free of her grasp, he gently returned her hands to her lap. "Why don't you like Rangers?"

She looked at him as if he were daft. "Because they're cold-blooded, and vicious, and dishonest, and—"

He held up his hand, fending off the words that slammed into his gut like blows. "Hold on a minute. I think you're confusing Rangers with bounty hunters. Or maybe even with the scum they bring in."

She gave a watery sniff. "As far as I'm concerned, there isn't much difference. They're all killers. And none of them has the morals of a scalawag."

He stiffened. He couldn't help it. He wasn't proud that he'd snuffed out a few men's lives, but he'd never killed a man who hadn't drawn on him first. Ever. "Those are pretty strong accusations. Do you have some evidence to back them up?"

She blinked incredulously at him. "Of course I do. I don't spread idle gossip."

"Well . . ." His heart kicked hard, but he had to know. Curiosity had been burning in his gut like a hot brick ever since she first denounced the Ranger force. "Let's hear it."

Her chin rose a notch, trembled, then sank again, falling nearly to her chest. "It's not easy for me to talk about it," she admitted finally, knotting her fingers and averting her eyes. "It involves Topher. And Topher's mother, Christine."

He held his tongue and waited out her silence.

"She was barely eighteen," she began, more bitterly

this time. "She was only a child; she didn't know any better! But that—that ranging lothario, Bill Malone, knew. He knew, and he didn't care."

"Was Christine some relation of yours?"

"No." She drew a steadying breath. "You'd think she was, wouldn't you, the way I carry on so. I guess I act this way because"—she smiled mirthlessly—"the first time I met Jarrod, I was only eighteen. And more naive than a babe. If I'd known Christine, maybe I could have helped her. God knows, I would have stopped her. She had her whole life ahead of her, and it breaks my heart to think that she . . . that she gave up the way she did."

Something noxious curled inside Wes's stomach. "Gave up?" he repeated uneasily. "What do you mean?"

Rorie's jaw grew harder. "Since Christine came from a good family, they put pressure on Malone to marry her. He promised he would, but his captain got wind of the affair—those Rangers all stick together, you know—and a team of them arrived with urgent orders for Malone to ride to San Antonio. A year or so passed. A peddler man rode into town one spring and started talking about the things he'd seen in Bexar County. He told Christine he'd met a Ranger there named Bill Malone, and that this Malone had a wife and a brand new son. I guess the humiliation must have been too much for Christine, because that night . . ." Rorie's voice trailed off, and she shuddered. "That night, she shot herself."

"Jesus," Wes choked.

"That law-abiding Ranger killed Christine as surely as if he'd put the gun to her head and pulled the trigger."

Wes ran rough fingers through his hair. "Maybe Malone didn't know—"

"About Topher?" Rorie's laugh was short and harsh. "Why else do you think he rode out of town like the devil's own pitchfork was prodding him? But you know what the worst part is?" She raised her eyes to his, and a single, silvery tear spilled down her cheek. "He denied up and down that Topher was his son. He wanted nothing to do with the boy. Christine's relatives were too humiliated by the scandal to want Topher either, so they packed him off to an orphanage. And—"

Her voice broke. He slipped a hand over hers, trying to ignore his guilt when her fingers wrapped around his, trying not to feel like the cowardly bastard he was as his long overdue confession shriveled up and dried on his tongue.

"And I would have died to give life to that child," she whispered hoarsely. "To any child. I—I can't have sons, Wes. Or daughters. That's why Jarrod left me."

The words tumbled out in an anguished rush, stunning Rorie as much as they'd clearly shocked Wes. She had never meant to reveal her shameful affliction, certainly not to a man who would never consider marrying her. When she saw his wide-eyed amazement, she couldn't bear to watch what might follow: pity, revulsion, contempt. Ethan's forthright discomfort she'd been able to endure. He was her suitor, and he deserved to know he wasn't courting any bargain. But Wes . . .

Oh, God, why did it hurt so much to realize he would never look at her again with hunger in his eyes?

"Rorie—"

She choked on a sob, unable to listen to the platitudes he would surely use to fill the awkward moment. Turning blindly, she tried to rise, to grope past her tears to the door, but his arms pulled her back, sealing her in a hard, fierce embrace that left her aching for more.

"Don't go," he said in a strangely thickened whisper. "Don't push me away."

"But I—"

"Shh." He caught her chin, urging her eyes to meet his. Some dark, pained emotion glistened there, one that looked surprisingly close to sorrow. "There's no way I'm letting you walk out that door to do your hurting alone."

She blinked as tears blurred his image. She had never expected him to care, much less understand, and a flood of feeling broke its dam, crashing through her in breakers of grief. First her resistance crumbled, then her knees. He swept her up, carrying her as effortlessly as if she were a doll made of rags.

Lowering her to his bedroll, he cradled her on his lap, rocking her as she clung to his neck. He let her tears spill in salty rivulets to the hollow of his throat, his big hands kneading the knotted muscles of her back.

She wasn't sure when her braid unraveled, or when his fingers began sliding through the weighty mass of her hair. She knew only that the gentle repetitions of his strokes were bringing her a comfort she hadn't known since early childhood.

They were bringing her something else too. As her tears dried, new feelings pooled in the secret places of her body. He pushed a strand of hair from her forehead. The touch of his fingers was followed by the lingering whisper of his breath. Slowly, hesitantly, his head lowered. He pressed his lips to her temple in a feather-soft kiss. She felt her heart leap as his other arm tightened, gathering her closer. When his lips touched the ticklish hollow of her ear, shivers tiptoed down her spine, leaving her shaken, breathless.

His palm skimmed her side, slowing almost wistfully as it brushed the exposed curve of her breast. His heart—or perhaps it was hers—leaped hard against her ribs, and when his cheek grazed hers, leaving a trace of moisture there, she dared to turn her head and gaze at him. She saw then the proof of what she'd suspected all along.

He'd shed a tear or two with her.

In that fraction of time, with his gaze so full of caring, some soul part of her stirred. It grew and expanded, bridging their worlds of books and guns, age and background, to bind their hearts in faith and trust. It was the most profoundly moving, spiritual moment she'd ever known.

Until he kissed her.

Wes filled his mouth with the taste of her, like a man hungering for sweetness. He'd known pain before, but nothing like the torment that had ripped Rorie up and clawed at his innards as if it were his own. He couldn't bear to think how she'd suffered, and he wished fervently that he'd found her first, loved her first; that he'd spared her from that selfish bastard, Sinclair.

Although Wes knew he could never replace what God had taken from her, he had the burning, irrational need to try. He wanted to pleasure her, take her hurt away, fill her with ecstatic joy. Nothing else mattered to him. Nothing.

"Rorie," he murmured, "I want you so."

And he did. He always had. The reason why Jarrod Sinclair had not mattered little to Wes.

He heard her breath catch, and he slanted his mouth across hers, coaxing her, possessing her, needing her to feel the same explosive desire that smoked through his veins, melting the rock-hard core of his restraint. He wanted to see the same hunger that he'd seen in her eyes when he kissed her beneath the magnolia tree, when she'd forgotten all her rational excuses, her heartaches, her fears.

Still, he sensed the battle raging deep inside her, the struggle between everything she believed and everything she wanted. He steeled himself to patience. If he could make her feel safe, then she would stay. That's what he hoped. He knew he could please her if she'd let him. He'd had a thorough education in making female bodies hum. Those other women had been just as well schooled, though, master teachers who'd graduated hundreds of students. He knew Rorie wouldn't give herself lightly to a man, and he never wanted her to regret this night, if she should choose to become his lover.

"You are so beautiful," he whispered, catching her face and gazing reverently into her misty eyes. He wanted her to know he spoke the truth.

When fresh tears glistened on her lashes, though, a knife twisted in his gut.

"H-how could I be?" Her voice was plaintive, cracking with self-doubt. "I'm so big and gangly and—"

Her protests trailed off, and her eyes grew impossibly round when he dragged her hand to the full, potent proof of his desire.

"Never doubt for an instant that I want you the way you are," he said, hoarse with what seemed like a lifetime of waiting to have this frightfully honest, heartbreakingly vulnerable woman. "I don't much like picking up a sweetheart or setting her on a tree stump so I can kiss her.

You're just the right size for me, Rorie. All of me," he added huskily.

His words recalled to Rorie's mind forbidden, secret fantasies, and she shivered irrepressibly, a tingly sensation that danced through her limbs. In the flames that were his eyes, an elemental yearning burned, holding her as helplessly captive as the hand that wouldn't set hers free.

He raised it to his lips. It quaked uncontrollably, from a sense of anticipation rather than any enfeebled cry of virtue. When his tongue slid between her fingers, tickling the sensitive skin there, she tried to rally her wits, to sever them from the heating furnace of her body. But the echo of forgotten need was too insistent, like a siren's call luring her to the sinful shores of no return.

"Touch me, Rorie," he urged, his words threading through her on a raspy ribbon of desire. "Touch me like you did before."

He trailed her moistened fingers across his angled scar and down his chest. His flesh looked like amber in the lamplight and felt like velvet against her skin. She needed no further coaxing to map the corded ridges and taut, hard planes of his torso.

He shrugged with feral grace, letting his gingham shirt fall from his broad shoulders, and it spilled across her thighs. His hand slipped beneath it, a prowling weight of squeezing, kneading textures that she couldn't see or control. His probing was the most unsettling enticement she had known. She squeezed her eyes closed against her guilt even though bloomers still protected her, and she trusted him to stop if she begged to be freed.

His mouth courted hers. Nuzzling and nibbling, it sought an open invitation. His tongue pushed past her lips. Fencing and caressing, it wooed hers with tender stabs until their tongues tangled, twined, and mated. He tasted of salt—the salt from their combined tears—and the memory of his compassion made her ache to know him, to be a part of him.

"Rorie, let me look at you," he whispered against her clinging lips. "Let me feel you flesh to flesh."

He'd raised her other hand to her bodice, and she

quaked when his fingers slipped a button free beneath her palm.

"Help me," he crooned, undoing another. "You're safe with me."

Her fingers obeyed of their own accord. With his persistent, skillful plucking, it didn't take long to wrestle ties or stays. Soon her gown sagged to her waist, and her corset had disappeared. Only her chemise remained, but he was slipping its straps down and murmuring reassurances, no doubt to mask his determination. When she shrank from the idea of her stark nakedness, his mouth lowered, steaming through the thin veil of fabric, teasing her nipple until the sheer touch of muslin chafed like rawhide on her straining, sensitized flesh.

"Wes, please—"

"Take it off."

"But the lantern—"

She gasped, suddenly blinded by darkness.

"There. No more excuses," he said silkily.

She swallowed. Exhilarated, tantalized, she couldn't help but be scared witless. Even at eighteen, she'd known enough not to let love play go this far. What was she doing? What was *he* doing? She couldn't see him in the ghostly twinkle of starlight.

"Wes, um, maybe this isn't such a good idea," she said, feeling obligated to say so, and hating every word.

A warm hand prowled over the muslin, peeling it slowly, provocatively from her flesh.

"There you go again, darlin', not giving a fella a chance."

He filled his palm with the weight of her breast, and she shivered with forbidden delight as his thumb began to toy with the jutting, tingling nub.

"Some parts of you think it's a very good idea," he teased, sliding his tongue inside her ear. "And all my parts have to agree."

She squirmed, choking back a laugh. He was so bad. And so good. A sticky warmth that had nothing to do with spring heat was lapping at her tender places. It would take divine intervention not to beg him to lay her down, to press inside her, to ease the torment that his grins and glances and stolen caresses had built inside her for days. Although she wasn't naive enough to think he truly found her attractive, she wanted to cling to that thought for a few minutes longer, to feel vibrantly feminine and alluringly beautiful in every fiber of her being. Jarrod had never made her feel anything but clumsy and horse-sized.

"Kiss me," he growled, sipping at her lips. "I want to taste you again."

Any doubt of his sincerity was dispelled when his mouth slanted over hers, feasting with relish. She raised a shaking hand, touching his cheek, sliding her fingers through the rich, coppery waves of his hair. How long had she been wanting to feel those shimmering strands? Since that first afternoon, when the sun had flared behind him and he'd seemed to wear it on his head like some crowning, autumn glory?

"God, woman." His breaths came less evenly now. "I do have a hunger for you."

He was weighting her down, pressing her into the rumpled pile of blankets and quilts. She heard the muffled crackling of the fresh straw underneath, felt the tender prickling of worn wool against her shoulders. Then another, more erotic sensation followed, the hot hard brass of his buckle, branding her belly with the fever of his arousal.

"You smell like wildflowers." His pleased, muffled tones came from the hollow of her throat. "Honeysuckle, I think."

And he smelled like leather and earth and wind and prairie.

"I love the scent of you, Rorie." He shifted lower, and his tongue, like wet velvet, licked between her breasts. "It keeps me up at night."

She flushed from head to toe, hearing a deeper, bawdier meaning in his words. Stretching out a hand, she sought to urge his lips higher to the safety of her mouth, but he delved out of reach.

She heard a clink and a rustle. A heartbeat later,

layers of fabric began peeling from her hips. When she tried to sit up, to preserve the last shreds of her modesty, his hands wooed her, gentled her, massaged the nervous tremors from her limbs.

"I just want to make you smile, sweetheart. Will you smile for me?"

She could see him again now, a silvery man-god kneeling between her legs. Starlight spilled over his Olympian shoulders and down the shadowed canyons of his ribs. It was then that she realized he'd shed his belt and jeans. She drew a swift breath. His naked flanks looked as hard and sleek as marble, and the maleness of him . . .

Her gaze flew to his, and his off-center smile made her secret flesh smoke.

"You're . . . beautiful, Wes," she said shyly.

"Thank you, darlin'. You know how I feel about you."

With that angel smile she'd come to associate with his devilish side, he lowered his head and sucked on her navel. The tickling of his tongue and mustache made her squirm with delight, until she felt a more intimate tickling against the nest between her thighs. When his long, exquisitely thick forefinger found the entry to her clinging heat, she sat bolt upright, gasping. He wrapped her waist in the prison of his arm, making her helpless to fend off his artful, plunging strokes. A slick welcome spilled from her traitorous core, and he made a thoroughly male, thoroughly satisfied sound.

"Oh, yes. Honey. You feel like molten honey."

With gentle pressure, he arched her back over his arm, and she groaned, digging her fingers into his shoulder blades.

"Relax, sweetheart. I've got hold of you. Just enjoy the ride."

She started a feeble protest, but her breath snagged when he sucked her breast into the steamy textures of his mouth, swirling his tongue over the shameless bud that was pouty and swollen, aching for his kiss.

"Trust me." His entreaty came faintly above the ripping of her breaths. "Let me lay you down."

Now he was exploring her body, learning what

pleased her. Every tender foray into her secret, guilty yearnings struck sparks from the deepest female parts of her, like a match strikes sparks from tinder.

"Wes, we can't keep doing this," she pleaded, knowing that to speak at all put her at terrible risk. She might beg him for every wanton delight she'd ever imagined.

"We can't?" His voice came in silky tones between each pinprick of his teeth, prowling up the trembling flesh of her inner thigh. "Why's that?"

A second finger joined the thrusting of the first, and wild pleasure streaked through her, making her writhe.

"P-people will talk."

"I don't plan on telling anyone. Do you?"

She didn't know whether to laugh or cry at his sinful persistence. She'd never been seduced before. "It's easy for you to jest," she panted, doing her moral best to twist away. "I'm the one who'll bear the brunt of the scandal. They'll call me a desperate old spinster who corrupts younger men."

"Still think of me as a barely weaned pup, do you? Hmm. Then let me show you something that might help to change your mind, darlin'."

He grabbed her hips and hiked them higher. Before she realized his intent, his lips settled on a place she'd only dreamed a man might kiss. Her startled, "What are you—?" fragmented into a high, strangled sound as his relentless, wickedly mobile mouth drove the itchy twitching inside her to a maddening frenzy.

Suddenly she was powerless to do anything more than arch and cry out as lightning splintered through her.

"Sons of thunder." She sank weakly beneath him, and he chuckled. Prowling higher, he planted nipping kisses from her navel to her ear.

"Liked that, eh? Then just consider it a sample—a very small sample, mind you—of what this younger man can do for you."

She shivered, as much from his silky promise as from the tiny jolts of sensation now shooting from her earlobe to her spine. "Wes, please," she moaned, shaking with her need. "Have mercy on me. I want you so much, I can't fight you."

He hesitated, and for a moment, she wished she'd still been too winded to speak sense.

"Rorie." He balanced himself on his arms, separating their steaming lengths, but not enough to keep his heat from lapping over her. "If you want me to stop, I will, but . . ." He smiled, an odd combination of wistfulness and raw desire. "Don't deny yourself pleasure just because some shriveled, dried-up old wasp in town is jealous of you. We're free, Rorie. Both of us. Who's it going to hurt?"

She swallowed hard at his reasoning. She'd always resented the way Jarrod could sin with whomever he pleased, while she was painted scarlet simply for thinking of the marriage act.

But her husband had divorced her. She couldn't become pregnant. Ethan had ridden off on his cattle drive, postponing the proposal he might never make now that he knew she was barren. Wes was right. She was painfully, *achingly* free.

"I . . ." She bit her lip. "I just want . . ." Tears welled up so thick and fast in her throat, she couldn't loose another word. There'd already been one casualty, although she couldn't bear to let him know it. She had fallen so hopelessly in love with him, that her heart broke every time she imagined him riding away, looking for a wife who could give him the redheaded children he wanted.

"What do you want, Rorie? Tell me. I'll do whatever you say."

"Oh Wes." A sob bubbled up past the knot in her throat. "I want you. Is—is that wrong?"

His expression grew so tender, so sweet with compassion, that she couldn't blink away the tears that slipped past her lashes.

"No, Rorie," he murmured. "Not between us. It will never, ever be wrong between us."

Easing his body down beside hers, he cradled her in his arms, kissing her cheeks, her eyes, her lips. She clung to him, needing his solace, wanting to believe that her love for him would make their union blessed, not profane.

"I would never hurt you, Rorie. Never on purpose," he added, catching her face in his hands and brushing away the last traces of her tears. "I want you to believe that. Do you?"

She blinked. There was something so vulnerable, so needy and urgent, pleading to her from the depths of his gaze, that she nodded yes without a second thought. His breath released in a rush.

"Good. Please try to remember that tomorrow, okay?"

She opened her mouth, but he gave her no chance to respond, much less to question what he'd meant, as his lips stole over hers. Sighing, she deepened the kiss, no longer reluctant to feed the primal hunger he'd restrained so fiercely to pleasure her.

She ran her hands over his back, kneading the taut, thick muscles and delighting in the small, tight curve of his buttocks. He made a throaty sound of pleasure when she gripped him harder, pulling him closer, wedging the hot, sleek proof of his passion between her thighs. When she slipped a hand down his body, she felt his smile against her lips. He wouldn't bear her petting for long, though, and pressed her shoulders down.

"Next time," he promised in a hoarse whisper. "Right now, I'm so crazy hot for you, woman, I might embarrass myself."

He gave her a thoroughly indecent grin, and she grinned back. She couldn't help herself, especially when she heard his breaths go harsh and shallow as she guided him unerringly to his mark. He needed little assistance. Gliding fast and deep, he sheathed himself completely inside her before he shuddered, tensing into rigid stillness.

"Oh God, Rorie, you're so tight."

She froze, afraid to move. Her husband had complained about many things regarding her body, but never of . . . of *discomfort*. Then again, Jarrod had been smaller in every conceivable proportion compared to Wes. Maybe she and her Olympian young man weren't quite as well-matched as he had first thought. Her spirits sank.

"Am I . . . hurting you?" she asked.

"*Hurting* me?" Dragging a whistling breath into his lungs, he threw back his head and laughed. The sensation of his mirth rolling through her was the most delightful intimacy she'd ever known.

"No, lover," he said, "you feel like velvet heaven. I was worried I might be hurting you. I, er, gather it's been a while since you've had a corruptible young man?"

She flushed from head to toe. Still, there was so much warmth glowing in those dancing, loving eyes that she could only nod.

"Give me your hand then."

Uncertainly, she obeyed, and he kissed it, twining his fingers through hers.

"Now make love to me," he whispered.

Holding her hand as if they were sweethearts, he moved inside her, slowly at first, watching every nuance of expression on her face. The great care he took to please her touched her almost as deeply as the light that poured from his eyes into the very heart of her soul. He murmured tender words to her, calling her every endearment he must have known. Bearing the soft, shy core of his own secret self, he confessed in a raspy whisper, "I've never been with a lady before. I just want to love you right, honey, so you'll always come back for more."

But soon even he grew too winded to speak. His heart beat with a musical frenzy that matched the dizzy drumming of her own. A glittering white heat spiraled through her, coiling tighter and faster inside her female essence. Time and place and questions of the mind spun far away, leaving only an age-old knowledge and the faith of a loving heart. It was as if they were meant to be, always had been meant to be, and heaven and earth and all the stars were there to help them know it.

Suddenly, she felt the hard, fierce grip of her lover's hand, the hot, swift throb of life. Then came an explosion of meteoric force, catapulting her into space, leaving her to streak and smoke across the ebony night to the sunbright source of all creation.

At last she collapsed beneath him, kissing him,

holding him, communicating all the wonder of their journey with a touch. She knew a feeling unlike any she had known before. It went beyond the realm of satisfaction. For the first time in all her thirty years, Rorie felt complete.

Chapter Fourteen

*H*e never should have done it.

That's what Wes told himself as he watched the sun's first rays creep past the chinks in the wall and streak Rorie's hair a tawny shade of gold.

He never should have made love to her. Especially the second time.

The first time had been almost forgivable, considering how she'd broken his heart into pieces with her tears. He'd always been as worthless a a four-card flush when a female started bawling.

It just wasn't fair that a woman who loved children as much as Rorie did couldn't bring a few little ones of her own into the world. As mothers went, she had to be the best he'd ever seen. And as fathers went . . .

Well, even a blind man could see her orphans were a sight better off without Jarrod Sinclair.

Wes scowled at the thought of Rorie's ex-husband, a man he'd never met but downright loathed. In fact, Wes wasn't sure who he despised more: Jarrod Sinclair or Bill Malone.

Shifting carefully, he gazed down at the woman lying so trustingly in his arms. An unbidden warmth—a soft, sweet swell of caring—surged through him. That's when he knew he was staring down the barrel of a real dilemma. What ever had happened to his motto, "No ladies, no complications"? What ever had happened to his brain?

As best as he could figure, it had gone stone-cold dead about one o'clock that morning. That was when Rorie had sheathed him inside a scabbard of silk. She'd been as slick and tight as a virgin, minus the awkward barrier. The fact that she'd proved herself an agile and versatile lover, once she overcame her initial reluctance, didn't surprise him in the least. He'd always suspected that girl had a fire banked inside her.

What did surprise him, though, was the power of their lovemaking. To describe it as earth moving didn't do it justice. There'd been something soulful, something downright spiritual, in fact, about gazing into her luminous eyes and feeling his heart float away. Ordinarily he didn't get so fanciful about coupling. His need for physical release was as necessary—and just as cyclical—as his need for food. Fortunately over the years, he'd learned to live with his hunger, since a Ranger's life didn't lend itself to regular female company, and he'd become resigned to feeling lucky if he found a woman once a week to bed.

Maybe that was why he'd been happier than a pup with two tails after making love to Rorie. When she didn't flee back to the house in shame, he'd started jabbering like a magpie. Lord, the things that had come out of his mouth. He'd told her about Zack and Aunt Lally, even a little about Fancy and Cord, and about the pranks he'd played back in the good-old days, before he had to leave the ranch forever. She'd listened so patiently, stroking his hair and smiling, that he'd blurted out what surely must have been another of his sins.

"You know the first time I wanted you, Rorie? It was Monday afternoon when I rode into the drive, and I saw you standing there so brave and fierce and hopelessly outgunned with that old unloaded six-shooter."

"That six-shooter was too loaded!"

He laughed at her indignation and pulled her closer as she tried to wriggle away. "Mercy me, it's a good thing you didn't shoot your foot off."

She gave up her struggles and glared at him in mock ire. "So you've been plotting the demise of my virtue all week, then?"

"Well now, there's a loaded question." He nibbled on her earlobe. "Lucky for you I'm not the kind to carry tales when I get fresh claw marks on my back."

"Wes!"

She heated like a furnace in his arms, and he chuckled at her rush of embarrassment, loving the paradox of the reserved schoolmarm by day, and the mewling wildcat by night.

"So tell me, darlin'. When's the first time you wanted to make love to me?"

"Wescott Rawlins, you are insufferable!"

She squealed when he snaked his tongue into her ear.

"Kind of makes you sticky warm all over, doesn't it?"

Her laughter was a husky, thoroughly female sound. It licked over him like tongues of fire and stirred more than just his pecker. Its joyful, carefree nature stirred his heart.

"Oh, very well," she said. "If you must know, the first time I wanted you was . . ."

"Well?"

She shoved his shoulder. "I'm thinking!"

"Hell, woman, you've only known me for a week. How much time do you need?"

"Your language, sir!"

He felt laughter ripple through her before she coughed delicately, as if to hide her mirth.

"Now, let's see. Where was I? Oh, yes. I suppose the first time I wanted you was when you were wrapping your arms around me, showing me how to shoot that impossible whiskey bottle."

"You mean it took a whole day?" His show of disappointment wasn't entirely pretense. "You didn't want me the first time you saw me?"

She stroked his chest soothingly, as if smoothing ruffled feathers. "Technically, I do believe the time between Monday afternoon and Tuesday morning can't be considered a full day."

"Damnation." He pressed her down, sinking into her tantalizingly lush breasts and concave belly. "That does it, woman. You're in a heap of trouble. Say your prayers, 'cause in about fifteen minutes, you'll be on your way to heaven."

"Fifteen minutes?" She took his flagging manhood in her hand and began coaxing it to full mast. "Why wait so long, lover?"

Wes grinned unabashedly at the memory. Then the magnitude of his blunder sank in, and he winced, stifling a groan. God, he was a jackass. It had been bad enough making love to a woman of principle—a woman of expectations—just one time. He'd gone and done it twice, and under false pretenses, yet! He worshipped the ground Rorie walked on, and he adored her orphans, too, but he wasn't ready to give up his badge. Not now. Not even for them.

Rorie, Rorie, I'm so sorry. I swear I'm not like Bill Malone. . . .

She started to stir, as if she'd heard him. A feeling of impending doom squeezed his throat. His mouth grew so dry, he tasted ashes. How had making a simple confession become so complicated? So painful?

She smiled shyly at him. Dawn had turned the ivory of her cheeks to pale amber, echoing the deeper, richer hues of sunlight in her eyes. Just to be touched by the warmth of her gaze made him ache with longing in ways that transcended physical desire. He'd seen Fancy look at Cord that way, and not long ago, he'd thought he would have given his life to see Fancy look at him that way too.

His feelings for Fancy were one of the main reasons Wes had left his family behind. Oddly enough, though, those feelings paled compared to the turmoil he felt when he thought of leaving Rorie.

"How long have you been awake?" she asked in a voice molasses-thick with sleepiness.

"Not long." He winced inwardly. That had been another lie. He was getting too damned good at them.

An awkward silence settled between them. He could

feel the nervous flutter of her heart. A flush tinged her breasts a primrose pink beneath his gaze. Whether she wanted to be or not, she was too damned tempting lying there against him, her leg twined carelessly with his and her nipples innocently brushing his arm with every breath she took. He could feel their tenderness begin to harden, even as his pecker did. He had to clench a fist to keep from petting her, tasting her, making love to her in ways that might shock her ladylike sensibilities and yet were guaranteed to take her to the pinnacle of paradise.

She stirred uneasily, dropping her gaze from his. "Shae will be hitching the wagon for, um . . ." her voice stumbled over the words, "church soon, so maybe I should get dressed."

He heard the unspoken question "Do you still want me?" in her words, and he half smiled at the bittersweet irony. Another ripple of desire swept through him, drawing him as taut as a bow, but he dared not act on it. Not when his lies still lay between them, and the clock was ticking off the minutes until someone else told her the truth. He knew his confession would put a wedge between them, but he was just optimistic enough to hope it would forge a bridge to bring them back together again.

"Stay awhile," he murmured, at last working the words past the lump in his throat. "We . . . didn't get to learn about each other quite the way I would have liked last night."

Her color heightened in the most endearing way—it was so easy to make her blush.

"Wescott Rawlins, you are incorrigible."

"Would you have me any other way?"

Glib words had always rolled easily off his tongue. He found them coming to his rescue now, steering him clear of the painful task that lay before him.

She laughed, rising on an elbow and shaking her head. A stream of hair spilled across his chest and shoulder, like honeyed shafts of daylight.

"God made you to torment me, I fear."

He fidgeted at her playful tone. As much as he would

have liked to deny it, she was in for a bout of hurting because of him.

"I prefer to think God made me to . . . protect you," he finished carefully. No longer able to resist the tiniest indulgence, he touched a gleaming strand of her hair. He closed his eyes for a moment, marveling at its silken texture between his thumb and forefinger, savoring its elusive perfume of spring and woodsy wildflowers. Releasing a long, steadying breath, he dared open his eyes once more. She was watching him with a mixture of shy pleasure and concern.

"Wes, I thought we had settled that last night. You were going to stop crossing the Dukkers so I could stop worrying about you being ambushed. Like Gator was."

He frowned. "No, we did not settle that last night. Sometimes a man has to—"

"—do what a man has to do," she chimed in. "Yes, I know. I've heard that before. Every widow in this country has heard that before."

"You're not a widow," he pointed out.

"Nor do I wish to be."

He flinched. Damn, there were those ladylike expectations he'd been worrying about.

"Rorie, you're not . . . I mean, you don't want . . ." *Hellfire.* All he had to do now was blurt out the rest: *You don't want me, sugar. I'm a Ranger, and I'll always be under the gun.*

But he couldn't say it. Not that way.

She was gazing at him expectantly, not to mention a tad coolly, and his heart kicked hard against his ribs. This was only a preview of her upset, and already he didn't like it.

Sitting up beside her, he combed rough fingers through his hair.

"Rorie, honey, look. You and I, we never did start off on the right foot. I mean, that first day when I rode in here, and you were waving that equalizer at me—well, those weren't the best get-acquainted circumstances, you have to admit. We never got to sit down, you know, just like regular folk and talk.

"Then things got kind of muddled," he rushed on, "downright tangled, in fact, and they just kept getting worse, so that every time I tried to do what I should have done in the first place, there was always something getting in the way." He glanced toward her uneasily, saw her perplexed frown, and gulped a bolstering breath. "What I'm trying to say is, Rorie, I, uh, have to let you know that I'm a—"

A loud thump came from the wall of the barn, then the scraping of wood on wood was joined by tuneless whistling. Rorie grew white and scarlet by turns.

"Shae!" she squealed. "Oh my God, he's got the ladder. He'll see us naked!"

Wes had to clamp a hand over her mouth to keep whatever other panicked exclamation she might squeak from floating outside through the hole in the rafters. Damn Shae. That boy had worse timing than a jilted beau bursting in on the bridal "I do's."

"Simmer down," Wes hissed, "and put your clothes on. I'll get Shae out of the way so you can hotfoot it back to the house."

Wes stabbed his legs into his jeans, grabbed his razor, threw his shirt over his shoulder, and hastily let himself out the barn door. His mind was already whirring in high gear, spinning another string of yarns, this time to protect Rorie and her honor. He wondered fleetingly if she'd appreciate the irony once he spilled the beans on his greater fib—the one that was bound to hurt her.

Grinding his teeth, he slowed his pace to a casual one as he rounded the corner and found Shae positioning the ladder.

With any luck his big lie would be out within the hour. It would have to be, Wes thought grimly, if he wanted at least even odds of parting from Rorie as friends.

Meanwhile, dressing frantically in the barn, Rorie was too mortified imagining Shae, whom she regarded as a son, catching her naked with a lover, to spare much thought for Wes's uncharacteristically awkward speech. She could hear his voice, glib and cocksure again, calling to Shae from the other side of the wall.

"Did the devil light a fire under you, son, to get you working on the Sabbath?"

She heard the creaking of wood, as if a boot had stepped down on a ladder rung, and she nearly bit her tongue in two to keep from shouting, "Go away, Shae!"

"I had to get up to fetch the wagon," Shae said. "Then I figured I might as well throw this tarpaulin back over the hole in the roof. Looks like the wind blew it off last night."

"Hell, that's what you woke me up for?" Wes snorted, and Rorie could almost see the amusement on his face. "There's not a sign of rain in those clouds, son. But if you're so jo-fired to get a job done, why don't you come down to the springhouse with me. That damned pipe's got so rusted it took a hammer to knock it loose last night. The womenfolk will have our heads if they can't take their shower baths before church."

Shae expressed surprise and a bit of irritation about the pump, which had been working just fine the day before, as Rorie knew well. Then the ladder rung creaked again, and their voices began to fade.

Holding her breath, Rorie cracked open the door, careful not to let its creaking hinges betray her. She spied Wes's bare chest in a burnt-orange blaze of morning as he strolled beside Shae's darker frame. They seemed to be chatting amicably as they headed for the springhouse.

Darting a nervous glance around the yard for spying children, she gulped a prayer, hiked her skirts, and bolted for her bedroom.

A quarter hour later, her hands still trembling from her close call, Rorie was dressing for church. She dreaded the hypocrisy of attending the service, yet she was certain that a change in plans would clue the world at large to her sin. Only a blind man or a total innocent would fail to recognize the evidence on her face: the starry light in her eyes, the glowing pink on her cheeks, the dreamy smile that kept curving her lips.

Every time she glanced in the mirror, she didn't know whether to giggle or groan. Never mind that she was a spindly crane with too-large bones, or a middle-aged goose without a lick of common sense, she felt beautiful. She felt changed somehow, too, although she couldn't quite put her finger on why.

All she knew was that if she didn't stop floating and start walking soon, her secret affair wouldn't be so secret anymore. She might be able to brave the scandal for her own fleeting chance at happiness, but she couldn't bear for it to hurt her children.

With a step she hoped was much less buoyant and an air she prayed was serene, she descended the stairs to practice nonchalance on her family. She proved to be a miserable failure during her first test. Rounding the corner, she collided with Shae on the landing. Their impact nearly tumbled them both down the stairs, and she giggled nervously—no doubt the first giveaway to her sin.

"Oh, Shae, do forgive me. I didn't hear you coming."

Steadying her with a wiry arm, he stepped back a respectful space. "Are you all right, ma'am?"

"Yes, yes, of course." She tried to wave his concern away, but he was looking her up and down for damage. She turned three shades of crimson, wondering if any of the love nips Wes had given her were visible above the high neck of her gown.

"I didn't expect you up so early after last night's fireworks, ma'am. Did you sleep well, then?"

She pressed her hand to her flaming face—another giveaway. "Fireworks? What do you mean?"

His keen gaze held hers. "Dukker's hurrah."

"Oh, yes. That." She looked away and gulped down air, silently berating herself for her idiocy. "Yes. Very well, considering," she added, wishing she didn't sound quite so flustered and hoping he would attribute her discomfort to their collision.

"Have you . . . talked with Rawlins since last night?"

"Talked with him?" She made the mistake of glancing upward at his gentle tone, and another burst of heat spread to the roots of her hair. "Why no. I've only just risen."

She'd never been good at lying, and she suspected the game was up completely, since Shae's look of concern softened to sympathy.

"Well, I guess there's still plenty of time for talk before church."

She nodded for no reason other than to placate him and flee. In reality, she wasn't certain church was still a good idea. After all, if she couldn't face Shae, how on earth could she face Preacher Jenkins?

Deciding a solitary spell of reflection was in order, she grabbed the egg basket from the kitchen and mumbled something to Ginevee about checking the hens. She'd no sooner started across the yard than Topher appeared, riding a broomstick nag around the corner of the chicken coop.

"I'll get you, you varmit," he shouted, threatening nothing in particular and aiming the cedar gun Wes had whittled for him. "Bang, bang!"

She cringed to think he might be hunting men instead of rodents, especially after the worshipful way he had chattered on the night before about Wes's markmanship.

The boy's face lit up when he saw her. "Morning, ma'am," he called, pulling the brim of his straw hat low over his eyes and spurring his pony to intercept her.

"A lady like you had best be careful walking all by her lonesome," he said solemnly, holstering his gun as he reined in. "That mangy cur Jesse James and his gang were sighted hereabouts. I've been sworn to bring them in. See?" he added eagerly. Flipping around his overall's twisted shoulder strap, he produced a battered badge.

Rorie started to smile, thinking Ginevee had gotten awfully good at cutting stars from the bottom of tin cans. Then Topher announced proudly, "I found it, ma'am. It's a real honest-to-goodness Ranger badge!"

The smile froze on Rorie's lips as his words registered on her preoccupied brain. Setting her basket on the ground, she knelt before the boy.

"Let me see that, Topher."

Beaming, he puffed out his chest as she reached gingerly for his strap. The weight of the star and the style of the insignia were genuine, all right. She'd met a half-dozen swaggering, loud-mouthed, lascivious lawmen wearing similar badges when they dropped in to "howdy" Gator.

Puzzled, she gazed up into the boy's excited blue eyes. "Topher, where did you find this?"

"Under a couple of dirty old boots Shae had thrown under his bed." He grinned, crowding his freckles together. "I reckon one of Sheriff Gator's Rangers friends must have lost it there."

Rorie's brows knitted in a frown. Topher's hypothesis was impossible. For as long as she'd been a guest in Gator's home, he'd never allowed a man, unmarried or otherwise, to bunk on the second story where she slept. Other than Shae, in fact, the only man she could recall bedding down in the room next to hers was . . . Wes.

A chilling sense of discovery crackled down her spine.

Wes couldn't be a Ranger. If he were, he would have told her, surely, when they'd first met. Besides, what possible reason could he have for keeping such a secret?

A niggling doubt pierced the armor of her denials.

She recalled uneasily how he'd ridden down the drive, carrying more firing power than the average cowboy. She remembered, too, his discomfort when she'd jested about his "lawman" talk. But most of all, she remembered the scar on his chest, the one that looked like half of a star.

"Am I in trouble?" Topher asked suspiciously.

She realized she was frowning at the child as if she meant to grab him by his ear.

"No, sweetheart." Her voice, coming from somewhere near her toes, croaked when it finally struggled past her lips.

"Then how come you look like you've been sucking on persimmons?"

Dear Topher. He'd always been able to read her much better than any book. He shared that ability with Wes.

Her stomach knotted at the thought, and she battled for control over her burgeoning dread.

"Topher, may I have the badge?"

His chin jutted, and he backed warily from her hands.

"You know the rules," she said as gently as her constricting throat would allow. "When we find something that doesn't belong to us, we try to find the owner before claiming it as our own."

"But those Ranger friends of Sheriff Gator are long gone!"

"You're probably right." *Lord, please let the child be right.* "But just in case, we owe it to Sheriff Gator's friend to ask questions, since he was our guest. If you had left your marbles at Nardo's house, wouldn't you want somebody to return them?"

"Oh, all right," he grumbled. "Here." He thrust the badge into her hand. "But I get first dibs if you don't find no Ranger."

She was too grateful for an end to the argument to bother correcting his grammar. "Thank you, Topher. Do you know where Wes is?"

"In the shower bath," he answered sullenly.

Her hand closed over the battered tin, and she couldn't quite repress her tremor.

"Would you mind checking on the hens for me, Topher? Then you'll want to put on your Sunday clothes for church."

He made a face. "I bet Rangers don't have to go to church," he muttered, snatching up the basket and stalking toward the chicken coop.

Rorie swallowed hard. She had no reason to believe the boy was wrong, and the implication of his words made her heart sick. Rangers didn't much care about morality or salvation. They lived by the gun. They did whatever pleased them.

Dear God, please don't let my Topher become a Ranger.

She fought off a hot quick stab of panic. Topher worshipped Wes. All the children did. What if he'd been using them? What if his friendship had simply been the means to an end—a tumble with her in the hay?

No! I won't believe that of him. I won't believe he's another Bill Malone.

Shaking, she started to walk, blindly at first. She

realized her feet weren't carrying her to the springhouse though, they were carrying her to the barn. *To the scene of his crime.*

She pushed that thought back in frantic desperation. Innocent until proven guilty, that's what the courts said. She had no right to condemn him. By some miracle, the badge might not even be his.

That's what she was praying when she found herself kneeling before his saddle bags, the voices of fear and reason shouting in her head.

"What, would you rob him of his privacy?" Fear taunted.

"If he's been lying all this time, he'll only lie again when I confront him with the badge," Reason said.

"What does that matter? You let Jarrod deceive you for years. You didn't want to know the truth then, and you don't want to know it now."

"No!" she sobbed. "I can't live that way anymore."

Pressing a hand to her mouth, she dammed the flood of tears. This time, it wasn't a matter of wanting to know. This time, it was a matter of having to, for the children.

"Wes, forgive me for prying," she whispered hoarsely, pulling the bags onto her lap and pushing back the flaps. Inside, she found everything he must own in the world: two changes of shirts, a slicker, a compass, a match safe, rope, first-aid supplies, and two letters written in a flowery, female hand. The first letter, well-worn and faded from handling, was dated December 2nd and was signed by Fancy.

> *Wes, we miss you. All of us miss you. Please come home for Christmas. Don't let this grudge between you and Cord go on through the new year . . .*

The second letter was even more plaintive than the first. Fancy had dated it six weeks earlier, April 10.

> *I pray this letter finds you. I pray you're still alive. An occasional message would help ease all our minds. . . .*

Cord heard from Captain McQuade that you were shot and almost died near Brownsville. My God, Wes, why didn't you send us a wire? Cord and Zack would have come for you. You didn't have to be alone. . . .

You're family and we love you. Please don't go on this way. All this bitterness, all this anger, it's not worth the pain. It's never too late to make amends, Wes. Please come home. . . .

Rorie blinked back tears, tears that she wasn't sure were for her, for Wes, or for Fancy. The woman clearly had deep feelings for Wes. Just as clearly, those feelings were torn between him and her husband. How sad that Wes called himself an orphan when he had more loving blood-relations than Rorie, Shae, or any of her orphans combined.

Folding the pages with trembling fingers, she slipped them carefully back into a pocket of his duster. Her doubts were eased, but not entirely relieved. She hadn't found a pair of handcuffs or the so-called black book, which Gator said Rangers read more often than the Bible, because it contained their list of fugitives.

"Why look further?" Fear whispered to her heart. "You found nothing to implicate him."

"Nothing except a letter referencing a Captain McQuade," Reason reminded her grimly.

Wes was clearly no army regular. The only other kind of captains she could think of in Texas were the kinds that commanded the loose military divisions known as Rangers.

She fought back another attack of dread. He could have hidden the manacles.

She remembered him the night before, shoving something beneath the straw when she'd surprised him at the door. A knife twisted in her chest. With numbing fingers, she forced herself to push the bags aside, to drop to her hands and search the stall floor where they'd made love two tender, blissful times.

It didn't take long to uncover the dingy white corner

of newspaper. When she shook the *Enquirer* free of stra
and spread its rumpled pages before her, it didn't tak
long to learn the full extent of his duplicity.

She crumpled the paper between her fists.

The bastard.

Chapter Fifteen

Standing beneath the shower bath sluice in the three-walled compartment Shae had rigged for privacy, Wes nearly jumped ten feet when he heard the springhouse door slam. Tossing the sodden hair from his eyes, he turned to find Rorie approaching him. A grin tugged at his lips. He thought about asking her to join him, until he noticed her pinched face and heaving chest. Hastily he turned off the rushing stream of water.

"Rorie, what is it? What's wrong? Has Dukker come—"

His words choked off when she halted, tossing his badge on his pile of discarded clothes.

"A Ranger, I hear," she said acidly, "isn't fully dressed without his star."

West felt his heart stall. Then it lurched painfully back to life. "Rorie—"

"No doubt it was just an oversight," she continued in that same acerbic tone, "your forgetting to pin it on every day since Monday."

The wall of the stall only came up to his waist. He gripped it hard for support. "I can explain—"

"There's no need."

Producing the *Enquirer* in the fist she'd held behind her back, she tossed it contemptuously on top of the star.

"You went through my bags?" he asked weakly, stalling for enough time to gather his wits for a defense.

"Yes, as a matter of fact I did, feeling guilty every moment of the shameful chore. Ironic, isn't it? There I was, trying to deny all the evidence, trying to believe every lie you'd ever told me. I was worried my behavior might seem like a betrayal, even though you'd as much as admitted you've been plotting to bed me from the moment we first met."

Wes flinched at her words. Things were bad—worse than he'd originally thought—if she was using profanities.

"Rorie, those things Faraday printed aren't true—"

"So you claim to know the difference? Isn't the development of a conscience rather convenient right now?"

His earlier sense of doom returned to squeeze his throat, making his breath wheeze. He didn't know where she'd found the star or how she'd put two and two together. He didn't know what he could say or do to make her understand him. All he knew was he had to try. The ice in her voice and the venom in her eyes were slowly killing him.

"Rorie, listen to me. There were extenuating circumstances. I couldn't tell you who I was right at first because I had to go undercover to investigate Gator's murder. And I never had any intention of driving you off your land without an inquiry. In fact, I'm working now to get a court order to keep Dukker from harassing you until this land dispute can be settled by a judge."

She looked dubious, so he added defensively, "Shae understands why I had to go undercover."

He could see by the shock on her face that she'd thought she was the first one to discover him. He groaned inwardly at his blunder.

"And do undercover Rangers make a habit of seducing their murder suspects?" she bit out, the higher pitch of her voice betraying the first hint of white-hot fury that seethed under her glacial calm. "Or do Rangers limit their rutting to schoolgirls and spinsters more trusting than babes?"

He stiffened. Her accusation cut him like a lash. "I

know what you're thinking. But I'm not like Bill Malone."

"Forgive me if I don't take you at your word."

"Dammit Rorie, I made love to you last night! What we did wasn't screwing. It wasn't anything *like* screwing," he added, his tone made harsh by his own hurt.

She swallowed convulsively. The sheen of tears darkened her eyes. For the first time since she'd stormed across the threshold, her wintry facade cracked, exposing the raw torment underneath.

"Yes, well . . ." Her chin quivered as she hiked it. "I hear you young people have a dozen or more colorful ways of describing how you mate with wanton women. You mentioned last night you'd never had a lady before. I'm afraid you'll have to search a little further. Apparently, you haven't had one yet."

"Rorie, don't."

Her smile was grim, lifeless, as barren as a snow-swept prairie. "Pray don't trouble yourself to feel sorry for me. I've been used before, and I've survived.

"Now, unless you have some other undercover"— her lip curled faintly at the term—"work to do for your investigation, I suggest you quit stalling and track down Gator's killer. I want you dressed and off this farm in fifteen minutes."

He muttered an oath as she turned on her heel. Grabbing his shirt, he tied it around his naked hips and bolted after her. He managed to intercept her, slamming the door closed before she could leave him choking on her trail of dust.

"Hold on a damned minute," he growled. "If Dukker really is the killer, you're in danger up to your eyeballs, and I'm not leaving you unprotected."

Standing her ground, she arched a haughty brow. "I should think it not very glamorous to play sentry to a household of orphans when the lure of a manhunt lies before you."

He winced. "You don't think very much of me, do you?"

Her smile was brittle. "Do us both a favor, Ranger.

Find the evidence needed to hang Dukker, and leave me and my family in peace."

"And in the meantime? Shae's got Creed gunning for him, so you can't count on him for your protection. The fact of the matter is, he's the one attracting all this trouble to your door."

"That may be true, but I trust Shae, and I know he has the good of the children at heart."

"Rorie." He made a concerted effort to gentle his voice. "Shae's in as much danger as you are, as you well know."

"Then . . . I'll go to Ethan, and I'll ask *him* for protection."

Her solution, which he secretly had to admit was a good one, ripped like a bullet through his heart. "That won't do you much good, either. The last I heard, your suitor was still on his cattle drive."

Her head shot up, and he could see teardrops clinging to her lashes.

"Then I'll find someone! Someone I can trust!" Her voice broke, and she clenched her fists. "Damn you. Did you ever once stop to think what you were doing, with your bedtime stories and your toys? Did you ever once consider what it might do to those children to watch 'Uncle Wes' ride away from here for good?"

"Rorie, I never meant to hurt you or the children," he said anxiously, reaching for her arm. "I never meant—"

"Don't touch me," she cried, recoiling as if she'd been burned. "Don't you ever touch me again!"

Spinning away, she wrenched open the door and ran outside. He glimpsed Merrilee, feeding an apple to Two-Step, and Topher, gingerly carrying a basket of eggs, before Rorie's next words ripped a piece from his soul.

"Merrilee, Topher, inside! Quickly, children."

Merrilee glanced toward the springhouse door. "Is Uncle Wes coming to church with us?"

"No. Uncle Wes is going away."

"Away?" Topher, too, glanced at the springhouse as Rorie caught his hand and led him toward the house. "But why? Where's he going? He's coming back, isn't he?"

"Those are enough questions for now, children," she said roughly.

The door slammed closed behind them with a resounding bang.

"Dammit, Rorie!" An avalanche of heartache thundered through Wes, and it was all he could do not to let it drag him to his knees.

He rammed a fist into the wall, but even that didn't make him feel any less battered by the pounding force inside him, a force so consuming and powerful he was afraid to give it a name.

"I had a job to do," he muttered, plunging his fingers through his hair. "I'm a Ranger, and I did what I had to do the only way I knew how to do it."

You're a miserable sonuvabitch, his conscience retorted.

He groaned, digging his fingers into his scalp. He had to get a grip on himself. He had to make Rorie listen to reason, if not for her sake, then for the children's. No one was going to listen to a word he said, though, if he stormed across the yard buck naked. He needed time to cool off, time to see his way clear to a solution. He didn't give a damn whether she liked it or not, he wasn't leaving her without protection.

And he sure as hell wasn't leaving her with the impression she'd been used as crudely as a whore!

Stumbling back to his jeans, he dressed himself as unhurriedly as his agitation would allow. Since his gut was still roiling with self-loathing, he decided he would pack his bags and saddle Two-Step next. If worse came to worse, he'd just hog-tie Rorie, put her in the wagon bed, and drive her and the children to a neighbor's—even if it had to be Ethan's.

The time he took concocting this outrageous plan helped him feel more in control of the chaos he'd created around him. He set his hat on his head, gritted his teeth, and stalked up the porch steps to pound a fist on the door. It was thrown open immediately by Shae, who barred his entrance.

"Out of my way, son. I've got business with Miss Rorie."

Shae braced himself as Wes tried to barrel past him.

"Hold on a minute, Rawlins. You aren't in any shape to be talking, and she's in no shape to be listening."

They grappled for a moment, each grabbing a fistful of the other's shirt, but Shae wouldn't back down, and Wes knew he'd have to beat the boy senseless if he wanted to force his way inside. Reason screamed loudly enough above the clamor of his fury to remind him of the consequences the last time he'd brawled with a man whom he cared out, over a woman he held dear. He released Shae and stepped back, cursing.

Shae nodded, relief stealing across his features. "That's better. Smart too. You might have done a foolish thing, but you're not anybody's fool." His smile was dry. "I was wondering why you were so insistent on getting me down to the springhouse. Then I saw her running across the yard."

"Jesus." Wes couldn't look Shae in the eye.

"She doesn't know I know," he said quietly.

Wes's face burned. "So why didn't you get your shotgun and—"

"Because she never would have forgiven me. Besides, I got a good look at her right after it happened. In the two years I've known her, I've never seen her so happy. It's a shame she found out about you the way she did, but it looks like she's got some mighty strong feelings for you. So if I were you, I'd give her time to remember them."

She had some mighty strong feelings for him, all right, Wes thought. Swallowing the lump in his throat, he stared at the wrinkles he'd made in Shae's linen Sunday shirt. "I need to make her understand that . . . I'm not like Bill Malone."

"Well, there'll be plenty of time for that, after she calms down. In the meantime, I just don't see any way around it. You're going to have to ride out of here."

Wes's head shot up. "The hell I do. Even if you could be alert every minute of the day, a time will come when you have to leave the farm, and Creed and his rough-riders will be waiting for you."

Shae met his gaze steadily. "I've already thought of that. There are a couple fellows I know, friends of mine around the county, who are tired of watching the Dukkers push their daddies around. I think Tom Parker and Jasper Wilson will be only too happy to bring their guns and lend a hand around the farm."

"Whoa. Slow down, son. Bringing in a couple of colored boys with guns is just the excuse Dukker needs to wage a full-scale race war."

Shae's eyebrows rose. "Who said they were colored boys?"

Wes grew even warmer under the boy's challenging stare. He decided to change the subject. "So Dukker's been causing trouble all over?"

"Let's just say he and his so-called deputies tend to take long rides out of town. Folks have learned to mind their own business. If they don't see anything, they can't talk; and if they don't talk, none of their women or children gets hurt.

"You may be the law around here until folks elect a county sheriff," Shae continued, "but that badge of yours isn't likely to loosen any tongues. Dukker's got folks too scared to trust the law. You're going to have your work cut out for you, when you go door to door recruiting witnesses. The way I see it, you're going to have to catch Dukker in the act."

"In the act of what?"

"Selling moonshine to the Injuns."

Wes's jaw began to twitch. So that's why the bastard had killed Gator. Gator apparently had found out about the smuggling, but since Dukker was his kin, Gator had probably just given the man a warning. Wes was willing to bet it was the last mistake Gator made.

"I'll do whatever I can to help you, of course," Shae added.

Wes gave the boy a narrowed, appraising stare. It wasn't any secret that Shae had an ax to grind with his cousins. Wes didn't think much of the Dukkers, either, but he had no license to take away their freedom without evidence of a crime. He wondered how far he could trust Shae not to shade the truth.

"No offense, son, but I need you here with your

scattergun. You just concentrate on taking care of your family. I'll concentrate on the Dukkers."

Shae's lips twisted. "Fair enough. I reckon this means we'll be seeing a lot of you around the county, then. If I were you, I wouldn't show my face back here for another week, though. Miss Aurora will need at least that much time to think things through."

"A week? Dammit, Shae, I can't leave here now the way things are between us!"

"And I'm telling you, you'll have to. If you go in there right now, you'll be making a bigger mistake than you made last night."

Wes stiffened. Shae had known Rorie longer than he had, so it stood to reason the boy would know better than he how she would react. Still, the thought of letting her believe the worst—that he'd used her and had no intention of coming back—didn't set right with him.

But you have no intention of coming back, his conscience reminded him. *Or rather, you have no intention of staying. All you'll be doing is giving her false hopes, making promises you can't keep, whether you go in there now or a week from now. Are you really such a bastard as that?*

Making a strangled sound, he turned and headed for Two-Step. His pulse was pounding so hard in his ears, he didn't at first hear the anxious cries behind him.

"Uncle Wes! Uncle Wes! Wait, don't go!"

His heart sickened when he saw Topher and Merrilee struggling to push past Shae. The boy's resolve weakened, and he let them pass with Nita, who ran with them across the yard.

Topher was the first to reach his side, and he grabbed hold of Wes's hand. "Where are you going?"

The child's panicked voice and desperate grip were nearly Wes's undoing. Then Merrilee reached him, throwing her arms around his hips, and he choked.

"Children," he said gruffly, squatting to bring himself to their level. "I have to go."

"But why?" Topher asked plaintively.

Wes drew a ragged breath. Shae had followed the others with Po in his arms. Now he stood beside Nita's quaking shoulders. Wes couldn't bear to look higher than that. He heard the sniffles the girl was trying so valiantly to repress.

"Because . . ." He hung his head. "Because I did a very bad thing. I lied about who I was. I thought it was more of a secret at first, a secret I had no choice but to keep, but now I see how wrong I was. I hurt Miss Rorie when I lied. I hurt her real bad, even though I didn't mean to. That's why it's so important always to tell the truth, children."

"Are you sorry you lied, Uncle Wes?" Merrilee's great eyes raised to his in concern.

"Yes. Very sorry."

She pressed her palm to his cheek. "Then I forgive you."

"Me too," Topher said fiercely.

Wes blinked hard. Glancing up, he cleared his vision in time to see a tear roll down Nita's cheek. Even Shae looked glassy-eyed.

"Thank you, children."

"We'll talk to Miss Rorie." Nita's smile was tremulous, pleading. "Don't go, Uncle Wes. We'll tell her how sorry you are. She won't be mad anymore, and then she'll let you stay."

He shook his head, wishing to God it might be that easy. "I have to go. I have to find the man who shot Sheriff Gator."

Merrilee caught her breath. "The bad man?"

The fear in her voice was more than he could bear. Nodding, he started to rise, but Topher and Merrilee clung to his shoulders, and Nita hugged his neck. He held them to his aching breast until he heard Po's giggle and the shuffle of escaping baby feet.

"Me play! Me too!" Po's gleaming black head poked its way inside the huddle. "Pick me up, Unca Wes!"

A tear slipped past all his defenses. He wrenched free, and stumbled blindly to Two-Step, throwing himself into the saddle.

"You're coming back, aren't you, Uncle Wes?"

He gritted his teeth against a lie, a false promise, and spurred the gelding down the drive.

"Uncle Wes?" Topher's voice rose again until it cracked. "Uncle Wes, come back!"

Urging the gelding faster, he closed his eyes and ears to their cries as best he could.

But there was no defense he could raise to keep them from his heart.

Chapter Sixteen

Wes never did put the events of that Sunday morning behind him. Fourteen days passed, fifteen nights dragged by, and still he could not shake his melancholy. Loneliness had sunk into his bones, leaving him lost and empty. It was a feeling not unlike the one he'd experienced eleven months earlier, when he rode away from Cord and Fancy for the last time.

Even the prospect of a rigorous chase after Dukker beneath the boundless Texas sky couldn't spark the kind of blood-tingling excitement he'd felt before when tracking an outlaw. He felt as if he'd lost another home, another family, the third one in his lifetime.

Common sense told him he was being absurdly maudlin, that six days were hardly enough time to forge an attachment to anything, much less a woman and four children. But for a man who had always prided himself on carefree living, his daily routine had become extraordinarily dull.

He tried to fill his daylight hours with interrogating, since his nights belonged to vigils in the cornfields within rifle distance of Rorie's front door. Steering clear of Elodea for the time being, he introduced himself to the small farmers and ranchers who were struggling to eke out a livelihood within a thirty-mile radius of town.

True to Shae's prediction, though, he found county

residents suspicious of his badge and fearful of his guns. No one had seen hide nor hair of Dukkers, Injuns, Doc Warren, or stills, or so they claimed.

As for Gator Boudreau, only a handful of people knew their sheriff had been gunned down. Apparently, gossip didn't spread quickly across the rolling hills and fertile woodlands of central Bandera County.

After a fruitless week of combing the county, looking for witnesses to testify to Dukker's moonshine smuggling, Wes returned to town. He figured he would find more dirt on Dukker closer to the man's home. Dukker might have silenced the Negro and Mexican farmers with his bullying and his riflemen, but someone, somewhere was bound to have a loose tongue—especially if whiskey was flowing. Wes started spending a good deal of time at Sultan's saloon.

"Yeah, sure," one old-timer told him as he helped himself to the bottle of rotgut Wes had bought to woo informants. "Everybody knows Hannibal and that boy of his got a couple irons in the fire. But you ain't likely to catch Hannibal doing something shady. He ain't fool enough to misbehave while a Ranger's nosing around."

Another saloon patron, a fidgety greenhorn who clerked for lawyer Callahan, confided there'd been rumors of misconduct during the latest election, when Doc Warren was officiating the balloting process. "Phineas Faraday was voted in as mayor, which split town council down the middle," the clerk confided. "Three fellows wanted to take Dukker's badge; Faraday sided with the two who feared for their families. Last I heard, that motion got tabled for good."

Wes found this piece of information interesting, and he decided to pay another call on Phineas Faraday.

His luck was on a roll that Monday afternoon. He'd sooner stepped up to the porch of the *Enquirer*, when angry voices drifted out to him through the open window. Two men were arguing behind the printing press. Moving stealthily away from the glass, Wes stood beside the door and listened.

"That's another favor you owe me, you lick-finger.

Don't think I'm not counting." Dukker's guttural voice wasn't hard to recognize.

"Now you hold on one damned minute! I never asked for any favors."

"Yeah?" Wes could hear the sneer in Dukker's voice. "Well, you got them anyway, Faraday. Your life got a whole lot easier when a certain election official went away."

"Your crimes have nothing to do with me."

"Think again, ink-slinger. If I go down, you go down with me. So you'd best ride a close herd on that highfalutin' daughter of yours—"

"Why, hello, Ranger Rawlins. Did you come to see Papa?"

Wes jumped, biting back an oath as Lorelei Faraday, dressed in lemon-colored silks and lace, approached her father's doorstep with a picnic basket over one arm and a parasol over the other.

Nodding irritably to Lorelei, Wes strained to hear more of Dukker's threat, but the argument inside had ended.

"I brought lunch for Papa." She smiled brightly at him, apparently unaware of her untimely distraction. "There's enough for two, though, if you'd care to join him. Fried chicken, cornbread biscuits, fresh peach cobbler—"

Suddenly the door was wrenched open, and Hannibal Dukker stood on the threshold. Lorelei gasped, edging a step closer to Wes, and Dukker curled his lip in the vague resemblance of a smile.

"What, no lunch for me, Miss Lorelei?"

She glanced uncertainly at Wes. He was just about to come to her defense when she raised her chin and squared her shoulders.

"I should think not, sir. The very idea is enough to rob one of one's appetite. Fortunately, I already broke my fast with your cousin—Shae McFadden."

Dukker's face turned an ominous shade of red, and Wes caught Lorelei's arm, pulling her safely behind him.

"You have something on your mind, Dukker?

Because I sure would love to hear it," Wes said, his hand straying toward his holster.

Dukker's eyes glittered like an ice-covered stream. He freed Lorelei from his glare and slowly, deliberately, raised his gaze to Wes.

"Cute little filly, ain't she? Sassy and wild. Not like that nag you've been riding, eh, boy?"

Wes tensed, and Dukker sneered.

"You folks have a nice day." Dukker turned, lumbering like a bear down the sidewalk toward the saloon.

Lorelei stepped forward, allowing herself a delicate shudder. "I can't imagine that beast of a man having any blood-tie to Sheriff Boudreau, much less to Shae." She shook her head and sighed. "I really wish you could find Sheriff Boudreau's will, Mr. Rawlins. I'm sick and tired of hearing Shae—and Mrs. Sinclair too—slandered by every tongue in this town. No wonder the poor woman stayed home in her bed."

Wes had been only half-listening as he watched Dukker push inside Sultan's swinging doors. At the mention of Rorie, though, his gaze snapped back to Lorelei.

"Mrs. Sinclair's sick?"

Lorelei nodded, her dark eyes sympathetic. "I'm sure you needn't worry, though. Mrs. Sinclair usually comes to town with Shae each Monday for supplies, but Ginevee accompanied him today. Ginevee said Mrs. Sinclair had a bit of a stomach upset, that's all. If I were her, I'd have butterflies, too, at the prospect of coming to this town. How she manages to face Mrs. Milner, my mama, and the other ladies every week is a mystery to me. But I suppose when one needs supplies, one can't trouble oneself over—"

"Lorelei."

Faraday had appeared on the doorstep, mopping his brow with an ink-stained neckerchief. Wes was quick to notice the agitated throbbing at the man's temple and the jerky movements of his hand.

"There you are, child. What's this I hear about you breakfasting with Shae McFadden?"

She grew pink and edgy by turns, clearly chagrinned that her father had heard her.

"Don't be angry, Papa. I didn't really eat with Shae.
I was just trying to put Marshal Dukker in his place."

"Child, you mustn't ever cross Hannibal. And certainly not in Shae McFadden's defense," Faraday added
with a dark glance toward the marshal's office. "Come
inside now. I've been waiting all morning to see what
goodies you've packed for our picnic lunch. Unless, of
course, you've promised your afternoon to some other
beau?"

When she gave her girlish laugh, the worry in his
eyes softened.

"Oh, Papa. Wait until I tell Mama what a rogue you
are." Her lashes fluttered as she gazed up at Wes. "Good
afternoon, Mr. Rawlins."

Faraday avoided Wes's gaze as he stepped aside to let
his daughter pass.

"Faraday."

The mayor hesitated, glancing after Lorelei before he
drew himself up another inch to face Wes.

"Yes, and what can I do for you today?"

Wes let a mirthless smile curve his lips. "I think you
know damned well. You've got information I want."

"I'm sure I don't know—"

"I was born in the dark, Mayor, but it wasn't yesterday. You can make things a whole lot easier on yourself—
and your family," he added grimly, "if you come clean
and cooperate in my investigation."

Faraday's double chin quivered, and he tried to disguise his agitation by adjusting his shirt collar. "I've already told you everything I know."

Wes scowled at the man's stubbornness. "And just
how much longer do you think you can appease Dukker?
How much longer do you think you and your daughter
can lead a charmed life?"

"Papa?" Lorelei called gaily from inside. "I've got a
peach cobbler waiting for you."

Faraday tensed, looking momentarily uncertain.
Then he turned, his fear apparently winning out over
good sense.

"Like I told you before, Rawlins, we Elodeans are

counting on you to rid us of the outlaw menace in ou town. Good day."

The brisk knock on Rorie's bedroom door that Monday afternoon made her want to groan. She didn't know which was worse: being forced to lie idle with a mind tha raced in circles around memories of Wes, or receiving well-meaning visitors with chicken soup and get-well posies, and a dozen or more questions about when their beloved uncle Wes would return.

Go away, I'm dying, she wanted to shout. *You can see me—and the few remaining fragments of my heart— when you pay your respects at my funeral.*

Of course, she didn't allow herself to say any such thing.

"Come in," she grumbled, wishing it wasn't so hot outside. She wished, too, she'd had sense enough to chop down Mrs. Boudreau's pathetic excuse for a shade tree, that half-shriveled, swamp-loving magnolia, and plant herself a nice, hearty Ohio buckeye to shelter her window from the sun.

Rorie held the heat solely responsible for her bout of nausea. Ginevee, however, had sagely pointed out that Rorie's sickness might have resulted from her feverish attempts to work herself into a state of exhaustion the past two weeks. All of Rorie's attempts to rid her thoughts and dreams of Wes had been futile.

Ginevee's wiry gray head pushed past the crack in the door. "I've got news," she announced, grinning much like Topher did when he had some shocking, toe-curling exploit to share.

Rorie shifted the arm she'd flung over her eyes just enough to toss her friend a withering glare. "You know I abhor gossip."

"It ain't gossip when you see it with your own eyes—technically."

Rorie didn't bother to argue. She went back to staring at the soothing grayness behind her eyelids.

"Are you going to mope, or are you going to listen?"

Rorie gritted her teeth. "If it will make you happy, and if it will make you leave, then I'll listen."

"That's the spirit."

A creaking floorboard heralded Ginevee's halt beside the bed. "He hasn't left the county yet."

"Who?"

Ginevee snorted. "Who have you been mooning over for the last two weeks?"

"I do not moon," Rorie retorted weakly.

"Child, you've got the worst case of cupid's cramp I ever did see." Ginevee sat on the side of the bed. "And I have half a mind to wring that boy's neck."

"Wes?" Rorie asked hopefully.

"No, Shae. Wes caught up with us as we were driving back from town today. That grandson of mine told him you were too sick for visitors and sent him packing."

"Bully for Shae."

"Aw, honey." Ginevee patted her hand. "I know you're hurting for Wes real bad. And judging by the ruckus he put up when Shae wouldn't let him ride out here to visit you, I'd say he's hurting for you too. Now that he's coming around again, why not invite him in and let nature take its course?"

Rorie winced. She'd been too ashamed to tell Ginevee the full story, that nature had already unabashedly taken its course. "He'd only ride away again."

"You can't know that."

"He's a Ranger, isn't he?"

Ginevee made an exasperated noise. "Child, I love you like you were my own, but sometimes you can be harder on a body than brand new boot leather. The boy lied about his reasons for being here, that's true. He suspected us of some awfully shady doings too. But that was all part of his job. You can't tell me in the week you took to know him you never noticed how sweet he was with those children, fixing their toys, telling them stories, playing with them like a great big kid himself.

"Then there was the way he stood up for us," she continued fiercely, "risking a bullet or two just to make sure you, me, and the children were all safe. Now I don't know what he may have done or said before he rode onto this farm, but while he was here, he showed he has a good and loving heart. I think he wants to make amends, and you're just being stubborn if you don't let him."

"You don't understand."

"I'm trying to, honey."

Rorie turned her face to the wall and tried to swallow her growing knot of tears. In the painful silence, she could hear the soft rustle of her breeze-blown curtains. She could see slanting shafts of afternoon light scattering colors across her eastern wall: silver violets on her wash pitcher, golden ivories on her chest of drawers.

Then the wind whispered again, and great oval shadows bobbed along the rose and lilac patches of her wedding ring quilt. Biting her lip, she traced a finger along one of those dancing silhouettes. She knew it belonged to a magnolia leaf.

"I know Wes wants to make amends," she said finally. "I've had a lot of time to think about the things he didn't say, and the things he tried to say. There were times when—when he asked to speak with me, but we were interrupted."

She squeezed her eyes closed, remembering the first time, when the lightning had chased her inside the night they'd kissed under the magnolia tree. The second time, she'd cut him off in her fear for the children on the night of Creed's hurrah. The third time, Shae's arrival had interrupted Wes's awkward, rambling monologue the morning after they made love in the barn.

A tear spilled down her cheek.

"I'm learning to forgive him," she said tremulously. "But it's going to take a lot longer to forgive myself."

Ginevee shifted uncomfortably. "What do you mean?"

Rorie drew a long, shuddering breath. "I mean . . . I let him make love to me."

There was a moment, an awful, lingering moment, when Rorie could feel her friend's shock reverberating through the sheets and mattress. Then Ginevee's hand, warm and kind with female understanding, settled on her shoulder.

"Aurora." She gave Rorie a gentle squeeze. "You're

a moral, Christian woman, and lying with the man you love doesn't change that. My Cecily, she loved Gator, and I loved my Jack. If I had it to do all over again, I wouldn't change a thing. Happiness doesn't always come inside a marriage, you know that. You deserve joy in your life, and you deserve love—that's all that God has ever wanted for his children. The real sin comes in wasting a life on bitterness and regret."

Rorie dashed the tears from her face as she sat up. "But don't you see? Caring about Wes hurts too much. When I agreed to marry Jarrod, I did it because I thought he loved me. But Wes . . ." She laced her fingers so tightly her knuckles turned bloodless. "Wes loves a woman named Fancy. Not me."

"Oh, honey. Are you sure?"

In answer, a sob bubbled up from Rorie's throat. A second and a third followed, and soon she wasn't able to dam the flood of tears. Ginevee murmured consolations, rocking her like a child. There was nothing more to say; nothing more that could be said. When a man didn't love a woman, he eventually rode away. Ginevee and Cecily had learned that lesson, and Rorie had too.

An eternity passed before Rorie's tears stopped flowing, leaving a barren, aching emptiness in their wake. Ginevee rested her chin on Rorie's head and stroked her hair.

"Maybe it's for the best then," the older woman said gruffly. "Your not seeing him, I mean. It'll be easier on the children too. They'll be more likely to forget a man if they've only known him for a week."

Nodding miserably, Rorie extracted herself from Ginevee's motherly embrace. The woman had put into words what Rorie had been thinking for days.

"I reckon you'll be glad when Mr. Hawkins comes back from his cattle drive, eh?" Ginevee lightened her tone. "Then you can put Wes behind you."

Rorie said nothing. She suspected forgetting Wes wouldn't be that easy.

Not when the sweetheart tree cast its shadow on her bed.

* * *

By the next Monday morning, Rorie was forcing herself to pick up the broken pieces of her heart. She used the same rigid determination she used to ignore sickness. Since her father had abhorred weakness, she had learned as a child not to make a fuss over minor maladies. Thus, whenever she suffered from a cold or stomach upset, she simply told herself she didn't have time for such nonsense and forged ahead with her routine. The same tactics, she decided, must be used if she were to free herself from the pain of Wes.

Whenever her immunity was threatened by some unwanted memory of him, she promptly reminded herself that loving Wes was impractical. Their union was an impossibility, a folly. She was not a foolish woman; therefore, she would not waste her time on hopes and dreams.

Besides, dreaming took too much energy—which probably explained why she felt so tired of late. Keeping up with the children and teaching their morning studies had become a supreme lesson in self-discipline.

It was that same self-discipline that kept her from crawling into her bed as she secretly would have liked when Shae hitched Daisy to the wagon for the weekly Monday-afternoon drive to Milner's General Store. Certain items, like canned peaches, she supposed she could do without. Flour, sugar, salt, and potatoes, however, were imperative.

Besides, she couldn't hide at the farm forever, avoiding Wes.

Thus, accompanied by Shae's young friend, Tom Parker, and Tom's ever-ready shotgun, Rorie and Shae armed themselves for the worst, said good-bye to a worried Ginevee, and drove the wagon into Elodea. The ride down Main Street proved to be uneventful. Apparently Creed and his bullies weren't as eager to cause trouble now that a quick-drawing Ranger was in town.

While Shae and Tom loaded dry goods onto the wagon bed, Rorie paid for their purchases. She was just congratulating herself on having survived with aplomb

Mrs. Milner's questions about Ethan, when the door's cowbell clanged behind her.

A broad, masculine shadow spilled across her shoulders to the counter, growing ever larger as it rippled forward over the canned fruits and vegetables stacked against the wall.

"Need a hand with your packages, Mrs. Sinclair?"

At the sound of that rumbling baritone, all her aplomb drained to her toes, leaving her knees weak and her stomach fluttering.

"Ranger Rawlins," Mrs. Milner cooed, "how good to see you again." Smoothing back her hair, the shopkeeper smiled in a way that left no doubt in Rorie's mind that Wes had indulged in a flirtation with her. He probably had with every woman in town, she thought uncharitably.

"Ma'am." The shadow on the canned goods tipped its hat.

Rorie managed to recover her wits, if not her equilibrium. She couldn't stand there quaking beneath his shadow all day.

"No, thank you, Mr. Rawlins," she said briskly, grabbing the last of her brown-papered bundles. "I can manage quite well without you."

A moment passed as she mustered the extra valor to face him, to bottle up her hurt and longing and keep it inside her chest. She forced herself to think of the children, and all the tears they'd shed in their grief at losing "Uncle Wes." She could not—*would* not—let her weakness for this man bring him back into their lives so he could hurt them again.

Drawing herself up stiffly, she hiked her chin and turned.

For an instant, Wes held his breath, hope of reconciliation quickening his pulse.

Then Rorie's eyes, as cool and clear as glass, met his, and his insides crumbled. Her face was a mask of ivory marble beneath her gingham bonnet. If not for the two bright spots of color staining her cheeks, he might have thought his arrival had no effect on her.

"Excuse me, Mr. Rawlins."

She nodded as she sidestepped him, trying to squeeze her way past his thighs and a column of pickle barrels. He'd be damned, though, if she brushed him off like some no-account horsefly. Plucking the two packages from her white-knuckled grasp, he smiled pleasantly to stave off the worst of Mrs. Milner's speculations.

"Why, it's no trouble at all, ma'am. I assure you."

Rorie's lips pressed together in defiance, so he held the door open, leaving her little choice but to keep her peace and step outside.

She sailed past him with a disdainful swish of her well-starched petticoats, her nose waving in the air. Her posture annoyed him even more than it hurt. For the last three weeks he'd been hoping for an opportunity just like this one, but she'd been avoiding town, as best as he could figure, and she had no inkling he and his Winchester held lonely vigils each night in her fields. At least, that's what Shae claimed. Shae had been keeping him company each night, and said Rorie changed the subject whenever his name was mentioned.

This news had made Wes even more despondent than before. Telling himself his guilt was to blame, and that he would never have peace unless he made Rorie listen to reason, he'd reconsidered his earlier decision to keep his distance and his silence. In fact, the need to see her, to speak with her, had him chomping at the bit. He'd practically camped out on the porch front across the street from Milner's that day, hoping the Sinclairs would make their traditional Monday visit for supplies.

He'd been certain he could convince Rorie to forgive him—until now. As if the hounds of hell dogged her heels, she crossed the sun-warped porch to the wheel-rutted street below, making a beeline for the wagon and Shae. The boy stood on the bed, watching their race with visible discomfort. Wes knew Shae's budding friendship with him couldn't hold a candle to his loyalty to Rorie, so he caught her arm and pulled her back to his side before she could call Shae to her rescue.

"Not so fast, ma'am," he said through clenched

teeth. "You're not running away from me again. It's time we had another talk."

"I have nothing more to say to you."

"That's just dandy. You can listen, then." Halting by the wagon's rear axle, he tossed Rorie's packages to Tom, who'd been passing flour sacks up to Shae. "Miss Rorie and I are going to take a stroll, boys."

She twisted, trying to break his grasp, but he ignored her struggles.

"You just holler if you need me," he added to Shae.

"How dare you—"

"You want to make a scene right here in the street?" he interrupted her, noticing that Shae had his hand on the sideboard, as if he intended to jump down and challenge him. "That's fine with me."

When her gaze flickered to Shae, she seemed to change her mind about calling in a champion.

"Very well. Let's get this over with," she said tersely.

She turned as if to march into the grocer's alley, an act of sheer orneriness. He'd never intended to have a side-street brawl with her. Frowning, he redirected her footsteps a block farther up the street to Gator's office. She maintained her seething silence all the way to his door, not even so much as glancing his way, until he released her into the cramped space that Gator had rented from the stagecoach master.

When he slammed the door shut, she rounded on him, looking as if her hand were on a hair trigger, ready to slap. He decided he would be wise to draw the shade on curious passersby.

"Not by any stretch of the imagination," she said, "would I consider your manhandling acceptable behavior."

"If you want to be treated like a lady, quit acting like a whampus cat."

Her eyes narrowed to dangerous slits. "I beg your pardon?"

"You heard me. You might get your kicks pretending to be a cold slab of marble, but I know the truth. You've got a lot of spit and claw inside you, girl, and I've got the scratch marks to prove it."

"You are no gentleman!"

"I never claimed to be," he flung back. "Now settle yourself down and quit flapping that jaw of yours long enough to listen to what I have to say."

Her mouth snapped closed, and she folded her arms beneath her breasts.

"That's better. Would you like to sit down?" he asked, striving for a more reasonable tone.

"No, thank you."

Was it his imagination, or had a blue norther just blown into the room?

"I heard you were sick."

She said nothing, just as he'd told her to. Faced with her silence, he wasn't sure it was the better option.

"I came by last Monday to talk with you, but Shae said you weren't up to receiving visitors. I wanted you to know that . . . you're never far from my mind. I worry about you and the children."

If he had thought this confession would move her in some way, he was sadly mistaken.

"Rorie, three beardless boys aren't going to be enough to stop Dukker and his roughriders if they come to the farm."

Still, she said nothing. She simply regarded him with that same unblinking stare. He supposed he'd asked for it, but her deliberate silence was driving him crazy.

"I've talked it over with Shae, and he agrees with me. Until I can find the evidence to throw Dukker in jail, I want to camp nights on your farm to protect you."

"Absolutely not."

Wes scowled. "Maybe you need to think on it a spell," he said. He wanted to camp nearer to the house in case of trouble, but his deeper desire was to close the painful distance that yawned between them.

"I've quite made up my mind, thank you."

"For God's sake, Rorie, will you be reasonable?"

Her smile was brittle. "Very well." She adjusted her arms and drew herself up taller. "If in your *professional* opinion you believe we are unsafe living on Gator's farm, then wire Ranger headquarters and request a replacement—

maybe someone a bit older—who knows how to separate his personal affairs from his investigation."

Wes stiffened. That had cut. That had cut deep.

"I am perfectly capable of handling your protection and Dukker's arrest too."

"Perhaps." Her voice thawed the tiniest bit. "But since you have an entire law-fighting force at your disposal, I see no reason for you not to request support."

He ground his teeth. "Rangers ride alone."

"Then Rangers are fools," she said with a quiet, grim finality.

His patience snapped. For her to attack the force again was simply the last straw.

"Maybe you're right," he said. "I suppose I was foolish to worry enough about your sensibilities to ask for your permission. I'm the law in this county until they elect a sheriff, and if I choose to camp in front of your house to keep your stubborn hide from a beating, rape, or worse, then I sure as hell have the legal authority to do it."

As he bluntly named her dangers, the color drained from her face. "You—you would be wasting your time."

"I'll be the judge of that."

"I see." She drew a long and shuddering breath. "It seems I have no choice then." She dropped her arms to her sides. "If that is all, I would like to go."

Without waiting for his answer, she headed for the door, her heels making a sharp, staccato sound. Her race to leave him tore up his insides. He moved quickly to block her way.

"Rorie, wait." He struggled to keep the hurt from his voice. "Do you really hate me that much?"

Her feet faltered only inches from his. When he searched her frozen facade for some hint of feeling, she blushed, tearing her gaze from his.

"What happened between us," she said flatly, "was a lapse in judgment on my part. You cannot be held responsible for that."

His heart quickened. He couldn't decide if her response boded well for him or not. "Rorie—"

He reached to touch her hand, but she recoiled so fast, the flash of heat and ice between them stalled his heart.

"However," she continued, "I shall not allow my poor judgment to jeopardize my children's happiness. I must insist you wait until after dark, when they are in bed, before you show yourself on the grounds. And I further insist that you ride off again long before they wake."

He hadn't expected these terms. In truth, he'd been looking forward to spending time with the orphans. In the past three weeks, he'd found himself worrying about Merrilee's nightmares, Topher's arithmetic problems, Nita's boy hunger, and Po's fondness for eating dirt. Not seeing them, not playing with them or talking to them, would be a bitter pill indeed.

"I don't want to cause trouble," he said in a strained voice.

"Good." She nodded, reaching past him for the doorknob.

"What about . . . us?"

She stiffened. He could have sworn he saw her hand tremble, but she controlled herself so quickly, he couldn't be certain.

"There is no 'us,' Wes." She met his gaze evenly, although her voice quavered a bit. "As I said, I made a mistake. I will not make it again."

"It was *not* a mistake, dammit." His jaw hardened. "You wanted me then and you want me now."

She yanked the door open so hard, the window shade flew up, sounding like gunfire in the room. When she smiled again, it was a mirthless, disillusioned expression that spoke volumes.

"I'm afraid we can't always have what we want, Wes. I suggest you learn that lesson now, before a more painful one comes your way. Good afternoon."

As he watched her walk stiffly down the sidewalk, a lump rose to his throat. Loneliness, desire, outrage, caring—they all coiled in on themselves, forming that painful knot. When he swallowed, it plummeted to his gut like a burning rock.

I'll melt you from that frozen fortress yet, Aurora Sinclair, he vowed. *When I get my hands on you—and I will—I'll fire up your blood so high, you'll beg me to lay you down. This isn't the end, I promise you.*

It's just the beginning.

Chapter Seventeen

The next ten days were the most frustrating ones Wes had ever known. Dukker was keeping his nose out of trouble, playing his lawman's role in an effort to woo voters. Faced with such a well-behaved suspect, one who didn't set foot out of town unless a political rally was involved, Wes found himself with plenty of time on his hands.

He'd never been much good at sitting idle; hence, he'd developed the fondness for whittling, fishing, and dancing girls.

But now his favorite pastimes seemed to inspire forbidden memories. He couldn't hold a knife in his hands without dreaming up some toy to carve or a new improvement for Merrilee's shoes.

He couldn't cast a line without concocting new stories to tell Topher about ghosts and Indians.

As for dancing girls, they all bored Wes to tears. He'd lost interest in their jaded propositions weeks ago, wanting only the class and sass of Rorie's clever tongue.

Even his adolescent dreams of Fancy had never compared to his fantasies of Rorie, all wet and wild and writhing. He would imagine her losing her ladylike control at his touch, arching and straining, shouting out his name in mindless ecstasy. It was enough to harden him in a white-hot flash of desire.

He would imagine, too, a slow and aching kind of lovemaking, watching her matchless eyes grow moist with feeling. He would dream of touching her deepest, most sacred part and becoming one with her, body, heart, and soul.

Thinking like that made him both sweaty-hard and scared. He'd never wanted a woman that way before. He didn't *want* to want a woman that way. With adventures to chase and legends to sow, he wasn't ready for a wife and children.

Why, then, did every moment without Rorie and her orphans make him crazy with loneliness?

Of course, loneliness was only part of his torment. Each night he would spread his bedroll beneath the magnolia under Rorie's window. When a muted glow bloomed behind the farmhouse's second-story windows, his pecker would stand up and take notice. He knew that Rorie was carrying a lamp or a candle as she walked down the hall, cracking open each door to check on her sleeping children.

Eventually that glow would spread across her own curtains. She would step alone into her bedroom, keeping the light just low enough for him to glimpse a tantalizing silhouette of breasts and buttocks while she hastily tugged on a nightdress.

One evening as he lay pumped up and aching, his every breath on fire with his need for her, it occurred to him he might need a new strategy for wooing. Maybe his brother Zack had the right idea after all.

Unlike him, Zack had never needed to ride into town every other night for female companionship. In fact, that boy rarely got close enough to a lady's skirt to let himself catch calico fever, although there was that one little filly who'd rattled Zack's horns. Barley McShane had had the audacity to outbid Zack for two hundred acres of prime, water-fed pasturage that bordered the Rawlins spread. Then, rubbing salt into Zack's wound, she'd loosed a herd of sheep on that land.

Wes snickered to himself.

Poor old Zack. A man with his limited lady experience would have his hands full with a neighbor like Bailey McShane. Wes wished he could ride home to watch the fun as Zack pawed sod for Bailey. He wished he could see Aunt Lally and Fancy, and his niece and nephews, and spend a quiet evening comparing outlaw stories with Cord.

Wes was never riding back, though. He'd just have to get used to the idea that he didn't have a home.

Or a family.

But he did have a new friend in Shae. The boy came into town every four or five days with one of his gun-toting friends, Tom or Jasper, while the other boy would stay at the homestead. The boys presumably rode into Elodea for supplies, but Wes knew Shae had other considerations on his mind—namely Lorelei.

Wes warned Shae away from the girl, as much for her sake as for his; and Shae, recognizing the danger his very existence posed to Lorelei, grudgingly conceded that a cooling-off period might be wise.

Lorelei, however, was not quite as cautious. In fact, Wes had discovered that the diminutive, porcelain-faced belle had a stubborn streak longer than the Continental Railroad.

As it turned out, Lorelei Faraday was bored. While her girlish heart might have genuinely beat with affection for Shae, Lorelei was even more fond of the adventure and high drama associated with sparking the town pariah.

At no time was this more evident to Wes than on the Thursday afternoon Shae stopped by his office. Struggling under the financial burden of keeping a roof over Rorie's and the orphans' heads, Shae had just visited the bank to dip into his dwindling savings. If Rorie knew Shae was risking his college education for her sake, Wes felt certain she would be mortified.

"I'm not here for a handout," Shae said quickly, turning a shade darker when Wes pulled his own meager purse from a desk drawer. "Just some advice."

"Hell, son. You know I'd give my life for Rorie and those children. I'm not going to miss a few gold pieces."

Shae's smile was thin. "I know. Thanks. But as a
anger, you can't be bringing home much more than
orty dollars a month."

He lowered himself into a tottering chair by the pot-
ellied stove. "If I can just get a clear deed to my pa's
nd," Shae continued hopefully, "I figure I can sell a
iece, and then we'll all live comfortably for a while.
hat's why I was wondering if you could wire the judge
nd see if you can't get that squatter hearing pushed up
n the docket."

"You figure your money's going to run out before the
ourt order expires?"

Shae made a face, averting his eyes. "Let's just say
ukker owns our creditors. And let's just say he'll get the
nd damned cheap when the bank decides to foreclose."

Wes frowned. Shae had once confided he'd led Rorie
> believe the money from her eggs and wildflower seeds
nd from Gator's last harvest were covering her family's
xpenses. But if money was really as tight around the
inclair household as Shae now implied, all Dukker
eeded to do was keep busy with his election campaign
nd bide his time. No wonder the bastard had done little
1ore than make threats when Wes had served him the pa-
•ers to bar him from Shae's land.

Wes was assuring Shae he would do whatever he
ould to sweet-talk the judge, when a pink parasol butted
gainst the door's window. Snapping her umbrella closed,
.orelei Faraday rushed inside, her dark eyes shining.

"Shae, it *is* you! I thought I recognized Daisy
•utside."

The boy rose, a shy grin stealing over his face.
'Hello, Miss Lorelei."

Her laughter was a sweet tinkle of sound. "Oh, Shae,
ou needn't be so formal. Ranger Rawlins isn't the old
uddy-duddy Papa is." She smiled brightly at Wes, but her
yes were all for Shae. "When I heard you were in town,
just had to find you. I have such a wonderful idea! I
now Ranger Rawlins will think so too."

Wes's brows rose at that.

"An idea for what, Lorelei?" Shae asked, sounding
;uarded.

"Why, to help you clear your name, of course. It o
curred to me this morning, when I was being ambushe
yet again by that pathetic Creed Dukker. He just doesr
give up, you know. He makes it rather difficult to wa
down the street. Anyway, Creed was asking me to tl
church barbecue this Saturday—" She broke off abruptl
"You will be there, won't you, Shae? I know Preach
Jenkins is still counting on your maw-maw to be the fi
dler at the hoedown. Oh, please do say you'll come."

Shae fidgeted. His expression clearly reflected h
struggle between temptation and responsibility. "Yo
know I can't leave Miss Aurora unprotected."

"Of course you can't. That's why you must convinc
her to come and bring all the children. Even Marsh
Dukker wouldn't dare cause trouble at a church socia
since the election's only three weeks away." Lorel
beamed at her perfect solution to Shae's dilemma. "B
sides, I'm sure Ranger Rawlins would help you watc
over the Sinclairs."

Shae half smiled at that. The boy was aware, even
Lorelei wasn't, that Wes was just itching for another op
portunity to make peace with Rorie. Wes hadn't forgotte
his vow to get his hands on her, but his night vigi
weren't proving as conducive to kissing and making up a
he'd hoped.

In fact, watching and waiting, stalking her shado
with his hungry eyes every evening while she undresse
for bed, was making him more dangerous than Red Ric
ing Hood's wolf. Rorie had to know he crouched unde
her window each night, hoping for an invitation. But tru
to her assertion that there could be no more betwee
them, he never once caught her peeking past the curtair
to give him a sign.

This time when Shae's eyes met his, Wes could see hi
own longing mirrored in the boy's gaze.

"I reckon if Miss Aurora's feeling up to it," Sha
said, "she might like to dance. But she's been tired a lc
lately. Mostly due to the heat, I think."

Lorelei nodded sympathetically. "I daresay our earl
summers must be hard on a Yankee. But I've strayed fror
my point!" She clasped her hands in girlish glee. "Sinc

Creed has been shadowing me like some kind of Pinkerton, it gave me the perfect idea. I'll just turn the tables on him. I'll spy on Creed!"

Shae stiffened. "What do you mean?"

She gazed at him through her lashes. "Why, I'll ask him where his still is, of course. And what happened to Sheriff Boudreau's will. I'm sure he'll tell me anything."

"Miss Lorelei." Wes was careful to keep his exasperation from his voice. The girl had been reading too many dime novels. "If Creed—or someone he knows—is involved in illegal activities, he won't want you to find out about them. And if you do somehow find out about them, then you're going to be in danger."

"That's right, Lorelei." Shae frowned. "I don't want you getting involved. You'll be hurt."

She laughed. "Oh, Shae. You're just jealous because I'll be spending time with Creed."

The boy's face darkened. Wes could see Shae and Lorelei had had this conversation, or one similar to it, before.

"Miss Lorelei," Wes said, "if you want to help me so I can help Shae, convince your father to come clean about the things he knows and the things he's seen."

Lorelei blinked at him, her mouth forming an *O*. "Papa? But what would Papa know about illegal activities?"

"That's what I'd like to find out," Wes said, careful to keep the accusation from his voice. "As Elodea's newspaper editor, I suspect he's done some detective work of his own to research his stories."

Lorelei's shoulders relaxed. "Oh. That. Well, Papa doesn't really have to research his stories. People tell him everything." She shrugged, smiling. "Anyway, I'm sure if Papa knew something important, he would already have printed it in the newspaper. He says telling folks the news is his duty and his Constitutional right."

Unless, of course, his own shady doings were the news, Wes thought grimly. Faraday was clearly waiting for a Ranger to eliminate the last witness to his election crime.

"All the same, ma'am," Wes said evenly, "I'd be

much obliged if you would speak to your pa—for Shae's sake."

Rorie knew all about the church barbecue.

Every other month, Preacher Jenkins tried to throw a community social, claiming it was the best way to keep townsmen and farmers feeling neighborly. In fact, the children had talked of little else since Wes had left the farm. They hoped to see him at the party.

Rorie, however, was dreading the prospect of facing Wes again. She was dreading it so much, in fact, she made herself sick. Attributing her latest bout of nausea to cowardliness, she tried valiantly to ignore the rumblings in her stomach when the time came on Saturday afternoon to drive into town. After all, Nita had sewn a brand new dancing dress, and Topher had collected river stones to trade with the town boys for their marbles. Rorie didn't want to disappoint the children.

A half mile from the farmhouse, however, she was forced to hang her head over the side of the wagon. Much to her humiliation, Shae turned the horse around and carried her up to her bed. Ginevee and Merrilee volunteered to nurse her, which made Rorie feel twice as miserable, so she insisted above their protests that they all ride on and have a good time at the party without her.

That had been nearly four hours ago. Now she was feeling almost human again—human enough for an attack of the jitters. The long, golden rays of afternoon were deepening to twilight streaks of orange. Soon it would be night. Soon Wes would come, and she would have only Shae's young friend, Jasper, to defend her.

She didn't doubt for a moment Wes would ride to the farm once he learned she was alone. Whether he came on the pretext of her sickness, or to keep her safe from Dukker, the fact remained: He would come. He would test every vow she'd ever made to stand strong against her endless aching for him. Even now, she sensed him lurking out there somewhere, preying on her nerves as stealthily as he preyed on her restless dreams.

The fact that he'd been prowling her grounds for eleven nights without a single attempt to seduce her

ankled. Her logical self knew he was only abiding by her
request to keep his hands to himself.

Her proper self heartily congratulated her for having
the conviction not to change her mind and creep downstairs to his bedroll, which he'd spread so invitingly a few
yards from her door.

Her lonely, hurting self, told her she deserved a little
happiness, and she was a fool to throw even a moment's
worth away.

That was why she'd come downstairs to sit on the
front porch with Jasper. Loneliness was an insidious and
clever companion, one that could tempt her to do regret-
able things, like lose her heart to a man who considered
her nothing more than a pleasant distraction.

Smiling bitterly at the thought, she plied her fan and
poured Jasper his third glass of lemonade.

"Would you like another slice of pie, Jasper?"

The boy grinned bashfully above his scrupulously
scraped, crumb-free plate. "If it ain't too much to ask,
ma'am."

She ignored his grammatical error. "Of course it's
not. You are my guest." *And my protector, God help you.*

She tried not to picture the boy squaring off with
Dukker. Jasper was a great big tow-headed teddy bear,
and she feared he wouldn't fare well in confrontations re-
quiring cold-blooded grit. That's why she had Wes to defend her.

She glanced anxiously past the thickening canopy of
the magnolia. The sun winked behind the breeze-riffled
eaves with all the earthy fire of a ruby. A flash of heat
spread through her, one which even the wind couldn't cool.

Wes was coming. Soon now. She felt him as surely as
she felt a rush of anticipation tingle all the way to her toes.

You goose. Nothing will happen, she told herself
firmly. *This night will pass as uneventfully as all the others, because Wes has accepted your conditions, and he respects your wishes.*

But oh, if he only knew what she really wished
for . . .

"It was so kind of you to stay behind, Jasper," she
said quickly, desperate to find some safe, polite topic that

would restore the genteel dignity she'd known before sh
first gazed into Wes's wicked, laughing eyes. "I'm su
you'd much rather be square dancing."

Jasper shook his head, mumbling between swallow
"Naw. I ain't much for hoofing, ma'am. I'd just as soo
hunt me a twelve-point buck. Besides, your sweet 'tater p
is heaps better than any old greased-up, barbecued pig."

Her stomach roiling at his imagery, Rorie neverthe
less managed a faint smile for his compliment. "Than
you, Jasper, but I'm afraid it's Ginevee's sweet *potato*"–
she pronounced the word carefully in the hopes he migh
correct his speech—"pie you're eating."

"Oh."

He made smacking noises as he licked his finger
which didn't set well with Rorie's hair-trigger stomach
Hastily, she turned her eyes away.

It was then that she felt a prickling at the nape of he
neck. Like a shivery, instinctive knowing, the sensatio
crept down her spine, causing her less alarm than uneas
She didn't feel in any danger, but she did feel as if sh
were being watched.

She knew then, in a blaze of raw, unladylike desir
that Wes had arrived.

Merciful heaven.

Her heart speeding like a runaway train, she glance
around the yard, trying to spot him without appearin
overtly concerned, or even worse, eager. In the dusky ros
and inky violet of twilight, she could glimpse no trace o
him, although she knew with a primitive certainty tha
her mate was nearby, hungry for her in the shadows. Sh
wasn't accustomed to knowing anything without clea
minded logic, and the blistering intensity of her intuitio
scared the living daylights out of her.

Since she couldn't ignore the persistent sense of hir
heating up her skin, she decided to do the next best thing
She directed her thoughts and her conversation towar
Ethan.

"Mr. Hawkins is fond of apple pie," she said. "He'
always so appreciative when I bake it for him."

Jasper blinked at her with pale, uncomprehendin
blue eyes. "Mr. Hawkins?"

She nodded vigorously, raising her voice so Wes could hear. "Yes, Mr. Ethan Hawkins. He has a rather prosperous cattle ranch a little ways south of here."

Jasper seemed to lose interest, his gaze flickering toward the privy.

Rorie's tongue quickened in direct proportion to her mounting panic. "It's true we're not exactly neighbors, but Mr. Hawkins was a close friend of Sheriff Boudreau's. I expect he'll take the news of Gator's passing very badly. Mr. Hawkins is due back from his cattle drive in a week or two, and then I'm sure you boys won't be needed to protect the children and me any longer."

Jasper shifted, grunting, "Uh-huh."

Rorie felt immensely guilty, holding him as a captive audience, but not guilty enough to dismiss him just yet. "Have you ever met Mr. Hawkins?"

Jasper crossed his legs. "Uh, not that I recollect. But Pa said he's a fair man, shrewd about business, but with a real generous spirit. He loaned the Parker family some seed money when a wildfire swept through their cotton crop. You know, after Mr. Parker took that Comanche half-breed as his second wife, there weren't nobody in Elodea who'd see fit to give him a loan."

Rorie nodded. Actually, she hadn't known that about Ethan, but she was glad to hear it, especially now, when she was trying so hard to remember why she was seriously considering a suitor more than twenty years her senior.

"Yes, Mr. Hawkins is a fine and honorable man."

"Ain't you two been sparking?"

Rorie felt her face warm, but she silently blessed the boy's indelicacy. "Why, yes. Mr. Hawkins has been courting me. No doubt you can understand why I am *so looking forward*"—she gave those last words added volume—"to his return."

The pining note in Rorie's voice was the final straw, as far as Wes was concerned. Hoping to see her at the barbecue, he'd made the dreaded trip to the barber for a haircut and shave. After learning she was ill, he'd ridden an acre or two out of his way, braving bees and thorns in

Gator's fallow north field, to bring her a bouquet of wild roses.

The last thing he'd needed, as he circled Two-Step to the front of the house, was Rorie sitting on the porch swing—which *he'd* repaired, by God—singing the praises of Ethan Hawkins.

That damned cowpoke hadn't so much as nailed down a loose board for her, not to mention his notable absence in the face of the Dukker threat. Still, Rorie sighed over the man as if he were another Ewen Cameron, the Texas legend whose heroics had led to the coining of *cowboy*. It made Wes mad enough to eat fire and spit smoke.

Flinging the hapless roses to the ground—and letting Two-Step feast on them for good measure—Wes yanked his hat brim low over his eyes and stalked around the corner. He arrived at the porch just in time to hear the slamming of the front door and the clicking of the bolt. He spied Jasper disappearing at a trot down the privy path.

Wes ground his teeth. If Rorie thought a measly little iron rod was going to lock her out of his reach, she had another thing coming!

With the ease of a man who'd spent many a night vigil perched high above a robber's roost, he swung up into the magnolia tree, vaulted over the veranda railing, and crawled through the open window of the first bedroom on the right.

Chapter Eighteen

*R*orie didn't go to bed immediately. As tired as she was, she knew she wouldn't sleep, not with her body parts so achingly sensitized, conjuring scents and sounds of Wes from thin air. She could feel his pervasive, hungry presence no matter where her restless feet carried her inside the house.

This unsettling sensation made her mind susceptible to unspeakable imaginings. The most shameful one was her fantasy that he would burst through the door, sweep her up into his arms, and kiss her with such tender savagery that she'd lose all sense of place and time—not to mention her lady's code of honor. What might happen after that, even her wanton nature dared not predict.

Maybe that was why she had to pull out both of the sloppy hemlines she had sewn, or why she had to reread the suffragette arguments she'd been studying.

Disgusted with her mending and her memory, she gave up on both and blew out her lamp. The waxing crescent of the moon had risen, so she decided she might as well dress for bed. The children weren't due back for another hour or two. She could catch a few winks of sleep before their excited footsteps woke her, and she went downstairs to hear them recount the adventures of their day.

Besides, if Wes was going to break down her door, he

would have done it by now. It was high time she started thinking and acting like an upstanding, moral Christian again.

Her feet well-accustomed to every warp and splinter in Gator's stairs, she needed no light to show her the way to the second-floor landing. It gleamed above her with the silvery translucence of moonshine. She suspected that pale glow poured in through her open window, and remembering the young man on watch outside, she decided to draw her curtain against prying eyes before striking a flame. She closed her shutters, too, despite the heat, since that niggling prickle of wariness had returned, growing stronger each moment she was in her bedroom.

Shaking her head at her addlepated trepidations, she fumbled along her dresser top until she found her matchsafe and candle. As the wick sputtered to life, she turned, only to blow the candle out with her gasp.

"Wes!"

Her hands shaking so badly she nearly dropped both match and holder, she somehow managed to relight her candle and set it on the dresser. Then she stared at the man who had invaded both her privacy and her heart.

As far as she could tell, he hadn't moved a muscle since she first spied him, sitting in a corner on her tipped-back chair, his boots propped up on a bedpost. His hat brim lay across the bridge of his nose, and his fingers were laced peacefully across his stomach. She might have thought him asleep, except for the uneven rise and fall of his chest. She had half a mind to grab his ear.

"What on earth are you doing in my bedroom?"

He raised his hat and had the audacity to look her up and down. "Now you just go about your business, ma'am. Don't you trouble yourself over me. I'm here to keep you safe and sound for that ranching paragon of virtue, Ethan Hawkins."

He let his hat slant back across his face.

"How dare you!"

Stalking to his side, she knocked his long legs to the floor and snatched off his Stetson. Too late she realized she'd been deceived. His relaxed pose and wiseacre drawl belied the anger smoldering in his eyes. For a moment, her own outrage ebbed as she watched him slowly unfold from the chair. He towered above her like Zeus on Mount Olympus, the threat of thunder rolling across his brow. She recognized his Ranger's edge, that unpredictable streak of ferocity that could trigger at the slightest challenge.

Still, she raised her chin. He was a lawman, wasn't he? Trespassing in a woman's sleeping quarters was a crime even in Texas courts, so he was legally bound to leave her in peace once she told him to march his impudent hide back to his bedroll.

"Since the doors are locked," she said, "I can only assume you climbed through my bedroom window. If I were a man, I'd call you out for such effrontery."

"If you were a man, I wouldn't have bothered," he said flatly.

"And I should be flattered by this?"

Wes scowled. As angry as he was at her for locking him out of the house, for refusing him contact with the children, for avoiding him as if he were some kind of rabid cur dog no matter how hard he tried to make amends, her indifference hurt even more.

It hurt so much, in fact, that he'd actually considered going on a forbidden bender to deaden the never-ending pain. Why couldn't she show him one-tenth of the Christian kindness she would have shown any other repentant sinner?

"You could do a helluva lot worse than a man like me," he growled.

"Indeed? You always were blessed with a healthy self-esteem. Just what do you think you're doing in my bedroom? Did Elodea's cathouse run out of—what was it you called me? Oh yes." Her eyes flashed. "Whampus cats?"

He gritted his teeth. She'd lived in Texas long enough to know the legendary whampus cat was part wolf, part badger, and part puma, not a full-blooded whore.

"Quit putting words in my mouth. I never called you an alley cat, and I've never treated you like one. What happened between us was special to me. I told you I've never been with a lady before. And I meant what I said about wanting you to come back."

She stiffened, her cheeks paling. "No doubt you do. No doubt it pleases you to have a conquest to help you while away the hours while you're searching for murder witnesses. But I will not be your paramour, Wes."

"That's not how I think of you."

"And yet you've come here tonight to fornicate, have you not? Let us call a spade a spade, sir. I am nothing more than a game, and when you get bored, you'll find new sport."

"That is *not* true, Rorie."

"You really don't know when to stop lying, do you?"

"Dammit, woman, I'm not lying!"

"No?" She swallowed, and her rigid body began to shake. "So what are you trying to say, Wes? That you won't ride away after you make your arrest? That I can count on you to stay here and help me raise my children?"

His heart slammed into his ribs. "No! I mean . . ." His brain froze in a desperate attempt at a better answer. "I can't give up Rangering!"

"Then what do you want from me?!"

"I don't know! I just know I want you more than I've ever wanted any woman in my life, and that scares the hell out of me!"

She swayed, and the last of her color drained from her face. Suddenly, she staggered, groping for balance.

"Rorie?" He caught her hand, but she sank, wheezing. Only his arm saved her from crashing to her knees.

"Rorie?" Fear squeezed his heart. "My God, what is it? What's wrong?"

She was gasping now, clawing at the buttons on her collar. "Can't . . . breathe." Panic glazed her eyes.

He didn't waste time thinking. Dropping to his knees, he rent her gown from bodice to waist. He wrenched apart the hooks on her corset. Her breath whistled through her teeth then, and she sagged, clutching great handfuls of his shirtfront.

"Damn," he muttered, relieved to see her color

returning. "I don't know why you women insist on wearing these things."

Without ceremony, he yanked the corset from the tangle of undergarments and tossed it across the room. Leaving her tattered gown and petticoats in a heap on the floor, he lifted her into his arms and carried her to the bed. She didn't protest for once. Instead, she rolled weakly to her side, shivering as she pulled her knees to her chest. Fearing she might go into shock, he kicked off his spurs and dropped his gunbelt, then climbed behind her on the mattress.

"You're all right, honey," he murmured, holding her against him. "Just breathe. That's it, sweetheart. Breathe deep for me."

He reached across her shoulders and pulled the quilt edge up, wrapping her clammy body in a cocoon of rose and lavender. She trembled, sinking into the warmth of his length. It was then that his reflexive calm—that gunfighter composure he'd honed over the past six years of facing sudden death—slipped away. Shuddering, he closed his eyes and buried his face in her hair.

My God. I could have lost her.

"I'm—I'm all right now, Wes."

"Shh."

"I didn't mean to scare you."

He smiled weakly.

"I swear I've never fainted before."

"Don't talk, honey. Rest."

She fell silent. He could feel her heart skittering beneath his arm, and he thought how typical it was of her, trying to reassure him when she was the one who'd had such a fright.

Smoothing back her tumbled hair, he felt the surge of raw feelings once more—feelings so volatile and confused, he couldn't immediately give them names. They whirled with cyclone force through his body, making his chest ache and his throat tighten and his stomach flutter in a giddy, unsettling way. He hadn't felt this needy and hopeful, this elated and scared, since . . .

Since he'd fallen in love with Fancy.

"Rorie, I'm sorry. I wouldn't have come to your room if I'd thought—"

"It wasn't your fault, Wes. Really. I haven't been feeling well all day."

He pressed a soft kiss to the nape of her neck. "What's wrong?"

She sighed wearily. "My lunch didn't agree with me."

He fell quiet. Resting his cheek against her hair, he watched the gleam of candlelight dance along the wavy mass and inhaled the sweet, lingering fragrance of honeysuckle. A heady warmth spread through him, one he couldn't recall experiencing in all his twenty-four years. Still, it felt ancient and familiar somehow. He wanted her to feel it too. He wanted her to know he cared so much more about her than about the pleasure they could share.

"I wasn't lying, Rorie, when I said you were special to me," he said huskily. "I care about you and the children. But I need time to . . . to sort things out. Please. Be patient with me."

Rorie held her breath, then slowly, tremulously released it. Words, she thought. They were nothing more than words. Nevertheless, her traitorous, hopeful heart quickened.

"I don't believe in promises anymore, Wes."

"I know." His rumbling voice flowed around her, over her, through her. "That's why I won't make you one I can't keep."

His lips grazed her temple. When he settled behind her once more, he folded her inside the sweetest, most tender embrace she'd ever known. Sickness, worry, and resistance melted from her mind, leaving her free to relax in his arms and to let his heartbeats lull her.

She must have dozed. Her eyes flew open with a start, and she realized the candle had guttered. Or maybe Wes had blown it out. She could see him standing bare chested and barefooted, gazing pensively out her window. The sickle moon, curving like a knowing smile among the magnolia leaves, threw his chiseled features into silver and charcoal shadows. She guessed the sound of the folding shutters must have woken her, for he'd pushed them back to join the curtains, which fluttered on a breeze. She couldn't help but notice how that whisper of wind stirred his hair, riffling the neatly cropped strands like harvest grasses.

He must have sensed she was watching him. When he turned, one short, damp curl fell endearingly across his forehead.

"I was hot," he explained sheepishly.

She realized she'd kicked off the quilt. Although she was clothed in nothing more than her chemise and bloomers, the room was just warm enough to make her want to strip naked for added coolness. The thought of him watching her made her flesh burn.

"What time is it?" she asked.

"Nine, I reckon."

"I thought you'd be gone by now."

He padded closer. "And leave you here sick?"

Sitting beside her, he stretched his big, callused hand to her forehead. The idea of the ferocious Ranger playing nursemaid made her smile.

"I'm feeling better. I must have slept."

He nodded. "How about your belly?"

His palm shifted to the waistband of her bloomers. In spite of the innocence of his touch, the weight of his hand stirred her stomach in ways that had nothing at all to do with illness.

"I'm fine," she said a little breathlessly. "Really."

"Good."

She decided she'd be wise to sit up, but his arm wrapped her waist, folding her against him as he lay behind her once more. This time, she wasn't quite as weary . . . or relaxed. The intimacy of his naked chest against her bared shoulder blades jolted sensations of pleasure—and warning—down her spine.

"You . . . don't need to stay with me anymore," she said, her throat constricting as she forced out the words.

"I want to, darlin'." His fingers strummed her ribs, massaging the last of the sore spots left by the whalebone corset. "I want to very much."

His lips brushed her cheek. She shifted uneasily as heat pooled between her buttocks and his thighs. She remembered the last time he'd held her, and how his gentleness had wooed her beyond all reason.

"Wes . . ."

"Hmm?"

His thumb slyly brushed the muslin shielding her nipple. She bit her lip, feeling the forbidden tingle as she hardened and jutted with wanton abandon into the welcoming warmth of his palm.

"We can't become lovers, Wes."

She imagined his smile as he nuzzled her hair.

"We already are."

His answer disconcerted her for a moment, and he took unfair advantage, tugging with enticing slowness on the drawstring of her bloomers.

"No, I mean—" She broke off, shivering with delight as his tongue snaked inside her ear.

"*What* do you mean?" he prompted in a husky whisper.

"I mean . . . not now."

She gritted her teeth. She had meant to say, "not again," but her tongue had betrayed her somehow. "Wes, please. The children—Shae—they'll be home soon."

"Then I'd say 'now' is the very best time, darlin'. Wouldn't you?"

His hand slid beneath her waistband, his warm palm gliding over her goose-prickling flesh. She tried to catch his wrist to end his provocative prowling. Her upper arm, though, was barred by the bicep that stretched across her hips, and her lower arm had tangled in a corner of the quilt. Desperately she fought off the languorous heat lapping at her.

"Wes, please—" In spite of herself, she loosed a throttled groan, feeling the telltale dampness on his fingertips as they teased the lush, swollen folds of her womanhood.

"I want you, Rorie."

She squeezed her eyes closed. She wanted him too. But she wanted so much more of him than stolen moments in a barn or on a mattress.

"Spread your legs for me," he urged.

She swallowed, but the lump in her throat remained.

"I know what you want, Rorie," he crooned in that same insidiously seductive voice. "I know what you like, and what you need. Let me love you."

"Oh, Wes." Tears stung her eyelids, threatening to steal her vision. "Then what?"

"Then I'll love you again," he murmured, dipping his finger inside her heating mound. "And again," he said when she arched, gasping. "I'll sheath myself inside the molten honey of your body." His plunging, serpentine strokes were milking away the last of her restraint. "I'll fill you with the life of me until we're both too tired to breathe."

He hooked a heel around her ankle, opening her thighs wider. She squirmed in sinful delight, her hips pitching helplessly against the steamy prison of his arousal.

"When you fall asleep," he promised, his voice sounding ragged above her harsh breathing, "you'll be fused to my body. You'll dream of my scent and my tang, only it won't be a dream, sweetheart, 'cause you'll wake to my wooing. Then I'll love you again till you flame, crying out my name in your wild, burning need for me."

"Oh, God," she gasped. She couldn't help herself. She didn't know what made her hotter: the words he'd growled into her ear or the spark he'd fanned into a bonfire between her legs.

She was quaking now, the cries of her reason consumed by a raging wildfire. "Wes, please," she whimpered. "Let me touch you."

He rolled her over, his mouth crushing hers as his weight pressed her down. The short, swift stabs of his tongue mimicked the snaking rhythm below that was driving her to a forbidden frenzy. Feverishly she groped for his belt, then slipped the buckle and shimmied his jeans from his hips.

"That's it. Make me yours, Rorie. I'm all yours."

He rose on his free arm, kneeling above her as she quivered, satiny wet with his expert petting.

"Now take off your bloomers."

She didn't think twice; she simply obeyed. His lips slanted once more across hers, sucking her tongue deep into the velvet pressures of his mouth. She tried to peel off her chemise, but his body weighted her down again. His left hand stretched her opposite hand above her head, and his fingers twined through hers, much like the first time they'd made love. This time, however, she dimly realized her right hand was useless, trapped outside their bodies.

"Wes—"

"Yes, lover?"

He rubbed his hips against hers in an ancient enticement. He was slick and hard, like satin steel, sliding with merciless patience against the moist, soft tangle of her hair.

"Please . . . don't . . . tease," she panted.

"No teasing," he agreed, the words throbbing with an earthy cadence. "But first, you have to make a promise."

"A promise?"

With catlike delicacy he kneaded the twitching knot he'd coaxed from her pool of satin fire.

"Just a little promise," he amended silkily, his breath hot and wet inside her ear. "Meet me tomorrow at midnight. In the springhouse."

"Wes, I can't—"

The rhythm of his hand changed: hard, deep thrusts, followed by leisurely withdrawals. She nearly crawled out of her skin at the sensation. When she tried to bring herself to climax, he changed his motions again. He seemed to know exactly how much to snake or thrust without pushing her over the edge. No matter how she twisted or strained, she couldn't get his dancing fingers to rub her pleasure bud again.

"It's too dangerous," she croaked, helpless to loose the volcanic explosion that steamed and seethed inside her.

"I'll protect you, sugar. You just come. Or rather," he taunted, his voice raspy, "I'll see to that. You promise to be there. I promise you'll be blissfully happy afterward."

She half sobbed at his wicked banter. God forgive her, she wanted him so.

But there was more at stake now than ever before. She had thrown her heart to the wind the first time, and it had come back to her in pieces. She couldn't bear to pick the fragments up again.

"Wes, I want . . . to meet with you. I do," she admitted between shuddering gasps. "But I'm . . . too afraid to let myself care for you."

"I know," He gentled his petting, giving her the tiniest reprieve. "Me too."

"You are?" She blinked, trying to see past her smoking desire. Was he speaking truth or more lies to raze her defenses?

His smile was dark and potently male, a feral, flesh-tingling expression with just a trace of entreaty.

"Baby, you've got me so tangled up inside I don't know which end is up. But I do know one thing: We've been given a chance. A moment in time. That's all anyone ever gets, Rorie."

She trembled, dangerously swayed by his reasoning, while he continued to caress her. A glittering starburst splintered through her. Like fragments of suns, it dimmed before it was allowed to shine. He kept dipping, milking, teasing her out of her mind, giving her glimpses of heaven while she teetered on the brink of hell.

She groaned. Her breaths fragmented over his name, and he kissed her voraciously, possessing her mouth with a tender violence that left her gasping and begging for more. Maybe he was right, she realized dimly. Maybe it was time to steal some happiness for herself, to hold the man she loved in her arms, to make memories that would last through the years if he rode away forever.

"Be my lover, Rorie," he insisted. "Fill my arms like you fill my dreams. Come to me. Promise. Promise me now."

"I promise, Wes."

"Thank God."

The swift, silken hardness of him thrust deep. Wave after wave of white-hot fire ripped through her, and she cried out, straining upward. He silenced her with his mouth, taking her again and again with his tongue. Shuddering, she sank, dissolving into tiny, erratic sparks of sensation.

Finally, he set her mouth free, and she gulped

greedily at air. Several minutes passed before she could gather her wits enough to realize he was watching her, every part of him bow taut with stillness except for the hammering of his heart. When their eyes at last locked, his heavy lidded and gleaming, he gave her his devilish, off-center smile and shifted inside her once more.

Her breaths unraveled all over again.

"You . . . You're still—"

"Powerful hot," he drawled, his voice rolling through her on an ocean wave of sound. "Not that I'm complaining. I love to watch you go all shameless and wild."

Her cheeks flamed, and he grinned, lowering his head. His dancing, hypnotic eyes held hers prisoner.

"A beauty like you can sure take a lot of pleasure from a man. I reckon I'll have to conserve my strength to keep all my promises. Even a young whippersnapper like me can only do this three or four times a night."

She knew her eyes had bugged out. "Three or four times?"

"My record is five."

"Five?"

He chuckled at her embarrassment. She didn't know whether his boast was a tall tale or not.

"But you must have been making love all night long!"

"Uh-huh."

He moved again, sweetly, seductively, his eyes alight with a mischievous glow that stole into the cracks of her heart and mended the pieces. "You weren't planning on getting any sleep tonight were you, lover?"

Later, as they lay twined and sated, they listened to the thunder of tiny footsteps on the porch and a childishly loud, "Shh!"

They had to smother giggles as Po, undaunted, ran up the stairwell shouting "bang bang," and Topher muttered an oath. A thud and a clatter was followed by a suspicious "ribbit" and a scrabbling from somewhere near the landing.

Ginevee caught up with the boys then, demanding the surrender of both the toy gun and the bullfrog.

Merrilee whispered something about catching flies for Elwood on the morrow, and Topher sullenly agreed.

The general commotion of clothes shedding was shortly followed by the murmur of prayers, the closing of doors, and the creaking of mattresses. At last the house was quiet.

Rorie released the breath she felt like she'd been holding for a quarter of an hour, but her guilt ebbed magically away when she ventured a glance into her lover's eyes. Behind his amusement glowed a warmth and a yearning that made her heart turn over.

"Thank you, Rorie. For letting me stay," he murmured, holding her close and kissing her with a lingering trace of passion.

Smiling contentedly, she lay her head on his shoulder and closed her eyes, letting his gentle hands soothe her into sleep. She dreamed she saw Apollo dressed in a Stetson and spurs. He climbed out her window with the coming dawn, leaving her with flowers and the sweetest good-bye:

"I love you, Rorie."

When she woke at last, sighing happily from her dream, the sun had risen and Wes was gone.

But on the pillow, in the hollow where his head had rested, lay one perfect, dew-kissed magnolia—the first of the season.

Chapter Nineteen

For the next two weeks, Rorie fairly floated through her days. Never in her life had she dreamed of such happiness. Making love to Wes was the most exhilarating, blessedly uplifting experience she'd ever known. She looked forward to their nights with a giddy, schoolgirlish excitement that left her too intoxicated for guilt or shame—or for practical considerations of the future.

At the stroke of midnight, without fail, she would sneak out the door, her blood fizzing through her veins like cherry sarsaparilla. Sometimes they'd meet in the springhouse. Other times they'd meet well out of sight and sound of the house, making love beneath the vast diamond field of the sky.

Her favorite rendezvous of all was Ramble Creek. She had to play the odds, then—a titillating proposition in itself—trusting her feet could carry her fast enough through the flower-studded meadow before Shae or one of his friends noticed her fleeing in the moonlight. Wes and Two-Step would be waiting for her at the woods' edge, and frankly, she didn't always get much farther.

At other times, he'd launch an insidious assault on her senses while she, a sitting duck behind his saddle horn, would tingle and tremble and squirm in feverish delight between the steamy prison of his thighs. On those nights, it was she who begged him to rein in and lay her down beneath the cedar canopy. He, however, wicked prankster that he was, always teased her without remorse, making her wait for whatever "surprise" he'd arranged for her pleasure beneath the limestone cliff that guarded the grassy banks of Ramble Creek.

In truth, Wes was full of erotic surprises. She'd thought that touching him, kissing him, holding him deep inside her, could never be surpassed by any feeling known to woman. She'd been wrong.

That second night, in the springhouse, she'd been surrounded by the flickering glow of at least two dozen candles, and the sweet, heady perfume of crushed rose petals on his bedroll.

The fourth night, in the meadow, he'd presented her with the most exquisite white eagle feather she'd ever seen. When, in her wide-eyed innocence, she asked what the feather was for, he'd flashed his fallen-angel's grin and dusted the feather across the pouting, sensitized nub of her breast.

"Oh, I'm sure you can come up with all kinds of uses, lover," he'd drawled.

Then came their first night by the creek. Stripping her naked on his lap, he'd treated her to a feast of blackberries and cream. Rorie still flushed and shivered by turns whenever she recalled those velvet droplets oozing down her skin, and the hot, wet sizzle of his tongue against her flesh. When he pulled her down to sheath his arousal in her, filling her with the sweet, sticky fruit of earth and man, she'd felt like Eve with her very own garden serpent.

As much as she enjoyed his bawdy ingenuity, though, she enjoyed learning all the ways to please him more. Every time she watched his eyelids flutter closed with the pleasure of her petting, every time she felt the pulsing shudders of his life force, or heard him gasp and groan her name, she soared to a new height in heaven. She didn't think it was possible to love a man so much.

She didn't think it was possible to fear losing him so much, either.

When he was apart from her, even during the most joyful moments, Rorie still struggled with the niggling doubt that he might never return. As midnight crept nearer, she would worry he might forget their rendezvous, that he would be detained in town—or worse, that the bullet of some wisecracking upstart would keep him from ever coming again.

When she dared to broach her insecurities, he'd laughed at them.

"Darlin', Satan himself couldn't keep me from you. Not for long, anyway."

He smirked, and her stomach fluttered. How could he speak so lightly of the permanence that was death?

"Aw, sugar." Pulling her across the rumpled wools and crumpled honeysuckle petals that covered his bedroll that night, he wrapped his big body around her. "Don't worry. I'm not about to let some two-bit moonshiner gun me down.

"Speaking of which . . ." His eyes danced like silver flames in the shimmering starlight. "We've got some celebrating to do."

She tried to put on a brave face. "We do?"

"Sure. I found young Dukker's still."

Her breath wedged in her throat. Considering that his discovery brought him one step closer to riding away forever, she found it hard to rejoice at his news.

"That's wonderful." She strived for a note of sincerity. "Where is it?"

He gave her a knowing, sidelong glance.

"Well . . ." Plucking a strand of meadow grass from her hair, he let it blow from his palm on a gust of westbound wind. "It's in a place near and dear to your heart, darlin'. Why don't you try and guess."

She didn't want to dampen his enthusiasm. "Cincinnati?" she joked weakly.

He chuckled. "Not this particular still, although I'm sure your Yankee neighbors have their fair share hidden on the Ohio River somewhere. Guess again, Queen City girl."

She smiled to hear him use the nickname of her birthplace. Most Texicans knew little about the lands beyond their borders, and they cared even less. How on earth had she ever let him bamboozle her into thinking he couldn't read?

"Ramble Creek?" she guessed after a minute or two of logical deduction.

He arched a teasing brow. "Since when did you like that muddy, smelly old fishing hole?"

Blushing to the roots of her hair, she ran a shy hand over the broad, hard planes of his chest. "Since . . . blackberry night."

"Blackberry night?" His expression turned wolfish. "Woman, you have a one-track mind."

"Now *there's* the pot calling the kettle—"

His mouth swooped down, and her words were devoured by his toe-curling kiss.

A half hour or so later, weak from loving and laughing, she sank beneath him.

"Now where were we?" he drawled, his breathing a bit on the shallow side. "Oh yeah. Creed's still. That lizard-tailed sneak's got more hiding places for his homegrown saloon than a squirrel's got stashes of acorns. But this time he got careless."

Wes smirked. "Yep, he flapped his jaw to a friend of mine, and she told me about some white lightning trading hands out by the boneyard. So I followed those fellows, see, back into town, and you know where they were headed?"

She shook her head uneasily. His reference to a female friend had not been lost on her.

"The schoolhouse," he said.

"*What?*" She propped herself up on an elbow. "Are you serious?"

"As serious as a hanging judge."

Outrage surged through her, scalding her skin. "So that's why the children of Elodea don't have a schoolmarm?"

"I reckon so. Too bad I didn't think of it sooner. The way that schoolhouse sits all by itself on that hill, with its fine new pump and its underground spring . . . Well, let's just say it's a moonshiner's paradise."

Rorie fumed. She had half a mind to tar and feather both Creed and his father.

"Don't worry, darlin'," Wes said, apparently reading her mind. "I shot up the kettle and twisted the tubing, and I smashed up an extra empty barrel just for you."

"Did you find Creed and Hannibal there?"

"No." He frowned, showing the first hint of his frustration. "And the two rowdies I arrested aren't likely to spill their guts as long as they're sitting in a jail as friendly as Pa Dukker's. But that's okay . . . for now. I want Hannibal Dukker on a hanging charge."

Rorie's stomach knotted. She didn't like the grim sound of his determination.

Touching tentative fingers to the damp swirl of hair that carpeted his chest, she chose her next words carefully. "But . . . is a murder charge really necessary? I mean, if you have the still, surely that's criminal enough to put Hannibal in a federal prison for a good, long time."

"You're right. Or you would be, if someone came forward with proof that moonshine earns him extra wages." His gaze, keen and assessing, locked with hers. "Besides, I thought you wanted Dukker tried for Gator's murder."

"I do . . . if he's responsible."

"Oh, he's responsible, all right."

"But Wes . . ." Her throat tightened, threatening to seal off the rest of her words. "Waiting to arrest that man for murder isn't worth risking your life."

He made an exasperated sound, sitting up and combing rough fingers through his hair. "Rorie, we've chewed the fat clean off that one. Try having a little faith in me as a man . . . and a lawman, okay?"

She flinched, mortified to realize just how much her worry sounded like doubt. "I do, Wes. I'm sorry."

Wes sighed. Spending the past two weeks loving Rorie hadn't made his job any easier, that's for sure. He'd known better than to care for her from the start, but he hadn't been able to rein in his feelings—or his hands.

Now she just kept getting scared for him, and he just kept getting angry, mostly at himself for breaking his cardinal rule: no steady sweetheart as long as he wore a badge.

Damn. How was he supposed to focus on Dukker when he had a woman and children nearby, vulnerable to kidnapping, brutality, or worse? And how was he supposed to stop Lorelei Faraday from playing detective for him when she was flushed with her first undercover success? The little fool had ignored his warnings, cozying up to Creed to smuggle information out of him. Because she hadn't gotten her fool head blown off this time, she was convinced she never would.

"Listen, Rorie. I didn't want to tell you this tonight, but since we're on the subject, I reckon now is as good a time as any. Remember when I told you I might have to ride off at a moment's notice?"

She nodded, biting her lip and sitting up beside him. The trepidation in her gaze was more than he could bear.

"It's not what you think," he snapped, then instantly regretted his harshness. "I'm coming back. I'm leaving only because I caught wind of a prizefight going on in Bandera Town. If Dukker has a lick of sense, he'll ride to the tournament to do some stumping and rustle up support. I'm going to tag along—at a distance, mind you— just to make sure campaigning is all he's doing. If I'm lucky, I'll catch him red-handed trying to extort or murder someone. Then I can throw him in the county jail and be back inside of a week—in planty of time for Elodea's Founder's Day celebration."

She fidgeted, tugging a corner of the blanket across her lap in a show of ladylike modesty that never failed to make him chuckle on the inside.

"That's good news." She glanced at him, then her gaze slid quickly away. "Do you suppose you'll meet up with Zack or Cord at the fight?"

He stiffened, his stirrings of amusement turning granite hard. He hadn't considered he might cross paths with Cord so close to home, and he bit his tongue on a particularly virulent oath.

"Not if I can help it."

He noticed how careful she was to keep her eyes averted as she reached for her blouse and chastely covered her breasts.

"If you see them there," she said, "it might be a good opportunity to buy them each a shot of whiskey and—"

"No!" His gut roiled with shame at the very idea. Seeing Cord would be hard enough. *Drinking* with him would be unforgivable.

"Wes." She slipped her free hand over his fist. "You miss them. You *love* them. They're your brothers. Whatever has happened between you and Cord, surely it can be put to rest."

"*No, it cannot.*" Snatching his hand away, he grabbed his jeans and climbed to his feet.

Thankfully, she fell quiet while he buttoned his fly. In fact, he dared to hope she'd dropped the subject. She stood with his blanket wrapped around her from her breasts to her knees, her hair spilling in luminous, glimmering waves to her hips.

"You love Fancy, don't you?" she asked quietly.

He gaped at her, wondering where the hell that question had come from. "Of course I love Fancy. She's family."

Rorie's smile was thin and fleeting. He had the sneaking suspicion she knew something about his past feelings that he didn't want her to know. Although he had finally admitted to himself he loved Rorie, he hadn't told her yet. Words like that were as good as a marriage proposal to some women, and he wasn't ready for a white picket fence. Not yet.

He glared at her in warning, trying not to notice how breathtakingly beautiful or fragile she looked, standing there in her defiance.

"If you love Fancy, then why have you let her worry all these months over you?"

He frowned. "What are you talking about?"

"That day when I was trying to find out if you were a Ranger, I found her letters in your saddlebag, and . . . I read them."

His jaw twitched. "You had no right."

"Maybe not, but the fact remains I did. And I think you're being selfish, not to mention cruel, to let a woman you love go on wondering whether you're dead. I suppose it would be too much to hope that you might show me more consideration than you've shown her, after you grow tired of our dalliance."

He sucked in a whistling breath. "That's a helluva thing to say to me, woman. A *helluva* thing."

"I know." Her voice trembled, as if she was fighting tears. "But it had to be said."

"Rorie, for the love of God—"

She dropped her eyes, and he muttered another oath. She still thought he only wanted to bed her!

"Rorie, don't cry. I told you I'm coming back, dammit, and I meant it."

She dashed away a tear, still looking miserable, which made him feel too low to look a snake in the eye.

"Come here," he ordered, pulling her into his arms. "Now you listen to me. The troubles between me and my family have nothing to do with us. You got that? Nothing. End of discussion."

He lowered his head to kiss her, but Rorie squeezed her eyes closed and turned her face into his shoulder.

Their discussion might have come to an end, but Wes was wrong about the rest.

The troubles between him and his family had everything to do with him and her.

During Wes's absence, Rorie spent part of every hour berating herself for losing her heart and her head over him. She'd foolishly allowed herself to dream of their life together, loving and laughing through the years, watching her children grow to adulthood. Somehow, she had forgotten Fancy.

Somehow she had forgotten, too, that Wes wanted redheaded children of his own. Clearly, a life with him would be impossible. Their affair was doomed.

As hard as Rorie tried to hide her misery from her family, everyone seemed to know something was wrong. Topher took special pains to do his chores and keep his reptile menagerie out of the house. Merrilee refrained from disappearing on her mysterious, woodland rambles and stayed close to home.

Nita volunteered to lead the children in their lessons, while Shae surprised Rorie by constructing the

blackboard she'd been longing to have ever since her arrival in Elodea.

Even Po, with his limited understanding, knew
enough to throw his arms around her knees and beam up
at her, shouting, "Me loves you!"

Rorie's brittle facade of cheer crumbled completely,
however, late one afternoon when Merrilee came to her
bedroom with a bouquet of magnolia blossoms.

"Don't cry, Miss Rorie," the child said, hurrying
across the room to sit with her on the bed. "Don't be
sad."

Sniffling in embarrassment, Rorie did her watery best
to smile at Merrilee, who was clutching her hand so wor-
riedly. "I'm sorry. I . . . uh, was thinking of the magnolia
tree."

Merrilee looked chagrined, glancing from the bouquet in Rorie's lap back to her tear-stained face. "But I
didn't hurt the magnolia tree, Miss Rorie. It's doing much
better now. Honest. Come see."

Holding fast to Rorie's hand, Merrilee dragged her to
the window and pointed outside. True to the child's
words, the tree had unaccountably flourished over the
past few weeks, while every other plant in the yard
looked beaten down by the sun.

"We need rain," Rorie said absently, staring in some
wonder at the profusion of alabaster blossoms on the
once semi-naked tree. Now even the tiniest twig bore a
great oval leaf or a pear-sized bud that was pregnant with
life. Rorie didn't know much about magnolias, but Mrs.
Boudreau had told her enough to realize that there was
something unusual about the way this tree withstood the
Texas heat.

And surely for it to blossom so late in the season was
another marvel of nature.

The sweetheart tree, Wes had called it. Maggie the
magnolia. Rorie almost cried again.

A gentle rapping sounded on her door, and she spied
Ginevee on the threshold. Girding herself against further
displays of weakness, she invited her friend to come in.

"Miss Rorie's sad again," Merrilee blurted out in all
her anxious innocence.

Rorie turned hotter than a branding iron, and Ginevee gave Rorie a curious glance.

"Again, huh?"

Merrilee nodded, then gazed up at Rorie one more. "If picking flowers makes you sad, ma'am, I'll just draw you pictures."

Her heart in her throat, Rorie knelt down and hugged the child to her breast. "I love your flowers, Merrilee, and your pictures too. But most of all, I love you, sweetheart."

Merrilee smiled shyly. "Thank you, Miss Rorie."

Ginevee came forward to pat the child's head. "Merrilee, honey, why don't you run on downstairs and help Nita set the table. I reckon we're going to have some company tonight."

Rorie started, rising, as Merrilee headed dutifully for the hall.

"Company?" Rorie's pulse quickened with the hope that Wes had returned. "Someone's coming to supper?"

Ginevee's cagey old eyes searched hers. "It looks that way. Shae spied a posse of riders heading this way across the north field."

"The north field?" Rorie repeated, still clinging to her ridiculous hope that Wes was among the horsemen, even though he had told her Rangers ride alone.

"A California sorrel is leading the way," Ginevee added.

Rorie's excitement abruptly fizzled. She should have known better. Hadn't she told Wes never to show his face on the farm before the children were in their beds?

"Ethan," she said.

"You were expecting someone else?"

Rorie sighed, turning back to the window. "No," she lied.

Since her bedroom faced south, she wasn't likely to see Ethan's approach until he and his men circled the yard to the front of the house. Ginevee moved quietly beside her, slipping an arm around her waist.

"I reckon they're on their way home from Abilene," Ginevee mused aloud, breaking the gloomy silence. "Mr. Hawkins probably figured he'd stop by to visit Gator and grab some grub, maybe even bunk here for the night, since his spread's another day's ride south. Of course, he probably doesn't know about Gator's passing, since he's been in Kansas all this time. You're going to have to break it to him, honey."

Rorie nodded glumly. She'd been thinking that was only one of the things she would have to break to Ethan.

She could see him now. Heading a column of eight riders, he sat astride his red-gold palomino with a military poise that even twenty years of cattle ranching hadn't been able to ease. Gator once told her Ethan had served as a scout at the tender age of sixteen under General Zachary Taylor in the Mexican War, and he'd received the artillery commission of colonel by the age of thirty-five, when he fought again for Texas in the War Between the States. At fifty-three, he was still a striking figure of a man, with his silver shock of coarse, cropped hair and his piercing sapphire eyes.

She watched him dismount with a brisk, fluid motion, and call to one of his men to corral his horse. Rorie cringed at the command. Ethan always seemed to be shouting, probably because he'd lost the hearing in his left ear.

"I could tell him you're feeling puny," Ginevee offered sympathetically.

Rorie's smile was brief. Somehow Ethan didn't strike her as a man who had much patience for weakness. He and her father would have gotten along famously.

"Thank you, Ginevee, but no. It's time I faced up to my responsibilities. And the truth of my situation."

She started for the door.

"Aurora . . ."

Ginevee shifted uneasily as Rorie raised questioning eyes to hers.

"Your heart's in the right place, child, so try not to let your head get so much in the way. Give Wes the time he needs. I still think you can convince him to stay."

Rorie's eyes began to sting, and she blinked rapidly to dam the tears.

"That might be true, Ginevee. But Ethan doesn't need convincing to stay."

* * *

As Wes reached the fringe of the woods, the first thing he noticed in the long crimson rays of the fading afternoon were the half-dozen horses grazing in Daisy's corral. The next thing he noticed as he spurred Two-Step faster was the sun-baked, leather-hard roughrider shouting orders. Wes's first inclination was to grab his Winchester, circle the house, and try to get the drop on the handful of men he saw scrambling to do their leader's bidding.

Then he spied Merrilee leaning over the top rail of the corral, offering carrots to a high-strung California sorrel.

Releasing his breath in a rush, he shoved his rifle back into its saddle boot. Whoever he was, the loudmouth wasn't any threat to the children.

Wes was debating whether or not to abide by Rorie's wishes and wait for the cover of darkness to challenge the longrider, when he heard a shriek of excitement from the vicinity of the house.

"Uncle Wes!"

Before Ginevee, Nita, or even Shae could collar him, Topher had dashed off the porch and bolted across the yard into the meadow. Wes's heart climbed to his throat. Turning Two-Step's head, he urged the gelding to intercept the boy.

"Uncle Wes!"

Topher was panting so hard, he could barely speak. Wes swept him up into the saddle, and the boy threw his arms around Wes's neck. For a moment, Wes could only hold the child as he battled a misty swell of feeling.

Topher began babbling between greedy gulps of air. "I *told* Merrilee you were coming back. I told Nita and Miss Rorie too. But they didn't believe me. *Women.*

"Say, you have to meet Elwood," Topher prattled on. "That's my bullfrog. And I got a brand new slingshot too. Well, it's almost brand new. I won it fair and square in a marble shoot-out with Abraham. He used to be champion."

Topher beamed, and Wes grinned, reining Two-Step to a slow walk.

"So I reckon that makes you marble champion now, eh?"

"That's right!" Topher bounced with glee. "You want to go fishing tomorrow? Mr. Ethan *never* wants to go fishing. He doesn't whittle or tell ghost stories neither. He just goes around barking orders all the time like, 'Stand up straight,' and 'Mind your tongue.' "

Wes's heart did a strange little skip before it quickened its beat. He phrased his next question as casually as he could. "Is that tall, rangy fellow there with Miss Rorie the Mr. Ethan you're talking about?"

Topher made a disgusted face. "Yeah. The one that was shouting orders. He's always going around shouting like that. Miss Rorie says it's because he's got an earache or something, but all that hollering scares the jeepers out of Merrilee. Most times, she tries to hide when he's around."

Wes's brow furrowed. He didn't like the sound of that.

"Boy, am I glad you're home!" Topher hugged him again. "Miss Rorie said Mr. Ethan might be staying for a few days, but now that we got a real *Ranger* around, I reckon we don't need him."

Topher frowned suddenly. "You ain't going to let her take us to live with him, are you? Nita says when a woman gets hitched, she has to go live in her husband's house."

Wes choked. "They're hitched?"

"Naw. Not yet. But Mr. Ethan asked her to marry him after dinner. Shoot. He shouts so loud, I didn't even have to listen at the door."

Wes swallowed hard. He knew he lost some of his color. "What was Miss Rorie's answer?"

Topher looked off thoughtfully, as if he were trying to recall.

"Well, she ain't as loud as him, you know. So I can't say that I heard."

By the time Wes and Topher rode into the yard, the whole household had turned out to greet them. Wes dutifully picked up Po, who scolded, "Me missed you."

He hugged Nita, Ginevee, and Merrilee, and he shook Shae's hand.

Then, stealing himself against his secret dread, he turned to greet Ethan Hawkins. Rorie nodded furtively, and Ginevee dragged the protesting children off to bed while Shae led Two-Step to the corral.

"So," Ethan said. "You must be that young Ranger Rawlins I've been hearing so much about." He stuck out his hand. "Hawkins is my name, but most folks call me Hawk. Or Colonel Hawk," he added with unmistakable pride.

Wes forced himself to shake the man's hand.

"I want to thank you, Ranger, for taking care of things around here for me while I've been away. I owe you a debt of gratitude."

Wes glanced at Rorie. When she averted her eyes, he battled a surge of pure, raw outrage.

"I've come to think of this place as home ... Hawk."

"And you'll always be welcome here, son."

Ethan clapped him on the shoulder, and Wes was hard-pressed not to punch his lights out.

Rorie cleared her throat. "Ethan knows your brother Zack."

"Yep." Ethan folded his arms across his chest. "I bought the finest bull I ever did own from that boy. Zack's got a keen eye for stock and a shrewd head for business." Ethan chuckled. "That boy damn near broke me on that deal, but it was worth it."

Wes glared at the old rancher. If Ethan thought Zack, at twenty-five, was a boy, it was pretty clear what Ethan thought of him.

Shae chose that moment to return from the corral, and Wes couldn't help but notice how Ethan's eyes narrowed as Shae approached.

"It's the damnedest thing," he muttered.

"What is?" Wes asked, ignoring Rorie's sharp, warning glance.

"The way that mulatto puts on airs. Calling himself Gator's next of kin. Hell, I knew Gator for twenty years and he never said a thing to me about siring any colored bastard."

Rorie shot her suitor a quelling look, but Shae must have overheard. He halted, giving Ethan a wintry smile.

"I reckon you and Pa weren't all that close, then."

Ethan's eyes narrowed. "Listen here, upstart—"

"Tell you what, Hawk," Wes interrupted, "before you start calling anybody names, why don't you and I have a private little talk and get some facts straight."

Ethan's eyes locked with Wes's, and panic made Rorie break out in a cold sweat.

"*Wes,*" she said with thinly veiled desperation, "I've already told Ethan about the missing will. And Doc Warren. And—and the court order." *But not about us.*

Her eyes pleaded with him not to push for a confrontation, and he scowled.

"Colonel Hawk!" An aging, tobacco-chewing cowpoke waved to his boss. "We've done finished drawing straws over here, and Hank and Rusty are going to take the first watch. You want to ride on out to Sultan's with the rest of us boys?"

Ethan had the decency to redden. "Er, I apologize, Miss Aurora. Seems like my men could stand to have a few more manners knocked into their heads." He tipped his hat. "Excuse me, ma'am. I won't be but a moment."

Air rushed from Rorie's lungs. Wes pressed his lips into a thin line. Shae glanced between them both and cleared his throat.

"I'll, uh, let you folks talk," he said, nodding his good-nights and turning toward the privy.

Rorie nervously laced her fingers together. Now the full intensity of Wes's unyielding stare was upon her. She could feel the upset radiating from his frame as if he were a mountain with a molten core about ready to blow. She didn't know what to say or where to begin, but he saved her the trouble. With a sweep of his hand, he gestured for her to walk beside him. She fell into step, and into an uneasy conversation.

"How was your trip to Bandera?" she asked, deciding not to chide him for showing himself on the farm before dark—even though she was sorely tempted.

"Uneventful." His tone was clipped.

She glanced at his profile and spied the tensing of his jaw in the fading light. She wished she dared touch him to soothe away his ire, but she was too keenly aware of Ethan and his watchful men—and the decision that now loomed before her.

"We didn't have any trouble with Creed while you were gone." She tried to keep her tone from echoing the agitation in her breast. "I suppose he must have been campaigning with his father."

"Actually . . ." Wes's lips twisted into a tight, dry smile. "Creed and his pa have had a falling out of late. Over a lady."

This news surprised Rorie, but when she would have asked him what else his investigation had uncovered, he halted before the magnolia tree.

As she watched him, all thought of the Dukker threat slipped from her mind. He placed his hand on the trunk and tipped back his head, gazing into the branches, much as she had done that night of the storm. The only difference was that this night, Maggie was bursting with life.

When he turned his head to look at her, they simply gazed into each other's eyes for an endless moment.

Finally, a sad little smile curved his lips. He reached for the nearest branch of the tree and eased a blossom closer.

"He's nothing like I expected, you know."

She watched the branch bow, its leaves spilling over his shoulders in a soft, loving embrace.

"Ethan?" she breathed, mesmerized by the relationship of tree and man.

"Uh-huh." He smelled the flawlessly formed blossom. "I didn't expect him to be quite so much older than I am." His gaze flickered to hers. "Or than you."

She shifted uncomfortably. Age *was* one of Ethan's drawbacks, but then, she used to think age was one of Wes's too.

"And I didn't expect him to be quite so . . . loud," Wes added in a feeble attempt at humor.

She secretly had to admit Ethan's booming voice annoyed her at times, but she always felt guilty immediately afterward, knowing the reason behind it. "He lost his hearing in one ear commanding a cannon brigade during the war."

"So that's what Topher meant."

Her face heated. "What else did Topher tell you?"

"Well, let's just say the boy doesn't like your Ethan very much."

"Topher doesn't like anyone who tries to discipline him."

Wes's amusement was fleeting. "I wasn't much under the impression Shae got along with him either."

Rorie couldn't rebut that argument quite as easily, but she had the hope that two reasonable men could learn to tolerate and respect each other. Wes and Shae certainly had.

"Ethan just needs time to get used to the idea of Shae being Gator's son."

Wes said nothing. He touched the flower again and it seemed to give itself to him, floating down into his palm.

"So you've got it all figured out, is that it?"

"What—what do you mean?"

"Topher told me about Ethan's proposal."

She cringed. *That boy.* Topher had as much delicacy as a charging bull.

"I'm sorry, Wes. I didn't want for you to find out that way. Topher had no business carrying tales."

He stared down at the stem he was twirling between his thumb and forefinger. "What answer did you give Ethan?"

She ached to hear the pain in his voice "I . . . asked for time to think on it."

His head shot up. The hope in his eyes made her knees weaken, in spite of all the rational arguments she had piled up in her head against him.

"You told me to be patient with you, Wes, and—" she struggled to keep the note of entreaty from her voice, "and to give you a chance. That was three weeks ago."

He grimaced. "I also said I wouldn't make you a promise I couldn't keep."

"I remember." She watched his reactions as closely as

she could through a growing mist of tears. "I remember, too, that I asked you what you wanted from me."

He ripped his gaze away.

"To wait," he said finally.

"For how long?"

"I don't know, Rorie. It's not that simple."

He pushed back his hat with a frustrated hand. "I've wanted to be a Ranger ever since I was a boy. Ever since . . . my parents were murdered. That dream has been a part of me for as long as I can remember."

His eyes begged her to understand. "But it won't always be my dream, Rorie. I want a wife and children too. Having a family is important to me, so important, in fact, that I don't want to ride away for months on end, leaving them behind. I want to watch my children grow and—and to share my nights with the woman I love.

"I grew up watching my brother's wife—his first wife, and then Fancy too—worrying about him," he continued grimly, "wondering if he was dead or alive as long as he wore this star. I don't want to do my woman that way. I don't want to do *you* that way, Rorie. That's why I swore to myself I would never take a wife as long as I wore this badge."

She stared down at her fingers. They were laced so tightly, the knuckles looked like white knots. How could she fault Wes for his reasons for waiting? And how could she stand in the way of everything he'd ever wanted—a lawman's career and children?

"Rorie."

Ever so softly, the petals of the magnolia grazed her cheek. His heart was in his eyes as he traced her jawline with the blossom, letting it linger just a hairsbreadth below her lips.

"I love you, Rorie."

A tear rolled down her cheek. She'd never, ever dared to believe she would hear those words from him.

"I love you too, Wes."

The first blush of his elation faded away, leaving his face gray and strained with uneasiness. "What are you thinking?"

She dragged her gaze back to her hands. They wer
trembling.

"I don't know. Like you, I . . . seem to have som
things to sort out."

A heartbeat passed. The magnolia blossom swan
back into focus. Through her tears, she watched hir
press it into her hands. Be patient with him, it seeme
to say.

"When can I come back?" he asked.

Oh, God, how could she let him come back? An
how could she be strong enough to let him go?

Ever the diplomat, her brain forced her paralyze
tongue to respond. "I think we shouldn't see each othe
for a while."

But the cowardly part of her couldn't leave things a
that. "You'll be at the Founder's Day celebration, won'
you?"

He nodded, looking greatly relieved.

"A week then."

"A week," she repeated.

Only seven days before she must give him he
answer.

She watched a tear splash onto the magnolia.

Chapter Twenty

*N*o matter how many times Rorie reviewed her dilemma, turning matters over, examining every angle, she always drew the same, bitter conclusion. She had to let Wes go.

As great as her love for him was, it would never be enough to hold him. From the father she had disappointed at her birth, to the husband she had disappointed with her barrenness, every man she had ever known had wanted sons of their own seed.

Even Gator had at last been willing to overlook Shae's color to reclaim the boy as his long-lost child, rather than let Creed, his second cousin, inherit the farm.

Rorie had heard Wes speak wistfully of children enough times to know he was no exception. So whether he stayed a Ranger or became a farmer or rancher, it wouldn't matter. The day would come when he would want his lifeblood carried on. And on that day she would have to disappoint him too.

Better to end the pain now, her ever-practical mind assured her. *Better to set him free rather than wait for that awful day when he turns to you with eyes clouded over with resentment. Do what's best for him and the children. Your heart will heal in time.*

Ethan might be a strict disciplinarian, but he wasn't cruel like Hannibal Dukker. He lived on a prosperous spread, far from the bigotry of Elodea, and he had three grown sons, all of whom were fathers to children her orphans could play with. Despite their age and cultural differences, he treated her with respect. She didn't love him but she could fulfill his need for companionship. As for the rest . . .

She supposed she could learn to forget rose petals, blackberries, and magnolias. She just prayed she could forget laughing green eyes and a fallen-angel's smile too.

On the morning of Founder's Day—which also happened to be election day—Ethan and two of his men arrived to help pack her and the children into the wagon. Rorie could tell by the way her suitor's eyes followed her that he was eager to end their courtship and take her as his wife and lover. She couldn't bring herself to give him the answer he waited for, though. Not then.

She told herself she owed Wes the courtesy of breaking the news to him first, before some nosy Elodean did. Ethan had made her wait more than two months for his proposal, riding off on his cattle drive to recover from the shock of her barrenness. She figured it wouldn't hurt him to wait a week and a day for her answer to his offer.

By noon, when Shae drove the rattling old buckboard into town, the streets of Elodea were swarming with townsfolk and county dwellers alike. Red, white, and blue bunting hung from the buildings on Main Street, and a brass band was playing in the center of Town Square. Every inch of shade seemed to be crowded with onlookers. In spite of the blistering heat, children ran and couples strolled from booth to colorful booth. The displays included tanned hides, a stuffed cougar, tortoise-handled knives, cornhusk dolls, and a variety of foods. The most popular attraction of all, though, seemed to be the free barrels of cider and lemonade and the keg of whiskey for the voters.

The orphans were so excited, they could hardly contain themselves.

"Where's Uncle Wes? Do you see Uncle Wes? He's going to be here, isn't he?" Topher chattered, scrambling to stand in the moving wagon bed so he could get a better view of the milling crowd.

Merrilee shaded her eyes, looking past Ethan and his palomino to the black-and-white targets set up for the shooting match at the end of Main. "I think I see Uncle Wes over there with Miss Lorelei."

"Where?" Topher had to be physically restrained from crawling over Ginevee's knees. "Does he have his Winchester, huh? Is he going to shoot in the contest, do you think?"

Nita sniffed, tossing her painstakingly braided, beribboned length of hair over her shoulder. "Not if he's with Miss Lorelei. I hear she faints at the smell of gun smoke."

One corner of Shae's mouth curved up.

"Besides," Nita said, "Uncle Wes is a Ranger. Gunfighters aren't allowed to enter the contest and claim the hundred-dollar prize. That means Shae's going to win that money hands down."

"I reckon that Dukker boy will be itching for the prize," Ethan called in a voice three times louder than necessary. "I hear he's a pretty fair shot."

Shae's humor ebbed at the old man's observation. Rorie tried to dispel the tension.

"I daresay every man in the county who fancies himself a marksman will enter that contest. One hundred dollars is a generous prize."

"Let's just hope Creed remembers to keep his gun pointed at the bull's-eye," Ginevee muttered.

By the time Shae found a livery and argued the inflated boarding price down to an affordable one, he and Ethan were glaring daggers at each other. Ethan had wanted to pay the full price and get on with the day; Shae had refused to be fleeced.

Of course, Topher hadn't helped matters when he took Shae's side, calling Ethan "an old cooter who's just showing off with his money."

Ginevee had to drag Topher away by his ear, Shae stormed off to register for the shooting match, and the girls ran to the pie booth to sign Nita up for her first baking contest.

That left Rorie with a snoozing Po and a fuming Ethan. She was just thinking matters surely could only get better, when Wes rounded the corner with a laughing Lorelei on his arm.

In spite of every common-sense argument against it, Rorie felt the fierce hot stab of jealousy.

For one stomach-knotting moment, the couples just stared at each other. Then Lorelei, who probably didn't have a clue that her County Fair Queen banner and tiara made Rorie feel twice as unattractive as usual, flashed her perfect smile.

"Why, Mrs. Sinclair, how nice to see you! And Colonel Hawkins. I haven't seen the two of you since Bonnie Sue Harrigan's wedding."

Rorie winced at the word "wedding," tearing her gaze from Wes.

Ethan nodded a cool greeting to Wes. To Rorie's agitated mind, their silent interaction seemed like the prelude to war. Ethan had not been pleased with the way she'd allowed Wes's magnolia to touch her face, and he'd privately boomed his feelings to her in his own inimitable fashion.

Doing her best to forget that last tender moment she was ever likely to share with Wes, Rorie forced down the lump in her throat.

"Yes, Lorelei, it has been awhile, hasn't it? You're looking lovely today."

"Thank you, ma'am." She blushed prettily. "This heat is so dreadful, isn't it? Papa's been worrying folks will drink too much of that free whiskey Mr. Jackson—or should I say *Sheriff* Jackson—brought to thank all the voters. Frankly, I don't know who's been to the tap more often, Marshal Dukker or our county's new sheriff."

Rorie's gaze flickered uneasily to Wes. So Dukker had lost the election. Between his hurt pride and his pickled conscience, he could become even more of a menace.

"Well, if a man can't hold his whiskey, he's not much of a man," Ethan said flatly.

For some reason, Wes grew extraordinarily red above his neckerchief.

"Tell Mayor Faraday," Ethan went on, "that I'd be

pleased to lend a hand if some of those hayseeds start popping off their guns."

"Much obliged, Hawk." Wes looked anything but grateful. "But until you're deputized, I suggest you leave the peace keeping to the law."

Ethan snorted. "Hell, son, there's only one of you and two dozen or more rowdies on these streets."

"Well now, that's what bullets are for, Hawk."

Rorie and Lorelei exchanged anxious glances as the two men glared at each other. Fortunately, Preacher Jenkins chose that moment to stroll past them with a cup of lemonade.

Spying his opportunity, Ethan nodded curtly to Wes and Lorelei. "Well, it's your funeral, Ranger. And you're welcome to it. I've got a preacher to see on business of a much more pleasant nature. Good afternoon."

Wes's jaw dropped. So did Rorie's. She knew Ethan was referring to the christening of his granddaughter, but Wes couldn't possibly know that. Shock, anguish, outrage, betrayal—she recognized them all as they flashed across his face. For a heartbeat, she thought to correct his misinterpretation, but his eyes stabbed her with such potent fury, she lost her nerve.

She lost her moment too. Ethan's firm grip on her elbow was guiding her away.

As she forced her numb limbs to move in time with Ethan, a bitter sense of irony washed over her. She had planned to tell Wes her decision in the gentlest way possible, but he had leaped to a conclusion—the right conclusion.

What was left for her to say?

"Colonel Hawkins is taking Mrs. Sinclair to the preacher," Lorelei whispered, her features growing animated with delight. "Do you suppose this means he has asked her to marry him?"

Wes, still reeling from the encounter, could only nod his head. Rorie had chosen Hawkins. She'd chosen Hawkins over *him*!

Pale and shaking, he felt a whirlwind of confusion batter his innards. He'd never dreamed she'd do this to him. Not after he'd told her he loved her. Not after she'd said she loved *him*!

Lorelei's eager monologue permeated the maelstrom in his brain. "Wait until I tell Marshal Dukker that Mrs. Sinclair said yes to Colonel Hawkins. He'll just be livid."

"No!"

Wes rounded on the girl, and she shrank back a step. He grabbed her arm and dragged her into a quiet, unoccupied alley.

"Lorelei, so help me God, don't you dare breathe a word about her to Dukker."

"B-but don't you see? If I tell Marshal Dukker, he'll get upset that she passed him over, and he'll be more likely to let the truth slip about Gator. It's perfect for our plan."

"*Your* plan, Lorelei." The blood pounded so hard in Wes's temples, she floated before him in a red haze. "I told you to stay out of my business. Pumping Creed about the still was dangerous enough. You've got about as much chance as a lamb in a wolf's den if you cross Hannibal Dukker."

Lorelei's pout was mutinous. "Well, *somone* has to enter the wolf's den to find poor Sheriff Gator's bones. Besides, I've gotten to know Creed a little better since I started helping you, and while I wouldn't necessarily let him *court* me, I don't think he's as bad as you and Shae want me to believe. I think you're just trying to scare me."

"You're damned right I'm trying to scare you! Detective work is not a schoolgirl's game! And you're talking about Pa Dukker now, not Creed. If Dukker killed his cousin, he won't have the slightest qualm about blowing off your silly little head. So if you've got half a brain rattling around beneath those curls, you'll stay out of my way. And out of Dukker's."

She snapped her parasol closed. "How dare you talk to me like that? Are you forgetting who my papa is?"

"I don't give a rat's fanny who your papa is. I don't get paid to entertain babes in bloomers when they've become bored chasing wedding bells."

She huffed, turning crimson. "I do not have to stand here and be insulted by the likes of you, sir." She jabbed her parasol into the dirt for emphasis. "You could stand to learn a thing or two about manners—even from Creed. Good day."

She flounced off with a swish of skirts and a glimpse of dainty ankle. Wes slammed a fist into his palm.

"Goddamned feather-headed *women*!"

He didn't know whose brain he needed to shake more sense into: Lorelei's or Rorie's. At least Rorie wasn't foolish enough to put her life in danger simply for amusement.

No, she just threw it away, he reminded himself brutally.

He rubbed a rough hand over his face, hoping the harsh contact of flesh on flesh would stave off the dreaded prickle behind his eyelids. How could she do this? Didn't she understand *he* wanted her, *he* needed her? How could she take away her love, her children, the only family he had?

The questions kept echoing in the frozen chambers of his mind. He couldn't think, he could only feel, and anguish, raw and blistering, lashed him up one side and down the other.

"I won't let you marry him," ground out through clenched teeth. "You're mine, Aurora Sinclair. So help me God, you'll fill the bed of some other man over my dead body."

Rorie walked numbly from booth to booth, seeing little and hearing less. Even Ethan's voice, booming at her side, registered as little more than a droning hum in her ears. Her entire being had retreated into the depths of her soul.

And inside her soul, she cried.

Outwardly, of course, she showed no sign of despair. She was the very picture of dignified serenity, if perhaps a trifle pale, as evidenced by her pinched reflection in a silver hand mirror that Ethan offered to buy for her.

She managed smiles and nods when appropriate, and her conversation with one of Ethan's daughters-in-law seemed to go well. The woman offered to take Po to her house so he could nap, but other than that, Rorie couldn't remember a single word that had passed between them.

If her family sensed her unhappiness, not one of them commented on it. Shae did gaze at her a little oddly during the horse race, when she stared glassy-eyed at the starting line long after the race had begun.

An hour or so later, Ginevee had to nudge her, reminding her to clap when Nita, bursting with pride, accepted the honorable mention for her age group in the pie-baking contest.

But it was Merrilee, intuitive, tender-hearted Merrilee, who finally roused Rorie from her emotional hibernation.

"I miss Uncle Wes too, ma'am."

Starting, Rorie gazed down at the child holding her hand. She couldn't imagine how Merrilee had appraised her situation. Ever practical, however, Rorie decided she must have given herself away somehow, perhaps by gazing at Wes while he kept vigil across the street. Arms akimbo, he stood rigid and foreboding, the epitome of lawful intimidation to keep the marksmen in line as they warmed up for the shooting match. To Rorie's consternation his gaze seemed to be riveted on her.

"Mama says missing Uncle Wes makes you sad," Merrilee went on earnestly.

"Mama?" Rorie repeated weakly. For as long as she could remember, Merrilee had talked to her mother as if she were a daily presence in her life. Rorie had patiently tolerated the child's fantasies in the hopes that Merrilee would outgrow them and her grief. Still, Merrilee's references to her mother never failed to trigger a painful feeling of rejection in Rorie—not to mention a prickling sensation of disquiet.

Merrilee nodded, her blue-black pigtails bobbing. "Mama says you'll be happy again soon, though. She likes you, Miss Rorie."

Ethan, who'd been frowning throughout this exchange, shook his head at the child. "Burro milk, Merrilee. Your mother is—"

"*Ethan,*" Rorie warned, shooting him her fiercest look.

He gazed at her in mild exasperation. "Miss Aurora, pardon my saying so, but it's downright nonsense, the child prattling on about her mother that way. The woman died three years ago."

Rorie bristled at his criticism of her child, but it was Merrilee who rose to her own defense, showing an uncharacteristic asperity.

"Just because *you* can't see Mama doesn't mean she's gone away, Mr. Ethan. But Mama forgives you for saying so. And I do too."

Ethan blinked at his comeuppance. Before he could argue his point, however, his son Nathaniel—the one who lived in Elodea—ran toward them through the crowd.

"Pa," he panted, "you just got a wire. Sounds urgent."

Ethan's eyebrows knitted together. Glancing at the contestants who were taking their places for the first round, he repeated reluctantly, "Urgent?"

"Yes, sir. I reckon you'll want to come see."

Ethan muttered something about poor timing. Sighing, he tipped his hat to Rorie and made his apologies, patting Merrilee on the head before he worked his way through the crowd to the telegraph office.

Merrilee watched the two men leave. "I don't think Mr. Ethan likes Comanches very much," she said thoughtfully.

"Who does, feather duster?" came a jeering voice from behind her.

Rorie turned to see Danny Dukker. His hands splayed on his hips, he stood with his legs spread, his feet bare, and his overalls rolled up to his scabbed knees. The faint tint of a shiner lingered under his healing left eye. The boy looked as if he hadn't seen a comb—or a bathtub—in several days.

"It's not nice to call people names, Danny," Merrilee said with adultlike patience.

Danny grinned at her, showing a broken front tooth. "Yeah? So what."

Rorie saw the gleam in the boy's pale gray eyes, and she suspected Danny was carrying a bit of a torch for

Merrilee. She didn't know whether to be amused or alarmed.

"Danny, where's your father?"

He leered at Rorie, giving her a ribald wink. "Whoring, most likely. That stupid Ranger spoiled Pa's fun, shooting up the whiskey barrel and saying everyone had had enough to drink. Pa looked mad enough to kick a hog barefooted when he walked out of the square. But I reckon he'll be back in time to see Creed whip that whitenigger of yours in the shooting match."

Rorie sighed, less surprised by Danny's vulgar behavior than she was saddened by it. Hannibal Dukker wasn't fit to raise a hound, much less a child.

"Yes, well, we're all looking forward to a fair contest, Danny."

The boy snorted.

Meanwhile, Mayor Faraday was climbing the steps of the city father's platform with Lorelei, whose job, as the reining County Fair Queen, was to kiss the winner and award the prize. Two town councilmen already sat beneath the shade of the white-and-yellow tent.

"Looks like they're about to begin," Rorie said, catching the eye of Ginevee.

She waved her friend forward, and Nita and Topher followed in her wake. Topher's face darkened considerably when he spied Danny. He picked up his pace, elbowing his way through the spectators.

"This view stinks," Danny said abruptly, scowling at his approaching rival. "I'm finding me a better spot. See you around, feather duster."

He yanked one of Merrilee's braids, and she squealed in surprise.

"*Hey!*" Topher was barreling through irritated bystanders now, intent on pummeling Danny.

"Hey yourself, toad," Danny taunted, exaggerating Topher's lisp. He made an obscene gesture, then laughed, disappearing into the ever-shifting crowd.

Rorie had to grab hold of Topher's overall straps to keep him and his flailing fists from charging after Danny.

Merrilee winced, rubbing her head. "Why does Danny always pull my hair?"

"Boys do that when they like you," Nita said sagely.

"They do?" Merrilee's eyes grew impossibly round. "But Topher doesn't do that."

"Well, I can start," Topher said, folding his arms in a huff.

Rorie was forced to hide the first smile she'd had all day. "That won't be necessary, Topher."

Ginevee chuckled, passing a basket of ice chips to the others.

Sucking on an icicle seemed to cool Topher off, although he did spend a frenzied minute jumping and shouting to catch Wes's attention. Wes tipped his hat to the boy, but otherwise his features remained carved from bronzed marble as he stood near the firing line. Rorie's heart twisted when his shadowed gaze bored into hers. She forced herself to turn away and watch the contestants.

True to her earlier prediction, there were twenty men of all backgrounds and ages competing for the hundred-dollar prize. The judging committee decreed there would be two preliminary flights of ten men each, and the top three sharpshooters in each flight would go on to the semi-final round.

Lots were drawn among the contestants, and Shae found himself pitted against Creed from the start.

Of course there other notable deadeyes in the lineup. Topher and Nita cheered for Jasper in the first round. His hunting practice had stood him in good stead, because when the smoke cleared, he was the only marksman from his flight to hit the bull's-eye. Tom Parker wasn't quite as fortunate, but he still claimed third place.

Then came Creed's and Shae's turns. Rorie noticed uncomfortably that a sweaty, sneering Hannibal Dukker had materialized with a whiskey bottle in his fist. He stood beneath the judging platform, as much a critic of his son's performance as the men who were officiating over the match.

"Give 'em hell, Creed!" Danny screeched, cupping his hands around his mouth.

Topher scowled, watching Danny. The boy stomped on a barrel and banged a stick against a metal drain pipe when Shae stepped forward to fire. Outraged, several spectators demanded the boy stop. During the resulting hail of insults and threats, Hannibal Dukker stalked over to keep the peace. The noise subsided instantly, and the spectators slinked off under the threat of Dukker's fists. Danny, his cheeks looking rather bleached for so much heat, huddled like a church mouse on his barrel.

At last, the judges finished inspecting the targets. Shae had made the second-closest bull's-eye. Creed had hit dead center.

"I think we should all scream and stomp next time Creed fires," Topher muttered.

"Children," Rorie said, "Shae can win without us cheating for him."

"Yeah." Nita nodded emphatically, but her eyes were anxious as she glanced at Ginevee. "Do you reckon Shae's just not used to Uncle Wes's rifle?"

Rorie started. She hadn't realized Shae had exchanged Gator's carbine for Wes's Winchester, and this proof of Wes's growing bond with Shae only made her feel more miserable about the decision she'd had to make.

For the semi-final round, more lot drawing ensued to determine firing order. The slates were wiped clean, and the six contestants faced new targets in the late-afternoon light. By some divine providence, Creed and Shae were placed at opposite ends of the line.

Ethan reemerged from the crowd.

"I got troubles back home, Miss Aurora. Rustlers got my damned best bull and a couple of stud ponies too. Me and the boys are saddling up now to track those brand blotters down. But I don't feel right about leaving you and the young ones by your lonesome. We'll see y'all home first, if you're of a mind."

"Go home *now*?" Topher's chin jutted. "Have you lost your cotton-picking—"

Ginevee's hand clapped over his mouth, garbling the rest. Nita's and Merrilee's eyes both pleaded with Rorie, and she secretly had to admit she didn't much like the idea of cutting her family's fun short so Ethan could chase down a bull.

"No, Ethan. We'll stay for the barbecue," she said

firmly. "I'm sure Tom and Jasper will be happy to see us home."

Ethan looked torn, but Nathaniel was holding the reins of the palomino and shouting for his father to hurry.

He finally nodded to her in exasperation. "Suit yourself, Miss Aurora."

Topher made a face at Ethan's back, and the girls giggled. Rorie sighed. Married life with Ethan would certainly have its challenges.

Meanwhile, Shae was stepping back from the line with his smoking rifle. When the judges proclaimed him the winner of the semi-final round, Topher, Nita, and Merrilee went wild.

In the glaring westward sun, the final round began. Shae leveled his rifle and fired three times in rapid succession. Creed, his lip curling, stepped forward and did the same. The other two contestants took their turns, and a hush settled over the spectators. Mayor Faraday and his daughter clambered down the platform for the final call.

It took several minutes for the judges to inspect and measure the four straw-backed targets. A lot of gesturing and headshaking ensued before they sent a young runner back down the street's two hundred yards to report the findings to Faraday.

The boy panted something into the mayor's ear.

"A tie?" Faraday's booming voice carried easily to every straining ear.

Whispers of speculation followed his announcement. Jasper and the other man stepped respectfully from the firing line as Faraday waved Creed and Shae forward.

"The hell there's a tie," Hannibal Dukker shouted in a slurred voice. "You old men need to wipe the crud from your spectacles."

Creed looked immensely uncomfortable. Mopping his brow, which was made high by thinning hair, he glanced sheepishly at Lorelei, standing only an arm's length away. Her eyes were only for Shae, though. Dukker took a threatening step toward the boy, and Wes moved unhurriedly to Shae's side.

Faraday cleared his throat. "As I was saying, boys." He raised his voice so every bystander could hear. "You'll need three more cartridges to break your tie. We'll draw straws to see who fires first."

Topher and Nita were almost beside themselves when Creed pulled the short straw and had to fire first. The boy resorted to complaints, protesting just about everything imaginable, including the sun's glare off a particularly distracting window.

"If you'd been man enough, boy, you would have won already," Dukker yelled at his son.

Red-faced, Creed fell silent, forced to take his place on the firing line. For the first time since she'd known him, Rorie's heart went out to the boy. As much as she wanted to see Shae win, she didn't want to see Creed publicly humiliated by his father. Even Lorelei looked sympathetic toward the suitor she'd once spurned.

When Creed's smoke cleared, Shae took his turn. Immediately, the judges scrambled to the targets, and more measuring, gesturing, and headshaking ensued.

The runners sprinted back to Faraday with the judges' decision. The mayor grew visibly tense, his smile strained.

"Well, folks, we got our winner. Taking first place in the hundred-dollar prize in Elodea's Twenty-fifth Annual Founder's Day Shooting Spree is . . . Shae McFadden."

The orphans cheered. County residents who knew and respected Shae loosed a ripple of applause. But for the most part, the faces around Rorie darkened. She felt Elodea's hostility so keenly, she grabbed Merrilee and Topher, pulling them protectively against her legs.

Lorelei was the one town resident who displayed unabashed delight at the announcement. Before anyone else near Shae could react, she bounded forward, her tiara twinkling like starlight, and reached up on tiptoe to kiss his cheek. She never got past the lip-puckering stage.

With a roar that sounded half bear's and half bull's, Hannibal Dukker lunged forward, grabbing her arm and wrenching her away from Shae.

"What's the matter with you?" he shouted at her. "Are you some nigger-loving whore?"

Stunned, Lorelei stumbled into her father's arms. Creed stepped hastily to her defense.

"Leave her alone, Pa. McFadden won the match fair and square."

Rorie held her breath. She thought everyone on the street did at that moment, except for Wes, who stood poised to draw his gun with his right hand and to slap Dukker in irons with his left.

"And I say you were *distracted*, you idiot." Dukker shoved Creed aside and turned his venomous stare on Shae. "You were distracted by the stench of this nigger."

"It's hard to believe," Shae retorted with the aplomb of a trial attorney, "that you could smell anything more than the blood on your hands. *Cousin.*"

The kinship dig, more than the other, set Hannibal into another spittle-flecked rage. He took a swing at Shae, who ducked easily. Before either man could throw another punch, though, Wes grabbed Dukker's holstered gun from behind and slammed him facedown on the ground. The older man squirmed, trying to roll over, but Wes's knee pinned him between his shoulder blades. His manacles clamped with a snap over Dukker's wrists.

It all happened so quickly, even Topher stood speechless, his heart racing beneath Rorie's forearm. As Wes hauled Dukker to his feet, the lawman screeched vulgarities, first at Wes, then at Shae, then at his son for standing like a half-wit and not "plugging the Ranger bastard."

Impervious to his prisoner's cursing, Wes spun him around and ripped the badge from his shirt.

"Hey!" Dukker writhed like a snake trying to shed its skin. "You can't take my badge. *Faraday!* You lily-livered prick, tell him who you made law in this town!"

"Shutup, Dukker," Wes said flatly. "You're under arrest for disturbing the peace . . . until I can find evidence of your other crimes."

"The hell I am! You won't get away with this, Rawlins. This here's my town, and no rooster-headed son of a—"

Wes shoved his neckerchief into Dukker's mouth. The town marshal turned purple trying to spit it and his threats out at the same time.

Wes pushed him forward, and the crowd parted in a mixture of shock and awe as the Ranger marched their marshal off to jail. Creed, thin lipped and ashen, hiked his rifle over his shoulder and stalked off in the opposite direction.

That's when Rorie noticed Danny. He was standing on the barrel again, his young face raw with upset as he looked from his father's retreating back to his brother's. Rorie's heart ached for the boy. She thought to call to him, to try to ease his hurt.

But the hardware store's owner was storming toward the boy with threats to cuff Danny for denting the drain pipe. Sticking out his tongue, Danny jumped down and bolted for the safety of the alley.

Minutes later, as Rorie was trying to calm her children and lead them safely through the angry crowd, she spied Danny slinking through the shadows beneath the jail's barred window.

Chapter Twenty-one

*T*he orphans all agreed it was time to leave town.

Even Topher only put up a token fuss when Rorie marched him to the livery and told him to wait there with Ginevee and the other children while she went to retrieve Po.

Shae, who had gone in search of Tom and Jasper, had promised to meet her back at the wagon in fifteen minutes. In light of the day's events, Rorie worried that even a quarter of an hour might be too much time to waste.

In spite of the no-gun ordinance, many Elodeans were carrying rifles, thanks to the shooting match. Some were openly belligerent toward her, their eyes and brains dulled by drink. She did her best to ignore their scathing words and glances as she hurried down the street. After all, she wasn't worried for herself. She was worried for Shae. Although slavery might have been abolished in Texas, bigotry flourished. There wasn't a white man in Elodea who thought a black boy deserved a hundred-dollar prize.

Especially at a white boy's expense.

Her uneasiness spurring her on, she was at a near trot as she passed Sultan's Saloon, where most of the rowdies appeared to be congregating. Ordinarily, she would have avoided this side of Main Street, but Wes's office

was on the other side with Elodea's town jail. Having
been stabbed repeatedly throughout the day by his pine
needle green glare, she decided she would much prefer to
brave a mob than bleed a single moment longer from his
stare.

Her timing, unfortunately, couldn't have been worse.
She'd no sooner reached the corner of Main and the ap-
propriately named Calaboose Alley, when the door of
Dukker's office squealed open and Wes emerged. The in-
carcerated marshal shrieked profanities after Wes, threats
that curdled her blood, but Wes ignored Dukker. As he
slammed the door and turned the key, she thought of
ducking into the blacksmith's shop to spare herself a confrontation. It was already too late, though. With the instincts of a wolf, he'd sensed her—his mate.

Her knees turned to rubber as his hot, fierce gaze
slammed into her. The hunger in his glare was as potent
as the anger. When he stepped into the street, his long,
lean legs chewing up the yards between them, she nearly
panicked. She might have turned tail and fled if she
thought it would save her.

He halted before her. Her tongue swelled and her
mouth grew unpleasantly dry. Perhaps it was his Stetson
or the muscles in his rigid neck and shoulders, but he
looked taller than she remembered—broader and more
dangerous too.

An electrical charge of some sort, a pulsating current
of elemental need, crackled between them. He caught her
chin in his hand, and her heart leaped to her throat. She
could feel the restrained strength throbbing through his
fingertips, but his grip was not hard, only firm. It left
little doubt in her mind that he could possess her instantly, if he so desired.

"Come with me."

Abruptly, he grabbed her hand and pulled it through
the crook of his arm. It remained there throughout their
walk. She didn't dare try to extract it, not when she could
feel the shivery tenseness of his bicep, like a warning, beneath her palm. His silence was unnerving enough.

He led her to the cramped ticket office that Gator
had turned into his Elodea headquarters. Recalling the

last confrontation she and Wes had had there, she glanced uneasily at his stony face as he held the door open for her. His features were shuttered, giving nothing away—except a hint of the Ranger ferocity, which he wore like a warrior's armor.

She didn't know which unsettled her more, entering the dim room with its shuttered window, or hearing the discordant clatter of his unwieldy key ring when he tossed it into a desk drawer and locked it inside. Turning reluctantly, she found him barring her escape, his legs spread and his arms folded as he stood in front of the door.

"If you're trying to punish me," he said, "you're doing a damned fine job."

"W–what do you mean?"

"I mean I can't help what I am. And I can't change overnight. But you—" his voice grew harsh and gravelly, "you just can't seem to see past all your hurt and prejudice to cut me any slack. What does it take, Rorie, to make you trust a man?"

"Wes." She struggled to keep her voice gentle, devoid of the blistering torment in her breast. He was dynamite on a very short fuse, and she could feel the explosion just waiting to blow. "Trust is no longer the issue between us. And I don't want to change you. I fell in love with who you are. I would never ask you to be something different—to become miserable in some misguided attempt to please me."

"Then dammit—" He battled visibly to leash his temper. "Why can't you be patient? Why won't you give me the time I need to work Rangering out of my blood?"

She sighed, dropping her eyes. She had known this wouldn't be easy. She might as well try to reason with a volcano.

"Because I have four children who need a father. Now."

"Your children need someone who can teach them, protect them, and love them too. They need more than a male figure to discipline them, Rorie, and that's all Hawkins will ever be to them."

"You're not being fair to Ethan."

"And you're not being fair to me!"

She cringed as his outburst nearly rattled the window. He stalked toward her, looking hell-bent on rattling her too. In spite of every common-sense command to keep calm and not feed his fury, she retreated before his advance.

Her buttocks struck the desk, and she turned anxious and angry by turns. How dare he trap her, throwing his size and strength around in an effort to intimidate her! Even in Texas, where swaggering male braggarts reigned supreme, a woman had the legal right to court, marry, and raise her children with whomever she pleased!

"Wes, that's far enough. I will not have you bullying me because you can't have your way. I'm marrying Ethan because that's the best course of action for everyone involved, yourself included. If you would take just ten minutes to calm down and think things through, you would undoubtedly see I'm right."

"That's the problem with you, Aurora. You think when you should be feeling."

"And you feel when you should be thinking," she fired back, her patience unraveling faster with each second that his looming presence bent her backward over his desk. "Put your childish jealousy aside for two seconds and kindly recall the facts. You want children. Redheaded sons and daughters of your own. Well, *I can't give them to you.*"

If she had thrown ice water in his face, she couldn't have stunned him more. His eyes widened; he drew a sharp breath. Straightening an inch or two, he allowed her to draw herself to her full height. She was glad for the chance to fortify her defenses, because she hadn't realized just how deeply hope had wormed its way into her heart.

But in that moment when dawning comprehension flickered across his face, he confirmed in her mind the bitter, dreaded truth: his need to have a son outweighed the love he felt for her.

Only then did Rorie fully and finally accept that Wescott Rawlins could never be her husband.

"And now," she said, choking down a sob, "if you'll excuse me, Wes, I have children waiting for me outside."

"Rorie, no." He caught her shoulders, anguish warring with the denial in his eyes. "It will be different between us. You'll see. We can—"

"We *can't*, Wes." A tear dribbled past her lashes. "I tried to conceive for seven years. My husband was a doctor, and even he couldn't find a cure for my condition. I can never be a mother. But Ethan doesn't need a woman to give him children like you do. He has three sons already, so he can take me as his wife without expectations or regrets."

"No! I won't let you marry Hawkins!"

Before she could protest, his mouth crushed hers, and he dragged her hard against him. Her senses sizzled as the familiar fire flared, showering sparks and fanning smoke between them. As his hand gripped her buttocks, grinding her hips into his arousal, she could feel the heat coursing through his length.

"Oh, Wes," she gasped, tasting tears and suspecting they didn't belong solely to her. "Don't."

She tried pushing against his chest, his shoulders, but his strength was too great and his need too strong. When she turned her face away, he made a guttural sound, his mouth hot and hungry as it fastened on her throat. She felt her heels sliding out from under her as he bowed her spine back; she felt her resistance melting as his fevered hands started grabbing fistfuls of her skirt and pulling it up her legs.

"Wes, stop."

She knew within seconds her will would be consumed, that she would ignite with the forbidden desire she felt for this man. If she didn't do something drastic, something shocking, his frenzied passion would drag her down. She would thrash and moan, as wanton as any saloon girl whether he took her on the desk or on the floor.

In desperation, she leaned back and struck his face full force.

He staggered back. His hand flew to the crimson stain on his cheek, and the hurt in his eyes nearly killed her.

"Let me go." Her voice cracked as she backed for the door. "Accept what cannot be."

Then she stumbled out onto the sidewalk, blinded by

a sun that was setting on her hopes and dreams, and turning her heart to ashes.

Wes reeled, his vision too blurred to see as he groped for support.

"Aurora . . ."

His hand struck the desk, and he sank heavily, perching on the scarred wood top.

She was gone. This time he had lost her forever.

"Rorie . . ."

His voice broke, and he buried his face in his hands, shaking with the helpless rage and grief that ripped up his insides. Not until she'd thrown sons in his face had he fully realized what her barrenness would mean if he pursued a future with her. And yet, how could he let her walk out of his life? How could he let her become some other man's wife? He loved her. He loved the children too. But she'd made up her mind for them both. She expected his heart to live with her choice.

Accept what cannot be.

The memory of her words was a private hell that burned through all the fibers of his body. Everything inside of him shriveled and crumbled, like the charcoal remains of a tree after the onslaught of a forest fire. It hurt too much to think, to breathe, to be.

He raised his head. Staring glassily out the open door, he tried to catch some last, fleeing glimpse of her. But it was a faded red-and-black sign that swam into focus.

He heaved himself to his feet. He reached for his hat and the Winchester Shae had returned. The crowd had largely dispersed, and the womenfolk were dragging their drunken men home. Now it was his turn to ride the bottle to damnation.

With a self-deprecating sneer, he headed for Sultan's saloon, never noticing the boy-sized shadow that cowered behind the potbellied stove in his office.

He never heard the scraping of a widdy in the desk drawer's lock, or the rattle of the key ring he'd thought was safe from theft.

* * *

Danny had never seen a man cry before. He'd seen women cry—mostly his ma, after his pa was finished beating her—and he'd even cried himself a few times, when his pa had given him a blackened eye or broken tooth.

But he'd never seen Creed cry. He'd never seen his pa cry, either. Danny should have known that sarsaparilla-chugging Ranger was nothing but a sissy.

Slinking through the alleys, heedless of their refuse, Danny crouched beneath the window of the jail and waited for some whooping, six-shooting cowboys to stagger out of sight. His heart raced with the excitement and the danger. The drunkards, not the Ranger, worried him. After all, Danny had seen what his pa did when he got roostered, and the memories scared Danny down to his bones.

Everything about his pa scared him sometimes, like the time Pa had threatened to kill him just for stealing a five-cent piece from the dresser to buy a couple of candies. Luckily, Creed had come home, and he'd sobered up right quick to find Pa's hands squeezing Danny's throat.

It bothered Danny that Pa and Creed fought like wild Indians, mostly over Miss Lorelei. Still, it was nice not to be hit, and when Creed was around, he would take the blows himself before he'd let Pa strike Danny.

But Creed wasn't around much anymore, now that he was chasing that little cockteaser—that's what Pa called Miss Lorelei. Pa didn't like the way Miss Lorelei put on airs, and when Pa didn't like something, he drank, which never boded well for Danny. But Danny figured Pa wouldn't try to hit him for a whole week, maybe even longer, if Danny was the one who got Pa out of jail.

Tiptoeing around the corner of the building, Danny fumbled with the lock and finally pushed inside. In the shaft of moonlight that spilled from the window into the holding cell, he could see two beady eyes, as red and wild as a javalina's, glaring at him from the lump of whiskey-stale flesh on the floor. Yellowed teeth glinted dully as Pa drew back his lips, and Danny edged uneasily forward. He knew that look. It meant trouble.

"What took you so long, boy?"

Danny winced as Pa's breath washed over him.

"Rawlins was fighting with that old schoolmarm."

"Yeah?" Pa lumbered to his feet, snatching the keys from Danny's inexpert hands and unlocking the cell door himself. "What were them two fighting about?"

Danny frowned, trying to remember. All that jawing and boo-hooing hadn't made much sense to him.

"Babies. And getting hitched, I think."

Pa's lips twisted in his I-got-a-rabbit-in-my-gunsights grin. "You don't say?"

He held out his hand, wiggling his fingers, and Danny carefully pulled from his boot the Remington he'd stolen from the Ranger's desk. Unhooking the safety, Pa spun the wheel and gave a satisfied grunt.

"I got your badge too," Danny said eagerly, plucking the tin star from his shirt.

Pa holstered his gun. "Good work, boy."

Danny beamed. Pa must love him again.

"Where the hell's that no-account, Nancy-boy brother of yours?"

Danny jumped up to sit on the desk, watching curiously as Pa heaved and cursed, pushing a stack of firewood away from the stove.

"Sultan's, I reckon. The Ranger went there, too, but now he's gone."

Pa looked up sharply. "Gone?"

Danny nodded. "Yeah. I saw him ride off with a whiskey bottle a little while ago, after his fight with the schoolmarm."

Pa snorted and knelt. He jimmied up a couple of loose floorboards, then pulled a cedar box from the cobwebs underneath the floor.

"Light the lamp, boy."

Danny scrambled to obey, then watched as Pa grabbed the crowbar he always used to "rattle the cage" when he was bored and his prisoners weren't much fun. Soon he'd pried the nails off the lid and was pulling a gunnysack, robe, and black cloth gloves from the box.

"What about McFadden?" Pa's lip curled over the name.

"Well, after Miss Lorelei gave him his kiss and his

rize, he made a beeline for the bank. I saw him drive off
little later with the rest of that half-breed trash."

"Little bitch," Pa muttered. "She ain't half as smart
s she thinks she is, cozying up with her questions and
er tits."

Pa was inspecting the gunnysack now. It had four
oles on one side, kind of like an All Hallow's Eve mask.
His grin came back, the one that always made Danny's
kin goose-pimply.

"I got a job for you, boy."

"Yeah, Pa?" Danny sat up with excitement. It wasn't
ften that Pa chose him for a job over Creed.

"Go over to the hoedown. Find the cockteaser and
et her outside, away from all the lights. But don't let her
now it's me who's waiting for her. Be real secretive like.
ay it's . . . McFadden. Yeah, McFadden. Think you can
o that, boy?"

Danny nodded, a little disappointed by such an easy
ask. "Sure, Pa. But then what'll I do?"

Pa smirked, pulling on his gloves and flexing one
and into a black fist.

"Well, son, then you can watch me give Miss Lorelei
ust what she's been asking for."

At ten o'clock, Rorie wearily blew out the sitting
oom lamp. Founder's Day had been the longest, most
rutal experience of her life, and she was glad it was fi-
ially over. Not that she actually thought she might sleep
vhen she climbed the stairs to her bed. Far from it. The
ook on Wes's face as she'd run out the door that after-
loon would haunt her the rest of her life. No amount of
ustification could erase the grief she'd caused him.

She'd tried her best to make the choice that would
erve the highest good for all. Yet even though she'd made
he most logical, fact-based decision possible, everyone in-
rolved was bitterly unhappy. How could something so
ensible feel so wrong?

She felt as if she was being punished. To make mat-
ers worse, her misery had upset her stomach again.
Ginevee had helped her out of the wagon during one of
everal retching-stops along the way home, and the dear

woman had stumbled over a gopher hole. Now Ginevee'
ankle was swollen twice its normal size. She was an eve
poorer patient than Rorie, and Rorie didn't know hov
she was going to keep her friend off her feet for the nex
couple of days.

A distant shout and the muffled pounding of hoove
distracted her from her worries. Glancing out the win
dow, she saw Shae emerge from the barn, where he'
been filling the animals' watering troughs for the night
He set down his bucket, squinting at the moonlit silhou
ette of horse and rider. She went out the front door to
join him.

"Do you think it's Jasper?" she asked hopefully. He
and Tom had been too indisposed for Shae to drag them
down from Sultan's second-story "Tea Room" when the
time came to leave. Rorie just hoped the boys wouldn'
catch any diseases from their "hostesses."

Shae frowned. "Not likely. I've never seen Jasper ride
like that."

Crouched high on his mount's neck, the rider was
pushing his horse hard, shouting encouragements mixed
with curses. An uneasy feeling slithered through Rorie's
innards. Something was wrong. Dreadfully wrong.

"McFadden!" It was Creed's voice, high and waver-
ing. His pitch was too shrill for belligerence; it sounded
urgent, even scared.

A muscle in Shae's jaw twitched. "Get inside," he
told her.

Running to the well, he grabbed his shotgun and
crouched down as Creed galloped up the drive.

"McFadden, don't shoot!"

Rorie hesitated, one foot on the porch stairs, one
foot in the yard.

"I've come to warn you!"

"That's far enough, Dukker," Shae shouted back,
raising his Whitney.

Creed swore, and his horse neighed, pawing the air
as Creed wrestled it to a halt.

"I don't have time to argue with you, boy! Lorelei's been hurt. She's been hurt bad. She . . . might not
make it."

Shae's shoulders tensed. "What do you mean, she's been hurt?"

"*Raped*, dammit, all right? Some bastard raped her!" Creed's voice broke, and his chest heaved. "Listen to me! Pa's getting together a posse. They're headed this way."

Rorie's heart stalled. Dukker was heading a posse? But surely Wes hadn't let him out of jail, even to avenge Lorelei.

In the distance, she could see a flickering of light. Those pinpoints must be a half-dozen or more torches. Dear Lord, what had happened to Wes?

Shae rose shakily to his feet. "But who—"

"I don't know! No one knows. She hasn't woken up since Danny found her. Now the whole town's out for blood—your blood, McFadden. Pa's got everyone convinced she kissed you, and you wanted more."

"That's a lie!" Shae's face looked unnaturally pale in the wash of the moon.

Rorie hurried to his side. She could feel him trembling.

"Shae's been here with me all evening, Creed."

"Hell, don't you think I know that? I saw you Sinclairs leave three hours ago, before the hoedown. But no one's going to believe you—or me either. I already tried. Your only chance is to ride out of here, McFadden. And don't go south to Hawkins's spread. That's the first place Pa will look once he leaves here."

The front door slammed, and an anxious Ginevee stood on the porch, surrounded by four pajama-clad children.

"What's going on?" Topher mumbled, knuckling the sleep from his eyes.

"Everyone inside," Rorie snapped, her brain whirring into action in her otherwise frozen body. "Ginevee, grab a canteen. Food. Ammo. Nita, get me a pen and paper."

"But—"

"*Now*, Topher. Everyone inside."

Shae, meanwhile, had spotted the torches. "Where's Rawlins?" he demanded uneasily.

"Don't know. I ain't seen hide nor hair of your

Ranger friend since he cozied up to a whiskey bottle
That was nearly two hours ago." Creed started to shorten
his reins. "Look, boy, I've done all I can do for you. Now
I got to go find my brother."

"Why aren't you riding with the posse?"

Creed looked over his shoulder at Shae as he wheeled
his skittering mount. "Because Pa's gone too far this time.
Too damned far."

As Creed spurred his horse back down the drive
toward town, Rorie grabbed Shae's arm.

"Hurry, Shae. Saddle Daisy."

Shae's grip tightened on his shotgun, and his gaze
shifted from the torches to her. "But what about Lorelei?
And I can't leave you and the children—"

"Don't argue!" She pushed him toward the barn.
"It's not us they want, it's you. Hurry! You can go to the
Rawlins ranch. It's not more than a day's ride north of
here."

Oh God, Wes, where are you?

In record time, Ginevee had returned, hobbling outside with a bulging satchel and Gator's Smith and Wesson
revolver. Heedless of the pain it must have caused her, she
limped down the stairs toward Shae, who was dragging a
recalcitrant Daisy from her stall. Ginevee glanced from
the torches, which were growing ever larger on the horizon, back to her grandson, and her eyes brimmed.

"Shae?" she whispered hoarsely.

The boy swallowed. "Maw-Maw."

He held open his arms, and she rushed to him, clinging to his shirt front for a moment.

"You be safe, boy." She pushed him away, her dark
cheeks glistening with tears. "Come back to me, you
hear?"

"Yes, Maw-Maw."

Rorie dashed off a few words of explanation to
Fancy as Nita hovered nervously nearby.

"Take this to Wes's sister-in-law," she instructed,
shoving the note into Shae's saddlebag as he mounted.
"Tell her—tell his brothers—what's been going on
here. Tell them Wes needs help."

Shae nodded. "You'll need a gun—"

"We've got the carbine. Don't worry about us. Go, hae, please."

His jaw hardened, and he pulled his hat brim down ver his eyes. "I'll be back in two days' time. I'll be back o get the sonuvabitch who did this to Lorelei."

Rorie clasped her quaking hands, watching as the oy who was like a son to her spurred Daisy toward the ield. She prayed to God she would see him alive again.

"Nita," Ginevee called hoarsely, "get the broom, hild. I need to sweep his tracks."

"I'll do it, Ginevee," Rorie said. "You need to get off our feet. Go inside with the children."

The old woman worried her bottom lip. "Aurora, ou can't take on Hannibal Dukker by yourself."

Rorie drew herself up stiffly. It was the only way she ould stop the trembling in her knees. "I have no intenion of taking on Hannibal Dukker. There has to be at east one reasonable man in that posse, and I'll appeal to is sense of decency. If we're lucky, Dukker will mistake Creed's tracks for Shae's. If not, maybe I can buy Shae :nough time so he can get to the cliffs at Ramble Creek. Dukker will have a hard time tracking him through here."

"And the children?" Ginevee asked, glancing anxously toward the porch, where Topher and Merrilee :tood on either side of Po, holding his hands.

"I'm sure even Hannibal Dukker wouldn't harm a :hild." Rorie struggled to sound convincing in the face of her gnawing doubt. "But just to be safe, take the carbine upstairs with you."

The two women's eyes locked. A silent understanding, age-old and maternal, passed between them. Rorie knew Ginevee would fight with her to the death for the children.

"Everybody back upstairs," Ginevee said, shooing the orphans before her.

Rorie took the broom and turned fearful eyes toward the ever-approaching flickers of light.

Wes, we need you. Please, please, come back.

* * *

Wes slouched down on his favorite Ramble Creek boulder and glared at a slew of green glass fragments and their dripping, golden contents. Now *there* was one damnable waste of a bender, that was certain.

He'd poured no more than three or four shots' worth of tarantula juice down his gullet before the whole con sarned bottle had slipped through his fingers, shattering on the rocky earth between his boots. The whiskey might be making the catfish howl, but he didn't feel one iota better as he watched it run into the murky waters.

In fact, he was thinking about heading back to town for another bottle. Or better yet, a keg. The damned moonshiners had the right idea, corking up wooden vessels. They were hard to break.

Two-Step, big moocher that he was, wandered over to sniff at the glass, then apparently disappointed, tried making a midnight snack of Wes's hat. Wes snatched his prized Stetson out of reach and scowled at his four-footed friend.

"What do you want, crow bait? I don't have any carrots or apples here with me. Merrilee spoiled you rotten."

Two-Step snorted, turning his head to regard Wes through one bright, curious eye.

"Think you know so much with all your horse sense, eh? Think I'm being punished for going back on my drinking oath, right? Well, that just shows you don't know nothing. I rode all the way out here so I could cut my wolf loose without hurting anybody. I got me a bottle and nobody's been jinxed yet, see? Nobody, except for me," he added miserably.

He'd been an uncurried fool to come to Ramble Creek, with its memories of loving and laughing with Rorie. But when he gave Two-Step his head, the old rascal had headed straight for Daisy's corral and home. It was just the sort of behavior a fellow should expect from his smart aleck pony.

"Only you aren't so smart, are you?" Wes muttered, pulling the velvet snout lower so he could glare into that eye. "I don't have a home anymore. And that means you don't either, fiddle foot."

Two-Step tossed his head.

"Yeah, well, I ain't too happy about it either, son."

Standing a trifle less steadily than usual, Wes let the world blink back into focus before he caught hold of Two-Step's reins. He was intent on heading back to Sultan's—and maybe even to the jail, to make sure his rabid cur of a prisoner hadn't chewed off some body part to escape. Then the distant sound of gunfire rolled across the hills and echoed off the cliff face.

Two-Step snorted, stomping. Straining his ears, Wes listened as the echo receded. He tried to determine the gunfire's origin, knowing that Gator's farm was only a mile to the east. The moon was still too dim for coon hunting, and that worried him.

He climbed into the saddle. Maybe hunters were just burning their powder, but Wes had the edgy, goose-prickling sensation that he needed to trot by Gator's farm, just to be sure. Just to prove to himself whiskey wasn't a curse every time it passed his lips.

A second rifle report sounded—rolling clearly from the east.

Merciful God.

With an oath and a shout, he spurred Two-Step hard toward the fringe of trees that marked the edge of Gator's property. The gelding bounded forward, chewing up the yards with long, powerful strides. For Wes, though, Two-Steps' breakneck gait wasn't nearly fast enough.

"C'mon, churn-head. *Come on!*"

Only a mile might have separated him from Rorie and the children, but it would be the longest mile of Wes's life.

Rorie stood with stiff, outward poise before Hannibal Dukker's five deputized Elodeans. Inwardly, however, she was queasy with fear. They'd already searched the storm cellar, combed the hayloft, and torn up the house looking for Shae. They had even shot off the lock on Gator's foot locker, hoping the boy might be hiding inside. Now, baleful and volatile, they were eager to vent their frustration.

Dukker stalked toward her. She was grateful for that. After his men had wrestled the carbine from Ginevee—

which had resulted in a misfire—they'd herded the chil
dren downstairs to huddle, trembling, on the front porch
As long as Rorie could keep Dukker's attention focuse
on her, she knew Ginevee and the children would be safe

"Search for tracks," Dukker snapped over his shoul
der at his men. Then he halted less than an arm's lengtl
from her.

She tried not to dwell on the stench of his rumple
shirt or the blast of stale liquor that struck her face. Sh
tried, too, not to telegraph any anxiety as she stare
squarely into the bloodshot eyes that glowed in the ma
cabre wash of the moon.

"All right, woman." Dukker tilted his head to glar
up at her, and she saw fresh scratch marks stretche
across his corpulent neck. "Where'd that murdering nig
ger bastard go?"

"I'm not Shae's keeper, Hannibal."

Swift as a snake, his hand lashed out, striking her
across the cheek. For a moment, she was so stunned by
this attack, all she could do was stumble backward, her
hand held to her stinging cheek.

"Leave her alone!" Topher shouted, struggling
against Nita and Ginevee, both of whom were trying to
keep him from dashing off the porch to her rescue.
Dukker had already cuffed the boy, raising a welt on his
temple, after Topher and his slingshot full of marbles had
defended the bedroom door against Dukker's deputies.

A cruel smile tugged at the marshal's lips.

"I reckon you know I mean business now, woman.
You want to tell me where McFadden went, or do you
want me to beat it out of your boy?"

Rorie repressed the urge to shudder. She couldn't
bear to think what an enraged Dukker might do to a boy
with Topher's sass.

"I'm sure you can't mean that, Hannibal. It's not the
sort of thing a lawman does, beating up a child."

He snorted. "Yeah? Well, that sarsaparilla-drinking
rooster you've been humping might be squeamish about
getting the answers he needs, but I ain't."

Rorie swallowed, glancing past him to the grumbling
townsmen whose mediocre tracking skills hadn't been

enhanced by the free whiskey they'd consumed at Founder's Day. She prayed Creed's tracks would catch the deputies' attention before the broom marks she'd left to obliterate Shae's.

"Topher doesn't know any more than I do, Hannibal," she said firmly. "He's been asleep for hours. All of us were sleeping, in fact, until you and your men broke down our doors."

"Is that so?" A sneer stretched Dukker's lips. "My cheating whore of a wife lied better than you do, Aurora. Hell, the Injuns who scalped my ma and pa lied better than you—till I grew up and cut their tongues out," he added menacingly, "and left their entrails for the buzzards."

Somehow, Rorie refrained from glancing at Merrilee, whose knees, she was certain, must be knocking.

"I'm sure I don't know what you mean, sir."

Suddenly, one of Dukker's men grew noticeably excited. "I found them! I found the tracks, Hannibal!"

Dukker didn't seem to hear. He didn't seem to notice, in fact, as his men mounted up, eagerly turning their horses in the direction of Creed's trail.

"Come on, Hannibal!"

Two of his five riflemen had already started toward town; the other three sat on their prancing, head-tossing horses waiting for orders.

Dukker licked his lips. He was leering at her, his eyes glazed and savage with a kind of half-crazed look.

"So you've been sleeping all this time, eh?"

He stalked even closer, but she stood her ground in spite of every screaming impulse to flee.

"If you've been asleep all this time, Aurora, where's your nightdress?" he taunted. "Under that day dress?"

Before she could suspect his intent, he reached out and grabbed her bodice, ripping it open and sending buttons flying.

"*Dukker!*"

It was Wes's voice. The earth shook with the pounding of Two-Step's hooves as the gelding broke from the cover of the house. His reins in his teeth, Wes rode as if he were fused to his mount as he raised his rifle stock to his shoulder.

One hapless deputy tried to turn a carbine on him only to have it—and his torch—blown from his hands.

Another man shrieked, his arm hanging limp as his rifle clattered to the drive. A second torch dropped.

Now there were two lines of fire, kindling the dry summer grasses that led to the barn.

"Dear God," Rorie whispered.

Above the pounding red rush of his fury, Wes heard Rorie's cries of "Fire!" Smoke swirled and flame whooshed, shooting up beneath Two-Step's hooves. The gelding obeyed the commands of Wes's knees, though charging down the fiery lines, scattering horses and riders.

"It's Rawlins! He's gone loco!" a wounded deputy shouted.

"I've got a wife and children. I don't want no trouble with Rangers!"

"Ride on, boys! Follow the tracks."

Seeing his deputies running like rabbits, Dukker bolted for his horse. Wes realized he had a choice: Gun down frightened townsmen who had no idea of their marshal's crimes, or draw blood from the bastard who'd dared to strike his woman.

"Dukker! Stand and fight, you sonuvabitch!"

Making an obscene gesture, Dukker shoved his rifle into his saddleboot.

It was more than Wes could bear. Denied the satisfaction of blowing Dukker to kingdom come, Wes spurred Two-Step closer. Just as Dukker was heaving himself into the saddle, Wes rammed his rifle stock into the marshal's gut. An oath wheezed from Dukker. Toppling from his horse, he landed flat on his back as his gelding shied away from Two-Step.

Wes snapped his rifle lever and took aim.

"Go ahead," Dukker panted, sneering up at him from his vulnerable, spread-eagle position. "Shoot me dead. Show the little kiddies what a big man you are."

"Wes!" It was Rorie's voice, shrill with panic. "We have to stop the fire!"

A tendril of smoke curled over Dukker's heaving

chest. Wes ground his teeth, fighting the murderous urge to end the bastard's life and be done with it. He'd fought too long for justice, though, to resort to vigilante tactics.

His grip tightened on his Winchester. "You're a dead man, Dukker."

For the first time, Wes saw fear in those wild, cur-dog eyes. It was enough to make him sick.

"Unbuckle your gun belt. Now!"

Dukker's hand shook as he obeyed.

"On your feet."

He rose unsteadily, suspiciously.

"You've got one minute to get off this land. Then I start firing."

Dukker scrambled for his horse.

"Not so fast! The rifle stays here. Toss it!"

Dukker hesitated, and Wes raised his Winchester again. He had the satisfaction of watching Dukker's weapon fly out of the saddleboot to skitter across the drive.

"Now you'd best run, old man. And you'd best say your prayers," Wes said savagely, "because there's not a place on this earth where I won't find you."

Dukker's face darkened and his eyes narrowed. His gaze flickered to Rorie, frantically beating at the snaking flames with a rug, then to the children, fighting beside her with buckets and shovels. His lips curled in an ominous sneer.

"I'll be waiting for you, boy."

With that, he threw himself into the saddle and spurred his horse to vault the flames, scattering Nita and Topher and nearly running down Ginevee.

"Wes!" Rorie coughed on the smoke as Topher doused the nearest patch of fire with a bucket of well water. "Get the watering trough from the manger! We can't lift it!"

He hit the ground running. Topher magically appeared by his side, helping him hoist the heavy, sloshing trough. They carried it outside and dumped it on the nearest blaze, which threatened a stack of cedar fence posts against the barn's new east wall.

With Wes's help, they contained the fires against the

gravel drive. Well water and a good deal of rug beating finally defeated the flames.

Soot-stained and grinning, Topher saluted Wes with a shovel. Nita caught Ginevee's arm and helped her hobble to the porch. Merrilee tried to hush Po, who'd been bawling ever since she grabbed him to keep him from charging into the fire.

Rorie dropped her rug. Turning as white as the magnolias in the tree behind her, she fainted dead away at Wes's feet.

Chapter Twenty-two

*R*orie woke to a bright haze of light, the acrid smell of smoke, and two anxious emerald eyes set in a bronzed and chiseled face.

"Did I . . . faint?" She shifted gingerly and heard the creaking of her mattress. "I did, didn't I? Oh, dear. But I never faint! I just can't understand—"

Two hungry lips silenced her, slanting possessively across hers. She gasped, and Wes's tongue pushed inside her mouth, fierce and sweet, demanding a response. A tear spilled down her cheek. Raising a trembling hand, she wove her fingers through his wealth of autumn-colored hair. She felt the bed sag as he knelt beside her; she felt his arms hard and tight around her shoulders.

In that moment, as he kissed her, there was no Ethan, no Dukker, no Shae. There was only her urgent, aching need to hold him, and the flutter of phoenix wings in the ashes of her heart.

"Miss Rorie?" Nita's voice was followed by a timid knock on her door. "Are you all right now?"

Growling in frustration, Wes raised his head. His pounding heart jolted through every fiber of her body. When she dared to peek at him, she saw the glint in his eyes and suspected it didn't bode well for interrupting children.

"They're scared, Wes," she whispered, doing her

best to sit up beneath his immovable chest. "Let them come in."

He cast her a narrowed I'm-not-finished-with-you look before he stalked to the door and threw it open. Four little bodies barreled past him, flinging themselves into Rorie's arms.

"I thought you were dead," Topher said shakily, burrowing into the curve of her hip.

"Me too," Nita whispered, clinging to her neck.

A moist cheek pushed against her throat. It had to belong to Po, since Merrilee's tear-stained face swam in the periphery of her vision. Despite her obvious distress, Merrilee nevertheless perched a respectful foot away on the edge of the bed. For a fleeting moment Rorie was disappointed by the child's physical and emotional distance, then Wes cleared his throat.

"I'm all right, children," she said quickly, glimpsing Wes's set jaw and folded arms above the heads of her sniffling cubs. "All that smoke made me light-headed and I fainted, that's all."

"But you *never* faint." Nita pressed a worried hand to Rorie's forehead.

The child's concern touched her deeply, since Nita's emerging womanhood often left her more interested in boys than her female caretaker.

Rorie mustered a smile for them all. "Yes, well, I'm sure it won't happen again."

"Good," Topher muttered.

"Where's Shae?"

Everyone stared at Wes's question. He wasn't usually left out of the children's displays of affection, and it pained Rorie to her core to realize he could never be a part of them again.

"There was some, er . . . trouble in town." Rorie chose words that, she hoped, would be the least upsetting to him and the children. "Creed rode out to warn Shae that he was in danger from Marshal Dukker's posse."

Wes looked incredulous. "*Creed* warned Shae?" His gaze flickered to the children, and he seemed to think better of whatever other exclamation of disbelief poised on his tongue. "Then what happened?"

"Well, Creed said it wouldn't be safe to ride to Ethan's, since that's the first place the posse would look. So I, um . . ." She drew a bolstering breath. "I sent Shae to your brothers' ranch."

"You did *what*?"

Although she'd expected his explosion, she cringed anyway. Even Topher cowered a little at his hero's outburst.

"Wes, I'm sorry, but I had to think fast. Dukker was already on his way. We could see the torches in the distance. Besides, I knew your brother Cord was a lawman once, and I figured he could help you find the man who hurt Lorelei Faraday . . ."

Her voice trailed off, and she swallowed, shaken by the blistering fury that crossed his features. With a scathing look that spoke volumes, he turned on his heel and stalked from the room.

Merrilee edged closer to Rorie. "Why is Uncle Wes so mad?"

Rorie managed a weak smile. "He's just worried about Shae."

She forestalled further questions by turning her attention to Nita. "Do you know where Ginevee is?"

The child's brow wrinkled. "Downstairs. I think she's having trouble climbing the steps. That's why she sent us to check on you."

Rorie shook her head. How typical that Ginevee should worry about everyone but herself.

"Well, you children tell Ginevee I'm just fine. And see if she needs anything before you go to bed. Tell her too that I'll be down shortly to help her upstairs. But first, I have to talk with Uncle—er, with Wes," she corrected herself.

She hated that she must strip him of that token endearment, but given the hostility between him and Ethan, she doubted her suitor would allow the children to continue calling Wes "uncle." She would have to speak with them about that on the morrow.

Rising gingerly as the children filed from her bedroom, Rorie glanced down at her shredded bodice and shuddered. Why Dukker had done such a thing was beyond her understanding, although the glint in his eye had not been entirely whiskey induced. Even if Dukker had been convinced by some misleading evidence that Shae was to blame for the heinous crime committed against Lorelei, there had been a frightening difference between the savagery Dukker displayed as a lawman and the ferocity Wes displayed.

In fact, having watched Dukker in action, she wasn't entirely certain he was sane. And her uncertainty made her doubly glad she'd called in assistance for Wes, no matter how angry her initiative had made him.

Donning a smokeless, soot-free gown, she hastily buttoned the bodice and crept downstairs. She wasn't looking forward to the coming confrontation with Wes, and when she saw him outside on the porch, his back rail-straight, she paused at the door, her hand on the frame. She wondered uneasily if it might not be wise to give him more time to calm down.

With that uncanny instinct of his, though, he must have sensed her presence. He turned his head, regarding her over his shoulder. When their gazes locked, her stomach did a strange little dance. Several heartbeats passed before she realized her pulse was racing.

Without a word, he turned his back on her again. Picking up his Winchester, he headed for the magnolia tree.

She fought off a searing disappointment. He was well within his rights not to speak to her, of course, yet surely he could stand to be a little more understanding! It wasn't as if she *enjoyed* tearing up his heart and tossing the pieces to the wind. She was hurting too—far more, in fact, than she dared to let him know.

Gathering the shreds of her courage, she stepped outside to follow him.

He wouldn't even look at her.

"Wes?"

His profile hardened at her gentle entreaty, and his chin jutted the tiniest bit. She could almost imagine Topher standing before her—at six-foot-four and weighing two hundred-odd pounds.

"I know what you're thinking. You're thinking I don't have any faith in you as a lawman. But that's not true. My sending Shae to your brother's ranch had nothing to do with your abilities to do your job. My only thought at the time was to find a safe place for Shae." She dragged a steadying breath into her lungs. "You have to know I did what I had to do. Just like you did . . . when you were working undercover."

She sensed rather than saw the tremor move through him, an electrically charged wave of heat that struck her flesh and left it smoking. She fidgeted in his stony silence.

"Wes," she tried again, "I know it cost you a lot to ride out here tonight after everything that passed between us. I don't know what made you come, but I'm grateful you did. *When* you did," she added, thinking of the tattered gingham on her bedroom floor.

"Did he hurt you?"

She started at the whiplike force of his words.

"No." She prayed he hadn't seen the knot on Topher's forehead. "None of us was hurt."

"What about Ginevee?"

His concern for an old black woman touched Rorie as much as it saddened her. As good a man as Ethan was, he still hadn't overcome his prejudice toward a people he'd once owned as slaves. "Ginevee twisted her ankle . . . er, earlier today."

He glanced at her sharply, and she blushed, not quite comfortable explaining the circumstances behind that event.

"Her injury had nothing to do with Dukker," she added firmly.

Wes pressed his lips together and went back to staring across the breeze-riffled meadow.

"And Lorelei?" he demanded.

"I'm sure Mayor Faraday must have let Dukker out of jail when Danny found . . ." Her voice faltered. Poor, sweet Lorelei. How did one speak of the unspeakable? "She . . . was violated, Wes."

He made a choking sound, growing pale before he darkened. "Who? Who was the bastard?"

"Creed said Lorelei hadn't regained consciousness to tell anyone yet and and—and that she might not live. Without a doctor in Elodea . . ." Rorie twisted her fingers into a knot. She didn't even want to think about the inevitable.

"You can imagine the bloodlust that ensued once the news spread," she said bleakly. "Dukker raised a posse to hunt down her attacker, because for some reason, everyone in town assumed it was Shae."

"No doubt that was Dukker's idea," Wes ground out. "Dammit! If I hadn't left town . . ."

"Wes." She touched his sleeve. "You can't blame yourself. It wasn't your fault."

"It was. I knew better than to go on a bender."

Her eyebrows knitted at this reasoning. "A bender? But what does your drinking—"

"It's a curse. Whenever I drink too much whiskey, someone I care about gets hurt."

"Wes," she chided in some concern.

"It's true! The first time I went on a bender, Zack and Aunt Lally were kidnapped by outlaws, and Fancy was nearly killed. The second time, my cousin Ginny miscarried her twins. Then there was the third time. And now this."

Rorie shifted uncomfortably. She had never put any stock in superstition, but Wes was clearly convinced he'd caused calamity by uncorking a bottle and draining its contents.

"You don't appear to be dangerous to me."

"That's because I only got three or four belts in me."

She sighed with relief. "Well, there, you see?" She used her most practical voice. "You didn't go on a bender tonight. So you can't blame yourself for what happened to Lorelei. Besides, Bandera County does have a new sheriff. One might question where the devil he was when all this happened."

Wes seemed reluctant to accept her perfectly legitimate rationale. He looked so miserable, in fact, that she suspected there must be some deeper reason for his guilt. Something he'd been punishing himself over for a long time. Perhaps she could make him see he wasn't to blame for that, either.

"Wes," she asked, "what happened the third time?"

He retreated closer to the tree trunk and folded his

arms across his chest. Starlight cast him in pewter shadow, making him appear more Olympian than ever. But unlike the fire-forged god he'd so often resembled, he was mortally—humanly—vulnerable. Her heart broke to see him so tormented. Edging closer, she struggled against the temptation to soothe him by stroking his hair.

"I'm not here to judge you," she murmured, "only to help."

Wes squeezed his eyes closed. Maybe it was true that his kinfolk's kidnaping and Ginny's miscarriage had been coincidental to those other benders. And maybe it was true he couldn't be held responsible for the cruelty perpetrated on Lorelei. After all, Dukker had been her most likely threat, and Wes had searched the weasel thoroughly for weapons and keys before locking him in jail. But striking Cord—For that, Wes had no one but himself to blame.

He sighed. His shame had been weighing so heavily upon him for such a long time, it was hard to find the words to speak, even to Rorie. He struggled for a minute, thinking better of saying anything, but somehow, the story began to tumble from his lips.

"I fell in love with Fancy when I was sixteen," he admitted, "when she saved my life. I even asked her to marry me once." He felt a stab of poignancy at the memory. "But she said I was too young, and besides, she was head-over-heels in love with Cord.

"There was a part of me that was glad to see them so happy," he continued earnestly, "but there was a part of me that was jealous too. It was hard to watch them together, even though I loved the devil out of them, and I would never, ever have done anything to hurt them.

"Or so I thought. Cord had finally got it through that thick skull of his that raising his family was more important than chasing down outlaws, but sometimes he'd get a hankering for the old days. It was during one of those times that the Pinkerton agent came along, offering to hire Cord as a scout to track train robbers into Indian territory.

"Fancy was beside herself," Wes remembered gloomily, "worrying Cord would get his wooden head blown off, but he wasn't listening to reason so . . . I had a talk with him myself. Only at eight o'clock in the morning and fresh from the saloon, I wasn't much good at talking. The things I remember saying were pretty awful . . . like Cord wasn't good enough for Fancy. And it would serve him right if she left him for a man who really loved her."

He swallowed hard, and Rorie's comforting arms slid around his waist from behind.

"He said I was drunk and tried to push me out of his way. That's when . . . I hit him." His voice broke with the horror of that memory. "I knocked him out cold in front of his wife and children and Zack and all the ranch hands . . .

"At first, I thought I'd killed him."

"Oh, Wes."

He hung his head. "Cord raised me, you know," he said thickly. "He taught me how to fight and shoot, and . . . how to be a man. But I guess I wasn't much of a man that day. I rode off right after he came to. I figured he'd never forgive me. I figured Fancy wouldn't, either."

"But she wrote to you," Rorie reminded him gently.

He nodded. "Yeah. The hell of it was, Cord decided not to chase any outlaws after all."

"You probably had something to do with that."

He shrugged, staring down at her soft arms wrapped so tenderly around his waist.

"And you might have even saved his life. Certainly you saved Fancy a lot of dread and worry."

"But at the cost of Cord's pride."

"Perhaps." She rested her cheek against his shoulder blade. "But if Cord taught you everything about being a man," she murmured, "he'll be the first to arrive on this farm in two days' time. And the first man to forgive you."

Wes sighed. If God—and Cord—were feeling generous, in two days he could have the camaraderie of his brothers again. He could frolic with his niece and nephews, and invent an outlandish enough tale to put the blush to cagey old Aunt Lally. Why, he could even go back to teasing the stuffing out of Zack until the man broke down and admitted he was lonely for a sweetheart.

The problem was, Wes couldn't be satisfied by just the Rawlins clan anymore. After facing the stark, harsh reality that Rorie had chosen a man she didn't love, that she was setting Wes free to find a wife who could make him redheaded babies, something inside of him had stood up and faced the facts. If Rorie could make such a sacrifice for his happiness, then by God, he could give up a few dreams to please her.

There was nothing on this earth he wanted more than Rorie and her orphans. His yearning for them was like a hole that needed filling to the bottom of his soul.

He plucked one of her long-fingered lady's hands from his work shirt and pressed a fervent kiss into the palm.

"I love you, Rorie."

He felt her tremor. Turning around, he seized the advantage and dropped to one knee. Holding her hand so firmly she couldn't possibly pull away, he gazed into her glistening eyes.

"Marry me, Rorie. Be my wife. I can't bear to live another day without you."

"Wes." Stunned, Rorie could only blink down into his hope-filled eyes. For a moment, her brain grew so numb, her heart took dangerous control of her tongue, feeding it the words, *Yes! I will gladly become your wife!*

But logic had always been a powerful adversary to her heart, and when logic joined forces with guilt, her heart was doomed to lose. She couldn't blissfully plan a wedding, knowing she had cost her betrothed his most cherished dreams.

"Wes," she repeated hoarsely, trying to pull him to his feet. When he resisted, waiting for her response, she touched a shaking hand to his hair.

"I love you so much," she whispered brokenly, "but . . . I can't be your wife."

He stiffened, and she wanted to cry. She could tell by the battle gleam kindling in his eyes that he would not make this easy for her.

"If you're worried about being promised to Ethan—"

"No." She shook her head. "I haven't told him my decision yet."

"That's a relief." He pressed another kiss into her palm.

"Wes, please. Don't do this. It hurts too much to argue."

"Then say yes," he murmured, "and I'll never let you hurt again. I promise."

He locked an arm around her waist, pulling her closer, and she felt the warm pressure of his mouth steam through the layers of her shirt and chemise to brand her navel. She swayed, squeezing her eyes closed as she clung to his shoulders for support.

"You've always been so impetuous."

"I know what I want, and it's you."

"No, you only think you want me because your feelings are running so high."

"Dammit, Rorie, I know my own mind." He freed her from his nuzzling and gazed up at her once more. "When you refused to allow my visits, I was miserable, crazy with loneliness. If those few weeks are any indication of what my life will be like without you, I'd rather be in hell. Nothing about Rangering is worth that kind of torment."

"But I can't have your sons—"

"Po and Topher are sons enough for me. Shae is, too, if he'll have me. And you know I can't live without Nita and Merrilee—or Ginevee and her pecan pie, either. I love your children, Rorie. I love them as much as I love you."

"But that's just it, don't you see?" He swam beneath her in a watery kaleidoscope. "They're not my children. There never can be children of my own."

"What are you saying?"

"I'm saying . . ." She struggled to steady her voice. "Someday you'll leave me, just like Jarrod did."

"Goddammit, woman!" He shot to his feet. "I am not like Jarrod Sinclair!"

She cringed. For a suspended moment in time, he loomed over her, his fists clenched and bloodless. Then he spun away, pacing beneath the magnolia tree.

"You're punishing me. You're punishing me because of Sinclair."

"No, Wes, I—"

"Don't deny it. He's your excuse. He has always been your excuse. You hide behind his irresponsibility so you won't have to face the truth."

"Th-the truth?"

"That's right. The problem isn't that I might run away, the problem is that you might. Or rather, you are."

"What are you talking about?"

He halted, his chest heaving as he glared into her eyes.

"You're convinced your barrenness makes you unworthy to love and be loved as a mother."

She gasped. If he had jabbed a fist into her gut, the air couldn't have fled her lungs faster.

"That's—that's not true."

"Isn't it?"

A chaotic rush of doubt rocked her to her core. Surely Wes's accusation was unfounded. Surely she didn't hide secret fears about her own capacity to love by heaping blame on Jarrod. . . . Did she?

She tore her gaze free.

"I love the hell out of you, Rorie, but I will not be the scapegoat for your conscience. Not when I love those children as much as I do."

He turned away, grabbing the rifle he'd propped against the tree.

"And another thing," he said in a low growl, pausing just long enough to look over his shoulder at her. "Don't think I'm going to toddle after you till the end of your days, begging you to marry me."

Stalking toward the barn, he left her dazed and confused and incapable of coherent thought, while above her, a wistful soughing started in the branches of the sweetheart tree.

Chapter Twenty-three

*T*ension and uncertainty cast their pall over Rorie's next two days. She worried whether Shae had made it safely to the Rawlins' ranch and whether Wes's brothers would respond to her hastily penned plea. She worried about Ginevee, who could barely limp on her sprained ankle, and about Merrilee, who'd grown more solitary and elusive, often disappearing for hours on end, particularly after meals. But her greatest uncertainty related to Wes. How could she make her heart do what her head knew was right?

Those two endless days contained some of the most poignant memories of her life: Wes acting as sentry with Topher and his slingshot by his side; Wes dozing on the settee with a napping Po cuddled in his arms; Wes carrying Ginevee up and down the stairs, flirting outrageously with her to stave off her protests; Wes suffering with good-natured gallantry through Nita's batch of scorched sugar cookies.

No matter where Rorie wandered in the house, she found some lingering reminder of his presence: the scent of leather and musk in the hall, a fresh spur mark outside Ginevee's door, the Stetson Topher proudly sported on his head, the guttered candle in the window where Wes had kept his vigil.

It was hard enough to keep from joining him each night, when every nerve in her body quivered for his touch. It was impossible to keep the children from falling more deeply in love with him. Topher had rebelled outright when she explained why they all must start calling Wes "mister" again, and the girls, observing Topher's mutiny, couldn't rally around him fast enough. Rorie finally gave up correcting their use of "Uncle Wes," mainly because she couldn't bear to see the hurt in Wes's eyes.

Thankfully, he didn't bring up the subject of Ethan or marriage again, although Rorie did happen to overhear Topher tell him, "I think you should get hitched to Miss Rorie. That way, I can have a real ma and a real pa."

And Merrilee gave Wes a detailed drawing of various farm animals and buildings. Beside each picture, she'd neatly written its name: cow, horse, barn, and so on. "Maybe if you study up on your reading," she said earnestly, "Miss Rorie will be so proud she'll *have* to marry you."

Overhearing that exchange, Rorie had felt like the lowest life-form on the planet. Her spirits weren't raised any when she spied a misty-eyed Wes slipping the folded diagram into his shirt pocket.

It seemed as if everyone was conspiring against her perfectly sound logic. What was worse, Wes had planted a seed of doubt in her mind, and now her rationalizations were sprouting like weeds. Of course she felt worthy to be a good mother to children who weren't hers by birth, she would tell herself fiercely. Of course she wasn't letting her secret rage about her barrenness punish Wes. *Of course, of course, of course.*

So why did she keep hearing the tiny bell of discord in her heart?

On the third morning, Rorie crawled out of bed far earlier than usual. She'd had a restless night, knowing this day would prove whether Shae was alive and unharmed. Wes had told her not to look for the boy until at least midafternoon, since Cord had probably tied him to a bedpost so Shae and Daisy could rest.

Thinking to steal a private moment with Wes—perhaps her last one ever—she dressed and crept downstairs. As she descended the steps, though, she heard hushed voices in the sitting room. In spite of the balmy temperature of predawn, she could hear the crackle and hiss of a fire and see the dancing indigo silhouettes of a man and child on the hall wall. Edging around the corner, she spied Merrilee huddled on the floor before the hearth in Wes's arms.

"This is the monster from my nightmares. He tries to eat little children," Merrilee said in a small voice. She handed Wes an ink drawing she had made on the newsprint he brought her. "And this is the monster who hides in the cliff. He comes out when it rains to hurt Miss Rorie."

As Wes gravely regarded the sketches, Rorie tiptoed farther into the room, sidestepping the creaking floorboard to peer over his shoulder. Her chest constricted to see what terrible visions plagued Merrilee's dreams. The first monster had fearsome eyes, sharp fangs, devil's horns, and a flaming six-shooter. The second one had a bear's body, a misshapen man's head, and great buzzard wings with cougar claws. Both creatures bore more than a passing resemblance to Hannibal Dukker.

Wes must have sensed her presence, because he glanced over his shoulder. His eyes narrowed when he spied her, but he'd been glaring at her a lot these last few days, especially whenever the children gathered around him. His message was loud and clear: "Ethan can't love them the way I do. When are you going to make up your mind to marry me?"

He turned his attention back to the child, who was still focused on the drawings she had made.

"These are very scary monsters," he said. "I would be scared, too, if they were in my dreams."

"You would?"

"Uh-huh. Do you know why I had you draw them for me?"

Merrilee shook her head, her wide eyes glimmering like polished onyx as they caught the flickering reflection of the flames.

"Remember I was telling you that I know a secret about how to get rid of them?"

Merrilee nodded. "Is that why you made the fire?"

"Yes, ma'am, it is. You see, you take the monster you drew and you tear him up into little tiny bits"—he demonstrated on a blank piece of newsprint—"then you crunch up all the pieces together in your fists just like this, see?"

Mystified, Merrilee followed his example, right down to the extra grimace he gave when he squeezed his fists.

"Then you throw the monster into the fire and watch him go up in smoke. That way he can't come into your dreams anymore."

Merrilee clasped her hands together, watching eagerly as her monster shriveled and blazed. Seeing the child's relief, Rorie silently blessed Wes and his homespun ingenuity. Lamps, dolls, adult roommates, even midnight searches under Merrilee's bed, had failed to convince the child she was safe from monsters.

Suddenly, Merrilee's forehead puckered. "Does your secret work with bad men, too, so they can't hurt little children?"

Wes wrapped the child tighter in his arms. "I wish it did, honey. But bad men have to be put in jail."

Digesting this information, Merrilee grew pensive. "But Marshal Dukker is a bad man. If he goes to jail, what will happen to Danny?"

Wes shifted, looking pained by the child's question, and Rorie stepped forward, placing a hand on Merrilee's shoulder.

"You mustn't worry about Danny, Merrilee. I'm sure Creed will take care of him."

Merrilee sighed, resting her chin in her hand. "That's what Mama said."

Wes raised his brows at Rorie, and she gave a small shake of her head.

"Merrilee, honey," she said, "Shae is coming home today with Uncle Wes's brothers. I'd like you to stay close so you can meet them. Please don't go into the woods."

Merrilee looked worried again. "But I have to feed my friend! I can't let him go hungry!"

Rorie steeled herself against a display of exasperation. Merrilee referred to any injured woodland creature
she found as a friend. God only knew what rodent or reptile was putting her at risk for rabies now. Although
Rorie had tried to stop Merrilee countless times from this
reckless behavior, warnings and punishments never deter-
red her. In this one regard, Merrilee could be as bullheaded as Topher.

"Merrilee," Wes interjected smoothly, "I have an
idea. Why don't you draw pictures to welcome Shae
home, and to say hello to Uncle Zack and Uncle Cord."

"Pictures?" Excitement tinged Merrilee's voice, and
her face reflected the war the healer in her was having
with the artist.

"Sure." Wes winked at Rorie. "I'll even help you
draw them."

"Well . . . okay."

Rorie breathed a sigh of relief, and Wes met her eyes
again. This time, the challenge was unmistakable in those
forest-green depths. He kissed Merrilee's hair, keeping his
gaze locked with Rorie's. She knew what he wanted to
hear. Her heart breaking, she swallowed and turned away.

"Riders coming!"

Topher's voice rang out above the creaking of the
corral gate he'd been swinging on. Wes glanced up
sharply. Against the backdrop of pewter and indigo thun-
derheads, he could make out four riders cantering across
the sun-fried grasses of Gator's fallow north field. In spite
of every strategy he'd planned for this confrontation, his
ribs suddenly felt too tight for his lungs.

"Is it Shae? And Uncle Cord?" Topher scrambled up
the gate as if it were a ladder and shaded his eyes for a
better view.

"I can't tell yet," Wes said, stepping across the post
hole he'd been digging and exchanging his shovel for his
Winchester.

"I never met a real live U.S. marshal before!"

Topher, in all his exuberance, was in serious danger
of somersaulting over the top rail. Wes grabbed him by
the seat of his britches and pulled him to the ground.

"He's not a U.S. Marshal anymore, son. Go inside and tell Miss Rorie we've got company."

"But—"

"Go!"

Topher's jaw dropped. Even Wes winced at the fire-cracker force of his tone.

"Hurry along, son."

"Er . . . yes, sir."

Wes gripped his rifle hard, letting the metal gouge his flesh. He hoped the discomfort would distract him from the lily-livered churning in his gut. He almost wished the riders were Dukker and his posse again, or a band of ne'er-do-well cowpokes riding back from Abilene. He'd feel a helluva lot more sure of himself then.

But the rider in the forefront was Cord. Wes would have recognized that stocky frame, square jaw, and slouching Carlsbad-style hat anywhere.

Zack sat taller in the saddle—at six foot one, he always had. His posture didn't radiate the don't-mess-with-me intensity of Cord's, though, since Zack tended to chase more dogies than outlaws. Still, Zack's easy manner was misleading. The middle Rawlins could be a surly, black-tempered, bullheaded cuss when he wanted to be. Sometimes it took Wes a whole day's worth of antics just to get Zack grinning again.

Between Zack and Shae rode a diminutive figure wearing a Renegade-style hat. Dusty boots clung to slender calves, and faded denim hugged rounded hips. Wes's eyes almost bugged out when he recognized Fancy's mare. Then he groaned. Fancy *and* Rorie on the same spread. God was hell-bent on punishing him.

Dread eating at his nerves, he held his breath as the foursome circled to the front of the house and reined in. Fancy practically flew out of her saddle. A pint-sized fury with flashing violet eyes and sable-colored hair, she stormed toward him before any of the men could touch a boot toe to the ground.

"Wescott Rawlins, your aunt Lally says I'm supposed to tan your hide and tack it to the nearest wall," Fancy said in greeting, flinging herself into his arms. She made a sound suspiciously like a sob. "Damn you, Wes, you gave us a hell of a scare."

When she tipped her head back to gaze up at him, he swallowed hard, waiting for the old surge of feeling, the bittersweet rush of adoration and lust, that never failed to seize him whenever he laid eyes on her.

To his intense relief, he was merely glad to see her. He grinned weakly, his hands spanning her waist as he set her back on her feet. That's when he made a startling discovery.

"Another one?" He gazed wide-eyed at her normally flat belly, which had blossomed into a familiar, sweet roundness.

She blushed, which was an unusual practice for Fancy. "You didn't think I was going to stop at one daughter did you? There're too many of you headstrong Rawlins men running around. It's time some women came along to even the score."

He chuckled. "Just what we needed. Three of you."

Her lips twitched into what her husband secretly called her "wicked-little-hellcat smile."

Turning, she peered at the porch with its various-sized onlookers. "Is that woman there the Aurora Sinclair who wrote to me?"

Wes started at this news, and his nerves' reprieve was over.

"Now, Fancy, you be nice. Rorie's a lady. No spitting and clawing, you hear?"

"So it's Rorie, eh?"

She arched a devilish brow, and he groaned on the inside. Fancy's lifelong distrust of other women tended to put her on the offensive in the company of females. He had hoped to have Rorie married and well briefed on his sister-in-law before allowing them to get within scratching distance of each other.

As if sensing his unease, Fancy patted his arm. "Don't you worry, Wes. Your Rorie's safe with me. These days I save all my spitting and clawing for Cord."

Winking, she sauntered with her usual sauce toward the porch. Wes was just wondering whether he should help his prim-and-proper sweetheart manage his world-wise sister-in-law, when a lanky, broad-shouldered shadow rippled into view.

"Hello, match-head."

The old childhood taunt made Wes smile sheepishly.

"I hear there's been some trouble too hot even for you to handle," Zack drawled, sticking out his right hand.

Wes gripped his brother's hand hard, his usual wise-cracks wedging as a salty lump inside his throat. God, but it was good to see Zack again.

"Well, you sure are a sight to behold, digging post-holes." Zack pressed his rare advantage, his brown eyes glowing with amusement. "I know of only two powers on earth that can move you to do an honest-day's work: Aunt Lally's pecan pie and calico fever." He shook his head in mock sympathy. "Son, you must have it bad for some woman."

A wave of heat rolled up Wes's neck. Zack had hit the bull's-eye and he knew it, which meant Wes would have to find a suitable comeuppance or hear about it until his dying day.

Fortunately, Merrilee, who had been busy passing out the pictures she'd drawn, wriggled under Wes's arm to greet his cattle-ranching brother.

"Hello, Uncle Zack. I am Merrilee."

Zack's chestnut-colored eyebrows rose at her familiarity, and Wes, laying instinctive, paternal claim to the child, stroked her hair.

"Merrilee's quite an artist, you know," he said proudly, ignoring the bemused expression on his brother's face. "Go on, Merrilee. Show Uncle Zack the picture you made for him."

With a trace of shyness, she surrendered the last tube of paper she'd been clutching to her heart. Wes waited expectantly as his brother unrolled the ink pastoral.

"*Woolies?*" Zack's outraged gaze snapped back to Wes, and he couldn't repress his snicker.

"Uncle Wes said you like sheep," Merrilee said uncertainly.

"Oh, he did, did he?"

Wes did a masterful job of looking innocent as Merrilee nodded.

"See?" She pointed to the picture. "I drew all these little lambs around the pretty ewe, and I named the mama sheep Miss Bailey, just like Uncle Wes told me."

Zack turned beet red, but he managed to recover with an aplomb that Wes was forced to admire. Lowering himself to one knee, he indulged the child by studying the drawing under her watchful, eager-to-please gaze.

"Well now, Miss Merrilee, this has to be about the finest woolie picture I ever did see. Is it for me to keep?"

She nodded again, beaming, and he smiled, slipping the artwork into his pocket.

As Wes watched Merrilee trot off hand-in-hand with Zack, his heart quickened to its earlier ramming speed. It gave him only small comfort to know Zack and Fancy weren't out to tar and feather him. He didn't dare hope the reigning patriarch of the Rawlins family would be so kind. Wes didn't deserve it.

Grim-faced, Shae stepped forward to shake his hand, as he asked for news of Lorelei. Wes had none to give, though, so Shae headed for the porch and Rorie.

Now there was no one else in the yard, no one left to help Wes forestall the inevitable confrontation with his eldest brother.

Since his arrival, Cord had stayed by the horses, watching Wes greet each of the others, waiting patiently for his turn. Now, Wes had a hard time meeting his brother's emerald stare. He tried to decide whether to make the first move, but Cord saved him the trouble, strolling toward him from the backdrop of lowering thunderclouds. Wes hastened to meet him halfway.

Wind rushed between them, grabbing at their neckerchiefs in the awkward silence.

"I . . . didn't think you'd come," Wes said finally.

"Well, knowing how good you handle your guns—and your fists," Cord added dryly, rubbing his jaw, "I didn't think you really needed some retired lawman getting mixed up in your Ranger business. But I figured I'd tag along anyway to meet this Aurora Sinclair who's been writing to my wife. I hear she thinks right highly of you."

Wes felt his cheeks heat at this second reference to some mysterious letter, and he had to bite his tongue to keep from asking just what Rorie had penned. His burning curiosity didn't make him any less pleased by Cord's compliment, though. Far from it. Now, more than ever, Cord's opinion mattered to him.

"She's a good woman," Wes said, choosing his words carefully, "and I want to make her my wife. But she's a Yankee with a stubborn streak a mile wide."

Wes held his breath, waiting anxiously for the impact of his news to sink in. *I found my own woman, Cord. Someone even more important to me than Fancy.*

"You don't say?" Dimples peeked in Cord's rugged face. "I remember some advice a kid brother of mine once gave me. Seems like you have to tell a stubborn woman you love her if you ever hope to get anywhere."

"I did." Wes couldn't keep the misery from his voice.

Cord arched a nearly black brow.

"It's complicated," Wes added quickly, unwilling to discuss Rorie's private burdens even with Cord.

"Does she love you?"

Wes shrugged. "I reckon. She says she does, anyway."

"Well ..." A spark of humor lightened Cord's searching gaze. "You could always try my original plan. The one I had for Fancy."

Wes's ears pricked up. Cord had never shared this story with him.

"What plan was that?"

"Hog-tie her and carry her to a preacher." Cord grinned.

Wes grinned back.

No doubt they were both sharing the same vision: two strong-willed, out-spoken women each flailing over her man's shoulder.

After a moment, solemnity crept back into Cord's features. "I've missed the devil out of you, son."

The sincerity in his voice made Wes's chest ache.

"Cord, I'm sorry. I never meant any of the things I said, and—"

"I know."

Wes drew a shuddering breath. Cord was smiling. He was even holding out his hand. Battling a misty swell of feeling, Wes reached to shake hands with the man who'd always been more father than brother to him.

In the next instant—he wasn't sure how it happened—Wes found himself wrapped in a bear hug with Cord.

Watching from a distance as the two brothers reconciled, Rorie wasn't sure whose shoulders slumped more in relief: Fancy's, Zack's, or hers.

She hoped Wes would sit down with his family for a meal before charging off on his manhunt, but another rider had appeared on the horizon. He was riding out of town, and as he approached the farm, Rorie felt Shae stiffen by her side.

"Creed," he muttered.

Riding parallel to the approaching storm, Creed was driving his horse with the same frenzied shouting and spurring he'd employed three nights earlier. Today there was a marked difference in his voice, though. It sounded shaky, as if the boy was close to tears.

"Rawlins!" Creed sawed back hard on his reins, and his gelding stumbled, nearly throwing him. "I've come about Danny! You have to help me. You have to help me find him!"

Topher snorted at this announcement, and Merrilee shrank nervously into the shadows.

"I'm more interested in finding your pa," Wes retorted grimly, "and teaching him a helluva lesson."

"Listen to me!" Creed's panic was etched in every muscle of his body. "Danny's been missing ever since he found Lorelei. Dammit, Rawlins, that was three days ago! I've looked in every hiding place in town. It's not like him to be gone for so long!"

Rorie felt outrage that Creed considered it normal for Danny to be missing at all. What on earth was the matter with Hannibal Dukker? Didn't he bother to see whether his child ate dinner? Or slept each night in his bed?

"Now calm down, Creed." Wes caught the reins of

he boy's restive mount. "Your pa's the one who should be helping you find Danny."

"You don't understand! It's Pa who ran him off, cursing him and beating him and—and threatening to kill him. I'm scared Pa might really do it!"

"Easy, Creed. I'm sure even Dukker wouldn't—"

"You don't know Pa! When he starts drinking and swinging, anything can happen. I think . . ." Creed's voice broke, and he struggled with a sob. "I think Danny saw what happened to Lorelei. And I think Pa tried to keep him quiet."

Wes and Cord exchanged tense looks. Shae and Zack stepped off the porch, hastily joining them.

"What are you saying?" Wes demanded. "Was your pa the one who hurt Lorelei?"

Creed seemed to realize he'd said too much. Fear flickered across his face. Then came fury, pain, and remorse. He glanced at Wes's badge and guns, then over at Shae, drawn so taut, he quivered.

"That's why you rode out to warn me, isn't it, Dukker?" Shae shook off Zack's restraining hand. "You knew your pa had done it all along!"

"No! I . . ." Something inside Creed seemed to crumble. He slumped. "I only suspected," he said brokenly. "When I saw the scratches on his neck."

Bile rushed so fast to Rorie's throat, she choked. Merciful God! She, too, had seen the scratches on Dukker's neck—and the half-crazed gleam in his eye.

"Danny must have let his father out of jail," she said shakily. "I saw him crouching under the window before I left town."

Creed nodded, his confession bleak. "Danny has a widdy. I gave it to him for his birthday. He could have jimmied the lock—"

"Or stolen the keys from my desk." Wes's brows lowered, making him look more dangerous. "Where's your pa now?"

"That's what I've been trying to tell you! I'm scared he's out hunting Danny so he can kill him!"

"Mount up, men," Wes said. "Creed, you're riding with me. Shae, you know this backcountry; you ride with

Zack and Cord. I want you men to circle back toward
town, see if you can pick up a trail. Danny will be on
foot, won't he?"

Creed nodded.

"Anything else they need to know?"

"Try the quarry," Creed said. "And Pearson's
burned-out homestead. Pa used to hide his still there until
Gator found it."

"What about the cliff at Ramble Creek?"

Creed shook his head. "Danny fell out of a tree once
and he's been scared of heights ever since. He'd never
climb way up there."

"All right. Then Creed and I will head first for the
schoolhouse," Wes said. "If we have any chance at all of
finding his trail, we'll do it before that storm hits. After
that—" Wes's voice grew positively ominous, "you boys
can hunt Danny. I'm having my showdown with
Dukker."

"No!"

The protest popped out of Rorie's mouth before she
could think better of it. Five narrowed pairs of male eyes
drilled into her, and she heated hotter than the Fourth of
July. Still, she thought it reckless of Wes not to take along
a posse, now that he had one available.

"Wes, there's no need to take risks—"

"Dammit, Aurora, that's enough!"

Wes was cinching Two-Step's girth strap. If he hadn't
been thus occupied, she sensed he would have tossed her
in the house and locked the door on her. In desperation,
she turned to Fancy.

"But it's madness! Say something to him, please."

Fancy's lips twisted in a mirthless smile. She glanced
at her husband, whose grimly set features so closely resembled his youngest brother's.

"Aurora, I promise you, there's not a woman on this
earth who can stop a Rawlins when he's wearing his
showdown glare." Fancy's eyes darkened sympathetically.
"But if it's any consolation, I know how you feel."

Rorie bit her lip to keep from saying anything more
that might frighten the children. They were already whispering anxiously among themselves.

As the men turned their horses up the drive, Zack separated from the group to retrieve the hat Topher had begged off of him. He nodded to Fancy and Rorie.

"Don't worry, ladies." He flashed a reassuring smile. "I won't let those two hotheads get into any trouble they can't handle alone."

With a tip of his brim, he spurred his horse after his eldest brother's, and Rorie was left wishing there were two Zacks—one to watch over Cord, and one to talk sense into Wes.

Chapter Twenty-four

Rorie spent the next half hour doing her best to be a perfect hostess to Fancy, although she could sense the woman wasn't entirely comfortable with pastry tarts and teacups. Perhaps it was just as well, Rorie mused, since she was too distracted by her worries to hold an intelligent conversation with anyone, much less the petite beauty who had held Wes's heart in the palm of her hand for so long.

"Fancy, forgive me," she finally said in exasperation. "I'm not very good company right now. Would you like to go upstairs and rest? Perhaps change into more comfortable clothes?"

Fancy looked amused as she set down her cup. "By that, I take it you mean skirts?"

Rorie fidgeted. She wasn't sure why, but she sensed she'd just made a grievous social error. She herself had never worn blue jeans, but she couldn't imagine how anything so tight could be comfortable, particularly since she'd had such trouble with her corset lately due to an inexplicable tenderness in her breasts.

"I just thought after all the hardships of your journey—camping all night and riding all day—that I was being insensitive to keep you talking."

"Wes hasn't told you much about me, has he?"

Rorie felt her face warm at this truth. "Well, I know

he cares a great deal about you. And he told me you once saved his life."

"Hmm."

"He dotes on your children too," Rorie said quickly, sensing that she'd somehow floundered again. "He's always talking about"—her hands twisted in her lap—"how much he'd like to be a father."

"Well, that's news. Wes was dead set on being a bachelor Ranger the last time we talked, which was nearly a year ago. You must have been a good influence on him, Aurora. Most of the women he's known—other than Aunt Lally, of course—have been like me."

Rorie was stunned to hear Fancy say such a thing. Even if Fancy had inadvertently said or done something that triggered Wes's love for her, he'd made it clear she'd been staunchly devoted to Cord throughout their marriage.

"Fancy, I'm sure you can't be blamed for what must surely have been a youthful infatuation on Wes's part."

Fancy's lips twitched. "It's kind of you to say so, but you misunderstand me. I meant to say you and I have led very different lives. At least—" she glanced meaningfully at the teacups, then over at Rorie's buttoned collar, "it would seem that way."

Rorie really didn't know what to say. So taking refuge in her hostess role, she reached for the tea server Ginevee had set between them on a tray.

That's when the floorboards began to heave. Nausea hit her fast, and she clutched at the serving table, trying desperately to fight the sickness off. Unfortunately, the table wasn't made to support her weight, and it toppled. She heard the crash of the cups and the serving platter even as she sank, mortified, to her knees.

"Aurora!" She felt a small, strong hand grip her shoulder. "My God, are you all right? Ginevee! Come quickly!"

Rorie protested as her friend arrived and helped Fancy lift her into a chair.

"Miss Aurora," Ginevee chided in motherly concern, "don't tell me you've gotten those stomach butterflies

again. Good heavens, child, this has been going on for
much too long."

Fancy awkwardly patted Rorie's shoulder. "Don't
worry, Aurora. It doesn't last."

"It doesn't?" she gasped, gulping air to settle her
stomach.

"No. I thought I was going to spend the rest of my
life in the privy when I was pregnant with my second son.
But with this baby, I've never been sick. Not even with a
headache. I do tend to get tired more than usual,
though."

Rorie and Ginevee both gaped at her. Rorie couldn't
possibly imagine how Fancy had leaped to such a conclusion except, perhaps, that her own baby must weigh
heavily on her mind.

She managed a feeble shake of her head. "Oh, no,
you don't understand. You see—"

Ginevee's hand tightened like a vise over Rorie's upper arm. "Wait a minute, Aurora. When was the last time
you had your woman's courses?"

"*Ginevee.*"

Face flaming, Rorie glanced at Fancy, but the other
woman just laughed.

"Believe me, Aurora, I'm the last person who would
judge you in a matter like this. Besides, I know Wes isn't
any monk."

The tremor in Ginevee's hand was increasing in direct proportion to her excitement. She looked like a child
on Christmas day. "You haven't bled for over a month
now, have you, child?"

Rorie, still dazed by her receding nausea, couldn't believe Ginevee was asking her such personal questions before a guest. Besides, Ginevee knew full well the state of
Rorie's womb.

"Ginevee, for heaven's sake. This is not the time or
place—"

"Miss Fancy, you say the sickness came on you too?"
Ginevee asked with unabashed eagerness. "Perhaps as
early as the second week?"

Gazing from the black woman back to Rorie, Fancy
looked puzzled. "Well, as a matter of fact it did. I had all

the symptoms with Billy—tenderness, nausea, swelling, swooning." She grimaced at this last symptom. "It was so humiliating. I never faint. Not for real, anyway."

Before Rorie could even comment on Fancy's observations, Ginevee clutched her hand and held it hard against her hammering heart.

"Aurora, don't you see? You've been suffering with the same ailments for nearly six weeks now."

Fancy frowned. "You mean you didn't know?"

Rorie's head was spinning—and not from sickness anymore.

"Well, no. I mean, you don't understand. My cycles have never been what you'd call regular, and . . . my husband was a doctor. He said I was barren. He said he was leaving me because I couldn't have his child—"

"The bastard."

Rorie's eyes locked with Fancy's, and something passed between them then. Something profoundly female. It transcended all barriers of experience and culture. In an instant, Rorie knew Fancy had also been brutally betrayed by a man.

"You know, Aurora—" Fancy squatted, the small protuberance in her belly brushing Rorie's knee, "not every man is up to siring a child. Did your husband have other children that you know of?"

She shook her head, still too afraid to dream, to hope, to *believe*.

"Well, six weeks is a long time to go without a cycle."

"It's been longer," Rorie whispered breathlessly, elation starting to get the better of her.

Dear God, was it true? Had Jarrod been the one with the affliction?

She'd never been with another man, yet on that first night with Wes, she'd known somehow, deep in the core of her being, that something had changed, that something was new.

She clasped her trembling hands, and Fancy, who'd been watching her reaction with shrewd eyes, nodded as if to dispel the last of her doubts.

"It looks like we have something in common after all, Aurora."

"Miss Rorie!"

Rorie started. The shout had been Nita's, pitched high with annoyance. Her footsteps clattered on the stairs.

"I can't find Merrilee anywhere, and it's her turn to carry the wash inside before it rains. You know Topher won't do it."

Rorie struggled to rally her wits. She'd been so busy trying to keep Fancy occupied that she hadn't checked on the children for—she glanced at the mantel clock—at least forty-five minutes now. She pressed her hands to her burning cheeks, and Nita, her fists on her hips, materialized in the doorway.

"I'm sorry to bother you, ma'am, but Merrilee just keeps disappearing, and it's about to rain cats and dogs outside. I even looked inside the barn, where Topher put Aunt Fancy's horse. I figured Merrilee had taken all those apples and that cornbread in there."

"Cornbread?" Rorie repeated uneasily. "Horses don't eat cornbread."

"Well, that's what I told her, but she just said her friend was hungry, and he was getting tired of apples. That's the last time I saw her."

"When was that?"

"Oh, I don't know. Right after Creed rode up, I reckon."

A queasy feeling, not unlike her earlier nausea, coiled inside Rorie's stomach. She remembered Merrilee's questions about Danny that morning and her talk of a hungry friend.

"Nita, send Topher here. Quickly, please."

Nita turned to obey, and Rorie glanced anxiously at Ginevee. "Do you know where Merrilee is?"

The old woman frowned, shaking her head. "No, but now that Nita's mentioned it, I did think it was strange when Merrilee asked for a basket to carry her apples. And last night I noticed a cup, knife, and fork were missing from the place settings she cleared."

A footstep touched off the creaking floorboard in the

hall, and Rorie looked up to see Topher standing rebelliously at Nita's side.

"I ain't doing no woman's work."

Rorie might have smiled if she hadn't been so worried.

"Topher, where's Merrilee?"

"Oh, is that all?" The boy looked greatly relieved. Folding his arms, he pasted on a scowl. "Well, you know how she's always wandering off somewhere, saying her mama told her to go, because someone's hungry, or hurt, or something." Topher rolled his eyes.

"Yes? And?"

He snorted. "She said her friend would be afraid all alone in the storm, so she headed off for the cave at Ramble Creek."

"Dear God." Rorie hastily stood, only to regret it an instant later when the floorboards spun beneath her feet.

Fancy gripped her elbow. "Aurora, maybe you shouldn't be standing so soon."

"No, I have to, don't you see? Merrilee's been feeding Danny at the cliff."

"*What?*" Ginevee gaped at her.

Rorie nodded absently, her mind racing. Somehow, she had to find the children and bring them back before the storm hit. "I have to go after them."

She started to turn, only to have Fancy tighten her hold on her arm.

"Wait a minute. If this is the same Danny that Wes went after, he won't be at the cliff. Remember what his brother said? Danny's afraid of heights."

"Apparently he's more afraid of his father," Rorie said grimly.

Fancy's brows knitted, and her gaze flickered to the children. Catching her eye, Ginevee shooed Nita and Topher into the hall and closed the door after them.

"Aurora," Fancy said, "if that's true, do you realize what kind of danger you could be in? Not to mention the risks you'll be taking for yourself and your baby in a rainstorm when you're climbing some cliff."

Rorie blanched, her hand flying to her womb. Still, the risks didn't matter. Merrilee was in danger.

"I have to go," she said firmly.

"But—"

"I have to go!" she shouted at Ginevee, who'd anxiously returned to her side.

Fancy's chin hardened. "I'll come with you."

"Don't be ridiculous, Fancy. You'll only be risking your own baby, and I can't have that. Merrilee's my child. I'll go. Alone."

"Do you have a gun?"

Rorie hesitated in midstride, the grim practicality of Fancy's question making her gut knot.

"Well, no, but—"

"My revolver's in my saddlebag. Take it and Frisco. She's gentle and a good climber, but she sometimes gets spooked by thunder. Keep a tight rein on her when the clouds burst."

Rorie nodded, glancing out the window. Forked spears of lightning were crackling ever closer, and the magnolia was shaking and moaning with the wind. She prayed the storm wouldn't unleash itself until she returned the children safely to the farm.

Her pulse jumping with every crash of thunder, she grabbed Shae's work slicker from the barn, shoved Fancy's .32 into a coat pocket, and mounted Frisco. The mare was none too pleased at the prospect of venturing out into nature's cacophony, but Rorie managed to spur her into a grudging canter.

The wind whipped her skirts and unfurled her hair; the sting of an occasional raindrop blurred her eyes. Or maybe that moisture was tears. Risking her baby terrified her, and yet she couldn't bear to think of losing the child she already knew and loved to lightning, a misstep . . . or Hannibal Dukker.

"Dear God, please keep Merrilee safe. Please keep Danny safe too."

Lightning crackled and popped above the canopy of trees, spooking Rorie almost as much as it did the mare. She had to grit her teeth and speak gently, threading her uneasy mount through the cedars and oaks. She wished there was some other route, but the grove was unavoidable. Dodging flying branches and wind-shorn leaves, she clung to the saddle with a will that defied even the wrath of the heavens.

At last breaking free of the grove, she urged Frisco faster beneath the roiling expanse of charcoal clouds.

"Merrilee!" She shouted the instant the cliff path came into view. "Danny!"

The wind ripped her cries from her lips. If they were dashed against the rocky walls, she never heard their echo.

"Help me, God," she whispered. "Help me find Merrilee."

"Mama!"

The word was nothing more than a murmur in the next earsplitting boom. Rorie reined in, pushing her hair from her eyes, and looked frantically around her. Tumbled slabs of limestone and scruffy sentinels of juniper were strewn all around. To her left lay an uprooted evergreen, rotting in a grave of scrubbrush and grass. To her right stretched the jagged rip in the earth that served as descent to the cave ledge below. There were hundreds of crevices and overhangs where a child could hide if he was afraid to venture down the slope.

"Merrilee, where are you?"

Only the wind responded, gusting past and carrying the scent of rain.

A tendril of dread wrapped around her heart. She urged her mount forward, toward the path, but a sudden icy prickle inched down her spine. The feeling was uncanny, like a primitive shiver of knowing, or an otherworldly finger, pointing her left instead of straight. It was compelling enough to make her rein in a second time. She peered toward the fallen juniper.

That's when she saw Danny and Merrilee sprint hand in hand from their hiding place among the browning needles.

"Run!" Danny shouted, tugging Merrilee behind him in spite of her stumbles.

Stunned to see the terror on their faces, Rorie dismounted, thinking to hurry forward and open her arms to them. Instead, she froze in her tracks. Rising out of the rocks behind the tree, like some creature from the bowels of hell, came Hannibal Dukker. His unbuttoned duster flapped around him like buzzard wings as he lurched forward, a sadistic, hulking monster who stalked the children in unhurried pursuit. He clutched a whiskey bottle in one clawlike hand, but his revolver, thankfully, was holstered.

Danny raced past her in stark panic, but Merrilee tore her hand free from the boys'.

"Mama!"

Rorie was knocked off balance when the child flung herself at her, locking trembling arms around Rorie's waist.

"It's the bad man! It's the monster!"

Tears threatened to steal Rorie's calm. She swallowed her fear, glancing at the sneering lawman as he advanced. "Merrilee, honey, I want you to run. I want you to hide."

Merrilee shook her head. "No. He'll hurt you! Like in my nightmare."

Dukker laughed, an eerie, rasping cackle that didn't sound human.

Rorie managed to detach Merrilee's viselike hold long enough to push the child behind her. "Hannibal," she said as firmly as her constricting throat would allow, "I have a gun and I'm not afraid to use it."

She drew the revolver, and he laughed again. The sound made her whole body stiff and clammy.

"So it's to be a shoot-out, eh, Aurora? You've been reading too many dime novels."

She didn't bother to contradict him.

"Merrilee, I want you to take Aunt Fancy's horse and find Danny. I want you to ride home."

Merrilee shook her head no, her slender arms practically squeezing Rorie in half.

"Stinking Injun cripple." Dukker took a swig of whiskey and wiped his sleeve across his mouth. "Now there's the thanks you get, Aurora, trying to raise Uncle Tomahawk's trash. You want the brat to mind you? Then backhand her till her lights go out. That's the kind of discipline a savage understands."

Merrilee's body quaked harder as she pressed closer,

and Rorie battled her motherly instinct to hold the child and comfort her.

"Merrilee." She spoke more sternly, every word ripping a piece from her heart. "Do as you're told."

Merrilee cringed, raising anxious eyes to her, and Rorie nodded, pushing her toward the mare.

Dukker's lips twitched in a cruel little smile as he watched the tearful child gather the reins.

"You don't really think I'm gonna let your papoose ride out of here, do you? You don't really think I'm gonna let her grow up like you, to breed more trash all over this county?"

Rorie's gut clenched. He couldn't possibly know about the baby, yet his threat triggered deep, primal instincts she hadn't even known she possessed.

She forced her chin higher. She hoped her defiance would hide the tremor in her arms, as the weight of the .32 began taking its toll. "You are in no position to be threatening me, Hannibal."

His lip curled. "You know, for a live dictionary, you ain't too smart."

She wasn't entirely sure what he meant, but it didn't matter. She listened intently for the sound of hooves behind her, praying that Merrilee could handle such a large horse.

"It's like I always said," Dukker went on, his grating words distracting her. "When a woman starts filling her head with ideas, she disturbs the natural order of things. That's why a woman needs a husband, to put her back in her place. But your old man mustn't have been much good with his fists, 'cause you're the snootiest bitch I ever did meet, except maybe for little Miss Cockteaser."

Merrilee, please hurry. Please find Danny and ride . . .

" 'Course, there's other ways to put a woman in her place." Dukker began advancing again. His glazed gaze ran down her breasts and hips as if she were a piece of beefsteak sizzling on his plate.

"That's far enough, Hannibal."

"Yeah? So stop me."

He tossed the whiskey aside. At the tinkling crash,

she flinched, her heart catapulting to her throat. For a moment, one chilling, numbing moment, her eyes locked with his. She could read his intent there as clearly as a sentence in a book.

"Can't shoot me, can ya?" His bowed legs stumped faster, closing the yards between them with alarming speed.

Dear God. She pulled back the trigger. Or rather, she tried. In panic, she dropped her eyes to the unfamiliar weapon to see what was wrong. That's when a fist lashed out, striking the gun from her hand.

"Told ya you were stupid."

She yelped. Another fist lashed out, colliding with her jaw.

"You never took off your safety."

Pain slammed next into her shoulder. She staggered, trying to duck and escape, but he caught hold of her fallen hair and spun her back for more.

"*Pa!* Stop it, Pa! Don't hit her like Ma!"

Suddenly pebbles were pelting her, and Dukker roared a curse. She reeled blindly away from the hail of stones even as Dukker's blows ceased.

"You little bastard!"

Danny had circled behind them, she realized dimly, and was now flinging every rock he could find at his father. To her horror, she saw Dukker draw his gun.

"No!" She lunged for Dukker's arm, and the revolver fired with a bone-jarring reverberation that rattled every tooth in her head. He tried to shake her off, but she managed to hold on, kicking and clawing and ramming a knee into his groin. He howled, doubling over. The gun dropped and skittered across the ground. She gave frantic chase, but it slid over the cliff.

"Mama!"

Skidding dangerously close to the edge, Rorie caught her balance, whirling in time to see Merrilee run for the .32.

"Merrilee, no!"

The child had reached the revolver. Merrilee, who had never even stepped on an ant in her short life, was aiming and trying to fire. Dukker saw her, too, and he cursed, limping toward her.

"*Dukker!*"

Rorie scrambled after him. She grabbed the jagged neck of the whiskey bottle even as Merrilee figured out how to unhook the safety. The hammer clicked and fire spat. The bullet zinged wildly off a rock, and the recoil slammed Merrilee into a boulder.

She crumpled, lying still.

Rorie's cry was lost in the echo as the explosion repeated again and again. Danny ran to Merrilee, and Rorie caught up with the hobbling lawman. Slashing at his back, his neck, his gun arm, she was desperate to distract him from the children and the .32. He rounded on her with a snarl.

The heavens chose that moment to rip open. Rain sheeted down, pounding her face and hands like tiny hammers.

"Bitch!"

The glass grew slippery, too hard to hold. She had to get to the gun, but Dukker stood between it and her, and she had no choice but to run. She could hear him panting, his boots scrabbling ominously over the rubble behind her. She stumbled on her clinging skirts, praying for a miracle, praying for the life she held inside her. The cliff was narrow and jagged at this end; she tried to veer back the way she had come.

That's when he tackled her, and they crashed into the uprooted juniper.

Wes reined in hard. Water poured off his hat brim. Rain rolled down his upturned collar, despite the protection of his slicker. He hardly noticed. Something was wrong. Dread was like a thousand needles stabbing at his gut.

"What's the matter?" Creed shouted over an earth-shaking crack of thunder.

Wes gazed to the east, toward Ramble Creek. They'd had no luck finding Danny or his tracks, and they'd decided to circle back to the house in the hopes that Cord and Zack had fared better.

"I was just remembering . . ."

Monsters. Nightmarish creatures with buzzard wings. They descended from the cliff during thunderstorms to hurt Miss Rorie.

". . . the Jenkins's puppy," Wes shouted.

"What are you talking about?"

"The children found Danny with it at Ramble Creek."

"I told you, Rawlins, Danny didn't steal—"

"I don't give a damn whether he did nor not! But Danny has been to the cliff before, and he might have gone there again!"

Wes wheeled Two-Step, every nerve in his body firing. He couldn't have said what made him so god-awful certain he'd find Danny at Ramble Creek. He couldn't have explained why he was giving a child's nightmare far more credence than it deserved. All he knew was that he heard a voice, an urgent whisper, begging him to hurry, before it was too late.

Creed thought he was an idiot to ride a mile and a half out of their way, and the boy minced few words in telling Wes so. Still, Wes noticed that Creed kept his horse racing neck and neck with Two-Step. He noticed, too, that Creed looked uncommonly wan in the drenching gloom.

The storm raged around them in all its elemental fury. But the risk Wes courted with each crackling blaze of light paled in his mind when compared to the mortal peril that might lie ahead for Danny. Wes squinted, trying to pick out landmarks through the opaque veil of water. There was the meadow, the fringe of woodland; now came the rocky rise, the tumbled boulders. He glimpsed the split in the cliff and the winding black ribbon of darkness that led to the cave below. Beyond it, tilting precariously over an eroding shelf of limestone, he spied the uprooted juniper.

A frenzied flailing grabbed his attention next. It looked as if two people were wrestling. They fell into the brittle branches, rolling dangerously close to the lip of the cliff. Wes had an impression of wet skirts and tawny hair, a flapping duster and muddy boots, then lightning slashed out of the heavens. It struck the tree's browning canopy, igniting it like tinder. The man screeched, rearing back, his coattails bursting into flame. The woman screamed, kicking frantically to rip her skirts free of the evergreen.

"Pa!"

"Rorie!"

Two-Step leaped forward even as Creed raced to extinguish his father's coat.

"Rorie, hang on!"

Wes's shouts were lost in the ominous cracking of wood. The rotted tree split, listing under her weight. He watched in horror, helpless to do anything more than spur Two-Step faster, as Rorie slid over the cliff edge in a hail of twigs and stones.

"No!"

He hit the ground running, his heart slamming into his ribs.

"Rorie!" He skidded to the lip, shouting again and again. He could see her rolling down the slope, banging against a bush or two, before she finally came to rest on a shelf about fifteen feet down. Limp and motionless, she sprawled a bare arm's length from the final plunge to the creek, a good fifty feet below.

"Dear God." He fought back a rush of panic. "Rope. I need rope."

He ran to Two-Step, wrenched open his saddlebag, and started to drag out his rope.

"Rawlins!" It was Creed's voice.

Wes spun, his right hand dropping to his .45. Creed was fighting his father now, rather than helping him. They were grappling over Creed's revolver, and Dukker, far heavier than his son, was about to roll on top of the boy and club his head with a rock.

"Creed!" From out of nowhere, Danny appeared, flinging himself at his father's back. The impact threw Dukker sideways. Creed's revolver went off.

Wes cursed. He couldn't tell if either boy had been hit, but he could hear Dukker bellowing like a wounded bull.

His heart in his throat, he ran to circle them, his clear shot foiled by the windmill of arms and legs.

"Drop the gun, Dukker!"

Dukker ignored him. Or maybe he hadn't heard. Lighting splintered and thunder cracked, making everything about Dukker's murderous intent more macabre. Danny yelped, rolling from the tangle. Creed slumped, and his father raised the gunbutt for another blow. Wes gritted his teeth and fired.

The bullet should have dropped Dukker. At the very least, it should have slowed him. But Dukker was maniacal. His shoulder blackening with blood, he staggered to his feet. Wes could see the bastard meant to kill somebody, and he called to Dukker again, reluctant to gun the man down in front of Danny's terrified eyes.

"Drop the goddamned .45!"

"You ain't taking me alive, Ranger!"

Dukker raised his weapon, and Wes fired again. This time, the bullet struck the lawman's knee, and he shrieked, buckling. His gun skittered into a crevice.

Wes bounded forward, grabbing the older man's collar and landing a cracking blow to his jaw. At last Dukker's head lolled, and he sagged.

Wes flopped the moaning lawman over. "I'm taking you alive all right," he ground out, snapping manacles around Dukker's wrists. "I'm even going to see you get medical help for those wounds, 'cause I want you to be healthy—perfectly healthy, you bastard—when you hang. Danny!"

The boy jumped.

Wes found Creed's pulse and released a ragged breath. "See to your brother."

Wes sprinted back to Two-Step. He couldn't waste time feeling relief, pity, or anything else related to a Dukker. He had to get Rorie. He had to carry her up the cliff.

Dragging the rest of the rope from his saddlebag, he wrapped one end around the pommel. He worried the rawhide might not be long enough to tie Rorie to his back and haul her up the fifteen-foot slope. To make matters worse, Two-Step wasn't a cowpony; he'd never been trained to lean back on his haunches and keep a rope taut under a load. Wes prayed fervently. He needed help. Or a miracle.

Two-Step pranced, choosing one helluva time to live up to his name. Wes had to grab the brute's head, dragging him back toward the fizzling fire. Wes cursed, and Two-Step neighed, his eyes rolling in mutiny.

Suddenly, Merrilee appeared at Wes's side. She placed a hand on the gelding's neck.

"Nice pony."

The cantankerous beast was instantly subdued. Wes gaped at the child. He couldn't imagine what she was doing on a cliff in the worst storm of the summer, but he didn't have time to ask. He squatted, grabbing her shoulders.

"Merrilee, honey, I need your help."

"Is Miss Rorie hurt?"

"I don't know, sweetheart. But you have to talk to Two-Step. You have to make him stand here, and keep this rope real tight while I go down the hill. Then you have to make him back up when I tell you, so he can pull me and Miss Rorie up the hill. Do you think you can do that?"

She nodded, water dripping from her nose and chin. Her immeasurable calm helped Wes get a grip on his own. He draped his slicker over her. Then, twisting the rawhide around his waist, he began the slippery descent.

Rorie was having the most amazing dream. She was sitting on a cloud, eating pastries and drinking tea with an angel. Only the angel wasn't the blue-eyed, golden-haired cherub variety. This angel was copper-skinned with great doelike eyes, raven-black braids, and a white buck-skin dress. In fact, she looked very much like Merrilee, except that the angel was perhaps fifteen years older.

Rorie couldn't remember much of what she and the angel discussed, although she did recall something about heaven and magnolia trees, green-eyed lawmen with dev-ilish smiles, and red-haired babies.

"A child's love is a sacred trust, and yet she gives it freely," the angel told her. "The true measure of mother-hood is not whether you can bear a child, but rather, how selflessly you can love her."

Rorie smiled—until all the implications of the angel's

words began to make her wonder. Why would a heavenly messenger tell her such a thing?

Something wasn't right. In fact, something was dreadfully wrong. She ached in every fiber of her body. She felt bruised and battered and cold and wet. Her back was being jabbed by a dozen rock-hard lumps.

Her eyes flew open with a start. Dear God, had she lost her baby?

"Rorie, don't move!"

She froze at the urgency in that voice.

"Wes?" She coughed on the rainwater that rolled down her throat.

"I'm coming, sweetheart. Hold on. Just don't move. You're right on the edge."

Her heart quickening, she dared to turn her head toward his voice. She could see him, soaking wet, lean and hard and straining as he descended the slippery limestone toward her. His boots scrabbled for a toehold. Pebbles dislodged, rolling down the hill to pelt her. He cursed.

"Rorie, I'm sorry. Can you see me? I'm almost there."

"I can see you," she said hoarsely.

She glanced to the other side. Blackness yawned as far as she dared look. She squeezed her eyes closed once more.

Thank you, God. Thank you for bringing Wes to find me. Please let me keep our baby.

"Rorie? Talk to me! Don't close your eyes!"

"I'm . . . all right," she lied feebly, wishing she dared move so she could truly assess her injuries. "Where's Merrilee? And Danny?"

"Up top. With Two-Step and Creed."

"And . . . Dukker?"

"I cuffed him."

Wes squatted, trying to reach her, but the rope wouldn't stretch that far. He muttered another oath, his fear for her warring with the love in his eyes. "Can you reach my hand?"

Gingerly she raised her left arm, straining for the fingers he offered as anchor. Several inches still separated them, and she shook her head, her temples throbbing with the effort. Panic began to seep into her veins. She fought it off desperately, clinging to the warm, caring depths of his gaze.

"I'm going to take the rope off. Can you reach it?"

She heard the rawhide slither closer, and she groped. Anxiously, she glanced upward to see where it led. Through the splashing raindrops, she saw the ceiling of the cliff's lip. Above that stood a stoic Merrilee, draped in a yellow slicker four times her size, and a disgruntled-looking Two-Step.

Rorie ran her gaze back down the brush-covered C shape of the slope. Merciful God. She had fallen down that?

"Wrap the rope around your wrist as many times as you can until it's tight."

Quaking, she obeyed, trying not to think about the void to her right, trying not to imagine what her tumble might have done to her baby. . . .

Wes eased closer, his hand running down the rope.

"Wes, be careful," she whispered as his big body filled every available inch of the shelf.

"Don't worry about me. Can you pull yourself up?"

Tentatively, she tugged on the rope. It held firm, and she inched toward it, wrapping the slack around her wrist until she could roll to her side and finally sit.

Wes's arm closed around her waist, locking it in an iron grip. She buried her face in his wet shoulder, biting her tongue on the blubbering urge to tell him how scared she was—and not just for herself. How could she tell him about the baby if she wasn't certain she still had it?

His heart was as loud as the thunder. It sounded to her ears like galloping hooves. Or maybe those hooves were real . . .

She glanced hopefully into his pale, haggard face for confirmation, but apparently, he hadn't heard.

"I've got hold of you," he murmured. "Now I want you to wrap that rope around your waist—"

"What about you?"

"I'll be fine."

He smiled, but she wasn't deceived. In this rain, he

needed the rope as much as she did to climb the summit of that hooked lip.

"It won't work," she said. "I won't leave you—"

"I'll be right behind you. Now. Can you stand?"

She clenched her teeth, knowing that arguing would only tax what little strength she had, and what remained of his. Gathering her courage, she tightened her hold on his shoulders, using them for balance as she swayed to her feet. Apparently nothing in her body was broken. That was a blessing. Maybe even a miracle.

"Miracles happen every day," he said, as if reading her mind.

She blinked back tears. If he only knew . . .

He straightened precariously, wrapping the slackened rope around his forearm. Edging behind her, he pressed her between the safety of the wall and his chest.

He was just bracing, preparing to lift her to the first toehold, when she heard a shout above the receding rumble of thunder. The hoofbeats she'd heard were real.

Suddenly there was a swish and a whisper, and a lasso fell neatly over her shoulders. She glanced up, stunned, and saw three horsemen peering over the ledge.

Wes let out a ragged breath, the first hint he'd given of his own unease. "Zack." He chuckled weakly, shaking his head. "That boy could rope the tail of a cyclone."

"Wes!" It was Cord's voice. "Don't move yet. We're tying the ropes to our cow ponies."

Wes grinned sheepishly, some of the color returning to his face. "Maybe you were right, darlin'." He cocked his head to glance back up the slope. "Maybe Rangers shouldn't always ride alone."

Another rope whispered down, this time over Wes. He wound it several times around his waist, and she followed his example. Soon his arms were around her again, and the horses were dragging both of them slowly, painstakingly up the curve of the hill. Several times her feet slid out from under her. She banged a knee and scratched an elbow, but Wes's embrace kept her safe until Shae grabbed her wrists and pulled her—sodden skirts and all—over the lip to flat, blessed earth once more.

Zack, Cord, and Shae all started talking at once, it

seemed, about how they'd ridden back to the farm and how Fancy had sent them out looking for her. Rorie barely heard them. She sank gratefully to her knees, and Wes sank beside her, drawing her hard against his chest for a hungry, celebratory kiss.

After a breathless moment, he drew back. Catching her face in his hands, he gazed into her eyes in a mixture of relief, joy, and mock despair.

"Woman, so help me God," he groaned. "Your swooning is going to be the death of me."

Chapter Twenty-five

Shae McFadden's life was still in dire danger. That fact was made blatantly clear the minute the Rawlins brothers rode into town with Creed and a wounded, half-conscious Dukker. A mob was congregating in Calaboose Alley, in spite of Preacher Jenkins's best attempts to send them home.

"We want justice!" the citizens cried, waving rifles and torches and swinging ready-made nooses. "We want McFadden!"

"Now hold on just a goddamned minute," Wes bit out, grateful he'd convinced Shae to stay with Rorie, Merrilee, and a shell-shocked Danny back at the house. While Ginevee had tended Rorie's bruises, Fancy had agreed to doctor Dukker. Otherwise, there might not have been a prisoner to charge with Lorelei's rape. "If you're so jo-fired up about justice, you can start looking at the facts instead of color."

"It don't take no blind man to see the facts, Rawlins!"

"Yeah! Danny Dukker saw it all. You tell him, Hannibal. Tell him how that half-breed nigger murdered Lorelei!"

Creed choked, turning sickly white at the news of Lorelei's death, but Wes didn't have the luxury to grieve for the girl he'd tried to protect. Striking with his rifle stock, he knocked back an overzealous gun waver. Cord and Zack snapped their rifle levers; Dukker cowered in his saddle.

"Now you listen to me!" Wes shouted, standing tall in his stirrups and making sure the loudest of the rabble stared down the barrel of his Winchester. "There's still a law in this town, and I'm here to enforce it! If someone has a problem with that, he can cozy up to my bullet."

That lowered the noise level to a hush.

"Shae McFadden did not, I repeat, *not* rape Lorelei Faraday. And he's got at least six witnesses to prove it. As for Danny Dukker—" Wes glared contemptuously at the boy's father. He'd say just about anything to please his old man. And we all know how much Hannibal Dukker would like to see Shae McFadden pay for being born. Now I suggest you folks go to the church and say a prayer for Lorelei Faraday. Say one for Gator Boudreau and Doc Warren too. Maybe folks wouldn't be dying in this town if you started showing each other a little kindness and respect."

Wes turned his most menacing glare on the men standing between him and the jail door. "You boys forget where the church is?"

Four or five merchants slinked out of his path; another half dozen scattered before the threats of Zack's and Cord's rifles.

Peering out of the jail a few minutes later, Wes was relieved to see the street was empty again—for now. He sent his brothers back to the farm to protect Shae and the women and to tell them he was escorting Dukker to the Bandera County Jail at first light. Wes figured once the truth got out about Dukker, the man wouldn't be safe in his own calaboose.

God, it was going to be a long night.

Ever baleful, ever defiant, Elodea's marshal sneered at him from his cell.

"You ain't got nothing on me, boy."

Wes didn't bother to point out that three attempted murders in one afternoon made for a weighty court sentence.

"There ain't no one in this town who will speak out against me."

"You're wrong about that, Pa," Creed said quietly. "I saw you kill Gator. And I saw you kill Doc Warren so you could destroy Gator's will—"

"Shut up, you jackass!" Dukker's face grew white and red by turns. "What the hell's the matter with you?"

"—And now I know you killed Lorelei," Creed finished numbly, as if he'd never heard. "You're a hateful, crooked sonuvabitch, and you tried to make me one too. But I won't let you turn Danny into the kind of man you made me."

Wes's heart twisted. "Creed, you're not like your father."

The boy hung his head, and a tear slid down his cheek.

"Christ, you make me sick." Dukker's lip curled as he scowled at his son. "But you're still my flesh and blood, so you ain't gonna be testifying at my trial. And McFadden can spout off all he wants. He don't have proof of anything." Dukker cackled, sounding mightily pleased with himself. "Yeah, that's right. You ain't got a thing on me, Rawlins."

A heavy footstep rattled the floorboards outside. Wes tensed, pulling a gun as the doorknob turned. He imagined some rabid Negro hater had returned. But when the door was thrown wide, a red-eyed, pale-faced Phineas Faraday stalked into the room.

"Hold it right there, Faraday."

The man's pudgy hand quaked as it hovered above the pocket of his black mourning coat.

"I've got something for you," he said hoarsely.

Wes eyed him narrowly, trying to decide if a derringer might be hidden inside that pocket. The man was strung tighter than a fiddle.

"What is it?"

"No doubt you heard . . ." Faraday's voice cracked. Hardening his features, he continued, "My daughter died tonight."

Wes nodded. "I'm sorry," he said more gently.

"She named her killer." Faraday pulled a sheet of paper from his coat and laid it on the desk.

The cell door clattered as Dukker suddenly grabbed

hold of the bars. "What's that, Faraday? What do you think you're doing?"

"Something I should have done long ago." He turned dull, lifeless eyes on Wes. "I've signed an affidavit. Everything I know about Dukker's extortions, the still, the murders . . . Oh. And I mustn't forget this."

He pulled a second sheet from his pocket. The stationery was pale blue with a pair of engraved doves at the top. In the bottom right-hand corner, a tearstain marred the shaky signature.

"Lorelei signed an affidavit too."

The ride to Bandera Town and the county jail was only a day's journey, but Cord advised Rorie that Wes would likely ride more slowly with a wounded prisoner. Cord further predicted that Wes would spend several days at the county seat, filing charges, writing reports, and answering the questions of the prosecutor and the county judge.

"It wouldn't be unusual," Cord told her, "for Wes to be gone for two weeks. But don't you worry about Shae, Aurora. Zack and I aren't going anywhere, and Fancy isn't, either. Aunt Lally's back home watching our children, so we can stay here just as long as you need us."

Rorie appreciated the Rawlinses' kindness, but she couldn't help worrying about Shae. The boy had insisted on attending Lorelei's burial, and even the threat of Zack's and Cord's firearms couldn't stave off the townsmen's hostility. Faraday and Creed had publicly defended Shae, but hatred and prejudice had deep roots in Elodea. Grim-faced and grieving, Shae finally conceded he could never live peacefully near that town.

The day after the burial, he announced he would sell the farm and put the money toward his schooling at Prairie View Negro College.

Creed, too, was anxious to leave behind Elodea and its heartbreaking memories. Although he planned to return for his father's trial, Creed confided when he retrieved his brother from Rorie's care that he still had an aunt and a couple of cousins in Louisiana. He planned to see Danny got a proper upbringing—and a couple more years in a schoolhouse.

Danny hadn't been too happy with that plan, but he had gotten excited when Creed mentioned the prospect of hunting alligators to earn a living.

As for Merrilee, she seemed a little sad to see Danny go, even though he still pulled her braids, called her feather duster, and goaded Topher into a brawling fit at least once every hour.

"Mama," she'd said, and it warmed Rorie's insides whenever Merrilee called her that, "do you think Danny and Topher will ever be friends?"

Rorie hid her smile from the child, who snuggled beside her on the bed with her drawing papers and pen.

"Well, sweetheart, stranger things have happened."

Merrilee seemed to consider this for a moment, then sighed and shook her head.

"Danny should stay away from alligators. They have too many teeth."

She proceeded to draw a ferocious, reptilian jaw beneath small, beady eyes. Rorie was a little surprised by the accuracy of the child's drawing. To her knowledge, Merrilee had never seen a live alligator, and Rorie was certain none of her books had pictures of one.

Before she could ask the child from where she'd gotten her inspiration, Merrilee turned the page over and began drawing something new. A likeness of the magnolia in Rorie's vase began to appear beneath the child's pen.

"I am glad you talked to Mama before she went away," Merrilee said solemnly.

Rorie started. Merrilee's mama had gone away? The poor child, she must have finally accepted her parents' deaths. No doubt Ethan's browbeating had weighed more heavily on Merrilee's thoughts than Rorie had first imagined.

She brushed stray hair from the child's brow, which was furrowed in deep concentration as she sketched the flower.

"Do you . . . miss your mama, Merrilee?"

She shook her head, her expression turning wistful as she drew. "Mama—I mean, my old mama"—she smiled shyly up at Rorie—"says I don't need her anymore. She says I have you now to teach me things, and Uncle Wes too. But Mama says she'll come back to help me, if I ever need her again."

A lump filled Rorie's throat. She didn't want to replace the child's mother, and yet, was it wrong of her to be pleased that Merrilee had finally accepted her as something more than a caretaker?

"I'm sure your mama will always stay close so she can watch over you, Merrilee. That's what angels do."

Merrilee nodded happily. "I know. I like angels. Does your baby have an angel to watch over him too?"

Rorie's jaw dropped. If the child had asked her about the birds and the bees, Rorie couldn't have been more stunned. No one knew about her baby except Fancy and Ginevee, and she'd sworn them to secrecy. They'd seemed to understand her need for circumspection, her reluctance to celebrate a miracle that might have been lost, so she couldn't imagine that either woman had discussed her condition in front of the men or the children.

"Merrilee," she asked hesitantly, "how did you know about my baby?"

The child smiled softly, gazing up at her with that older-than-her-years wisdom that never failed to mystify Rorie.

"My old mama told me before she said good-bye."

"Rider coming!"

Rorie's heart still jolted every time Topher bellowed the warning cry. Now, as she watched him leap off the fence, his face starbright with elation, her stomach did a somersault.

"It's Uncle Wes!"

With a wave and a whoop, Topher charged off to intercept Two-Step almost as fast as Rorie's pulse was racing. She heard the front door slam as Fancy and Ginevee came outside with Po; Merrilee and Nita dropped their dolls to run for the drive; the men all set aside their guns and strolled from the porch into the yard.

Rorie drew a shaky breath. Kneeling in the twilight beneath Maggie's cooling shade, she gazed down at her gloves, stained with damp, fertile earth, and the bucket o seed pods she'd been gathering. The minute Shae had an nounced his intention to sell the farm, she knew she had to collect every flower the tree dropped. Magnolia sap lings weren't likely to thrive on a dusty cattle ranch, bu she would plant hundreds of them and hope that one—a least one—would prove as hearty as Mrs. Boudreau' sweetheart tree.

Of course, Rorie had concocted this plan based on the premise that Wes still wished to marry her. "I need to work Rangering out of my blood," he'd once told her Had arresting Hannibal Dukker cooled Wes's gunfighter' passion, or had the old thrill fired up again?

Two weeks. She'd waited two nerve-racking weeks to know. In that time, her cuts and bruises had healed. She and Merrilee had, miraculously, suffered nothing more debilitating than head colds from their trauma in the storm.

Spared from fever, or worse, pneumonia, Rorie had been acutely lucid, which meant she hadn't been able to escape a plague of worry. Breathlessly, anxiously, she'd waited every day for the dreaded contractions, the spot ting, the evidence of her miscarriage.

But after fourteen days without her woman's courses, she'd dared to conclude her baby was healthy.

She was healthy, too, except for an occasional bout of nausea. Rather than fretting, though, she rejoiced in those episodes now. She just prayed Wes would.

Marrying a woman with four children and a fifth child on the way would surely be daunting to a young man who'd spent as much time as he had on the roam. She'd consider herself fortunate when she broke the news if he didn't vault back into the saddle and gallop to the nearest saloon.

Rising nervously, she shook the mud clots from her knees, pulled off her gloves, and waited with twined fin gers for him to finish greeting the others and come to her.

She didn't have to wait long. Excusing himself from his family, he covered the ground between them with long, purposeful strides. A rope was slung over his shoulder. The no-nonsense determination on his face made her stomach flutter. She lost some of her nerve.

"How—how was your trip?" she asked, reluctant to broach her news until she could better gauge his mood.

He halted, and the hint of a smile softened the businesslike gleam in his eyes. "It got a whole lot better once I rode up the drive."

"I suppose Dukker was a lot of trouble."

"I'm used to prisoners bellowing and cursing."

"Oh." She blushed. She didn't know why, but she sensed his comment had a double meaning, especially when he let a coil of rope slide to the ground.

She cleared her throat. "Creed said he would be back for the trial. After everything he and Danny have been through, I can't help but feel sorry for him. He's torn between testifying for Gator's and Lorelei's sakes, and keeping his father from hanging for Danny's. Dukker might have been the worst kind of villain, but he's still the boys' father."

Wes's jaw hardened the tiniest bit. "With Lorelei's and Faraday's affidavits, a jury won't need Creed's testimony to convict Dukker of murder."

He took another step closer, abruptly changing the subject. "Now that all the excitement's over, I've been meaning to ask you . . ."

Rorie caught her breath, her heart leaping. She'd been waiting for this moment, this question, for weeks.

"Just what did you write about me to my sister-in-law?"

She blinked, momentarily stunned. "You mean, the letter?" Air rushed back into her lungs, but she still felt deflated. Laughing weakly, she waved his question away. "I just told her you wanted to make amends, but that you didn't know how. And I said you would probably never forgive me for telling her so, but I couldn't bear to see you go on hurting."

She bit her lip, searching his face for signs of an impending explosion. "Does that make you angry?"

He folded his arms across his chest. In the fading light, with his hat's shadow falling cross his chiseled jaw, she couldn't tell what he was thinking.

"If it did make me angry, would you sneak off with me to the shower bath tonight so we could make up?"

Her face heated a couple hundred degrees. Glancing over his shoulder, she spied his brothers and sister-in-law watching in unabashed amusement.

"You're joking, right?"

"Hell no. I don't ever joke about keeping the peace."

She grew even warmer, if that was possible.

"All right, woman, enough of this chitchat. Are you, or are you not, going to marry me?"

Her heart bumped. For a moment, she was so happy to hear him propose again that she couldn't even think.

"Before I say yes—" she swallowed, blinking hard so she wouldn't embarrass herself, "I have a confession to make."

"And what might that be?" he asked silkily, fingering the coils of his rope.

"Well, it seems that I'm . . . er . . ." She gulped a bolstering breath. "I'm not quite as barren as I once thought."

She waited anxiously, her heart in her hands, and watched the dawning of his realization. He stiffened, his eyes widened, and his chest rose with a huge breath and held. Grabbing her shoulders, he searched her face wildly for confirmation.

"You mean—?"

She nodded. "I'm having your baby, Wes."

The widest grin she'd ever seen slowly split his face. "When?"

"In about seven months."

His whoop startled her. He picked her up and spun her around. She gasped, then laughed, her feet flying out from under her. Her pulse was soaring when he set her back on the ground, and he kissed her hungrily, making her dizzy and breathless all over again.

"You know what this means?" he asked, nibbling on her ear.

She was tingling from head to toe. "No, what?"

"*I* don't fire any blanks."

"Wes!"

He laughed and spun her around again. She giggled,

clinging to his neck, too happy to heed the conventions.
For once, her heart was in control, and when he hugged
her closer, she couldn't imagine why she'd ever let logic
guide her instead of love.

"Boys," he shouted, pulling off his hat and waving it
at his brothers, "there're going to be five new additions to
the Rawlins family." He grinned, tossing her a sideways
glance. "Make that six."

She pressed her palms to her face, and Topher, racing
ahead of the others, joined them beneath the magnolia tree.

"What's going on?" the boy asked eagerly.

"Well, son—" Wes squatted, gathering all of the children around him, "seems like you, Nita, Merrilee, and
Po—and Shae and Ginevee too, if they're of the same
mind—are going to come live with me and Miss Rorie.
Only I reckon you can't call her 'Miss' anymore. I reckon
you'll have to call her 'Mama.' "

Merrilee tugged shyly on his jeans. "Does that mean
we can call you 'Papa'?"

"Sweetheart, I wouldn't have it any other way."

He hugged them all, winked at Cord, then rose to
slap Zack on the shoulder.

"Son, it looks like you're gonna have some catching
up to do."

Zack laughed good naturedly, congratulating her on
the engagement. Cord and Fancy took their turns, then
Shae and Ginevee hugged her.

Wes didn't let his family monopolize her for long,
though. Taking her by the hand, he hurried her back to
Two-Step as if she were a renegade running from the law.
She laughed at him as he boosted her into the saddle.

"You aren't afraid I'll change my mind, are you?"

"Nope." He vaulted up behind her, his mustache
tickling her ear. "It's the shivaree," he whispered in mock
dread. "After the things I did to Cord on his wedding
night, those boys are going to hound us but good."

"But we're not even married yet!"

"Yeah? Try telling them that."

He wrapped his arm around her waist, and a delicious shiver gusted down her spine. "Besides," he

drawled, "I have a surprise waiting for my sweetheart by the blackberry bush."

She knew she reddened at the earthy promise in his voice, but she was too elated to care. He loved her, he wanted her, and he'd given her everything she'd ever dreamed of having.

Since he'd come into her life with his devilish laugh, his wicked flirtations, and his fallen-angel's smile, her days had been a series of miracles, one right after the other. She was a woman who counted her blessings. She would cherish him until the end of her days, and if he chose to continue Rangering, she would find some way to accept his decision. After all, she understood the importance of having dreams and making them come true.

As if reading her thoughts, he slipped a hand behind her, fishing in the pocket of his vest.

"Hey, Topher!"

"Yeah, Pa?"

"I've got something for you."

A flash of metal tumbled in the fading light, and Topher caught the object in his hand. His eyes grew as round as silver dollars when he gazed down at his palm.

"It's your Ranger badge!"

"That's right, son. I won't be needing it anymore."

Rorie's heart tripped. Tilting her head back, she gazed up at him through a shimmering rainbow of tears. "But Wes, Rangering means so much to you. Are you sure you want to give it up?"

He chuckled, spurring Two-Step out of the yard and into the dancing orange and yellow flowers of the meadow.

"Darlin', I'm through chasing bad men." His hand strayed down her ribs in the naughtiest, pulse-stirring way.

"Now I just want to be one."

ABOUT THE AUTHOR

After earning more than thirty awards for journalistic excellence, ADRIENNE DEWOLFE finally yielded to her love for fiction and started writing romance. Adrienne is a native of Pittsburgh. After receiving her journalism degree from Ohio University, she migrated to central Texas, where the rolling hills and lush green belts are reminiscent of the Pennsylvania woods she still loves. When she isn't hiking, she volunteers for numerous civic organizations.

For Adrienne, writing historical fiction is one of her greatest joys. She welcomes correspondence and invites readers to write to her in care of Bantam Books, 1540 Broadway, New York, NY 10036.

Look for the next thrilling historical romance from Adrienne deWolfe as she delivers the passionate and captivating follow-up to TEXAS LOVER and the third book in the Rawlins Brothers series, TEXAS WILDCAT, coming soon from Bantam Books.

A terrible drought has set the cattlemen and sheepherders of Bandera County at one another's throats, each vying for enough water for their thirsty livestock. When Bailey McShane, owner of the largest sheep ranch around, finds two hundred of her sheep killed, she wants revenge. But Zack Rawlins, her neighbor and president of the Cattlemen's Association, gives her a better idea—a minirodeo between sheepherders and cattlemen to settle the conflict. And Bailey and Zack will go head to head in the herding competition—herding pigs, that is!

Here is an excerpt from this exceptional romance.

The whole of Bandera County must have turned out for the Independence Day Rodeo. The usual events—roping, riding, broncing, and racing—were among the draws, but the main attraction for the phenomenal crowd, as Bailey well knew, was the long-awaited competition between the sheepherders and cattle ranchers.

The sun-beaten grandstands were filled with cowboys, sheepmen, farmers, and townsfolk, each group assembled in their own loosely defined cheering section. A few early-morning arrivals had rigged canopies over their buckboards, but other than the occasional lady's parasol, little else offered relief from the sun.

The lack of shade coupled with the blistering heat made Stumpy's barrels of whiskey extremely popular throughout the long day. Nick Rotterdam proved to be Stumpy's biggest customer, and Hank had to heave his firstborn into the river to soak some sense into Nick and keep him from breaking his fool neck in the bronc-busting contest. Luckily for Nick, his twin brother, Nat, got up enough nerve to say he'd ride Widowmaker, keeping the Rotterdam ranch and the cowboy team from forfeiting.

Bailey couldn't have been more pleased. As she'd predicted, the fence-stringing competition had gone to the sheepmen, the shooting match to the cattlemen. If Nat lost the bronc-busting contest, the sheepherders were practically assured of winning the day. All Bailey had to do was beat Zack at pig herding.

No big task, right?

Shifting from foot to foot, she stood nervously behind her rival at the rear of the arena, where he leaned against the high cedar fence connecting the competitor's ring to the horse barn. The sun was at five o'clock now, throwing Zack's long, lean shadow into the ring. He'd already competed in the countywide bull-riding competitions, putting on a tremendous show. He hadn't been gored, trampled, or thrown by his longhorn, and she wondered a little hopefully if being named champion bull-rider for the third year in a row might have tuckered him out.

He didn't look tuckered out, though. He looked downright relaxed. Taking off his Stetson, he balanced it on his saddle, which he'd thrown over the fence's top rail. An occasional puff of wind ruffled the short-cropped waves of his chestnut hair; his pale green shirt cleaved damply to his broad back. When he raised his forearms to the fence, she enjoyed watching his muscles ripple beneath the clingy cotton of the shirt.

Even more, she enjoyed trailing her gaze over the taut derriere above his brown-and-white cowhide chaps and the hard, corded thighs filling his denim blue jeans. He was a fine specimen of a man, Zack Rawlins was.

Because Zack had a good view of the ring in a nice piece of shade, she was sorely tempted to go share it with him. But that meant she would have to talk with him, and she always had the damnedest time talking to Zack Rawlins.

She blew out her breath. Well, one thing was certain: she'd never been one to back down from a challenge.

Marching up to the fence, she climbed the bottom rail and gazed out at the arena. They stood shoulder to shoulder, and a minute or two passed. She noticed her heart was hammering ridiculously hard. Still, Zack didn't say anything. He didn't even glare at her. She wondered if she had to climb another rail just to get his attention. Hell, she wasn't that short, was she?

Finally, she cleared her throat. "You ready for the herding contest?"

He cast her a sideways glance. The touch of heat in his mahogany eyes sprinkled goose bumps all the way to her toes. She wasn't entirely opposed to the sensation, and she felt a fleeting disappointment when he let his gaze slide away again.

"Yep," he answered. "Are you?"

"Yep."

More silence. Now what? She steeled herself against

fidgeting. Why did this have to be so difficult? After all, she wasn't thirteen any more, nurturing a school-girl's infatuation for the man.

She sighed, and Zack arched an eyebrow at her.

"Change your mind?"

She raised her chin. "Not on your life."

She glimpsed his dimples and caught her breath, not quite prepared for one of his rare smiles.

"Miss Bailey McShane," he chided in his whiskey-smooth bass, "are you over here fraternizing with the enemy?"

Those heart-stirring dimples deepened to crescent moons, and she shook herself, realizing she'd been staring.

"I didn't come here with a bribe, if that's what you mean," she said in her best businesslike voice.

His smile abruptly faded. "That's not what I mean."

He went back to gazing at the arena, and she suspected she'd irritated him. She always seemed to irritate him. Why did he have to irritate so damned easily?

"I just . . ." She struggled not to sound exasperated, or worse, hurt. "I just wanted to wish you luck. That's all."

"Hmm."

Suddenly, the chute flew open. Nat's mount didn't lunge cleanly, and Bailey had to grip the rail tightly as the fence shook with the force of the stallion's striking hooves. Nat's hat flew off, but he clung to the hurricane deck, twisting and jerking like a rag doll as Widowmaker spun beneath him.

Bailey held her breath as the spectators roared. For the fleetest of seconds, she prayed for the contest victory that would prove her merit as a rancher and end the cattlemen-sheepherder feud.

Then Widowmaker's flank slammed into the fence at the far side of the arena. Every bone in Bailey's body jolted with the impact. Nat managed to hang on, but Widowmaker whirled, hurtling himself into the rails again.

"Oh, God." Bailey's heart leaped, and she dug her fingers into the soft cedar. The stallion's intention was frighteningly clear. Bucking and thrashing, Widowmaker was doing his deadly best to smash Nat against the fence.

"Choke the horn, Nat!" she shouted, fear making her voice shrill.

Dimly, she felt Zack tense beside her as the rodeo clowns jumped onto the fence beside Nat, shouting and waving their hats at the bloodthirsty stallion.

With a shrieking neigh, Widowmaker veered for the center of the ring. The clowns had done their job, but Nat, weakened by the pounding blows, lost his grip. Suddenly his body was bouncing down the rails, caught between the fence and the stallion's vicious rear hooves.

"Nat!" All Bailey could see was dust as a cowboy galloped after Widowmaker and wrestled him away from the fallen rider. Terrified for her childhood friend, she scrambled up the fence, planning to run to his rescue.

"Hold on, girl."

She struggled futilely as Zack's iron-hard hand grabbed the back of her belt and dragged her down. She felt her spine pinned against the unyielding breadth of a powerful male chest as Zack's forearm wrapped her waist, holding her prisoner between his hammering heart and the railing.

It all happened so quickly. She squirmed, straining to see past the swirling dust, past the straw wigs and polkadotted bandannas of the clowns who had raced to Nat's aid. In the breathless silence, she could hear Zack's quick, warm breaths against her ear. His hand tightened anxiously over her belt, and she could feel the tantalizing heat of his knuckles against her back. She could feel the tender chafing of her jeans against her femaleness. It made her shiver.

Finally, the dust cleared. Nat rose shakily to his feet. He looked pale beneath his layer of dirt as he limped toward the gate, and heartfelt cheers came from the cattlemen, even though he'd clearly lost the event.

Bailey unleashed the breath she felt like she'd been holding since Christmas.

"And you say sheepherders are crazy," she muttered at Zack. "Bronc-busting is child's play compared with bull-riding."

She tried to turn so she could glare at him—a mistake, for she lost her foothold. She might have bruised her back sliding down the fence if Zack hadn't caught her in time, his hands at her waist, his thighs anchoring her hips to the rails.

Now they were face to face, heart to heart, steamed together by a heat that was only partly a result of the merciless sun. Momentarily stunned by this intimacy, Bailey could do little more than blink into the gaze that melded with her own. He had chestnut-colored lashes, she realized with an awestruck kind of pleasure, and tiny flecks of amber glowed in the sienna depths of his eyes.

"You worried about me, neighbor?"

His voice rumbled in his belly, vibrating into hers. She felt the flutter of butterflies she'd thought she'd banished in her childhood.

"Er . . ." Distracted by a white-hot glitter of sensation on her skin, she realized his gaze was roaming down her length to rest on the fusion of their thighs.

"I reckon that would make us even, since you always seem to concern yourself with me," she rallied weakly.

"As I recall, I always get an earful for it, too."

"Well, that's only because . . ." She hesitated, tingling all over with the return of his smile. She didn't want hasty words to chase it from his face again. "Never mind. It's Nick I'm mad at, not you. Nat nearly got himself killed, thanks to his weasel of a brother. Nat's not the rider Nick is, and everyone knows it. Nick should be drawn and quartered for getting too roostered to bronc—"

"Maybe he did it on purpose."

Bailey blinked at Zack. She didn't know what confused her more, his reasoning or the disappointment she felt when he eased his hips from hers and steadied her on the ground.

"Come again?"

"Maybe he wanted to lose."

"Nick would never . . ." Her voice trailed off as her heart leaped painfully, lodging in her throat. Damn Nick, he just might have done it.

"Zack, you won't do that to me, will you?" she

asked urgently, grabbing his sleeve before he could step past her, out of reach. "You won't cheat so I'll win?"

Looking a tad uncomfortable, he turned his body sideways, his back filling most of her vision. "If Nick did throw the contest, I'm sure he thought he was doing you a favor—"

"Nick was doing himself a favor! He's a selfish little toad. Zack, please. Promise you won't let me win at herding."

His lashes fanned lower, but even half closed his eyes held a magnetic intensity as he regarded her over his shoulder. He seemed to be studying her, sizing her up.

"The outcome means that much to you, eh?"

"Of course it does! I want our event to be square. When I win, I don't want any cowboy coming back and saying you lost on purpose."

He chuckled at that, and for the first time, Bailey glimpsed the gentle humor that lurked behind his fierce, no-nonsense businessman's personality.

"All right, Bailey. I won't let you win."

"You promise?"

"I promise."

He stayed there for a moment longer, then someone yelled his name. Nodding to her, he settled his Stetson on his head, grabbed his saddle, and walked away. Bailey might have stood there staring after him until dark, if her foreman hadn't brought her dog over to her.

A white paw pushed against Bailey's thigh, and Pris panted up at her, a question in her liquid brown eyes. Bailey half smiled, bending over to scratch the border collie's black ear.

"Just wait 'til they get an eyeful of you," she told the dog affectionately.

Zack was waiting for her by the pigpens. They drew straws under the watchful eyes of their judges, all nonpartisan farmers and townsmen. When she triumphantly pulled the longer straw, she selected her hogs first, a litter of Berkshire shoats and their grand dame. Left with ten cantankerous specimens of spotted pork-on-the-hoof, Zack elected to ride first. Tramping off with coils of rope and a bag full of corn, he led his black gelding, Boss, into the starting chute.

Seeing those yellow kernels made Bailey a wee bit nervous. Even though Zack had spent the last month driving his steers north, he'd apparently found time to learn something about swine. Still, he couldn't possibly have gotten much practice herding.

But Bailey and Pris had.

She smiled a little smugly, scratching the collie's head. At first Pris had been skittish around all those grunting quarter-tons of lard, but now the forty-pound collie rounded up petulant pork just like she rounded up mutton. Of course, pigs, unlike sheep, were awfully canny creatures, and Pris was still new at matching wits with the beasts. . . .

The bell rang, and the chute flew open. Ten hogs charged the ring, squealing in mass confusion, and Zack whooped, spurring Boss from an adjacent gate. The gelding cornered instantly, heading off a beady-eyed boar with nasty-looking dewclaws. But rather than follow their leader like nice, well-behaved steers, the other nine hogs raced off in all directions. Bailey couldn't help but grin. Zack had only three minutes to chase all the hogs into their pen.

The cattlemen's grandstand roared with encouragements, and Boss wheeled. Bailey watched in admiration as Zack hugged the big horse, his powerful thighs commanding the cow pony to turn, cut, or run. His rope rose and fell in his right hand, slapping the spotted flanks that raced by; with his left hand, he rummaged in his burlap bag for a fistful of corn.

The first fling did little more than scatter the squealing hogs and start the whole whooping-wheeling-galloping process over again. The second fling was apparently less frightening and lured the pigs into loose formation.

Bailey bit her lip. Two minutes had passed.

The hogs' leader was beginning to put two and two together: The big black animal had food. The boar trotted warily behind Zack's stirrup, his snout upturned and his pink nostrils twitching. This behavior was quickly mimicked by the sows, and poor Boss could hardly put a hoof down without endangering a curly tail. With a few deft switches of his rope, Zack managed to guide the spotted cluster of rumps to the open pen. A half-minute remained.

Unhooking the corn bag from his saddle horn, Zack heaved it over the top rail of the pen. The burlap broke, the corn scattered, and the boar rushed greedily inside, closely followed by his harem—except for one independently minded sow. She chose instead to snuffle outside in the dirt for overlooked kernels. Zack mouthed an oath as he slammed the gate closed behind the herd. Bailey felt a resurgence of hope.

The loiterer oinked in terror when she saw Boss bearing down on her, this time carrying an angry-looking cowboy and a twirling rawhide lasso. She bolted, but Zack's lariat caught her rear leg, and she toppled, thrashing, to the ground. Boss backed up, tightening the rope like a good cow pony, and Zack cursed again. Clearly, Boss couldn't drag the pig all the way across the arena to the pen. Zack jumped down, wresting a second rope from his saddle horn, and Bailey snickered as he tried to throw a leash around the sow's flailing head.

The three-minute bell rang. The sheepherders cheered, and Zack scowled in defeat, releasing his squealing quarry with obvious disgust.

Bailey did her best to wipe the unsporting smirk off her face as Zack passed by her gate, leading Boss across the arena to the stalls at the rear of the ring.

She vaulted into her saddle. Her very first rodeo, and she was going to win, not only for herself but for sheepherders everywhere!

Agonizingly slow, the seconds dragged by. Her mare, Sassy, tossed her head, stamping with excitement, and Pris ran back and forth along the gate, sniffing eagerly at the animal smells beyond. Twisting in her saddle, Bailey strained to see how many of the ten pigs still needed to be chased into the adjoining chute. Instead, her gaze was pulled upward, away from the hogs as if by magnetic force.

She spied Zack, standing with Wes by the judges'

platform. He was watching her, and when their eyes met, she felt an electric crackle like lightning flicker down her spine. She caught her breath, not quite prepared for the surge of heat and smoke that spiraled outward to her toes and fingers.

That charge was the last thing she remembered before the gate flew open, and Sassy bounded with Pris into the ring.

Zack didn't know which was worse: letting swine make him look ridiculous in front of the entire county, or acting like a fool in front of Bailey McShane.

God, what was wrong with him? Two years ago, he'd barely noticed Bailey had a rump, much less the saucy roundness of it. Today, he'd practically had to rope his hands to his sides just to keep from exploring that taut little fanny.

Of course, she hadn't helped him any by squirming and wriggling, butting his pecker as she'd tried to scramble over the fence. Bailey McShane was a handful—more than a handful, God help him—and he didn't want her messing up his life. If he had wanted his peaceful existence turned upside down by a wildcat, he would have courted her long before now.

Wes pushed back his hat, giving Zack a cheeky grin as Bailey thundered past them on her palomino. "I don't suppose you let that pig run by you on purpose, eh?"

"No, I did not," Zack growled.

"Hmm."

Bailey whistled, pointing, and Pris charged the wheeling right flank of the hogs, cutting off their retreat before the chute gate was closed.

"Kind of funny, isn't it," Wes drawled, "her being female, her dog and horse being females, and you and Boss . . . Well, you're both males."

Zack grunted something noncommittal, secretly impressed with Bailey's command. She rode in a circular pattern, shouting orders like a five-star general, while that collie of hers raced to obey, barking and snapping at the stragglers until they joined the formation.

" 'Course, it's probably just a coincidence," Wes

continued cheerfully, "you and Boss being up against all females. Too bad that sow got away. You would have figured she would have followed her boar."

Zack shot his brother a withering glare. "If you're trying to make me feel better, you're doing a damned poor job."

"I am?" Wes did a masterful job of looking contrite. "Here now. Don't go swallowing an overdose of woe. This contest isn't over yet. You still got that cougar to bag, and he's male. 'Course . . ." Wes shook his head, loosing a lusty sigh as Bailey pointed, and Pris charged off after the last recalcitrant shoat. "There won't be any living with our womenfolk if Bailey wins. They're gonna ride us boys but good."

"This business has nothing to do with you and Cord," Zack said grimly.

"It doesn't?"

"No."

By now, Bailey's battle strategy was paying off. Pris had marshaled the sows shoulder to shoulder behind the grand dame, and the whole troop was trotting, somewhat irregularly, toward the gate and the slop troughs at the rear of the pen.

Suddenly, one shoat broke ranks. Ignorant of the consequences, she ran merrily ahead to forage, no doubt scenting the corn kernels Zack's swine had overlooked. General Bailey, of course, didn't tolerate this breach of discipline. With a slash of her arm, she pointed out the delinquent to Sergeant Pris, and the collie bounded forward, her white tail fluttering like a battle banner.

Barking orders, which the pig either ignored or couldn't comprehend, Pris raced ahead, rounded on the yearling, and flashed all her fangs. This warning was only mildly effective. Even at her tender age, the shoat was twice Pris's size, so the miscreant ran on. Incensed, Little Napoléon charged after her and nipped at a ham hock.

One would have thought that pig was going to the slaughterhouse.

With a squeal that would have rung tears from a statue, the baby turned tail and ran straight to her mama. The grand dame bristled. Gnashing her teeth, she bellowed a battle cry that would have done a wild boar proud. Suddenly, all ten hogs were on the stampede.

"Pris!" Bailey spurred her mare out of the way. "Pris, come around!"

Canine pride must have been at stake, because the collie ignored the command. Planting her paws, Sergeant Pris lowered her head and barked riotously at the mutineers. They grunted back swine obscenities and charged her at ramming speed.

Clearly shaken, Pris stopped wagging her tail. She retreated a step. Then another. In the next heartbeat, Zack and Wes were laughing uproariously with the rest of the cattlemen as Pris shot like a black-and-white bullet into the pen, all ten pigs in hot pursuit. Bailey slammed the gate; Pris vaulted the fence; and the shoat's defenders were left to oink their outrage until they discovered the tasty tidbits waiting for them in the slop troughs.

"Good girl, Pris," Bailey called, leaning down to ruffle the dog's fur.

Pris wagged her tail in sheepish relief to see her mistress in such high spirits. Zack, still grinning, cocked an eyebrow at the judges. They'd gathered together, all muttering and shaking their heads. He glanced at his brother, and Wes shrugged, equally mystified.

"Miss McShane," Bandera's mayor boomed through his megaphone, "kindly report to the judges' circle."

Amidst the disgruntled applause of the cattlemen and the wild cheering of the sheepherders, Bailey cantered to the platform and reined in with a flourish. "Mayor Strathmore means the *winner's* circle." She tossed this smug taunt at Zack as she dismounted.

Zack folded his arms, equally smug. He didn't know what had happened, but a second glance at the judges convinced him their decision wasn't in Bailey's favor. "If I were you, I wouldn't embarrass myself with premature claims, neighbor."

"I beat you," she retorted, her eyes agleam like polished sapphires. "It's as simple as that."

"'Fraid not, sweetheart."

"Weren't you watching?"

"Oh, I was watching all right. Watching you lose."

"What?" That jewel like gaze flashed in warning as she rounded on poor Mayor Strathmore. "What's he talking about?"

"Well, Miss McShane," the judge said uncomfortably, wiping a handkerchief across the back of his neck, "it seems you didn't quite abide by the rules—"

"The hell I didn't." Her glare snapped back to Zack. "What kind of game are you playing, cowpoke?"

"Me?" He felt his jaw harden. Wasn't it just like her to cast the blame on him? "You sheepherders had just as much input making up the rules as we cattlemen did."

"That's right, Miss McShane," Strathmore interjected hurriedly. Pushing his spectacles up his perspiring nose, he pointed to a paragraph at the bottom of the contest contract. "It clearly says here the contestants will herd ten pigs into a corral—"

"That's what I did. I herded ten pigs."

"Uh, no, ma'am, you didn't. Your dog was supposed to herd the pigs, not the other way around."

Her jaw dropped. *"What?"*

Zack was hard-pressed not to chuckle. Strathmore did have a point, as convoluted as it was. No wonder he was a law wrangler.

"That's ridiculous!"

"Now Miss Bailey," Strathmore said a bit indignantly, "both sides agreed beforehand. The judges' ruling stands. Why don't you get out of this hot sun and go cool yourself off for a spell?"

She shook his hand off her arm. Stalking closer to Zack, she wagged a finger under his nose. "You put them up to this, didn't you, Rawlins?"

It was his turn to gape. "Now wait just a consarned minute—"

"You said you wouldn't let me win, and you didn't!"

"You made me make that promise."

"Yeah?" Standing toe to toe with him, she actually jabbed her finger into his chest. "I should have known you'd made that promise too easily. No wonder you've been over here all this time standing by the judges' platform!"

He felt his cheeks flame. Well, *that* put the spurs to

his temper. He didn't take kindly to being called crooked, and he sure as hell didn't like to be prodded.

"You know what your problem is?" he ground out, lowering his face to within inches of hers. "Your daddy spoiled you rotten."

"He did not!"

"He spoiled you and coddled you. What he should have done was turn you over his knee."

"My daddy knew how to treat a woman," she flung back, "which is more than I can say for you, Rawlins!"

That was it. The final straw. He'd borne her public insults too many times. In a surge of primal instinct, he grabbed her shoulders and pulled her hard against him. He heard her gasp as her heels left the ground; he saw shock widen her eyes. Then his mouth swooped to cover hers.

Suddenly, his anger was snuffed out in a flare of desire as her hands clutched his shirt sleeves. He slanted his mouth, demanding an entry to the enticing wetness that lured him deeper.

Her lips trembled open, and her rigid spine softened, arching, letting him mold her length to his. When she pulled him closer, his heart tripped; when his tongue thrust, she parried.

She was kissing him eagerly now, hungrily, demanding a response that every sizzling part of him ached to provide. But not here. Not now.

Abruptly he pushed her back, setting her on her feet. She blinked up at him, her eyes brimming with wonder.

He heard a buzz. Growing, crescendoing, it thundered to a roar. Boots were stomping, hands were clapping, spectators in the grandstands were howling with mirth. Dumbfounded, he stared at the lips that were so moist and swollen from his. Shame burned through him. How could he have lost control?

He swallowed hard, thinking he should apologize.

A fist slammed into his gut like a miniature locomotive. He wheezed, unprepared for the punch that nearly blew a hole through his spleen.

"Dammit, McShane," he gasped, clutching his searing midsection.

Without a word, she turned on her heel, red-faced and tight-lipped as the snickering judges parted before her.

Wes gave Zack's shoulder a commiserating slap. "You sure handled her, son. Yep, you handled her real well."

Now that you've been captivated by

—— TEXAS LOVER ——

be sure to look for

TEXAS OUTLAW

by Adrienne de Wolfe

"A stunning debut . . . kept me on the edge of my seat."
—*New York Times* bestselling author Arnette Lamb

With her violet eyes and sultry smile, Fancy
Holleday knew there wasn't a man alive she
couldn't charm, seduce, or just plain outsmart
—and that included federal marshal Cord
Rawlins. He had sworn to throw the lady train
robber behind bars—until he discovered that
beneath Fancy's wicked ways lay a secret sorrow and a desperate longing that could steal
his heart.   __57395-0 $4.99/$6.99 Can.

- -

Ask for this book at your local bookstore or use this page to order.

Please send me the book I have checked above. I am enclosing $____ (add $2.50 to
cover postage and handling). Send check or money order, no cash or C.O.D.'s, please.

Name _____

Address _____

City/State/Zip _____

Send order to: Bantam Books, Dept. FN 7, 2451 S. Wolf Rd., Des Plaines, IL 60018.
Allow four to six weeks for delivery.
Prices and availability subject to change without notice.   FN 7 9/96

DON'T MISS THESE FABULOUS
BANTAM WOMEN'S FICTION TITLES

On Sale in August

Available in mass market

AMANDA

from bestselling author *Kay Hooper*

"*Amanda* seethes and sizzles. A fast-paced atmospheric tale that vibrates with tension, passion, and mystery."

—CATHERINE COULTER

_____ 56823-X $5.99/$7.99 Canada

THE MARSHAL AND THE HEIRESS

by *Patricia Potter*

"One of the romance genre's finest talents." —*Romantic Times*

The bestselling author of *Diablo* captivates with a western lawman lassoing the bad guys—in Scotland! _____ 57508-2 $5.99/$7.99

from *Adrienne deWolfe*
the author *Romantic Times* touted as
"an exciting new talent" comes

TEXAS LOVER

Texas Ranger Wes Rawlins comes up against the barrel of a shotgun held by a beautiful Yankee woman with a gaggle of orphans under her care. _____ 57481-7 $5.50/$7.50

Ask for these books at your local bookstore or use this page to order.

Please send me the books I have checked above. I am enclosing $_____ (add $2.50 to cover postage and handling). Send check or money order, no cash or C.O.D.'s, please.

Name _____

Address _____

City/State/Zip _____

Send order to: Bantam Books, Dept. FN158, 2451 S. Wolf Rd., Des Plaines, IL 60018
Allow four to six weeks for delivery.
Prices and availability subject to change without notice.

FN 158 8/96

DON'T MISS THESE FABULOUS
BANTAM WOMEN'S FICTION TITLES

On Sale in September

TAME THE WILD WIND

by ROSANNE BITTNER

the mistress of romantic frontier fiction

Here is the sweeping romance
of a determined woman who runs a stagecoach inn
and the half-breed who changes worlds to
claim the woman he loves.

_____ 56996-1 $5.99/$7.99 in Canada

BETROTHED

by ELIZABETH ELLIOTT

"An exciting find for romance readers everywhere!"
—AMANDA QUICK,
New York Times bestselling author

Guy of Montague rides into Lonsdale Castle to
reclaim Halford Hall, only to be forced into a
betrothal with the baron's beautiful niece.

_____ 57566-X $5.50/$7.50 in Canada

Ask for these books at your local bookstore or use this page to order.

Please send me the books I have checked above. I am enclosing $_____ (add $2.50 to cover postage and handling). Send check or money order, no cash or C.O.D.'s, please.

Name _____

Address _____

City/State/Zip _____

Send order to: Bantam Books, Dept. FN159, 2451 S. Wolf Rd., Des Plaines, IL 60018
Allow four to six weeks for delivery.
Prices and availability subject to change without notice.   FN 159 9/96